CONRAI

To Lisa
Best wishes

GerriCon Books Ltd

First published in Great Britain in 2010
by
GerriCon Books Ltd
Orford Green
Suite 1
Warrington
Cheshire
WA2 8PA
www.gerriconbooks.co.uk

Copyright © 2010 Conrad Jones

Names, characters and related indicia are copyright and trademark
Copyright © 2010 Conrad Jones

Conrad Jones has asserted his moral rights
to be identified as the author

A CIP Catalogue of this book is available from
the British Library

ISBN: 978-0-9561034-9-9

The places named in this book are real. The fictional events are based on
factual ones but have been changed by the author.
Any similarity between the fictional characters and people in
the public domain are coincidental, and are generated purely
from the imagination of the author.

All rights reserved; no part of this publication may be reproduced or
transmitted by any means, electronic, mechanical, photocopying
or otherwise without the written permission of the publisher.

Cover Photos: ©istockphoto.com

Cover designed and typeset in Minion 11pt
by Chandler Book Design
www.chandlerbookdesign.co.uk

Printed in Great Britain by
Ashford Colour Press Ltd.

1

The Mosque

Nick was sweating as he sat and watched the rain run down his windscreen. The wiper blades squeaked annoyingly as they moved back and forth relentlessly, struggling to move the deluge from the glass. His nerves were jangling with excitement and anticipation, while fear pumped his veins full of adrenalin. He could smell the explosives that were packed into the back of the rusty white panel van, two hundred litres of hydrogen peroxide and a nitrogen-based fertilizer filled three oil drums. Surrounding the canisters were huge bags of two-inch wood screws, and steel ball bearings, which would become a maelstrom of deadly shrapnel when the device detonated. A smile crept across his face as he caught his reflection in the rear view mirror. Nick was ridiculed for most of his childhood, because of his Aboriginal type facial features. There were no Aboriginal genes in his family anywhere, he was plain unlucky. He had a wide flat nose, protruding brow bones and a thick angular jaw-line. In the weeks before, he had grown a thick beard and dyed it blond. He tinted his hair and eyebrows to match. Thick black spectacles completed the disguise. He waited patiently for his targets to appear from inside the building. The bomb-maker had done a good job, but then he always did, a proper little

Einstein. They didn't always see eye to eye, but they shared a single goal. Sometimes he had to be put in his place, but generally, they were a good team.

Nick scanned the front of the building. It looked nothing like a mosque; however, it was the first of its kind in Britain, built in the previous century by a lawyer in the Everton area of Liverpool. He had converted the interior of a Victorian terraced property into a place of worship for the followers of Islam, and in its heyday, prayers were held five times a day. Christmas Day, 1889 was the original opening day, but his attempts to champion Islam were not welcomed by local residents. Prejudice, which often erupted in violence against the founder and his followers, finally forced the lawyer to close up, and move abroad. In the 20th century, the building was used as a registry office for a while, before it fell into disrepair, and the facade began to crumble, as it tumbled into dereliction. Recently, the leaders of the local Muslim community decided to buy the building and renovate it to its former glory, because of the historical significance as Britain's first mosque, and today was the official reopening.

Parking close enough to the entrance for the device to be at its most effective had been a hurdle to overcome, and Nick drove the vehicle to the ideal spot the previous day, leaving it there overnight. He received a fixed penalty notice for his trouble; the yellow parking ticket lay discarded in the passenger foot well. Movement caught his eye as the front door of the mosque opened, and three photographers jostled for the best position to snap the guests as they walked down the wide stone steps, smiling and shaking hands with the other VIP's as they left. Small groups began to form along various parts of the pavement as the departing guests made small talk and promised, half-heartedly to keep in touch with each other. Nick waited patiently for his targets to appear, but they hadn't left the building yet. His mind drifted back to his school days, where he had first become involved with the bomb-maker and his family. Their lives were scarred by events from the past, and their future was inseparably entwined. A loud rap on the window snapped him back to reality.

Nick cursed under his breath, realising that a traffic warden caused the knocking. He hated people in uniform. They made him nervous. Nick served fifteen years of a life sentence, and the stigma of being subservient to uniforms became engrained in him. The traffic warden's image was blurred by the pouring rain, but he could tell that she wasn't best pleased. She gestured to him to open the window, which he did reluctantly.

"You're parked in a restricted zone," she barked. Rainwater dripped from her peaked cap in tiny rivulets onto her saturated jacket. Angela Williams hated being a traffic warden, her childhood dreams of being a police officer were dashed by her asthma. She thought that becoming a parking attendant would fulfil her desire to work in law enforcement, but it didn't. Her first day in the job was a whirl of excitement, the uniform, the authority, gave her a rush. By lunchtime, she had been spat at, sworn at and verbally abused by strangers in passing cars. The novelty wore off quickly.

"Get a proper job you slag!" If she had heard it once, she had heard it a thousand times. Every day was a constant battle with the public, verbal abuse was a frequent occurrence. Her bosses set unachievable targets every week, forcing her to issue tickets wherever possible. Angela couldn't sleep at night, worried about the stress of working the next day, every shift became a trauma. To top it all her husband was recently made redundant, his drinking was spiralling out of control, and her marriage was going down the toilet.

"This is a restricted zone."

"I've broken down." Nick lied.

"Have you arranged for the vehicle to be repaired?"

"Yes, they're on their way."

"How long will they be?"

Nick was becoming annoyed with the woman. He looked up and down the street and considered punching her in the throat, before bundling her into the back of the van. There were too many vehicles on the road, and the crowd from the mosque were lingering around. He looked in his wing mirror and spotted his targets emerging from the building. Panic set in and forced him into action.

"I'll go and call the breakdown company again." He opened the door and steeled himself against the rain. He slammed the door closed and pushed past her, breaking into a jog as he crossed the road.

"I've already issued this vehicle with a fixed penalty notice," the pedantic warden called after Nick as he crossed the road away from the van. She lost sight of him as a double-decker bus trundled by, spraying the rusty van and the hapless warden with surface rainwater. Her boots and socks were deluged, freezing cold water seeped between her toes, and she swore as she removed her ticket machine from her sodden jacket. He was getting another ticket now, and she would enjoy issuing it too. Just when she thought, her day couldn't get any worse the rusty panel van was ripped apart as the fertilizer bomb inside it exploded remotely. One second she was unhappily doing her job in the teeming rain, the next her head and limbless torso dangled from spiked iron railings, impaled through the throat.

2

Aftermath

Alec Ramsey stood on the steps of the mosque, inspecting the aftermath with an expert eye. After twenty years service, he had reached the dizzy heights of Superintendant and was the Senior Investigating Officer with the Major Investigation Team. His department was tasked with analysing the scene of the bomb blast, alongside the Counter Terrorist Unit. His blond hair was dishevelled, and a breeze from the river blew strands into his blue eyes, annoyingly. When he frowned, his forehead furrowed with deep lines, his chin dimpled. His friends and colleagues teased him constantly that he looked like the celebrity chef that was his namesake. The protective hood and suit were doing little to keep the wind out as he inspected the scene. He studied the pattern of the blast damage. Shrapnel from the explosive device pockmarked the front elevation of the building. Chunks of render were blown away by the impact of steel ball bearings travelling at four thousand feet per second, and blackened screws were embedded in the front door and window frames. A senior officer from the uniformed division approached him, dressed in a white paper suit. Alec recognised him as Chief Carlton, a key player in the divisional hierarchy. They'd been involved together in several cases over the years, and their relationship was one of polite tolerance.

"What are your first impressions?" the Chief asked, his face etched with deep worry-lines, dark circles shadowed beneath his eyes. The workload of senior personnel in Britain's police forces took its toll mentally and physically, especially in the big cities. The economic downturn was biting at every level of society, and crime was on the increase. Carlton looked like he was feeling the pressure.

"The device was built by a competent bomb maker. They used household chemicals and fertilizer. As long as you know what type you need then it's available at any discount warehouse. The shrapnel could have been purchased at any home improvement store, and the detonator was a simple remote, possibly from a toy or a mobile phone."

"The internet has a lot to answer for," Carlton mumbled. He was referring to the dozens of websites that carry instructions for homemade explosives. "Anyone using a search engine could find 'fertilizer bombs' and put that together."

"I'm not sure that this is the work of amateurs." Alec pointed to the wreckage. "The van was modified to aim the blast at the pavement, by welding metal plates into the side and the floor of the vehicle. The bombers directed the blast toward the pavement, and the mosque," Alec said. He stepped around a congealing pool of blood, walking toward the remnants of the van. Alec was tall, and the Chief struggled to keep up with his long strides.

"It's a miracle more people weren't killed," the Chief replied. He grimaced as he navigated his way between the blood and gore. The bodies had already been removed, but smaller particles, human and otherwise, were still being collected by a small army of forensic scientists.

"What was the final body count?" Alec Ramsey asked. He had no idea how many fatalities there were, for now it wasn't the priority. Finding out who built and detonated the device was uppermost in his mind. Superintendant Ramsey spent seven years working in a combined unit, investigating bombings in Ireland. He knew how to follow the evidence, and piece together the details that added up to the bomb maker's signature. From what he had seen so far, the perpetrators of this attack were well versed in their trade.

"Four dead so far, and one man is still critical. Most of the guests had left, thank God," the police Chief shook his head as he spoke. "A minute or two earlier and dozens could have been killed. It's a good job their timing was slightly out."

Alec wasn't so sure that their timing was out. He studied the scene again from a position next to the wreckage of the van.

"Do you have the initial photographs?"

"I've got some of the early shots here," Chief Carlton took a small digital camera from inside his protective suit. He turned the viewing screen toward Alec. The Superintendant compared the crime scene images taken immediately after the explosion. One of the casualties was a female traffic warden, obviously in the wrong place at the wrong time. The head and torso dangled from the railings, her peaked cap still in place. Two bodies lay close to the stone steps, and two more were nearer to the van, their clothes shredded by the blast.

"Who are they?" Alec asked, pointing to the images.

"The two men here were photographers, one died instantly, and the other is hanging on by the skin of his teeth in intensive care." Chief Carlton referred to a notebook before he continued. "This is Amir Patel and his wife Mina, both died at the scene, and that poor soul impaled on the railings is Angela Williams, a traffic warden."

Alec caught sight of his number two, Detective Inspector Will Naylor, picking his way through the rubble, towards them. Will was talking on the telephone as he approached. Chief Carlton nodded a silent greeting, which Will returned as he ended the call.

"Your forensic teams can take the van, we've got all the information we need from it for now," Will said abruptly to the police Chief. Initial tests had been done, and now the wreckage belonged to the Counter Terrorist Unit. Chief Carlton wasn't accustomed to being spoken to so curtly, especially by a fast track detective. Will Naylor was one of the new breed of detectives that enter the force on the back of a university degree, and then fly through the ranks at a rate that is offensive to time served, senior officers. Chief Carlton had spent more time on the beat than Will had on the force in total. He saw him as insolent and disrespectful.

"Did they find anything of use?" Alec ignored Carlton's discomfort, confused as to why they were allowing the terrorist division to claim vital evidence already.

"It has been bleached inside from top to bottom. They tested every remaining flat surface, and they're all positive for sodium hydroxide. The vehicle has been sterilised."

"I'm sure that a thorough analysis of the wreckage will reveal vital pieces of information, Detective Naylor. I wouldn't be so quick to dismiss it at this early stage," Chief Carlton tried to recover his damaged self-esteem.

"That's why we investigate major incidents, and you chase burglars. The vehicle has been wiped clean, Chief Carlton," Will replied politely. His mobile rang and he turned away to take the call before the Chief could manufacture a suitable reply.

"That man is beyond belief," he fumed. His lip quivered as he spoke. It wasn't the first time he had been on the receiving end of his tongue. "He has no respect whatsoever!"

"He's a good detective, Chief. I'll have a word him about his people skills."

"I'd have him disciplined."

"What are your thoughts on a plan of action?" Alec ignored his remonstrations. There were bigger priorities to deal with.

"I intend to collect all the evidence from yourselves, and the terrorist unit, evaluate it, and then react with the appropriate measures," Chief Carlton blustered. He sprayed saliva as he ranted. "I'll send our findings onto you, when we're finished assessing it." The Chief turned to walk away, stumbling off the kerb as he did so. Alec followed him with his piercing blue eyes, doubting that forensics would find anything incriminating. The bombers had planned this operation with precision. They'd also planned it so that they wouldn't leave any evidence behind. Will disturbed his thoughts.

"Now Sherlock has gone, what do you think?" he asked.

"The first mosque in Britain reopens, and a bomb goes off outside, Uniform Division will arrest the usual suspects, local fascists, neo-Nazis and right wing sympathisers. They'll shake them up and see what falls out."

"Okay, now answer the question. What do you think?" he raised his eyebrows as he spoke. The corners of his mouth twitched slightly, just the ghost of a smile behind his words.

"If I had planned this attack, I'd have loaded enough explosive into the van to blow the front off the building. There would be forty dead, not four."

"My thoughts exactly, something doesn't smell right," DI Naylor grinned, looking more like a young football star than a senior detective.

3

Richard Bernstien

SCHOOL DAYS

Fifteen years earlier, Richard Bernstein waddled down the stairs of the three-bedroom semi-detached that he shared with his parents, older brother and younger sister. He was fourteen years of age, fat, spotty, and Jewish; not a great combination for making friends and keeping a low profile in the schoolyard.

"Straighten your tie, Richard," his mother fussed. "Tuck your shirt in for heaven's sake. Have you brushed your teeth properly?"

Richard rolled his eyes skyward and screwed up his face as he walked into the tiny kitchen, making his older brother laugh. His brother was his hero, slim and handsome, and as hard as nails, which was very handy at school. He never teased Richard about his weight, unlike his sister, who teased him all the time. The kitchen was warm, and he could smell the familiar odours of toast and strong coffee. His father was reading the Daily Telegraph, a broadsheet which almost hid him completely from the rest of the family. It was his barrier at the breakfast table, and no one spoke to him unless the newspaper was folded up and put down on the table.

"Here Einstein," his brother David laughed as he handed him a small plate loaded with four pieces of hot buttered toast. Einstein was his pet name, because of his unusually high IQ. Richard Bernstein was top of every class he studied. He was also the best chess player in his year, only a few of the older students could still beat him, and he was improving every year.

"You're so gross," his sister Sarah moaned. Richard shoved half a piece of toast into his mouth in one go, and then showed her the contents of his mouth as he munched it. He loved his younger sister, even though she avoided him like the plague at school. She was part of the trendy set in her year, and far too pretty to be associated with her nerdy fat brother. She had beautiful deep brown eyes and dark hair, inherited from her Jewish ancestors. Richard noticed with humour that her school skirt seemed to get shorter every term, and boys flocked around her like bees to a honey pot, much to the annoyance of his brother David. David got into a few schoolyard scraps with boys who were pestering her. Mr Bernstein was also becoming aware of her ever-decreasing hemline.

"I need a note for games, Mum," Richard said. Toast sprayed from his mouth as he spoke.

"Do not speak with your mouth full, Richard Bernstein," his mother scolded him. She clipped him gently behind the ear. Richard worried her. He was by far the most intelligent child that she had ever encountered, but he was a loner. She knew why he had no friends; it was because he was fat and Jewish. He had no confidence and was awkward in company. The only real friend he had was his brother David, but he was growing up so fast, and she didn't think he would be around forever to look after his younger brother. "Why do you need a note for games?"

"Because he's too fat to run," Sarah sniped. She pulled out her tongue and grinned.

"Sarah!"

"I'm only joking," she said. Richard blushed and sat down, staring at the piece of toast in his hand. He laughed but the comments always hurt inside. Another dollop of lime marmalade numbed the pain slightly.

"Well, you're not funny, young lady. That was very cruel," his mother cleared the plates and dumped them in the sink. Richard managed to salvage one last piece of toast as she whizzed past him.

"We're supposed to be doing cross-country running today," Richard explained. He hated all sports, full-stop. Getting changed in front of his schoolmates was far too traumatic. Not only embarrassed by his weight but also he was not as sexually developed as his classmates were. Most of them had pubic hair, but he had none yet. He had a small penis compared to the other boys that he had seen naked. Some of them had hair on their arms and chest already. His body was way behind the average adolescent, which the other boys were very quick to point out. Richard would rather sit in the warm library and read than run anywhere.

"Why would they want you to run across country, you're such a clever boy?" his mother tried to sooth his embarrassment. "It's such a waste of your brains, I'll write you a note before you leave."

Sarah rolled her eyes and pretended to vomit, making both her brothers giggle. A knock at the front door prompted a flurry of activity. David slipped on his blue, fur-lined parka, kissed his mother and ruffled Richard's hair as he left.

"That'll be Nick," he said as he opened the door. "Hiya mate." David high-fived his best friend, which wasn't easy because Nick was so tall. He towered above his schoolmates. His height and exaggerated features made other students wary of him.

"Why don't you let Richard walk with you to school?" his mother shouted after him. She tried hard to slot Richard into the mix with his brother at every opportunity. David looked at his brother uncomfortably. Nick and David had a crafty cigarette when they walked to school in a morning, and he didn't want his younger brother to see him.

"I'm not ready yet, and I need my note for games," Richard smiled at his brother, knowing that he had let him off the hook. David smiled back and put up his thumb.

"See you later, Einstein," David shouted. The front door was still ajar, and Sarah made a dash for it, before her mother made her walk to school with her fat brother.

"Bye, Mum," she called as she slammed the door.

"I don't know why everyone is in such a rush these days," his mother muttered. She fumbled in her handbag for a pen, finally rescuing one from the deepest reaches. "I'll say that you have a chest infection, and you're not to do games for a month."

"Thanks, Mum," Richard felt a wave of relief sweep over him. School was torture. He enjoyed the academic side of things but he was the target of bullying and ridicule from morning to dusk. Things had become almost unbearable lately. There was an influx of Asian kids the previous year, and they were particularly cruel to the white students, and especially to Richard because of his religion. They called themselves the 'Asian Invasion', and they ran riot at school, ridiculing pupils and teachers alike.

"Here, get yourself some sweets from the shop on your way to school, and don't tell your sister," his mother winked at him, handing him a crisp green pound note. She knew that she shouldn't encourage him to eat rubbish, but she could tell that school life was going to be difficult for her middle child, and if she could brighten his world, then she would do it.

"Thanks, Mum," Richard kissed her on the cheek and struggled into a grey duffle coat as he headed for the door. The toggles stretched over his chest and belly. "Bye, Dad." He shouted as he closed the front door, knowing that his father would grunt from behind his paper.

It was a bright and breezy morning, and Richard called into

his favourite shop on his way to school. They sold mixed bags of toffee for twenty-five pence each. He bought three bags, and two packets of salt and vinegar crisps, leaving enough change for a tin of Panda Pop cola. The cola was nowhere near as good as the real thing, but it was half the price, meaning that he could afford more sweets. The wind was biting as he headed across the park, and he pulled up his hood to keep the cold off his ears. Sefton Park was a mile across, and it was a kidney shape. Richard loved the walk to school, especially passing the boating lake. There was a full size pirate ship in the middle, inspired by the tales of Peter Pan. As he walked by, he would imagine being onboard, sailing around the lake repelling all boarders and firing the cannons at his imaginary foes.

"Hey, Richard Head," a voice called out from his left. He recognised the voice and his heart almost froze with fear. "What is short for Richard?"

"I think it's fat head."

"No, It's Dick."

"Oh, you are right. I know, Dick. Dickhead!" The taunting continued. He glanced toward the source of the abuse, his throat went dry and he had a sick feeling in his stomach.

Richard pulled his hood tighter around his head and picked up his pace. He could see his abusers walking along an adjacent footpath. It was the Asian kids from his school. There were seven of them in total. Their leader was Malik, and he was the toughest kid in Richard's year group. He was also the best footballer, best cricketer and most successful boy with the girls. Everything Richard wasn't.

"Have you got any sweets fatty?" another voice called out. Richard stuffed his toffee's deeper into his coat pocket. 'They're not getting their filthy hands on them', he thought. The gang neared, laughing and jeering at him, egging each other on. Richard wanted to run but he couldn't out run them. They were fit and athletic. He looked around for help, maybe David would be in the park with Nick somewhere, but there was no one around.

"I said have you got any sweets you fat bastard," a lanky kid called Ash snarled. Richard ignored him, putting his head down and walking faster.

"Hey Jew boy, I'm talking to you," Ash kicked the back of his trailing leg, and Richard stumbled onto his hands and knees. His knees stung, scraped by the impact with the concrete, and one of his trouser legs was torn. Richard tried to stand up.

"Are you deaf?" Ash stamped on his fingers. Richard felt his fingers throbbing. He tucked his hand under the opposite arm and concentrated on not crying. Malik and his gang always tried to make other kids cry, but Richard was determined that he would not.

"Leave me alone. What have I done to you?" Richard whimpered. His voice cracked as he spoke. Clumsily he stood up, still clutching his injured fingers beneath his arm. His pants were wet and torn at the knee, his hands muddy. Tears welled up in his eyes and he could feel his chubby cheeks reddening with embarrassment and anger. He hated being fat, more than being Jewish. The other kids always picked up on one or the other, and usually both.

Ash didn't attempt to reply; instead, he punched Richard in the face. The blow stung like hell, stunning Richard. His eyes watered involuntarily, and he could feel blood running from his nose. The second punch hit him square in the mouth, splitting his top lip against his front teeth. Richard fell backward and landed heavily on his backside.

"What a shot," Malik patted Ash on the back. The youths roared with laughter.

"That must sting, does it sting fat boy?" Ash taunted Richard.

"Fucking bully," Richard spat blood on the floor, trying to right his bloated frame. Tears of anger ran down his cheeks.

"What did you say?" the baying teenagers fell silent. Ash leaned over Richard threateningly. His dark eyes flashed with hatred and anger.

"I called you a bully, you Paki," Richard sat up. Blood and mucus smeared around his nose and mouth. Months of abuse had finally forced him to strike back in the only way he could, with his words.

Ash pulled a lock knife from his trendy Farah pants and opened the blade slowly. Richard remembered wishing that he hadn't called him that. He wasn't a racist, being Jewish taught him that prejudice was evil, but it was the only thing that he could think of at the time. There was no way that he could fight Ash, let alone the gang behind him. Richard wet his pants as Ash approached with the glinting blade. He remembered being surprised at how many times he could be kicked and punched in the head without being rendered unconscious. The blows came from all angles, and he was sure that he was going to die. Richard struggled to stand up at one point, but the beating was relentless and they hammered him back down again, and again. Ash used the knife several times; if not for his thick duffle coat, the slash wounds would have been much deeper, probably fatal. A voice called from the distance.

"Hey! Leave him alone!" A dog walker interrupted the melee.

"Mind your own business, Mister."

"I'm calling the police, I know which school you are from." The dog walker ran toward a red telephone box. He fumbled for change with shaking fingers. Someone was taking a terrible beating, and he wished he had the courage to do something about it himself, but he was no fighter. He called the emergency services and ran back toward the fight. The boys were a writhing mass of arms and legs. The body on the floor twitched with every blow.

"I've called the police and an ambulance!"

"Leave it Ash, split up and let's go!" Malik Shah gave the order to leave, and the attackers scattered in different directions.

The Good Samaritan kneeled next to Richard Bernstein and covered the injured victim with his coat while he waited for the ambulance to arrive.

"You hang on there. The police are on their way. You're safe now."

Richard was semi-conscious when the ambulance team cut off his clothes and dressed his wounds to stem the bleeding. He remembered thinking that his mother would be mad that they'd cut his grey duffle coat. It had cost a fortune. The ambulance journey was a blur of blue flashing lights and sirens. His mind became numb as the drugs circulated through his broken body, and seven names flashed through his mind over and over again.

4

The Major
Investigation Team

"Morning, Will." Superintendant Alec Ramsey walked into a large open office space, which housed the Major Investigation Team. It was just past seven in the morning and he was all set to face the trials and tribulations of the day ahead. They were three floors up in the fortress-like Canning Place building, situated on the banks of the River Mersey. It was the home of the county's uniformed and Special Departments senior hierarchy. The MIT office was L-shaped, and the windows were full length, giving it a bright and positive feel. The ambiance helped to lift the team's spirits as the cases they investigated were the worst possible. It was all too easy to become de-motivated when the details of a gruesome case weighed heavy on their minds. Chasing human monsters could be relentless and frustrating. A handful of dishevelled looking detectives were sat in a semicircle around DI Will Naylor's desk area.

"Morning, Guv," Will replied. He looked tired and his appearance was shabby. It was a sharp contrast to his usual razor sharp demeanour. His shirt collar was undone, and his sleeves rolled up to the elbows. Dark stubble suggested that he hadn't shaved for a couple of days. In contrast, the Super looked and smelled like he had just stepped out of the shower.

The scent of Fahrenheit wafted in with him.

"Have you been here all night?" Alec raised his eyebrows, knowing what the answer was.

"We've been doing some digging, Guv."

"Well if one of you good men would like to put the kettle on. I'll make you all a brew and you can fill me in on what you've found out, and then you will all go home, get showered and shaved, have a few hours sleep, and I don't want to see you until this afternoon. Is that clear to everyone?"

"Right, Guv," a ginger haired detective saluted and headed into the kitchen area. "Does everyone want coffee?" he mumbled as he left the group.

"By the look of them we'll need the full pot," Alec shook his head and patted each of them on the back as he followed. He was proud of his team. In his opinion, they were the best detectives on the force, and their dedication and commitment never failed to impress him. He returned a few minutes later with a pot of strong black coffee. The ginger officer followed him with a tray holding six mugs. "Right then, what's so important that you haven't been to bed?"

Alec poured coffee into all six mugs, and handed them out to each of his detectives in turn. He picked up the last one for himself and sipped the scalding black liquid as he waited for his DI to gather their findings together. He looked through the full-length window and watched a ferry leaving the Pier Head, white foam frothed behind it as it headed across the river.

"The plates on the van were genuine, Guv. It's registered to a landscape gardening outfit in Sussex. We ran the usual checks and the company doesn't exist. The postcode belongs to a derelict factory unit, which hasn't been used for five years or more according to the local plod."

"Sounds a little too clever for our skinhead goose-stepping friends," the Super commented. Top of the list for the Counter Terrorist Units were Neo-Nazi organisations. Alec knew that they would be interrogating every name on the activist list for the next few weeks. There would be some tough skinheads wetting their pants right now.

"Uniform division have come up with zilch as far as known extremists are concerned, and the intelligence service say there has been little to no information from their undercover agents regarding planned activity for the groups they monitor," Will sipped his brew. "The Counter Terrorist Units are working closely with MI5, but so far no one has claimed responsibility, making it unlikely that it's a political gesture."

"Okay, we thought as much." Detective Superintendent Ramsey doubted from the off that the bomb was the work of right-wing groups. It was too sophisticated.

Will continued. "Initial reports from forensics on the van and the bomb fragments are very interesting, Guv."

The Superintendent raised his eyebrows and slurped his coffee. "I'm all ears, Detective," he smiled. Will Naylor's tenacity made him chuckle to himself. His enthusiasm rubbed off on his team hence they had not been to bed yet.

"The fertiliser mixture was a very special blend. It had been cooked and dried to remove all the moisture, and then mixed with aluminium powder and diesel. Forensics haven't seen a mixture that well prepared since......"

"Northern Ireland," Alec Ramsey interrupted. Everyday fertiliser absorbs moisture from the atmosphere, and will not burn or explode as a result. There are only certain grades of ammonia, or nitrogen-based compound, which are suitable for bomb making, and they need careful painstaking preparation before they can be turned into explosives. The Superintendent was familiar with bomb makers' signatures. "Every bomb maker has their own individual method of mixing the ingredients, some more successful than others. Cooking and mixing the fertiliser is the sign of an experienced bomb maker."

"Exactly, Guv. They have also found evidence of a mercury

motion switch, and remnants of a photocell trigger switch. Forensics reckon this one was created by an expert, nothing of this type has ever been attributed to any extremist group."

"A mercury switch would have triggered the bomb if the van was towed away, and the photocell would have detonated the bomb if the back doors were opened."

"Yes, Guv."

"That bomb was going to explode no matter what happened."

"It was, so why risk being close to the van to trigger it by remote?" Will pushed his sleeves up as he asked the question.

"Unless they were targeting someone specific?" Alec Ramsey answered thoughtfully. He stroked the dimple on his chin with his thumb. "What does the guest list tell us?"

"We've checked, and double checked the guest list for the opening of the mosque," Will handed a list of names to his Detective Superintendant.

"Anything interesting?"

"Nothing at first glance, Guv."

"Nothing stands out at all, until we looked at the casualties." He handed another shorter list to Alec. Alec sipped his coffee as he read the list of names. The list contained the two photographers, the traffic warden, and the Patels. At first glance, it was not a remarkable list.

"The photographers and the traffic warden are collateral, so I'm assuming that the Patels have something more to them than meets the eye?"

"Correct, Guv." Will handed a pile of papers over as he explained. "Amir Patel is the director of two limited companies, both haulage businesses with international contracts."

"Looking at this everything seems to be above board," Alec flicked through details information downloaded from Companies House, and the Inland Revenue sites.

"It is, Guv," the ginger detective nodded as he spoke. "I've been through it with a fine toothcomb. His tax returns are submitted on time, his VAT is spot on and he has never appealed any decision that has gone against him."

"What are you saying, Smithy?" the Superintendant looked up from the paperwork.

"It's too neat and tidy, Guv." Carl Smith, or Smithy as he was known, had spent years on the fraud squad, before joining the MIT. "He's turning over millions, and never questions a single tax demand. It's screaming 'don't look at me'. If I was laundering money, then my accounts would look like that."

"So we can rule out the Inland Revenue as possible suspects," the Superintendent joked. The group of detectives laughed and the coffee pot was refilled, and then shared out between them.

"That's not everything, Guv," Will said, taking another gulp from his mug. The caffeine was having the desired effect. "Patel is also on the board of directors for another six limited companies. Now this is where it gets interesting."

"Come on, come on," Alec made a winding motion with his arm. "Get to the point, Smithy wants to get to his bed, eh Smithy?" The detectives laughed. They liked working with the Superintendant; he got the best out of people.

"Two names appear on the director's lists again, and again, Malik Shah, and Ashwan Pindar."

"Their names have cropped up many times over the years, drugs, prostitution, one or two gangland murders that I can remember, but the Patels don't mean anything to me." Alec shrugged.

"They didn't to me, until Smithy remembered Shah was being investigated in the late nineties, linked to importing engine blocks full of smack from the Far East."

"What happened," Alec turned toward the ginger officer.

"Nothing, Guv, there was nothing concrete and he walked. He didn't even get charged, but Patel was questioned about a large sum of cash which was deposited into his business account at the time. I had to follow the money trail, but it was a dead end. He bought legitimate properties in Spain and the Algarve with it. The DI was adamant he was money laundering, but they couldn't touch him, Guv."

"It's all a bit tenuous at the moment, but if Shah and Pindar are smuggling heroin into the country, then a couple of international haulage companies under their umbrella would be handy," Will looked excited as he spoke. "I've spoken to the DI at the drugs squad, and he thinks Shah and Pindar are responsible for bringing in most of the heroin and ecstasy that comes into the country. They've been watching them for years, but so far they haven't put a foot wrong."

"Well now that changes everything," Alec ran his fingers across the dimple in his chin. "This could have nothing to do with the Mosque being a target, the evidence tells me it's a hit?"

"It makes sense, Guv. What do you think?"

"I think you have all done a good job. Now go home and get some sleep, we'll crack on later this afternoon."

The detectives moved as one, packing up papers, moving files and putting on jackets. Superintendant Alec Ramsey watched the team drift off toward the elevators. As they left, the day shift were beginning to arrive. He greeted them and headed to his office to mull over the new information. It was going to take the investigation in a completely different direction. It looked like Malik Shah and his associates could be the targets, and that changed everything. At the moment, CTU and MI5 were running the show, but if the bombing turned out to be the assassination of a high profile crime family member, then it would fall to MIT to investigate. Detective Superintendent Alec Ramsay felt a cold shiver run down his spine. He had a gut feeling that this was going to get messy.

5

Mamood

A week after the bombing at the mosque, Mamood checked his reflection in the mirror. He smiled to check that his teeth looked clean. They should be, he had brushed them four times since getting home from school. His hair was jet black and shone with freshly applied hair gel. It was cut short at the sides and back, and spiked on top. Mamood stood side on to the mirror and breathed in, pushing his chest out and tensing his biceps. He was only fifteen, but he played most sports at school and kept his figure toned by lifting weights. His dad had been tough all his life and he pushed Mamood to follow his lead. Mamood looked up to his father, and respected him for what he had achieved in his lifetime. He always wore designer clothes, holidayed abroad regularly, and changed his Porsche every year. One day Mamood would enter the family business, whatever it was they did, and he would have all the flash trappings of wealth that his father had. He wasn't a hundred percent sure what his business entailed, only that it was an import, export company. Whatever he did, it paid a shitload of money.

In a few years time he would be borrowing his father's car to pick up his dates, and a few years after that he would have his own. The future was bright. Mamood was vain, to say the least, and he worked hard to keep his appearance manicured. He opened the wardrobe door and flicked through his favourite shirts. The white Armani was very cool, but it could become marked where he was going. He selected a navy blue Versace and slipped it on, fastening the buttons up to the neck, leaving his gold chains visible. A pair of faded Levis and his new Air-Walk trainers finished the ensemble. He picked up the letter and read it again. Perfume wafted up to him from the pastel coloured paper.

The letter was from Vicky Stanton, who was in the year above him. She was a very sexy chick, with a growing reputation for putting out to her boyfriends. The letter was posted the day before, and it was waiting for him when he got home from school. Vicky said that she had fancied him for ages, but was too shy to approach him. If he was interested then he had to meet her at the reservoir. She said that she would make it worth his while. She hadn't included her mobile number, but she said that her father didn't like her getting text messages from boys. There were a couple of old lock-ups close to the reservoir, where teenagers met to kiss and canoodle. Mamood was hoping for a bit more than that tonight, and he checked that his parents weren't around before slipping a packet of condoms into his Levis. Vicky's reputation promised a lot more than just kissing. He checked the mirror one more time and slid the letter into his back pocket. Three long squirts of Ralph Lauren, Polo, topped the grooming. Mamood walked down the stairs with a spring in his step, nervous but excited at the thought of a sexual encounter.

"Where are you going, Son?" his father asked.

"Got a hot date, Dad," Mamood smiled and winked at his father.

"You be careful, and don't do anything that I wouldn't do," his father went to touch his hair.

"Hands off, Dad, don't mess up the hair!" Mamood danced backward on his toes and put up his hands like a boxer.

"You're still not big enough to take on your old dad," his father followed suit, and raised his guard.

"Leave the boy alone, Ash," his mother walked out of the kitchen. "Where is this hot date then?" His mother asked a little concerned. His mother was old fashioned. Her religious values had been passed down from generations, and were deeply engrained in her. She found it difficult to think of her son being in a relationship with a female, her husband was her one and only sexual partner. He was far more 'Westernised', his Muslim background long forgotten. She knew that he didn't share all her ideals, especially where their son was concerned.

"None of your business, Mum," Mamood skipped over to his mother and picked her up by the waist. He was tall and gangly like his father had been at that age. He kissed his mum on the cheek and spun her around. She was pretty for her age, and always dressed to impress, sometimes, in modern designer gear, and others in traditional Pakistani silks. "Don't worry about me, I'll behave."

"It'll be dark soon, Mamood," his father said seriously. Ash wanted his son to have as much freedom and fun as he could, as long as he kept safe. He knew the dangers of being that age from firsthand experience. The world was a dangerous place, especially so for the young and vulnerable. Ashwan Pindar dealt with death and danger everyday of his life, but he kept it separated from his family.

"Oh, Ash, stop fussing," his mother laughed. Her teeth were straight and white, and her smile made little creases form around her beautiful brown eyes. Her father's lifelong friend and business partner introduced her to her husband. The first time she saw him she fell for his dark good looks, and they were married six months later. Ten months after that Mamood was born. She realised over the years that her husband was no angel, but he treated her like a princess and doted on their son, Mamood. He was secretive about his business dealings, but they lived well, and as the years went by, it became less important to her.

"See you later, much later if I get lucky," Mamood joked as he headed through the front door.

"Like father, like son," his mother tutted. Lana Pindar was inexperienced sexually when she met her husband, but he overcame her embarrassments and shyness, teaching her and coaxing her. She soon became comfortable, even confident of her prowess in the bedroom, but the thought of her son engaging in sex made the hair on her neck stand on end. It seemed like yesterday she was cradling him in her arms, fixed to her bosom. Now he was a handsome young man, off on a date. "Where have all the years gone?" She shook her head, happy and sad, at the same time.

Ash watched through the window as his son walked away. He was a good boy, never involved with gangs at school, unlike Ash. Ash had been involved in gangs all his life in one way or another. A tight knit group of school friends, bonded by their ethnicity, grew up into a powerful crime family. It had been a dangerous but, lucrative career, and not one he wanted his son to emulate. A chill went down his spine and the hair stood up on the back of his neck. He couldn't explain it but he had strange feeling that something bad was going to happen.

6

Sefton Park
SCHOOL DAYS

When Byron ventured out at night, he stayed on the paths that skirted the perimeter of the park. He walked his dog, Lulu, three times a day, wind or shine, without fail, but he never entered the park after dark. The park was a hive of leisure activity during daylight hours, but at night, it took on a darker persona. Drug dealers, prostitutes and perverts trawled it after sundown. Once, one of the most affluent areas of the city, the suburbs around the park were spiralling into a mire of poverty and deprivation. The dregs of society were attracted into the area when the tall Victorian terraces were bought up by property developers, and turned into bedsits.

Byron, saddened by the decline, was trapped in his one bedroom flat by negative equity. His only companion was Lulu, a French poodle, named after the television star and pop Diva. He had never been married, never been in a steady relationship with a woman, but he didn't think that he was gay either. Byron enjoyed his own company, and didn't really have any sexual urges. His life was simple but happy. He had inherited the proceeds from the sale of his mother's house, when she died. She had spent the last few years of her life in a nursing home, wasting away while senility took her brain and her memories from her. Byron spent the money on his humble apartment, where he enjoyed life's simple things.

At least it had been simple, until last week. It wasn't simple anymore. Byron had stumbled across a group of Asian youths, attacking a young fat boy. They were like a pack of animals, kicking the prone body. His dog, Lulu, had gone mad barking and pulling at the lead. Byron was the last man to get involved in someone else's business, but he had tried to intervene, he couldn't walk past. There was so much blood that he thought they'd killed the boy. He called the emergency services from a phone box. As they dispersed, the Asian youths had given him some verbal abuse, 'faggot', 'dirty queer', and a couple of 'bummer' references, probably because he was walking a poodle in the park. He thought that Lulu may have bitten one of them on the leg, but he couldn't be sure. When Byron called the emergency services, and reported the incident; the police and an ambulance arrived, and before he knew what was going on, he was making a statement describing the attackers, without considering the consequences. Since then things became weird. 'Queer' had been daubed on his front door in yellow paint. A brick smashed his front window, and when he walked the dog, he felt as if someone was following him. Lulu wouldn't settle at all, either on the lead, or at home. She seemed to sense danger was close by. As he walked around the park, he was mulling it all over in his mind when a voice called out.

"Bummer!" a voice shouted out of the darkness, deep in the park. Byron could hear people laughing, but he couldn't see them.

"Queer boy!" echoed across the park. Byron couldn't be certain that the abuse was aimed directly at him, but he had a gut feeling that it was. He walked a step quicker, but he could hear chattering voices and sniggering keeping pace with him from the darkness, behind the tree line.

"Nice poodle, you big puff!"

"Arse bandit," this time the insult was hurled from the opposite side of the road. Byron turned and looked for his abuser, but there was no one in sight. The insulting references to his poodle left him with no doubt that he was the target of the abuse. He immediately made the connection with the Asian youths that he had encountered the week before, and the resulting police investigation. 'They couldn't know that he had given a statement, could they?' he thought.

"Don't bend down, when Byron is around, or you might get a penis up your arse!" several voices sang in unison. His abusers adapted a song from the football terraces of the day, especially for him. Shadows moved against the darkness, just out of his range of sight. The voices belonged to young, teenagers.

Byron shivered. They knew his name. The police assured him that his identity would be kept secret, obviously not. He was a half-mile from home, and the pavements well lit all the way. 'There is nothing to be frightened of', he told himself.

"You're dead, faggot!" another voice shouted. This time the abuse came from the opposite side of the road. There was a grassed area parallel to the pavement, planted with thick rhododendron bushes. Someone was hiding behind them, he could hear them rustling.

"I'll call the police as soon as I get home, you don't frighten me," Byron tried to sound assertive, but he did not. His voice was reedy, almost camp. People often mistook him as a gay man because of his voice and demeanour. The streets were empty and the traffic was sparse. There was no one he could turn to for help.

"You talk to the pigs too much, bum boy," a reply came from the park again. Byron turned sharply, the voices nearer this time. His heart raced, pounding in his chest. He had seen the level of violence that this gang of teenagers were capable of first hand, and he had no wish to become their next victim. The young boy that he had rescued was slashed and beaten to a pulp by them.

Byron walked on quickly, surrounded by a dangerous entity that he could feel tingling his skin, even though he couldn't actually see them. Lulu knew that they were there, and she was barking, snarling and standing on her hind legs, trying to protect her master. She could sense his fear.

"Don't bend down when Byron is around, or you might get a penis up your arse!" the gang sang as one from the shadows.

"Shut up, I'm not gay!" Byron shouted, scared and offended. How dare these teenagers follow him and abuse him, intimidating a grown man walking his dog, how dare they? He turned toward the park, staring into the darkness. His eyes became accustomed to the inky blackness, but he could see nothing but shadows.

"You need to shut up, grass!" this time the voice came from across the road. Byron turned around to face his abuser, droplets of sweat formed on his brow, and shivers ran down his spine. His stomach felt like it was being squeezed by the icy fingers of an invisible giant. He still could not see anyone.

"You are nothing but cowards, all of you. Spineless cowards!" Byron shouted toward the darkness.

A figure emerged from the shadows dressed in a black tracksuit, black trainers, and a hooded Parka. Then another two appeared. Another three came from the trees on the left, two more from the right. Byron swallowed hard, his heart racing with fear. The gang were all around him, emerging from the night. A Ford Cortina slowed as it past, and Byron waved to the driver for assistance but he sped up and drove on. He heard footsteps running toward him and he turned around, Lulu yanked the lead and almost pulled him off balance. A hooded figure appeared from the bushes, squirting a liquid from a yellow tin. Suddenly flames shot toward him. Byron couldn't comprehend what was happening. The figure clattered into him, knocking him over. Lulu snarled at the fleeting figure but he was gone in a flash, and then she howled like a banshee as her fur began to burn. Byron stared in disbelief as his dog burst into flames before his eyes, stripping his coat instinctively he wrapped it around the howling dog. He rolled her on the grass, desperately trying to extinguish the flames.

"Next time it'll be you that we burn, bum boy!"

"Don't bend down when Byron is around, or you might get a penis up your arse!" some of the voices trailed off, laughing hysterically, and the hooded figures disappeared into the blackness.

Lulu whimpered, she was hurt, but not fatally. Byron picked her up and ran the rest of the way home. He grabbed his car keys and took the whimpering poodle to the emergency vet. On her hindquarters, there was a weeping bald patch the size of an orange. The vet thought the burn was caused by lighter fuel, sprayed like a flamethrower. Byron didn't care what the vet thought, the terrible experience had scared him to death. It was frightening how vulnerable he felt, despite the assurances of the police. After hours of mental debate, he called the police that night and dropped his witness statement.

7

Richard Bernstein

SCHOOL DAYS

When Richard woke up he was in the intensive care ward on the top floor of Liverpool's Royal Hospital. He remembered the scuffle with Ashwan Pindar, and then he remembered being swamped by a barrage of punches and kicks. At first, he thought that his head and face were bandaged, because he couldn't see properly, but as his memory kicked in he realised that his eyes were swollen, narrowing his field of vision. His mother sat close to his bed, holding his right hand tightly. Her grip hurt his bruised fingers. His brother and sister, David and Sarah sat to his left, away from the bed, near the wall. When he moved and opened his eyelids for the first time, his mother gasped and cried, while his father called a nurse for assistance.

Richard wasn't aware that he had been unconscious for nearly a week. The swelling on his brain had nearly killed him. His mother's fussing echoed around his confused mind. The familiar voices of his family sounded metallic and fuzzy.

"Richard, can you hear me darling?"

He blinked his eyes but couldn't find his voice yet.

"We've been so worried about you," she squeezed his bruised fingers and he grimaced.

"Hello, Richard, everyone's been very worried about you," a portly matron leaned over the bed, shining a torch into his eyes. He flinched from the painful beam, closing his eyes shut. "I know this is uncomfortable, Richard, but I need to see that everything is working as it should be."

"I'm thirsty," Richard croaked. His throat felt like he had been swallowing sand for a week. His vision began to clear and the sounds around him came with more clarity.

"Do you know where you are?" the matron asked, shining the torch again. He squinted at the probing light, wanting it gone. His head ached enough as it was. The smell of disinfectant drifted to him as his senses began to jump back to life.

"Hospital," he groaned. His broken teeth ached and he hurt all over.

"Good boy," she said patronisingly. "Sip this, don't gulp it."

Richard sipped the soothing liquid, the plastic cup hurting his split lips. Scabs had formed on his wounds but they were painful to the touch. His body felt strange; there was pain and numbness all over.

"Is he going to be okay?" his father asked.

"It's too early to make any predictions yet, but he seems to be aware of where he is, and his reactions are normal. I'll get the doctor to see him immediately." The matron left them, her starched uniform rustled as she walked across the highly polished flooring, and she left a waft of Charlie behind her.

"He could be brain damaged," Sarah said a little too loudly.

"Shut up you stupid girl!" her father snapped. David senior was becoming increasingly short tempered with his daughter.

"I think she was brain damaged at birth anyway," David said. Richard laughed painfully, and his mother had to hide her smile. Mr Bernstein wasn't as amused as his family, but that was the norm. David Senior despaired at his children, especially the youngest two. Richard was clumsy socially, and hideously overweight for his age. He was bright and intelligent, but David Snr knew he would be hampered by his weight if he did not sort it out before he got older. His wife spoiled him, and was a major part of the problem. She encouraged his overeating by buying bulk packets of cookies, crisps and sweets. Sarah was a constant worry, becoming very aware of her sexuality far too young for her father's liking. The attack on his youngest son was a shock, and he was finding it difficult to cope with while maintaining his decorum.

"Welcome back Einstein," Richard heard, as his brother stood up and walked to the bedside. He took his left hand gently. "Who did this to you?" David looked after his younger brother and sister at school. Physically he was tough, socially he was popular, and he utilised both to protect his siblings, although sometimes his sister wasn't happy at being protected, especially if she was being protected from good-looking suitors.

"David, he has only just opened his eyes, leave that for now," his mother scolded. Sara Bernstein loved her children with a passion. Richard needed more support than the other two, and she overcompensated by smothering him. Seeing him unconscious, swollen and cut with a knife broke her heart. Sara tried to protect him every day of her life, and she felt as if she had failed him.

Richard looked into his brother's eyes and a silent message passed between them. Although they were like chalk and cheese, they loved each other a great deal. Richard struggled to answer questions if he was embarrassed, much to the annoyance of their father, who saw his silence as contemptuous. David would wait until they were alone, and he squeezed his hand gently to let him know that he understood. 'Later, bro'.

"How long have I been asleep?"

"You weren't asleep, you were sparked out!" Sarah chuckled.

"Sarah!" Mr Bernstein snapped.

"Well it's not asleep is it?" Sarah protested. "George Forman doesn't put people to sleep does he? No. He sparks them out!" She shrugged and looked at her older brother. He smirked and shook his head in warning. Mr Bernstein was not in a joking mood.

"Very funny, how long?" Richard asked again.

"Nearly a week, young man," his doctor arrived. "Can I see the patient please?" He approached the bed, and David stepped away.

"A week, that's not good," Richard commented on his own condition. "Sub cranial haematomas no doubt?"

"Several, young man, you are lucky to be alive," the doctor smiled at his young patient's knowledge.

"Did he cut me?"

"Who?"

"I remember a knife," Richard mumbled. "I don't remember who it was, but I remember a knife."

"You have a number of knife wounds, Richard, some we stitched, and some we stapled," the doctor checked his eyes again.

"How many stitches?"

"Hundreds," the doctor answered, pressing his stethoscope to his chest.

"Can I look?" Richard was eager to see his injuries in a mirror.

"Not right now, I think we should allow some of the swelling to go down before we do that," the doctor replied.

"You look like the Elephant Man, except you're purple," Sarah joined in the conversation.

"Sarah!" her father said angrily.

"I know. Shut up you stupid girl," she mimicked her father and folded her arms sulkily.

"I don't know what has got into you. I'll deal with you when we get home. For now, be quiet. If you can't be polite then be silent," Mr Bernstein added.

The doctor completed a series of checks, and noted his findings on the chart at the end of the bed. He agreed with the young girl, his patient did look like a purple Elephant Man, but he kept his opinions to himself. The boy had been very lucky indeed. It had been touch and go for a while as they battled to keep the swelling on the brain under control.

"I'll be back to see you in the morning. If you suffer any discomfort, or headaches, then tell the nurses straight away," the doctor smiled at Mrs Bernstein before heading off on his rounds.

"Thank you, Doctor," she said after him. She turned to her son.

"How do you feel, Richard?"

"Hungry," Richard moaned. His older brother sniggered.

"Typical Einstein, he's on the mend," he said laughing. "Be back on your feet in no time."

Two plain clothed detectives entered the ward. They spoke briefly to the doctor, and then approached the Bernstein family. Mrs Bernstein frowned as the stale odour of cigarettes and alcohol reached her. She met the detectives briefly when Richard was attacked, and she had noticed it then too. It didn't instil confidence in their ability to catch her son's attackers.

"How is the patient?" Detective Wallace asked. He had a broad Liverpool accent.

"Hungry," Sarah spoke first, receiving a dig in the ribs from her older brother. Her father gave her a withering stare. Richard giggled, but the pain it caused in his face cut it short, becoming a gasp. Everything felt like it was happening in slow motion.

"We need to ask him a few questions," Detective Sergeant Aspel added. "It shouldn't take too long."

"Really, Detective?" Mrs Bernstein asked concerned. "He's only just woke up, surely it can wait a few days."

"I'm sorry, Mrs Bernstein, but the trail is going cold. This was a very serious assault. We need to ask Richard some important questions," Wallace nodded as he spoke, to reinforce the point. He had gaunt features, sunken cheeks and deep-set eyes, which gave him an intense look. Richard thought he looked scary.

"Five minutes, and no more," she said reluctantly.

The detectives shuffled uncomfortably to the bedside. Aspel was the senior officer. He was older than his partner was by twenty years, and he wore his grey hair in a military crew cut. His nose was bulbous and red, the effect of years of whiskey drinking. He removed his leather bomber-jacket and pulled up a plastic chair. It made a loud scraping noise, attracting the attention of the matron. She gave them a scathing look, and pointed to a sign on the wall. 'Four visitors to a bed'.

"I'll take Sarah to the canteen for a coffee," David offered.

"I want to stay here and listen to the interrogation," Sarah protested. Her father glared at her, his face was furious. "Okay, I get the message." Richard tried to laugh again as his brother and sister left the bedside.

"Later, Einstein," David said.

"Later," Richard tried to sound normal, but he actually sounded like he had a mouth full of marbles.

"What can you tell us about the assault?" Wallace got the ball rolling, frustrated by the family's concerns. They'd been waiting a week to talk to Richard. Now he was awake they needed to ask him what he remembered.

"Not much. I remember being tripped up, and a knife, that's all," Richard was hesitant as he spoke. He remembered everything but he hadn't decided whether he wanted to reveal who his attackers were. His brother David could handle himself, but Sarah was young and vulnerable. Part of his rational was to protect his siblings, but deep inside, the real reason that he could not tell was his own white-hot fear of retaliation if he grassed. What would they do to him next?

"A witness recognised a school tie worn by one of your attackers. He identified it as your school, Richard," Wallace pushed. He could spot a liar at a hundred yards, and the boy was lying. "He also said that they were Asian boys."

"I don't remember," Richard mumbled. "I'm thirsty, Mum. Could I have a drink please?"

His mother tutted and reached for the plastic beaker that was next to his bed, knocking over several greeting cards as she did so.

"He's in no condition to be interviewed," she fussed. Richard slurped the water and swallowed hard before taking another sip. The liquid cooled his thirst, but he was craving a can of coke. His body was missing the sugar.

"We know that you're frightened, it's only natural. We can protect you, but you have to tell us who did this to you," Aspel tried with a softer tone of voice.

"I can't remember anything."

"Do you know any of the Asian boys at your school?"

"No, I think I'm getting a headache."

"Tell me about the knife," Wallace jumped in.

"What do you mean?"

"The doctor said that you remembered a knife. Was it a flick-knife? A sheath knife, maybe a kitchen knife like your mum would use? What colour was it?" Wallace tried to pressurise information from him. He had volunteered that he remembered seeing a knife, so he decided to use it as a lever into the truth

"I don't remember," Richard closed his eyes and a stinging tear ran down his swollen cheek.

"You asked the doctor if he used a knife, who was he?"

"I don't remember."

"Was he Asian, Richard, Indian, Pakistani, Black?"

"I don't remember," his lips quivered and Richard Bernstein began to sob openly. He was in shock.

"That's enough," Mr Bernstein stepped in. He couldn't watch his son crying, he had been through enough. It was difficult not to become upset himself. He swallowed a lump in his throat.

"It is vital that we find out what Richard can remember," Wallace turned toward him, angry at the interruption.

"I said, that's enough for now, Detective Wallace."

"You have a witness, ask him," Mrs Bernstein insisted. "The boy has been through enough. Surely, you can see that. "

The detectives looked at each other; Aspel shrugged his shoulders and took Mr Bernstein by the arm, leading him away from the bed.

"Look, Mr Bernstein, we don't have a witness anymore," he explained in a hushed voice. "He has withdrawn his statement."

"I don't understand, Detective," Mr Bernstein said. He looked at his son's face, swollen to the size of a football.

"Our witness withdrew his statement, all we have to go on is your son's evidence," the detective squeezed his arm as he spoke. Mr Bernstein shrugged him off and stepped backward.

"What do you mean?" he hissed angrily. "How can he withdraw his statement?"

"It appears his windows were smashed, and his pet dog was set on fire. He thinks that it was a warning," Detective Aspel whispered the last sentence.

Mr Bernstein put his hand to his mouth and bit his knuckles. Blind fury, a father's angst at his son's predicament. The sheer helplessness of the situation was mind numbing.

"There must be something you can do," he shouted. All heads turned to the detective and Mr Bernstein as they faced each other. The portly matron marched over to them.

"I need to remind you gentlemen that this is an intensive care ward, some of these patients are dying. I will not have their families disturbed by your nonsense," she spoke with a clear, calm but determined voice. The two men turned together and walked out of the ward into the corridor beyond.

"We have nothing to go on, Mr Bernstein," the detective

held up hands to placate the angry father. "We need Richard's evidence, or we can't do anything."

Mr Bernstein walked toward a window and looked out over the city. The St. John's Tower was illuminated in the distance. His mind raced through the possible scenarios as he watched the lights on a cargo ship sailing off to sea. He wondered where in the world it was heading, he also wondered what type of people set fire to a pet dog? A brick through the window could almost be understood, but burning someone's pet. The answer was clear, the type of people who set fire to a helpless animal were also the type of people that had beaten his son to within an inch of his life. What would they do if Richard testified against them?

"If my son remembers anything I'll call you," Mr Bernstein said quietly.

"Mr Bernstein?"

"You heard me, leave us in peace," Mr Bernstein walked away from the detective and back to his family. It was a decision that he would live to regret.

8

M a m o o d

PRESENT DAY

Mamood crossed two lanes of the dual carriageway, which separated his school from Knowsley Safari Park. He cut through the school grounds on his way to the reservoir. The light was fading but the bulk of the rush hour traffic had melted away. Crossing the road during peak time was impossible, but now it wasn't difficult, and it would save him ten minutes. He climbed through a gap in the railings and jogged up a grassy bank, which led into the grounds of the safari park, and the reservoir beyond. A gravel track snaked through a copse to the water's edge. His heart beat faster as he thought of Vicky Stanton waiting for him. He couldn't believe his luck. Of all the girls in the year above him, she was the one he fancied the most. She certainly played her cards close to her chest, barely giving him a second glance in school time. Vicky could take her pick of the boys in school, and she certainly hadn't shown any interest in the students the year below her. Still he wasn't one to look a gift horse in the mouth, and he was one of the best looking guys in his year, after all. Maybe she was embarrassed about being seen with a younger guy, and so she had kept it quiet. 'Who cares? ' Mamood thought to himself. She had put pen to paper and written him a perfumed letter. It had to be a sure bet.

The light was fading fast when he turned the final bend in the road, and he could make out the silhouettes of the lockups about five hundred yards away. There was no sign of Vicky. It was growing cooler though, and he guessed she would be waiting around the corner, sheltering from the evening breeze, which came off the water. He wondered what she would be wearing. Mamood had seen her in town once, wearing tight black leggings and knee-high boots, turning every head in the place. He hoped she was wearing a skirt tonight, easier to get into, and he didn't want to be fumbling around with buttons and zips. She would think he was an inexperienced virgin. He was, but he didn't want her to know that. Mamood had come close a couple of times, but never actually gone all the way. Tonight was the night. In her letter she had promised to make it worth his while, what else could she mean?

He reached the water's edge and picked up a flat stone. Mamood cocked his throwing arm and skimmed it across the surface. The lockups were less than a hundred yards away now, once used as boatsheds, they'd been empty for years. A number of drownings one summer prompted the reservoir owners to stop all leisure activities on the water, but people still came here because it was picturesque. The double doors of the lockups came into view, one of them almost intact, the other broken and shattered. A dull light flickered and glowed from behind the missing panels. She was already in there. His mouth went dry, and he put his hand in front of his mouth to check his breath was fresh. He broke into a jog, eager and excited, only stopping as he neared the buildings.

Mamood peered into the gloomy lockups. Boat racks were fixed to the walls, cobwebs and dust now hung were canoes and paddles once lived. There was a smell of decay in there.

"Vicky?" he called into the gloomy interior. A paraffin lantern dangled from an ancient roof truss. The light from it glowed orange, flickering and inviting, tempting him inside.

43

He stepped through a gap in the rotten planks, ducking low to avoid banging his head.

"Vicky, it's Mamood. I got your letter," he tried to sound cool. His hands were shaking with nervous anticipation. She had gone to a lot of trouble. He hoped that he wouldn't disappoint her when the time came. Malik told him to think of his dream England squad for the next World Cup; that way the sex would last longer. He wasn't sure he wanted to think of anything else, but then Malik had already had lots of girls, so he should know. The older girls in school were scathing about their sexual encounters, especially if they'd been disappointed, of jilted. A guy's reputation could be ruined in a lunchtime break.

A shifting noise from the back of the lockup brought him back to reality. There was a doorway fixed to the back wall, probably leading to a storeroom. The door was ajar, and he could hear a radio playing quietly, the disc jockey was chatting aimlessly to his co-presenter, between tracks.

"Vicky," he called a little louder, uneasy about penetrating the gloom at the rear of the lockup. She would think he was a Nancy boy if she saw him dithering. He steeled himself and walked to the rear of the building. "Vicky, it's Mamood, I got your letter."

"Meet me at the reservoir, and I'll make it worth your while," Nick stepped from the darkness as he mimicked a female voice, sounding nothing like one. There was an evil sneer across his face.

Mamood froze and inhaled sharply, confused and frightened. The man was tall, well built, and somehow, he knew what Vicky had put in her letter.

"Who the fuck are you?" Mamood tried to sound aggressive, but he didn't. "Where's Vicky?"

"Vicky is probably at home, tucking into her spaghetti bolognaise. She will not be coming I'm afraid," Nick spoke in a monotone voice. His face was distorted by a nylon stocking. His nose looked flatter and elongated, his chin hooked with a dimple in the middle. The beard and hair he had grown for the bombing were cropped to the bone, exposing his high cheekbones and Neanderthal forehead. Nick was ugly, frightening to look at, especially in the flickering shadows, even more so with the stocking pulled tight over his features. "Do you know why you're here?"

"Get out of my way, weirdo!" Mamood shouted. He was scared witless. The man was between him and the doors, and he was freaky looking. How did he know about Vicky's letter?

"You're here because you're vain, little Mamood, just like your father," Nick walked toward him as he spoke. Mamood wanted to move away but his legs ignored his brain. "How is Ashwan? Is he still a fucking wanker?"

"What do you want? How do you know my father?"

"Oh that's a long story, Mamood. Your father is a bad man, a nasty piece of work, and now it's time for him to pay for his actions," Nick moved a step closer, his shadow smothered Mamood.

Mamood cowered, shuffling backward against the boat racks. The man towered above him, wearing army camouflage fatigues and combat boots. He had something in his right hand that Mamood didn't recognise. His mouth opened in a silent scream as two conductive darts pierced his chest, and fifty thousand volts surged through his body. The stun-gun did its work quickly and efficiently, Mamood collapsed in a heap. "Maybe your father will listen now. Your life depends on it," Nick growled.

9

Richard Bernstein;
SCHOOL DAYS

Richard Bernstein spent Christmas, and the best part of the following three months in the Royal Hospital. Recurring infections hampered the healing process, and the surgeons struggled to make skin grafts take. His parents hired private tutors to further his education, and his father gave him a computerised chess game to pass the hours. The game was a challenge for the first month or so. When he left the hospital, he could beat the computer within twenty minutes, taking just twelve minutes at his record best. Richard loved the game, draining the power from a dozen batteries a week. He managed to lose nearly two stones in weight too, a combination of a healthy diet and less chocolate, although his mother brought him daily treats. The police had kept their distance, as requested, and Richard's memory of the incident had not shed any light on the matter. He never disclosed the names of his attackers, and no one pushed him to.

Life outside the hospital carried on without him. His brother David did well in his final exams, and he had been awarded the captaincy of the school's First Fifteen, rugby team, which was an honour indeed. Mr Bernstein turned out every Saturday afternoon with his flask of coffee to watch his son play. Sarah continued to be the bane of her father's life, late nights and an ever decreasing hem lines were driving him demented. She began to hang out with the older set, and came home several times, smelling of cigarettes and alcohol. All was not well in the Bernstein family home, and Richard could sense a change in his sister as soon as he arrived home. She looked older, and somewhat tarty. Mr Bernstein wasn't a religious Jew, in that he didn't frequent the Synagogue regularly, weddings and funerals mostly. He was a member of the chamber of trade, as were many of his Jewish friends. On several occasions, he noticed raised eyebrows and hushed whispers when his back was turned. Sarah was becoming a regular topic of conversation.

"Nice belt, Sis!" Richard joked about the length of her miniskirt. He had been home a fortnight and already put back on the weight he had lost in hospital. His mother fed him at every opportunity, 'to build up his strength', she said.

"Shut up, Richard," Sarah retorted nastily. "Dad is always on my back, and I don't need you joining in thank you." She twirled three hundred and sixty degrees, checking out her outfit in her bedroom mirror. "This is called a waistline, something you'll never have to worry about." She said pouting, her hands on her hips.

"Just kidding," Richard mumbled. There was no mirth in her voice anymore. She had always teased and joked with him, but things had definitely changed. Her remarks were becoming nasty. She wiggled past him in her bedroom doorway, trying to emulate the catwalk models on the television. He tried a different tack to engage his younger sister in conversation, pretending to be sensible. "Are you going anywhere nice?"

"Mind your own business," she looked at her reflection in the hallway mirror, pouting and looking way too sexy for a fourteen year old girl.

"I'm just being friendly, Sis," Richard smiled at her, but she didn't look at him. "Are you going to a party?"

"What is it you want exactly?" Sarah turned on him. Richard hardly recognised her anymore. "If you're fishing for an invite then forget it. It's definitely not your scene Einstein. There will be no........." She stopped.

"What? Fat kids?" Richard finished off her sentence.

"Why don't you go and eat a Mars Bar or something?"

"Take a chill pill, Sarah. I was trying to make conversation, forget it," Richard snarled. He headed into the kitchen and opened the refrigerator. There was a packet of sliced pepperoni sausage open on the middle shelf, next to a triangle of cheddar cheese. He broke a chunk of cheese off, and wrapped it up in a slice of pepperoni, before stuffing the tasty parcel into his mouth. A large gulp of gold top milk from the bottle added to the mix of flavours.

"Richard Bernstein!" his mother's shrill voice came from the hallway. "What have I told you about snacking all day long?"

"I'm hungry," Richard blushed. He wasn't hungry at all. Sarah had been nasty, so the pepperoni and cheese made him feel better. Comfort food.

"You should not drink milk from the bottle, young man."

Richard crossed the kitchen to meet her. She held four carrier bags full of groceries in each hand, having come back from her weekly supermarket trip. His father was following close behind her, loaded to the hilt, and trying to close the front door with his foot. Richard's parents were creatures of habit, always dressed in sensible, practical clothes. His mother had a chocolate coloured anorak, and a matching headscarf; his father wore a navy-blue anorak, and a matching flat cap. They looked like extras from a seventies sitcom.

"Where's your sister?" Mr Bernstein asked, emerging from the hallway. Mrs Bernstein plonked her shopping down heavily on the kitchen table.

"She was in the hallway two minutes ago," Richard answered, a little surprised.

"She had better be in her room, or she will be in big trouble," Mr Bernstein muttered. "She's grounded after her performance last week."

"Please stop moaning at the girl, for heaven's sake!" Mrs Bernstein scolded her husband. "She is growing up. We were young once too."

"You didn't prance around in clothes that should belong to a tart," Mr Bernstein mumbled under his breath. He plonked down his shopping and struggled out of his anorak, leaving his flat cap on his head.

"Don't use that word please, especially not about your own daughter."

"She did look like she was dressed up to go to a party, now you mention it," Richard stirred the issue. He looked in his mother's shopping bags for treats. "Dad is right about her clothes, Mum. Her skirt barely covered her arse!"

"Richard Bernstein! How dare you use language like that in front of your old mother, and about your sister too?" Mrs Bernstein clucked around like a mother hen, banging tins into cupboards to show her annoyance. As much as she loved Sarah, she was slipping out of control. She was losing respect for both her parents, and her tutors. School reports and parents evenings were becoming a trauma. Her attitude toward Richard was downright nasty.

"Sarah!" Mr Bernstein shouted up the stairs. There was only silence in reply. "Sarah!" He repeated, but to no avail. Sarah had sneaked out seconds after her parents had returned. "I'm at a loss with that girl."

"Where has she been going while I've been away?" Richard found a packet of chocolate-chipped cookies, his favourite. "Can I have one of these?" he asked, already ripping into the packet.

"You will not eat your dinner if you pig out on biscuits, Richard." His mother gave him three, took the packet from him, and placed it into the cupboard. "She's been hanging around with some older kids, and that's why your father is not happy about the situation. He thinks that she is drinking and smoking."

Richard stepped behind his mother and opened the cupboard quietly, removing three more cookies with a deft touch. He slipped them into his pocket, silently. His father saw him and gently nudged him in the back.

"Caught red-handed," he whispered, so that Mrs Bernstein couldn't hear him. He smiled at his son. Sarah's recent behaviour made him appreciate his sons more somehow. Richard had weight and confidence issues, but he was never disrespectful, and he never got into trouble.

"What are you two whispering about?"

"Nothing, Mum." Richard laughed and moved away from the cupboard. "Who is she hanging around with then?"

"A couple of the girls from your year, I think. They've been going to parties at the weekends, with a group of Asian boys," Mrs Bernstein put the chilled items into the fridge as she spoke. "Have you been eating the cheese?" She asked, noticing a large chunk was missing.

"Asian boys?" Richard Bernstein felt a cold shiver run down his spine. "Which Asian boys?"

"I'm not sure, but she keeps mentioning a boy called, Malik, or something like that. I think she has a crush on him."

Richard shoved his hands deep into his pockets and sulkily walked out of the kitchen. He decided that he wanted to play chess against his computer, in his room. Of all the boys in school for his sister to get a crush on, it had to be him. Malik Shah was building a reputation as the best drug dealer in school. Apparently, his gear was cheap and strong, not that Richard touched anything like that. If Sarah was running with that crowd, then it would only be a matter of time before she experimented with drugs. Richard didn't think things could get any worse, but very soon they would be. Much worse.

10

Major Investigation Team

Superintendent Alec Ramsay briefed his troops about the findings that Will Naylor's team had discovered, and he set them the task to find out as much information as they could about Malik Shah and Ashwan Pindar. The investigation was to be covert. No one would approach them directly, or their associates for now. They had to gather information from other departments, other constabularies, and international law enforcement agencies. There was no shortage of suspected crimes allegedly committed by their criminal organisation; however, there was no hard evidence against them. They were smart. Malik Shah hadn't been arrested and questioned since the late nineties. His record was clean. It was just before three o'clock when the entire Major Investigation Team was present at their desks.

"Half past three, ladies and gents please, let's have a quick update. I don't want anything overlooked, no matter how insignificant it might seem now," Alec brushed his blond fringe back from his head. Grey and ginger strands were creeping into his mane; he had read that the 'hair industry' called it salt and pepper. 'Getting older', he called it. His hair was parted down the centre, and while it was still thick, the roots always appeared darker, greying blond. The afternoon sun was sinking fast in the west, its warmth was gone now, but its glare was annoying through the full windows. In the near distance, the river looked slate grey in the fading light. Heads nodded in confirmation of the Superintendents order, and several small clusters of officers formed as they collated their team's information. Alec had been kept up to speed all day as news came in, but each team needed to be completely aware what avenues their colleagues were following. Hundreds of man-hours could be saved by frequent briefings. They stopped people working on the same issue, or heading down a dead end that others had already been to. Alec had the bit between his teeth, and the longer they investigated the bombing, the less likely it seemed that it was a terrorist attack. He needed the Divisional Commander to have the same opinion, or it would be left to the Counter Terrorist Unit to deal with.

"Guv," Will Naylor held up his telephone. He looked sharp and refreshed after his break, as did his team. Even Smithy looked half-tidy.

"It's the Commander, Guv."

"Patch it through to my office please, Will."

Alec stepped into his office and clicked the door closed behind him. He couldn't make his mind up whether he wanted to be the lead unit on the bombing or not. It was a massive case, which carried volumes of kudos if it ended with a conviction. The careers of the entire team would be enhanced by working on a case like this. They could also be damaged beyond repair, if mistakes were made. Alec was too long in the tooth to be a glory hound, but he relished a challenge, and his detectives were the best.

Alec was convinced it was a targeted hit. The problem was both the protagonists and targets lived in the world of organised crime. It was a world of secrecy and silence. There would be no informers, no tip-offs, and no witnesses. Malik Shah appeared to be made of Teflon, nothing stuck to him, and

Alec would bet a year's wages his enemies would be made of similar material. The police hierarchy would want results and convictions tomorrow, if not sooner. Alec couldn't see either coming quickly.

He lifted the phone and pressed a button to connect the line. "Commander."

"Detective Superintendent, how are you Alec?" Alec and the Commander went back years. Alec had always been a few rungs down the ladder, but the two men had a mutual respect that can only grow over decades. Alec had been pulled out of a few close scrapes during his years on the force, and though he was never certain, he had a hunch that the Commander was his guardian angel.

"Not so bad, Bob. How's Sally?"

"Fine thanks, and how's Gail?"

"Still trying to poison me with organic everything. I'm still not sure what organic actually means, but I'll live forever at this rate." Alec was force fed a healthy diet by his long-suffering wife, whether he wanted it or not.

"Heaven forbid! Why would you want to do that? By the time we retire our pension funds will have been invested in an Icelandic bank. It'll be worth peanuts."

"Probably, but as long as they're organic, the boss will be happy." Alec Ramsey had been married twenty years, and he'd never strayed once, which he was proud of. He'd had plenty of offers over the years, a mixture of power and personality made him attractive to his female colleagues, but he'd never succumbed to the temptation.

The Commander laughed and then said seriously, "All joking aside, Alec, how's the investigation going?"

"It depends on where you're looking at it from," Alec rubbed his chin as he replied thoughtfully. "What are CTU saying?"

"They have nothing solid worth shouting about. You know what they're like, cards very close to their chest and all."

"Do they think it was an extremist attack?"

"I'm assuming from that comment, Superintendent, that you don't," the Commander batted the question back.

"No, Commander, I don't." The two old friends slipped into their professional standings comfortably. "Have you seen the preliminary forensics?"

"Yes. What do you make of it?"

"Did you pickup on the mixture?"

"I did indeed, Superintendent." The Commander had spent a number of years in Belfast. "Echoes of our Republican friends?"

"Without a doubt, Commander, I haven't seen or heard of a cooked mixture since our time across the Irish Sea."

"You're ruling out any Irish involvement, I presume."

"I can't say for definite, but what would their motive be?"

"I agree, so where does that leave us?"

"I think it's a hit, Commander."

"The Patels being the possible target?"

"It's a possibility that needs to be investigated. Patel has some very dubious business associates."

"Malik Shah, I believe," Alec thought the Commander sounded like the bulldog from the car insurance adverts on the television. "That man has been a thorn in my side for as long as I can remember."

"It could be a coincidence, Commander, but the extremist tack doesn't sit right. It's a hunch, but the evidence tells me it's a hit."

"Was Patel of value to Malik Shah?"

"According to Smithy, the drugs squad had him down as the bookkeeper for the entire operation, but they could never follow the money trail to anything solid."

"Do you think Shah could have taken him out, maybe he was skimming off the top?" The Commander speculated.

"Who knows, it's way too early to tell, but my money is on a link to Shah, rather than right wing extremists, Commander."

"I tend to agree, but if it is, then the ball will be in your court."

"Yes, Commander, I thought as much." Alec swept his hand across his mouth and eyes, rubbing them.

"I think the joint departments meeting will iron out where we go with this."

"We're working our way through the possible options, Commander. If it falls to us then we'll hit the ground running." Alec swallowed hard, and loosened his tie. It seemed that that case was about to drop into his lap.

11

Lana Pindar

PRESENT DAY

Lana floated in and out of a troubled sleep. Her dreams were real and worrying. She dreamt of a lake and a rowing boat. Mamood had fallen into the water, and no matter how hard she rowed, the boat drifted further away from him. Lana called his name and shouted for help, but he was being carried away by an unseen current. There wasn't anything she could do to help him. He became a spot on the horizon, just before he disappeared beneath the dark waters. She awoke with a start, out of breath and covered in a thin sheen of sweat. The red glow of their digital clock told her that it was past three in the morning, and she hadn't heard Mamood coming home. She didn't make a fuss when he was late, but she didn't sleep soundly until she knew that he was home safe. Lana thought that maybe he'd sneaked in quietly, while she dozed, but she dismissed that as wishful thinking. She knew when her son was home, and when he wasn't. It was a mother's intuition. Lana lifted the quilt and slipped out of bed. Ashwan murmured and turned onto his back. He could sleep through an avalanche without waking. She tiptoed across the thick white carpet to the door, where she removed her dressing gown from its hook and pulled it on.

Lana moved quietly down the landing, thick carpet cushioned her footsteps. She hoped she was overreacting as she pushed open her son's bedroom door. Amir Khan, the Asian boxing hero from Bolton snarled at her from his place above Mamood's bed. His Manchester United quilt cover lay unruffled. There was no sign of a sleeping teenager beneath it. Lana bit her lip and her stomach twisted and sank. She felt physically sick with worry. He had been home late from parties before, but never this late. Midnight was his allowed time, and he never pushed the deadline much past half-past. Mamood had been so full of life and excitement when he'd left that evening. The thought of his prospective date had made him high and giddy.

Maybe he'd got lucky, she thought, remembering what he'd said before he left, but then maybe he was in trouble. Lana was his mother, and she was bound to worry about her only son for the rest of her days, that's what mothers do. She sat on his bed and touched his pillow. He was growing up so quickly, and staying out late with girls was something that she would have to get used to, whether she liked it or not. Lana thought about waking up Ashwan to tell him, but he would probably laugh and say, "That's my boy," or something equally macho and crass.

Lana crept downstairs and walked down the long, wide hallway into a large open kitchen area. Their home was huge, and the kitchen was bigger than most people's gardens. The floors were tiled with Egyptian white marble, and it felt cool beneath her feet. She opened the American refrigerator and took a glass from the cupboard, filling it with milk and then sipping it as she debated what to do. She leaned against a granite worktop and chewed her manicured nails as she debated in her mind. Finally she decided to ring Mamood on his mobile, after all that's why he had it. To let them know where he was, and to keep in touch. If she was worried then it was his own fault for not letting them know that he would be late.

Lana dialled the number from memory. It clicked straight onto answering machine, voice mail. She tried again, just in case, voice mail. She bit her lip as she replaced the handset, remembering the nightmare she'd had before she woke. Lana tiptoed back to bed and slid gently under the warm covers, next to her husband, scolding herself for being overprotective of her child. She tried hard, but she could find no peaceful dreams that night.

12

Abdul

PRESENT DAY

Abdul Salim ground a cigarette butt into the pavement. A steady evening rain had started to fall, but he did not go inside to shelter. Salim was a teenage drug dealer and there were customers to serve, rain or shine. He was tucked between two empty shop units, which were situated beneath a gargantuan tower block. A service alleyway snaked between them, connecting the lockups to a delivery bay behind them. The tower blocks were once the architect's solution to overcrowding and a simple method of providing state housing, but they actually became vertical human zoos. The tenants either were unemployed or in low paid jobs, easy pickings for drug dealers and loan sharks.

Across the street, two police cars passed by and their uniformed occupants strained to look out of the steamed-up windows. Salim watched as they drove off down the street. The police knew what he was doing. Sometimes they left him alone, sometimes they didn't. He always carried just enough drugs to qualify as being for personal use, never more. The rest of his stock, his takings and his weapon he kept stashed with a young runner.

Like his parents before him, Salim was an Asian pioneer, but instead of settling down to the hard-working toil of previous generations of Asians, Salim and others had blazed a new trail into the violent world of drug dealing. Hard drugs had arrived in Britain's Asian communities, and were rapidly creating a social problem of spiralling crime rates and increased numbers of addicts. It had led to the emergence of Asian drug gangs who were willing to use violence to carve out territories and defend the enormous profits the trade can bring. On the streets of some northern towns, gang shootings had led to public killings, executions, and a climate of fear that the drug dealers were only too willing to encourage.

Salim knew that it was not a problem confined to the North of the United Kingdom. The previous year, police in London smashed a huge crack and heroin dealing operation in the East End of the capital city that controlled a trade worth millions of pounds. The gang, based on several large Asian families, had run a twenty-four hour operation supplying drugs to thousands of the capital's users. Tower Hamlets, which has a large and deprived Asian community, had slowly become the 'heroin capital' of the country. If he could progress through the ranks of the organisation, and make money for his boss, then he would eventually be given his own area to manage. Drugs were everywhere, and where there are users, there is money to be made.

Successful Asians left the rundown areas, as did the educated ones. Once they achieved a degree course at university, they up and left for pastures new, using their qualifications to escape the ghettos. What they left behind were poor, vulnerable and isolated communities: places that were easily invaded by gangs. They brought with them a culture of extreme violence and ostentatious wealth that seemed more at home in the ghettoes of Los Angeles. Salim knew who his role models were, and they were not his parents. They spent their lives slaving away in a small corner shop, which they called their family business. Salim could make more money in one night than they did in a week. His role models were the gold-chain wearing drug traffickers with their new BMW cars, souped-up hi-fi systems and latest designer sportswear. The only way he could achieve his material aspirations was through crime.

Salim was a street dealer, near the bottom rung of the ladder, but he was highly thought of and he would soon reach the next level. The 'next level' is a violent place, where the culture of 'saving face' among drug gangs can lead to the slightest perceived insult being punished with horrific violence. Salim wanted to be as rich as his boss Ashwan Pindar was. Aspiring to be at that level, was like standing at the bottom of a mountain, and looking up at the peak. Malik Shah was the man at the top of this particular mountain. He controlled several successful crime families across the country. His gangs were highly organised and stretched from the inner cities of Britain to the poppy fields of Afghanistan. At the bottom of the pile were the 'runners', usually young teenagers who make drug deliveries on specially bought mountain bikes. Then come street dealers like Salim, supplying runners and customers with their fixes. Above him were the murky upper echelons of the gang world, often using family ties with Pakistan to arrange the courier routes that bring the drugs back to Britain.

The callousness of Malik Shah was staggering. He groomed girls as young as thirteen to be mules, bribing their families to be complicit. He sought the financially destitute people of his communities, and pressed them into service. Malik would offer them loans at impossible interest rates, and then force them to act as mules in order to repay their debts. Those that refused were terrorised. As his gangs grew, they became more sophisticated. Over the past months, Salim noticed crack cocaine make its first appearance among the Asian gangs. It led to friction with other drug gangs, but the potential profits were just too great to ignore.

"Salim," a voice behind him disturbed his train of thought. He turned to see one of his young runners approaching from the blackness of the alleyway on his bike. He was a skinny Bangladeshi kid known as Rozzo. Rozzo looked up to Salim in the same way Salim respected his superiors, hoping one day to be working in his shoes.

"What?" Salim was angered by the fact that Rozzo had arrived unannounced. The rules of the business were clear. The runner sent a text message first, and then came for the drugs, carrying the buyer's payment. Rozzo had broken the protocol. "What the fucking hell are you playing at, Rozzo?"

"A weird looking bloke has been asking questions in the park, Salim. Questions about you, I've never seen him before. Don't think he's a dealer. He's not a pig, no way!"

"Take it easy," Salim lowered his voice to try to calm his frightened associate. "What was he asking about?"

Rozzo spat on the floor, and a string of saliva hung from his chin. He wiped it excitedly away with the sleeve of his black tracksuit before answering. "He was asking who worked for Ash, but he's not a pig. I swear he's not a pig."

"When was this?"

"Five minutes ago, Salim. I came straight here!" Rozzo smiled a toothless smile. He had lost his front teeth to an angry customer who wanted credit for a hit, but was refused. His line of credit was revoked when he failed to pay his debts on time. It was one of the hazards of the job. Rozzo was convinced that he had done the right thing by alerting his boss immediately. Salim was smarter, and he knew it was a mistake. Rozzo had led the inquisitor straight to him.

"What did you tell him?"

"Nothing, Salim!" Rozzo pulled a three hundred and sixty degree wheelie on his bike. "I told him to fuck off!"

"What did he look like?"

"He's a fucking weirdo, mate! Army pants and boots, and

he's a real ugly motherfucker! Massive head like a caveman!"

"Did he follow you?" Salim reached into his white Nike windbreaker for his phone. White was his colour of choice. Salim thought it made him stand out from his colleagues, who always opted for black hooded shell-suits. He dialled quickly, looking left and right along the empty street. It was time to acquire his weapon. A young voice answered the call.

"Bring me the ten, and bring it fast," Salim spoke quickly, trying to keep his cool. His runner kept a reactivated Mac-10 machine pistol in a duffle bag. He kept the weapon safe, constantly circling the area on his bike, in the event that Salim would need it for protection. "Have you seen anyone wearing combats?" He asked the runner on the telephone. Salim nodded his head at the reply and ended the call with a stab of his finger.

"Could he have followed you?" He asked turning back to Rozzo.

"No way, Salim, I'm too fast," Rozzo bragged proudly, pulling the bike into a wheelie again. He was about to speak again when a nine millimetre hollow-point smashed into his back. It was as if he had been hit with an invisible sledgehammer. Salim thought that he had tumbled off his bike for a moment, but as a dark pool of blood spread quickly from beneath his body, realisation hit home.

Salim froze to the spot in panic, it was every dealer's worst nightmare. He was under attack, and unarmed. He couldn't tell which direction the bullet had been fired from, because Rozzo had been spinning the bike when he was hit. Salim flattened himself against the wall and scanned the area for his attacker's possible hiding places. The street was empty. He reached down and touched Rozzo's neck, checking for a pulse. There was none, he was long gone. Salim looked down the alleyway, which ran between the tower blocks. The darkness was impenetrable. His mobile vibrated and he looked at the illuminated screen. It was his runner. He was a minute away, bringing Salim his machinegun. The sound of rubber tyres approached, a splashing drone as rainwater sprayed up from the tarmac. A mountain bike approached at high speed. The young runner was standing as he pumped the pedals as fast as he could. Salim felt adrenalin pumping through his veins now as his weapon neared. The Mac-10 would even things up. Whoever this clown was, he would be sorry that he crossed paths with Salim. He was destined to be a famous gangster. Malik Shah and Ashwan Pindar would be impressed when they heard that Salim had taken out a rival. He could taste the street-cred a kill would bring to him.

Salim broke cover and sprinted to meet the runner. The runner reached inside his black hooded top, and pulled the weapon out. He lifted it out in front for Salim to grab it. A silenced shot spat from the darkness, and a nine-millimetre dumdum hit the cyclist straight between the eyes. A jagged black hole appeared in the runner's face and the back of his skull exploded as the bullet exited carrying lumps of grey brain matter with it. The mountain bike carried on without the rider, and it clattered to a halt at the entrance to the alleyway. The runner was blasted backwards off the bike and he dropped like a dead weight onto the pavement. The Mac-10 clattered away into the night, lost in the shadows.

A second silenced dum-dum round hit Salim in the left thigh, the bullet flattened and fragmented on impact, ripping through muscle and sinew. A crimson pattern widened across the white tracksuit, a ragged black hole at the epicentre. Salim dropped his cell phone and it clattered across the paving slabs noisily. He leaned his back against the wall of the alleyway, and slid down it into a sitting position. Blood was pumping through his fingers as he tried in vain to stem the flow. Two figures emerged from the darkness. They grabbed the dead body of Rozzo, and pulled him out of sight of the road, and then they returned to Salim and his runner. Salim gritted his teeth together in agony as they dragged him by the legs into the darkness of the alleyway. His fingernails ripped and split as he clawed desperately at the concrete. He was badly wounded and helpless as they pulled him off the street and into the urine stinking blackness.

"What do you want, you bastards!" Salim cried through the pain. His question was answered by a hard punch to the bullet wound in his leg. He screamed and flailed helplessly at thin air, trying to grasp anything that could stop the men taking him further into the blackness. "I'll tell you where the money is!"

The two men stopped momentarily; they glanced at each other silently. Salim took their reaction as a positive. Blood had soaked through his underwear and saturated the back of his hooded top. He was losing too much blood to survive this attack for any length of time.

"The money and drugs are hidden in the bike frames," he gasped. He thought that giving up the information would buy him some time. "Pull the seats off, it's all in there. Take it and fuck off!"

One of the men stopped pulling his injured leg and headed off in the direction of the discarded mountain bikes. Salim almost breathed a sigh of relief, until the other man began to drag him alone. He tried desperately to struggle, but his energy was fading as his life force bled away. The stabbing pain in his thigh was excruciating, and white-hot bolts of fresh agony pierced his brain with every movement.

"Did you have to shoot him there?" A voice came from the darkness. Salim was slipping in and out of consciousness. "There will be blood everywhere."

"Shut up, Einstein!" The man dragging Salim replied abruptly. "That's why we brought the plastic isn't it?"

"We brought the plastic because I told you to. There will be blood all over the alleyway."

"Bollocks, open the doors."

Salim heard vehicle doors being opened, and then the crinkling, crackling sound of a polythene sheet being dragged across the delivery bay. Another shaft of pain shot through him as he was dragged onto the plastic by the legs. He tried to scream but a choked gargle was all that he could manage. Time was running out, and there was nothing he could do about it.

"Where is he?" Einstein asked angrily.

"He's getting the drugs and the money," came the snarled reply.

"What for? We've got what we came for." Einstein moaned. "Can't you two ever follow a fucking plan?"

A hooded figure emerged from the alleyway. He had the bike in one hand and he dragged the body of the dead runner in the other. He dropped them on the loading bay and then returned for the other.

"What are you doing?" Richard Bernstein hissed, looking at the dead boys. He was shaking his head in disbelief.

"Change of plan, Einstein." The man replied calmly. "We're going to leave these little bastards here, with the drugs, and a message for the police. I want everyone to think that this was a drugs hit. The scumbags will take this personally."

He rummaged through Rozzo's pockets and recovered a small notebook and a biro. He ripped a blank page from amongst the illegible scrawling, and penned a note, sticking it to the dead boy's forehead with a piece of discarded chewing gum. "That should put the pressure on Malik Shah and his friends for a while, anything that we can do to spotlight his activities is a good thing."

Einstein could see the sense in it immediately. If Malik, Ashwan and their associates had the police crawling all over them, then it would make it very difficult for them to step out of line. They would have to do as they were told, or face the consequences, just as Amir Patel and his wife had done.

They didn't follow the instructions they were given, and they paid the ultimate price. Malik Shah would realise that his dark empire was under attack, but he would be helpless to stop it while the police scrutinised his businesses. If this were a game of chess, then Einstein had all his strong pieces in the right places, and this game would have only one ending, checkmate. The dead boys were a bonus for now, and he could see the benefit. The big man couldn't but he rarely did, he just followed orders. At first Einstein was worried about killing, but as the years went by and he watched Malik Shah and his empire grow, he realised that anyone connected to them was evil, and equally guilty. There would be collateral deaths too, but that was to be expected.

Salim could hear the conversation around him, but it didn't make much sense to him. In his mind he didn't believe that this was a drugs hit by a rival gang. The shooter was a marksman, no doubt about that. He did believe that his number was up. He would become a statistic. Abdul Salim was to become one of the legions of dead teenage victims of the ever growing number of drug gangs.

"Put the memory stick into his pocket," the man called Einstein said. His voice seemed distant now. Salim felt rough hands placing something into his top zip pocket. His vision cleared for a moment, and the face of his murderer appeared. The man was ugly to say the least. His features were broad and exaggerated, his forehead protruded. A sneer crossed his attacker's face.

"Give this to Ashwan from me, and be sure to tell him that Mamood will die slowly, unless he follows these instructions to the letter."

"Wrap him up. He isn't going to live long enough to tell anybody anything, thanks to you. We'll dump him outside Ash's house, as we planned." Einstein moaned.

Salim heard the words echoing in his mind as he felt

himself being cocooned in plastic. His vision distorted as the layers built up. He was turned over and over, breathing became difficult, and then impossible. Salim died as many of his young customers had, helpless and alone in the darkness.

Ronald Theakston held his breath and tried to stay as still as he possibly could. He shuffled backwards against the fire door, and made himself as small as he could, praying that the men in the van wouldn't turn around and see him. The doorway had been his home for the last three months, reasonably dry and faraway from the eyes of passersby. Ronald had been on the streets for as long as his alcohol-addled brain could remember, but it hadn't always been that way. He was a veteran of the first Gulf War, a Royal Marine. Civilian life didn't suit him and he drifted from one dead-end job to another, before finally falling off the wagon completely and drinking himself into oblivion whenever he could afford it. He was registered to a homeless shelter, but he rarely went there. The Social Security gave him the minimum allowance allowed, and he received a nominal pension from the Marines, which enabled him to stay drunk seven days a week, if he didn't eat of course. He was drunk, tired, and very scared. It had been a long time since he had fired a gun, but he could recognise the deadly spitting sound of a silenced nine-millimetre pistol. There were three men by the looks of things, and two dead, at least. He'd heard the name, Einstein, and something about a message for Ashwan. Ronald closed his eyes and allowed sleep to take him.

13

Sarah Bernstein
SCHOOL DAYS

Sabah Barakat was in his last year of high school, and he couldn't wait to leave. His family, who were originally from the United Arab Emirates, had high hopes for their eldest son, but their aspirations were not the same as Sabah's. They had dreams of him reading law, becoming a solicitor or even a barrister. His mother talked incessantly about him becoming an eminent surgeon, despite the fact he had dropped biology as a science subject. He hated science. In fact, he hated studying completely. Sabah had dreams of his own, and he had already taken his first tentative steps into a life of crime. His friend Malik Shah was buying cannabis and acid tablets from some of his older cousins, and then making a huge profit selling them to the other students at school. If anyone needed drugs for the weekend, Malik and his sidekicks were the suppliers of choice. Sabah was making good money already, and he hadn't finished his final exams yet. He could buy new trainers every week if he chose to, and his collection of gold bling was growing month on month. Being part of the supply chain had its benefits in other ways too, primarily of the female kind. The young girls on the periphery of the gang were drawn to the male members like moths to a flame. Sarah Bernstein was one of those unfortunate girls.

Academically Sabah was gifted, but he had no interest in his studies. The only school activity that he enjoyed was the annual chess competition. He saw it as a mental boxing match, a chance to demonstrate his superior intellect. His father was a magician at the game, and he introduced his son to it at a very early age. Sabah was by far the best player in the school, and the summer saw him smash his way through the opposition to reach the semi-finals of the competition, without losing a single leg. The final was in his sights, and regaining his title as school champion looked a fore gone conclusion. Sabah sniggered when he saw who his next opponent was to be. Richard Bernstein stood in his way, the fat Jew-boy that they'd beaten to a pulp in the park a year before. He was also Sarah Bernstein's brother, and Sabah knew her well, most of the gang did. Sabah couldn't wait to play him. He was going to enjoy every minute of it, or so he thought.

Richard Bernstein and Sabah Barakat were twenty minutes into the first game of their semi-final, and things weren't faring well for Sabah. Richard Bernstein had always done well in the open competition, but he was a year younger than Sabah, and being beaten by a younger pupil was embarrassing. There were teachers drifting around, watching and refereeing, and a small crowd of onlookers, seated at one end of the sports hall, sat and watched in silence. The hall was used for a multitude of events by the school, and it smelled of polish and bee's wax. It had a stage at one end, used to show the schools theatrical productions. When not in use it had the headmaster's podium on it, from where daily assemblies were directed. Sabah had used his strongest opening moves, but Richard Bernstein had a counter measure for everything that he tried. Sabah was in danger of losing a game, so he decided to apply a different tactic when the teacher's backs were turned.

"How are the scars, Bernstein?" Sabah tilted his head to one side to gauge the impact of his words on the younger boy.

Richard's eyes flickered upward for a second as the verbal assault landed, but he was toughened by years of abuse and bullying by others, and he retreated into the safety of his mind. He moved a knight, trapping Sabah's bishop, and rook in a fork. The move meant that Sabah had to sacrifice one to save the other. Richard ignored Sabah and stared hard at the board. Sabah shifted uncomfortably in his seat, disturbed by the lack of response from Richard, and by the position, he found himself in on the board.

"You never grassed us up, did you?" Sabah sneered. He moved the rook begrudgingly, knowing that Richard was about to take his bishop. "Fucking good job or you would have been really sorry." He leaned forward and whispered across the table. He slapped the palm of his hand on the desk as he spoke, and a slapping sound echoed across the sports hall.

Richard captured Sabah's bishop with his knight. His facial expression never altered. A teacher walked by them, alerted by the sudden slapping sound. He stopped to study the board. Both boys planned their next moves mentally in silence. Sabah made his move. The teacher tutted and shook his head as he walked away, indicating that it was a poor move. Sabah frowned and tried in vain to see his mistake, but he could not. He could feel anger rising in his belly.

"Check," Richard said, moving his queen into an attacking position. Sabah had left his king exposed. Sabah twisted in his seat, and bit his lower lip in frustration. He glared at Richard but his opponent never took his eyes from the board. Sabah had such a mastery of the game that being outplayed was totally alien to him. His thought process was thrown out of kilter.

"Sarah is your little sister, right?" Sabah moved his king out of check. He stared at Richard, but Richard wouldn't make eye contact. "She's a real party girl."

Richard Bernstein concentrated on the board. He had Sabah on the ropes, and it felt good. For once in his life, he felt that he was his attackers' equal. Sabah had been there the day he had been attacked and slashed. There was no remorse, no apologies, no forgetting the incident. The bastard was still attacking him now, over a game of chess, and Richard was not going to be bullied out of the game. Not by one of his attackers. The chessboard was his domain, and he wouldn't be intimidated there.

"She's Malik's bitch mostly, but he shares her around when she's stoned." Sabah had a twisted smile on his face as he spoke. He kept prodding, probing, looking for a chink in Richard's mental armour, but none was forthcoming.

"Check," Richard didn't flinch as he attacked Sabah's pieces again. The words had sunk in, but he wasn't really surprised if the truth was known. His parents suspected that his younger sister was 'partying' with Malik and his crowd, but he doubted that they thought she was sexually active, and being 'shared', as Sabah had so eloquently described it. Sarah had changed dramatically as she reached adolescence. She had turned from a pretty, young girl into a sexy young woman in the space of a few months. Richard had seen the changes more than his family, because of his time in hospital. They couldn't see what was under their noses.

"I had a dabble myself, and I can tell you that she is talented orally. You understand what I mean don't you? Or are you still a virgin fat boy?" Sabah whispered the last sentence. He moved a pawn to block the attack, but Richard Bernstein was playing in a class above Sabah. His game had improved dramatically in the months that he was in hospital. "Most of the guys agree that she could suck the skin of a banana."

"Check-mate," Richard swooped in and trapped Sabah's king. Game over. Sabah's face was a picture of confusion; he hadn't seen the move coming. It's one thing knowing that your being beaten, but another when the killer blow comes out of the blue.

"Take the move back now, Bernstein," Sabah hissed through clenched teeth. He leaned over the board aggressively, trying to intimidate his younger opponent. "Take the piece back or you're dead when we get outside!"

Richard sat back in his chair and raised his hand in the air to attract the attention of a teacher. He reached into his pocket with the other hand and took out a Wagon Wheel biscuit. He bit the wrapper from it with his teeth while he waited for the teacher to arrive.

"I'm warning you, Bernstein! Keep your mouth shut!" Sabah couldn't believe that Bernstein was being so blasé about his threats. He was going to teach him a lesson, one he had never forget. He was so angry that he couldn't get his words out properly.

Richard looked through his tormentor as if he wasn't there, and kept his hand up. He took two bites from the chocolate Wagon Wheel, and he munched on them while he studied the board.

"I'm going to fuck you up, Bernstein, just you wait, fat boy!"

"Yes, Bernstein?" a teacher approached. He wore a tweed jacket with stitched on elbow pads, and clenched an unlit pipe between his teeth. The pipe was never ignited until he was in the staffroom, but it was always there in the art teacher's mouth.

"Checkmate, Sir," Richard said pointing to the board. Sabah's face darkened with anger.

"Yes, indeed it is. Well done, Bernstein, one game to you." The teacher began to reposition the pieces ready to begin the next game. "Is everything alright, Sabah?" the teacher added, noting the anger on his face.

"Sabah has just threatened me, Sir," Richard added.

"What?"

"He threatened me, Sir, and tried to make me withdraw the final move. He said he would kill me, Sir." Richard looked hard into Sabah's dark eyes and took another bite from his snack. He chewed the chocolate snack noisily, allowing the mashed up contents of his mouth to be viewed by Sabah.

"Is this true, Barakat?" The teacher asked, removing the pipe from his lips, and raising his eyebrows in surprise.

"You're dead, Bernstein," Sabah leaned back and pointed two fingers at him, making an imaginary gun. "You're sister's a slut, and you're a fat Jew-boy." He reached out and slapped Richard's biscuit out of his hand. For the first time Richard looked offended. He stood up and retrieved the Wagon Wheel from the floor, taking another bite from it. He screwed up his face and opened his mouth wide, taunting Sabah while the teacher had his back turned.

"Barakat!" The teacher was astounded by the venom in his pupil's words. "You are disqualified from the tournament, and you're suspended! You will report to the headmaster's office tomorrow morning!"

"Shove it!" Sabah stood up, knocking his chair backwards as he did so. He swiped the pieces from the board and scattered them across the wooden floor. Then he squared up to the shocked teacher. "Are you going to make me?"

"He's also one of the boys that attacked me in the park, Sir," Richard said nonchalantly. The other teachers had gathered around, as had most of the spectators. The crowd fell silent at Richard's revelation. Sabah turned toward him open mouthed. They were all convinced that they'd got away with Richard's assault. It had been nearly a year since the police visited the school, looking for suspects. "My memory of it has come back. Sabah was one of the boys, and there were six others with him including Malik Shah and his cousins. Ashwan Pindar had the knife."

"I'm calling the police," the art teacher said. He grabbed Sabah by the scruff of the neck, but he struggled wildly, breaking his grip. Sabah bolted from the room, kicking chairs over, and slamming the doors as he left.

"You're fucking dead, Bernstein!" Sabah's voice echoed down the corridor as his footsteps faded.

The remainder of the day went by in a whirl. The two detectives from the hospital quizzed him for an age. His father was there, as the responsible adult, and he remained silent throughout. Richard thought that he had seen a tear in his father's eye, although it was gone as soon as it had appeared. The headmaster then had his turn, gathering the names of the attackers, and convincing himself that the accusations had substance. Suspending Asian pupils would be a potential PR disaster, if he got it wrong. Four hours later the inquisition had died down, and his shell-shocked parents drove him home in silence.

The atmosphere at home was icy. His mother cried for hours, and his father was sullen and withdrawn. Richard's brother David freaked completely. He disliked the Asian crowd intensely, because of their drug dealing, and blatant arrogant behaviour. The fact that they'd assaulted his younger brother made his blood boil. He telephoned his big friend, Nick, and he had a whispered conversation with him for twenty minutes. Sarah sat in her father's armchair with her knees tucked up under her chin, and her arms wrapped around her shins. She cried nonstop, sobbing like a child into her mohair jumper. It was a while before her demeanour was deemed to be unusual, a slight over reaction to the news.

"What's the matter with you, Sarah?" David asked sarcastically. "Are you pretending to be bothered about your brother now then?"

"Perhaps she's realised that she has a family that cares about her. It might make her stop being so bloody selfish." Mr Bernstein mumbled. His daughter was definitely in the bad books.

"Leave her alone, it's been a shock for all of us. She has

feelings too." Mrs Bernstein sat on the arm of the chair and stroked her daughter's hair. "Everything will be fine, darling. Richard's memory has come back, and the boys that hurt him will go to prison for a long time."

This brought on another round of sobbing, and fresh tears streaked her pretty face. She rocked back and to.

"Don't worry about me, Sis. I'm glad I've told them what happened," Richard walked into the room eating a handful of chocolate chipped cookies. He munched as he talked, and sprayed crumbs everywhere.

"The boys that attacked you, Richard, are they the same boys that Sarah hangs around with?" Mr Bernstein hadn't connected the dots until now.

"I'm not sure," Richard mumbled. He looked at the beige carpet and took another bite of his biscuit. "There are lots of Asian kids at our school now."

"Yes they are, bastards!" David clenched his fists. His mother took a sharp intake of breath. "There is only one Malik Shah in our school, and Sarah hangs with them at the weekend."

"David Bernstein!" Mrs Bernstein wailed. Profanity was taboo in the Bernstein household. "I'm sure Sarah is as upset as the rest of us, David."

"Well you will not see them ever again, and mark my words, young lady, you will do as I tell you from now on!" Mr Bernstein unleashed his frustrations.

"I will see him!" Sarah shouted.

"You will not my girl!" David senior flushed purple with anger. His eyes were wide, almost popping out of his head. She had gone too far this time. "Go to your room."

"No!"

Mr Bernstein took a deep breath and walked toward her. She looked up at him with a determined look on her tear-streaked face.

"I'm pregnant!" Sarah screamed at the top of her voice.

"I couldn't give a flying fuck about that fat waste of space!" she pointed at her brother. Richard's mouth opened wide, displaying the half chewed cookie inside. He looked around the room and his parents and older brother had similar expressions on their faces.

"What did you say?" Mr Bernstein asked.

"I'm pregnant." Sarah folded into a sobbing wreck. "They raped me."

"Oh my god!" Mrs Bernstein choked. "Who raped you? Who raped you!"

"Malik?" David Bernstein knew that his sister had a thing for Malik. He put two, and two together, and came up with five.

"No! I love Malik! It was his friends. They drugged me."

Mr Bernstein staggered backward and collapsed heavily into his armchair. The material on the arms of the chair was black and shiny in places, a sign of the age of it. He looked from his daughter to his wife, and then stared at the floor. His little girl changed so much over the last six months that he had begun to question if she was the same person. Now she was claiming that she had been raped, and that she was pregnant. It was hard to comprehend.

"Phone the police, David. Phone nine, nine, nine, and do it right now."

14

Lana Pindar

PRESENT DAY

Lana was dreaming again, when the sound of the front door bell invaded her consciousness. It melted into her dream. She was standing by the front door and a huge shadow appeared at the glass, blocking out the light. She panicked and backed away from the door, wanting to open it and to look at the sinister shape that was there, but not daring to. The shadow belonged to something evil, yet the urge to look at it was irresistible. The tiled floor turned into an escalator, no matter how fast she back peddled, the escalator carried her toward the door. As she neared it her arms reached out to open the door. She couldn't stop them, they had a mind of their own. Her hand touched the cold brass handle, and it felt like ice, chilled by the omnipresence beyond the glass pane. Ashwan's voice called to her, waking her from her nightmare.

"Lana, stay there," Ashwan shook her from her slumber.

"What?"

"I said, stay there."

"What time is it?"

"Half five, stay there, do you understand me?"

"Yes, what's the matter, where's Mamood?" The memories of her son not returning flooded back to her as she woke, "Oh my god!" Lana realised that she had heard the doorbell.

It was the middle of the night. All kinds of images flashed through her mind, policemen bringing Mamood home in disgrace, drunk or on drugs. A female office with her head bowed, come to tell her that her son had been found injured, or dead. Lana panicked.

"Oh my god, Ash, what's going on?"

"Why are you asking about Mamood?"

"I checked on him earlier. He wasn't home."

"What time was that?" Ash looked at his Rolex.

"It was gone three o'clock, why?" Lana wiped her eyes and looked confused. "What's going on?"

"I don't know yet, Lana. Stay where you are."

"I'll do no such thing! He's my son, and I want to know what has happened." Lana seldom answered Ash back, but she was distraught, frightened, and confused. Her head was still fuddled with sleep and dreams. "Something terrible has happened."

"Lana, listen to me." Ashwan held her face in one hand. It's late at night, and the doorbell has rung. Mamood may have left his keys or it could be trouble. Now stay there and do as I tell you."

Lana tried to take it all in but she was disturbed. Disturbed by her dreams, and disturbed by the lack of sleep, and the late night visitors. She sat up and nodded her head slowly. "Okay, but I want to know what is going on," she murmured.

Ash didn't answer, he was already through the bedroom door and halfway down the wide sweeping staircase before her head had cleared. He opened a closet door, which was set near the front door, and reached for the baseball bat that he kept there. He wished he kept a gun at home, but Malik forbade it. It made perfect sense not to, as the police would find it if they ever obtained a search warrant, no matter how well hidden it was. Malik was paranoid about the police finding any incriminating evidence. He had been so careful over the years, and that was why they were so successful as a crime syndicate. The law had never been able to touch them. Right now though, he wanted a gun in his hand. Ash hoped it was Mamood, drunk and keyless, but something told him that it wasn't.

"Who's there?" Ash stood with his back to the wall at the side of the door. If a random bullet was fired it would miss the target by miles. "Who is it?" He peeped a quick glance through the glass, but he couldn't see anything. Lana appeared on the staircase, hugging her dressing gown tightly around her neck with both hands. If an attacker fired a twelve-gauge shotgun through the door, then she was in the line of fire, and could be hit by the spray of lead shot. "Lana!" Ash hissed. "Get back up the fucking stairs, now!"

Lana was torn. She was worried sick about Mamood, but the site of her husband wielding a baseball bat did not do anything to allay her fears. Why was Ash being so skittish? What did he think was beyond the front door?

"Move, Lana!" his voice boomed up the stairs, and she turned and ran to the top of the landing. She stooped to her knees and peered between the balustrades so that she could see the front door. She looked like a child peeking through the rails. Ashwan flicked a light switch near the door. Security floodlights illuminated the front lawn. To his left was the study. It had bow windows protruding out from the main elevation. Ash kept close to the wall as he crept into the study. He navigated his way across the polished oak floorboards, around the leather topped desk, to the widow. He moved the heavy velvet drapes a fraction and peered out onto the lawn. The curved bay windows allowed him a clear view of the garden, and the porch area. The front door was visible, and there was no one there. He swept the grassed areas and caught his breath. There was a rolled object dumped near the double garage, to the right of his vision. It could be a carpet, or a large refuse sack. It could also be a body. Ashwan thought about Mamood, and blood pounded through his brain. He gripped the baseball bat so tightly that his knuckles went white.

"Who is it, Ash?" Lana's voice made him jump.

"For fuck's sake, Lana!"

"What's going on, is it Mamood?"

"Get back up the stairs, Lana!" Ash shouted at the top of his voice. "Get back up the fucking stairs!"

"Don't use that language to me, Ash!" Tears filled her eyes. Ashwan was secretive and sometimes moody, but he never abused her, verbally or physically. Something was very wrong. "Don't ever swear at me Ashwan Pindar!"

Lana stared at her husband, and she didn't recognise him. The veins in his neck were stretched to snapping point. His temples pulsed visibly with the pressure. She backed out of the study frightened, hot tears spilled over her eyelids and ran down her cheeks. She had never seen Ash this scared before. What had he seen through the window? Why was he acting so bizarrely? Where was her son? Lana sat on the bottom step and bit her fingernails as her husband opened the front door. He looked around cautiously, and then walked out into the night with the bat cocked ready to strike.

Ash walked slowly toward the double garage. He looked left and right, scanning the dark beyond the reach of the security lights. Nothing stirred. The roll looked plastic, reflective in some way. As he got closer, the shape of a body took shape beneath the cellophane wrapping. There was blood pooled from the waistline down, blurring the outline of the legs and feet. He moved closer, praying that it was not his son. His life was a charade, a family man on one side, and a gangster on the other. Ashwan's enemies were many, and his biggest fear was that one day they might come looking for him in his family world. He was staring his fears in the eye as his two worlds collided. The time had come to reap the rewards for the suffering that he had sown over the years.

Ash could make out a face through the plastic. The facial features were squashed and misshapen by the wrapping. The eyes were wide open, rolled backward into the skull, only the whites showing. Ash lowered the bat as he stared at the dead boy. He was a boy, a teenager, certainly no older. The mouth was fixed wide open in a silent scream. It was a surreal sight to behold. There was a dead teenager wrapped in plastic, dumped on his driveway in front of his garage. Ash looked closer. His eyes widened as realisation struck home. It was Abdul Salim, one of his junior dealers. There was now no doubt in his mind, someone was sending him a message, a bad one for sure. How had they connected a street dealer to him? It had to be a rival gang; no one else would pull a stunt like this. Abdul Salim worked the tower blocks in Netherley, and they were lucrative market places, constantly under threat from neighbouring crime families. It looked like one of them was making a serious bid to take over the area.

Ashwan's brain raced at warp speed. One of his dealers had been wasted, and then dumped on his front lawn. Someone was sending him a message but who? Perhaps it was another dealer? Ashwan was furious. It was one thing killing one of his most promising dealers, another to dump the body in front of his home. His wife would be mortified and there would be more questions and accusations than the Spanish Inquisition. There would have to be savage repercussions to avenge this strike, but right now, he had to clear up this mess, before Lana did something stupid, like calling the police.

Was it a coincidence that a dead body had been dumped, and his son hadn't come home? Ash turned and looked toward the front door. Lana was stood on the porch with her hands covering her eyes and face. She was visibly shaking.

"Lana." Ashwan said calmly to get her attention. She looked at him but he wasn't sure she'd registered what she was seeing. "Go and see if Mamood is home."

Lana shook her head from side to side. "I've just checked. He hasn't come home." Lana put her head onto her shoulder and dropped to her knees slowly, as if a heavy weight was pressing her down. "What's going on, Ashwan?" Her body quivered and tears ran freely down her cheeks. She began to wail like a scalded cat.

"Get a grip, Lana," he hissed. "I'm not sure what is happening, Lana." Ashwan said, opening the garage door. "Go inside, this is not Mamood." He looked at her with a face like thunder. Lana could tell by the look on his face that he was serious. "Turn off the security lights and get inside, do it now!"

"What is going on, Ash?" Lana wiped her running nose with her dressing gown sleeve. "What have you done?"

"Get inside, and turn off the lights." Ash hissed and his face turned to a snarl. He grabbed the plastic and dragged the body toward the garage. The security lights went out as he closed the metal door. He needed to call Malik. Someone had declared war.

15

The Bernstein Brothers

PRESENT DAY

Richard Bernstein sat at his desk in the basement of a Victorian farmhouse. It was set in the centre of twenty-five acres of grazing land, surrounded at the perimeter by deciduous woodland. Richard fell in love with the farm the first time he had seen it, as a teenager. As a young man he used to fish in the stream, which ran through it. Carp and chub swam in the gentle waters, and he came to escape the traumas of his family disintegrating. He sat on the bank in the sunshine alone, dreaming of owning the farm one day when he grew up. He rarely caught any fish, but he loved the peace and quiet. The setting was idyllic, and it offered the owner privacy, while not being completely isolated from the main arterial routes.

Many years later when Richard had grown up, the farmer could no longer make a living from the land, subsidies from the European Union were slashed dramatically, and he decided to sell up and retire. Richard paid the full asking price for it, before the 'for sale' sign had gone up. It was ideal for a loner like Richard. The farm had a cellar network, outhouses, a workshop and stables, and he put them all to good use. When he left school, he studied at college, and then went on to complete a chemistry degree at university. He stayed and completed a Masters, and then a Doctorate. Work in the chemical industry was easy to find, and a brain like Richard Bernstein came with an expensive price tag attached.

Richard's career was well documented. He worked on several new pesticides and fungicides, all of which he owned the patent for. He licensed his formulas across the globe, bringing him a substantial passive income every month. Now he spent his time as an advisor to the agricultural industry as an eminent scientist developing fertilisers and animal feeds to compliment his patented products. In his own time, he used his extensive chemical knowledge to develop other things, things that explode.

The farmhouse cellar was an extensive warren of rooms and corridors, once used to store seed and grain. Part of it ran beneath the farmyard and underneath the barn. Richard had set up an office area, and a workspace, as well as a chemistry lab and electronics benches. Over the years, he added extra equipment as he polished his art. Explosives, and their behaviour became his passion, and revenge was his driving force.

Richard was sitting at his desk working; the only light in that room came from the screen of his laptop computer. He'd been searching for information about limited companies that he'd found on the register at the Companies House website. The list contained all the corporate details of every tax-paying company registered in the United Kingdom, and Richard had found over a dozen associated firms connected to Malik Shah's empire.

"Apparently crime doesn't pay, this list would prove otherwise," Richard said. He picked up a Yorkie chocolate bar and snapped off a thick chunk. He forced the chocolate briquette into his mouth in one piece, and struggled to chew on it. His white cotton shirt was open at the neck, and his sleeves were rolled up to the elbows revealing pudgy hands and forearms.

"How many of his companies have you found, Einstein?" David looked over his shoulder as he worked. He noticed that his younger brother was sweaty, a strong odour drifted up to him.

Richard held up his hand while he tried to break down the contents of his mouth, making David smile. It was a full minute before he could reply. "Four registered to Malik alone, and another nine associated companies with the others listed as directors, and company secretaries."

"They've been busy bees haven't they?"

"The drugs trade is obviously flourishing." Richard clicked on his e-mail message box. "We'll wait for contact from Ashwan Pindar."

David moved closer to the screen to read the information. The companies ranged from computer software retailers, to aggregates and mineral exporters. They all looked well established and financially buoyant. Einstein stored the information onto a memory stick, and shut the programme down.

"I've got all the names and addresses we need. Once Ashwan has found his dealer on his lawn, things should start to move pretty quickly," Richard bit another chunk of chocolate from the bar.

They'd dumped the dead body of Abdul Salim on the lawn of Ashwan's family home, and then waited patiently for a reaction to their gruesome message. "What do you think he will do?" David asked thoughtfully.

"I think he'll be very offensive, threatening, and downright rude to be honest!" Richard chomped as he spoke. "I think he'll shit his pants and phone Malik Shah, especially when he realises his son is missing." The brothers laughed as they looked at the screen. "I don't think Shah will be very happy about his dead dealer, do you?"

"I think that he'll soon realise who is in charge, and that the police are all over his business interests, that will change his mind." David turned his head toward the door. He could hear muffled sobs coming from deeper in the basement.

"Does he have to do that?" Richard frowned his distaste at the noise, as he typed a ransom request to Ashwan. He pointed the angry dealer in the direction of his dead employee's pocket. In it, he would find a memory stick, which contained some very disturbing photographs of his son, Mamood. Richard knew that dumping Salim's corpse on Ash's garden would have the desired effect, especially when he realised that the killers had his son. It had been simple finding an e-mail address to contact Ash, and sending untraceable messages via multiple servers was easy to do. By the time Ashwan had seen all the photos of his son, he would be dancing to whatever tune Richard played.

"We'll see how he reacts when he opens the picture file." He sent the message. A muffled cry echoed down the corridor. It was creepy in the darkness.

"Mamood doesn't sound happy. Nick has been telling him what his father does for a living. He has some of the police photographs from punishment hits they have been associated with, and he's spelling out how his father was involved. I think it's a habit he picked up in prison, mentally torturing his cellmates. " David said. Nick had developed an evil streak during his spell in prison.

"I think it's strange. The poor young lad will never look at his father the same again!" Richard feigned concern. He shuddered at the thought of what Nick was doing to Mamood, but somewhere inside the fact that he was suffering pleased him. It would go some of the way to paying the debt that Ashwan, Malik and the others owed to Sarah.

"Don't worry there is nothing that will link back to us."

"He hasn't let Mamood see his face. I almost feel sorry for the boy." David raised an eyebrow in surprise. Richard shrugged and shook his head. "Well he will be suitably enlightened when he leaves here. I wonder if he knew what his father was involved in, not what he expected, I'll bet you. He'll never look him in the eye again."

"Just remember that they never had a second thought for Sarah. None of them did. Tell him to hurry up will you. We need to go over the ransom money pickup again." Richard turned on the light illuminating a large workshop area. There were two long tables in the centre of the basement, neatly stored tools hung on a pin board nailed to the wall.

"The rest of the devices are ready to go."

David walked to the first table and looked closely at an oil filter.

"Will this fit onto their cars?" David asked.

"No, but it will fit onto their delivery vans, and there's enough Tovex in there to blow a vehicle to bits. It would never be spotted, and it would take a forensic team a month to piece the remnants of the filter back together."

A pile of large padded envelopes sat next to the filters. David reached for one. They were letter bombs, ready and waiting to go.

"Don't touch them, David," Richard shook his head and his fat cheeks wobbled as he spoke. "They're stable, but the circuit wiring isn't fixed yet."

David nodded and smiled. The table stretched fifteen yards, and it was littered with mobile phones, vehicle stereos, digital cameras and an assortment of homemade limpet mines. They were all explosive devices manufactured from the fertile mind of Richard Bernstein.

A Blackberry on the desk rang, and the screen flashed. David reached for it.

"BANG!" Richard shouted, and grabbed David's shoulder. He jumped back from the table.

"You wanker, Einstein!" he laughed. David shook his head as he looked along the benches. They were lined with a plethora of household objects; every one of them had been converted into a deadly explosive device. "Nice work, Einstein. Nice work indeed. We are going to blow Malik Shah and his house of cards to smithereens."

"It's payback time bro!"

"We've waited a long time."

"I know, but it's the right time," Richard said seriously. "We had to wait for Nick's release. They ruined his life too."

16

Sarah Bernstein

SCHOOL DAYS

Detective Sergeant Aspel raised his head toward the grey clouds that obscured the sky, and breathed in deeply. He was trying to calm down, but it wasn't working. His job was becoming more impossible every year, and the frustration had already given him two ulcers, and an alcohol problem. Two months ago he would have lit up a Marlborough when he was stressed, but he had quit and now he used breathing techniques to make the cravings go away. It was having limited success.

"Does it work?" Detective Wallace asked.

"Does what work?"

"The deep breathing, does it work?"

"No."

"Do you want a cigarette?" Wallace took his packet of Bensons from his brown leather jacket. He constantly tempted his boss to lapse back to smoking, much to the annoyance of his superior. "Go on have one, it'll make you feel better."

"Fuck off, Wallace."

"Charming, I'm sure." Wallace drew deeply on his Benson and made a fuss of blowing the smoke out slowly. It drifted on the breeze toward his ex-smoking colleague.

"I don't know how you smoke that shit," Aspel frowned at his colleague. Bensons were the strongest end of the cigarette market, and certainly not the detective's smoke of choice. "If I ever smoke again it will not be that crap."

"You know you'll probably get hit by a bus?"

"What the fuck are you talking about?"

"Now you have given up smoking, you'll probably get run over by a bus, instead of getting lung cancer."

"Thanks for that encouraging thought, with friends like you who needs enemies?"

"What do you think the Crown Prosecution clowns will do?" Wallace asked seriously, all levity gone from his voice. The Crown Prosecution Service had the final say as to whether a case would be taken through the courts, or not. Their role was to protect public finances by highlighting cases with weak evidence, or evidence that couldn't be submitted. If they felt that a prosecution would not end up with a conviction then they would not step into the courtroom. The police were constantly at loggerheads with them.

"We'll have to wait and see." Aspel closed his eyes and breathed deeply again. When he opened them he was looking into the stony gaze of Queen Victoria. Her bronze statue was situated outside the main court buildings in Liverpool city centre. The passing of time and the salt air had turned the metal statue green. "The whole thing revolves around Sarah Bernstein's testimony. The boss thinks that she will be crucified in a courtroom." He looked at his wristwatch. There were groups of people scattered over the square, some of them shopping, others having a break from work. Life in the big city went on regardless of the traumas taking place in the city's courthouse.

Wallace stumped out his cigarette and the detectives walked in silence back toward the courtrooms. They showed their identity cards and bypassed the queue for the metal detectors, which provided the first line of defence against terrorists and hit men. The queue moved slowly as people waited patiently inline. The Bernstein family were inside, seated to the left hand side of a large waiting area. Four courtrooms led from the lobby area, and a number of interview rooms and anti-chambers were situated to the rear of the ground floor. The entire area was panelled with dark walnut, making it seem austere and intimidating. It was the type of place that made people speak in whispers automatically, almost cathedral like. The detectives navigated their way through the seating area, attracting several abusive comments from local lags and their families. Many of them had encountered the officers before during their criminal careers. The seating area was full of people waiting, wearing a mixture of cheap suits and designer sportswear. As they approached the Bernstein family, a cloaked court usher entered the waiting area and called their name. Mr Bernstein stood and acknowledged the court official.

"Mr Bernstein?" the usher greeted him. His wispy grey hair greased back against his mottled scalp. He was tall and skeletal, and his black cloak of office made him vampire-like. "We need your daughter, and either you or your wife as the responsible adult."

"We would both like to be present," Mr Bernstein replied. He glanced nervously at his wife. Mrs Bernstein nodded her head in the affirmative. She wanted to be next to her little girl while she suffered this terrible ordeal.

"I'm afraid that it must be one or the other. We have to keep the meeting as informal as possible."

The detectives neared the family and Mr Bernstein turned to greet them. Detective Sergeant Aspel shook his hand firmly, and he noted how clammy his hand felt. He was obviously worried for his daughter.

"They are saying that we both can't go in with Sarah?" Mr Bernstein was looking for some support.

"It's probably better if you go, Mr Bernstein. Your wife doesn't need to hear the gory details."

"I'm not sure I do either," Mr Bernstein said grimly. "I'll go with her." He turned to his wife and placed his hands on her shoulders. He leaned over and kissed her cheek. As he pulled away, a tear ran down her face. "Come on, Sarah."

Sarah Bernstein stood up. Her hair was braided into two plaits, making her look her age. She wore a bottle green pleated skirt, below the knee, and a green tweed jacket, which hid her bump. To anyone watching she looked like a prim and proper young schoolgirl. The prosecution barrister had been very specific about how her appearance needed to be at the meeting. The Crown Prosecution Service had to be convinced that she had been violated against her will. The slightest hint that sex was consensual would blow the case out of the water. Her mother grabbed her hand and patted it gently; a sudden sob brought more tears to her eyes.

"This way please," the usher said firmly.

"Will you be there?" Mr Bernstein asked the detectives.

"I'm afraid not, Mr Bernstein. The Crown need to be convinced that we haven't coerced the victim in anyway. There should be no pressure on the victim during the interview."

Mr Bernstein nodded and turned slowly to follow the usher. He waited a moment to allow Sarah to walk in front of him. Detective Wallace saw the look of distaste on his face as his daughter walked away. If things were bad between them now, then this meeting would compound things further, but it had to be done. Wallace had seen enough rape cases to know that the defence lawyers would tear a victim to pieces on the stand if there were any inconsistencies in their allegations whatsoever. The purpose of today's interview was to verify that the evidence was watertight. Wallace didn't think that it was, in fact her evidence had more holes in it than a Swiss cheese. He looked at his colleague and the look in his eye told him that he felt the same way.

17

Major Investigation Team

Superintendent Alec Ramsey positioned himself to the left hand side of a bank of screens. The suns dying rays were reflecting from the screen, blurring the images for some in the room.

"Pull the blinds, Linzie please," Alec called to a raven-haired detective at the back of the room. She was a looker, and several heads followed her shapely form as she crossed to the window.

"Yes, Guv," she flicked a switch on the wall and the blinds closed automatically without making a sound. The blinding sun was gone and the room was cooler. There was a tension in the air as the Major Investigation Team prepared to collate their findings.

"Okay, let's start at the beginning." A picture of the Mosque appeared. "What have we got on the Mosque?"

"The building is owned by the British Muslim Council, Guv." A bald detective spoke. He had a Mexican moustache that gave him a look of the gay biker from the Village People. "They bought the building from Liverpool Borough three years ago, and refurbished it. It's significant because it's the first building in Britain where Islam was practised. The refurbishment was paid for by private donations. We've checked the list of donations from local businessmen, and Malik Shah is on there."

"How much did he donate?" Alec asked, not knowing what the significance was, but he wanted to know.

"Undisclosed, Guv."

"Has he attended this Mosque?"

"Not as far as we know, Guv, but we haven't finished trawling through the visitors' books yet.

"Does he attend any Mosque?" Alec thought aloud. They needed to build a full profile of Shah, and his associates. Their habits and behaviour had to be studied and analysed.

"Not that we know of, Guv."

"The donation would explain why Imran Patel attended the opening. He represents his boss, Shah."

"I think so. Patel and his wife were pictured at the opening of a boxing gym in Huyton, six months ago, and at a nursery school nearby in May last year. Both projects were funded by donations from local Asian businessmen." The detective looked up from his notes. "Shah's name is on both lists of donators."

"Is he now? He's a proper Robin Hood!" Alec shook his head. "If he keeps his local community happy, they're less likely to inform, I suppose. What else on the Mosque?"

"Pretty much it, Guv."

"Okay, the casualties," Alec clicked the remote and the crime scene pictures flicked onto the screen.

"Angela Williams, graduated from Chester University, failed her police entrance selection programme due to a chronic asthma condition. She became a traffic warden, last year, and she has no discipline on her record. Her husband is unemployed, no criminal record either, Guv." Trevor Lewis put down one file, and picked up another. Lewis was a red-faced man, at least thirty pounds over his fighting weight. "James Horrace, a forty year old photographer for the Echo. He had one conviction for possession of cocaine, twelve years ago, Guv, and then there's the Patels obviously."

"Okay, Trevor, concentrate on the Patel family. I want to know everything there is to know about them," Alec nodded to reinforce the point. He was certain Imran Patel was the target, but they had to explore every avenue.

"What have we got on potential bombers?"

"I've got a list from the Counter Terrorist Unit of possible suspects, Guv," Nickie Weaver crossed her legs and smoothed her trousers with her hand as she spoke. "There's a small chapter of Combat 18, based at a pub in Bootle. There are nine registered members, and twenty-three affiliates. Grievous, ABH, burglary, affray, nothing jumps off the page, Guv. CTU have their meeting room bugged, and they have nothing to indicate that they could pull off an attack like this one."

"They bugged their meetings?"

"Yes, Guv." There were a few muted giggles around the room.

"I bet those recordings are priceless!"

"Do you want me to get hold of one, Guv?"

"No, Nickie, I'll give it a miss this time," he smiled and motioned for her to continue.

"There used to be a fairly large following of the National Front, around the Toxteth area, but its dwindled down to a half a dozen or so members. One of the original founders, Michael Street, stood as a BNP candidate in the last local elections. He seems to be a hard-core racist, Guv, criminal damage, riotous affray, assault with a deadly weapon, and incitement to riot. He served six months in ninety eight, for the assault charge. His medical records show that he has been treated for alcohol addiction."

"Our bomb maker isn't a drunken thug," Alec dismissed Street as a serious suspect immediately.

"He's on record threatening to burn down any Mosques that are built in the city, Guv."

"Okay, have CTU pulled him in?"

"Everyone on these lists has been pulled in, questioned and released, Guv."

"Are they looking elsewhere?" Alec wanted to know if the terrorist unit were spreading their net wider, looking for other possible extremist groups further afield.

"Yes, Guv, so far nothing to report."

Alec wasn't surprised. This bomb wasn't the work of egg throwing racist skinheads; It had been set off by experts. The image on the screen changed again, and the devastated van appeared on the screen.

"What do we know about the device itself," Alec looked to Will Naylor. His team had the newest information from forensics.

"Forensics found the remnants of at least six detonators, Guv. The explosive compound had been cooked and mixed, with aluminium powder, and diesel, which increases the heat on detonation and ensures that all the fertiliser explodes. There were three metal drums packed with explosive, and wrapped with homemade shrapnel, ball bearings, and screws."

"Why would they need so many detonators?" Smithy asked. His ginger hair was ruffled and unruly.

"Guv?" Will wasn't sure what the answer was. He knew the Super had extensive experience of bombs from his days in Ireland.

"Good question, Smithy," Alec swept his fingers through his hair and frowned. Deep lines creased his forehead and chin as he prepared the answer. He didn't want to lecture his team, but it was important that they realised how good the bomber was. "The problem with fertiliser bombs is they don't always explode, especially if the mixture is moist. Any moisture at all will stop it exploding. This bomb maker painstakingly cooked the compound to remove all the moisture, and then mixed it. They used three drums. The detonation of one drum would not have triggered the others hence two detonators were used for each drum. Each drum was an independent device."

"So there were two detonators in each bomb, to make sure they all exploded?" The Super nodded. "Talk about belt and braces," Smithy was impressed by the bomb maker's skill.

"Whoever set this bomb, Smithy, left absolutely nothing to chance. Carry on, Will."

"The devices were attached to a mercury motion switch, and a photo-cell trigger." Will Naylor looked up at the confused faces around the room. "If the van had been towed or moved, it would have set off the mercury switch. If the back doors were opened the photo-cell would have triggered the devices."

"The bomb was going to explode, no matter what happened," Alec added. "Which begs the question as to why would the bombers use a remote detonator, and risk being near the scene, unless he needed to see a target before he detonated it."

Eyebrows were raised, whispered thoughts were shared and nods of agreement spread around the room.

"Smithy," Alec turned toward the ginger detective.

"Guv?"

"Pick five detectives with a knowledge of figures and money trails, and find me a reason why Imran Patel and his wife were blown to pieces," Alec was convinced that the motive was money. Organised crime families like the one headed by Malik Shah were worth billions, but a life is cheap. A hit could be ordered for a three-figure sum.

"I'm on it, Guv," Smithy pointed to five of his colleagues with his pen, and they nodded keenly, happy to be on his team. Some detectives got off on forensics, others interrogation techniques, but it was bank accounts and electronic transactions that did it for Smithy. With the best detectives and some time, he would find something.

"Will, I want you and your team to focus on Shah's enemies. Find me someone that wants to kill his accountant, cripple his business, and is capable of building this device." Alec pointed to the van wreckage.

"Guv," Will smiled. He wanted this part of the investigation. It would involve pulling some of the city's biggest scumbags in to the cells and rattling them around an interrogation room for twelve hours or so. Now that was something to look forward to.

"The rest of you work on Malik Shah, and Ashwan Pindar. I want to know what they eat for breakfast, dinner and tea, what colour underwear they're wearing, and I want some hard evidence that they're criminals. I want these two men off the streets."

Alec Ramsey looked around the room and made eye contact with as many of his team as he could. Whatever happened with this investigation, Malik Shah was firmly in his sights.

18

Malik and Ashwan
PRESENT DAY

Malik Shah pulled his cashmere overcoat tighter around himself. The wind from the River Mersey was howling through the railings that lined the front lawn at Ashwan Pindar's house. The river was half a mile away down the hill, and he watched the dark green waters flowing lazily past into the Irish Sea. White horses tipped the waves, caused by the propellers of the passenger ferries, which crisscrossed the river heading to Ireland. The streetlights reflected from the murky waters like blurred yellow torches. His dark brown eyes were full of anger, and frown lines creased his forehead.

"You have no idea who is doing this?" Malik turned to his colleague. Ashwan looked into his eyes momentarily, but the anger in them frightened him, and he looked down at his black shiny brogues. Malik frightened Ashwan; he had always dominated him since school. He had a violent temper, and Ash had witnessed its ferocity on many occasions.

"Get rid of that," Malik said kicking the dead body of Abdul Salim. Two bruisers moved in silence, one at the feet and one at the head. They lifted the body into the back of a Renault van. The van was sign painted with the name of a funeral parlour, one of three in the city owned by Shah's limited companies. They were very good businesses, and handy for transporting bodies across the city.

"What about the runners?" Ashwan asked. Once he had alerted Malik to the problem, he'd sent men out to find out what was happening. The news wasn't good.

"Both dead, and both connected to us," Malik snarled. He spat on the floor in disgust.

"How have we been connected?" Ash asked.

"According to our men, the killers left a note pinned to Rozzo's forehead, naming us as his employers. The police are all over the place," Malik punched the garage door and it rattled. The funeral parlour van pulled out of the driveway, and Ashwan noticed Lana watching them from the front bedroom window. Malik followed his gaze. His eyes narrowed. "What has she said?"

"Nothing," Ash swallowed hard. It was a stupid answer, but he couldn't think straight.

"One of your dealers is shot and dumped on your lawn, and your son is missing, presumed kidnapped, and your wife hasn't said anything?" Malik shook his head slowly in sarcastic disbelief. "I bet she's had plenty to say."

"Fucking hell Malik!" Ashwan snapped. He took the picture of Mamood out of his pocket. "This is my son tied to a chair, Malik. We are going insane with worry, what do you think she has been saying?"

"Let's calm down and go inside," Malik softened his voice for a moment. He wanted to speak to Lana. He had to speak to Lana. If she telephoned the police then all hell would break loose. Someone had crossed the line. He was under attack, there was no doubt about it, and he couldn't for the life of him think who it was.

Both men headed for the front door. Malik wore an expensive designer suit and a long overcoat. Ashwan was still wearing jogging bottoms and an old sweatshirt. Lana was walking down the staircase as they entered the hallway.

"Who was that poor boy?" she asked.

"No one we know," Malik lied. His face was like stone, his eyes dark and narrow.

"Why haven't you called the police?" she looked directly at Ash. He shook his head and bit his bottom lip. The thoughts of his eldest son Mamood were consuming him. The kidnappers told him where to find a memory stick on the murdered dealer that'd been dumped on his lawn. It contained pictures of his son, bound and gagged; he looked terrified, and his eyes were reddened from crying. The photographs played constantly in his mind, each one worse than the next. Three of his employees had been butchered in order for this message to be sent to him, and he was under no illusions that his son was in grave danger. What he didn't know was who was responsible, or why he had been targeted specifically. The kidnappers had made contact, but no ransom demands received yet.

"We think someone is trying to set us up, Lana," Malik interrupted before Ash could answer.

"How so, Malik?"

"One of our business rivals is out to cause us trouble," Malik found it hard to hold her stare. Her eyes were red from crying. She was desperate to call the police and report her son's kidnap. Ashwan had pleaded with her to wait for Malik to come. He would know what to do.

"Are they the same people that have Mamood?"

"I'm guessing so, Lana," Malik needed to keep her on side. "I've asked Ash to think of someone that has been disgruntled or upset. An ex-employee or a rival that has lost a contract?"

"What type of people do you do business with, Ashwan?" she looked bitter and angry. Her expression was pure contempt. Her son had been kidnapped; a boy had been murdered and dumped on their lawn, and her husband wouldn't call the police. What type of father was he? What type of husband was he? She didn't know what to do or think. "What type of businessmen would take your son, kill a teenager and dump him on your lawn, Ashwan?"

"I don't know, Lana" Ashwan turned his back and walked away from her.

"Why haven't you called the police, Ash, or am I missing something?"

"Mamood would be in grave danger if you involve the police, Lana," Malik leaned his back against an oak Welsh dressing table. He was cool, almost cold about it. "The kidnappers said, 'no police or he dies', correct?"

"Why haven't you called the police, Ashwan, what have you got to hide?" Lana ignored Malik. She hated the man with a passion. He was evil, and bullied Ash at every opportunity. Ashwan was his partner in name only. Malik Shah made all the decisions, and Ash was his whipping boy. He made her skin crawl the way he looked at her sometimes. "Tell me, Ash. What type of business associates would do this to you?"

"Think hard, Ashwan," Malik grinned. His whitened teeth seemed too straight to be real, but the Hollywood smile looked more like a sneer to Lana.

"I have no idea, Malik. I've racked my brains trying to think who could do this, but I haven't got a clue," Ashwan shrugged his shoulders and tears filled his eyes. "Mamood has nothing to do with our business, why have they taken him ...why?"

"Get a fucking grip of yourself!" Malik hissed. He couldn't stand weakness in a man. "There are hundreds of people who would want to hurt you and your family, absolutely hundreds." He pointed a well manicured finger toward Ashwan's Porsche 911, which was parked fifty yards away on the driveway. "Do you think you'd be driving that if we sold newspapers?"

"No, of course not, Malik, but..." Ash mumbled and tried to compose himself.

"What do you do, Malik?" Lana tilted her head slightly.

"Shut up, Lana, you're not helping," Ash tried to calm her,

but she shrugged him off and stood eye to eye with Malik.

"Tell me what my husband does for you?"

"We import and export commodities," Malik sneered. His patience was wearing thin. "You should be grateful, Lana, it pays for your nice house."

"Look, that's not important now. Mamood is in danger," Ash walked over to his wife and tried to hold her. She froze and held up her hands.

"Don't you touch me, Ashwan Pindar."

"I know you don't understand, Lana, but..."

"But nothing, Ashwan!" Malik had enough. He grabbed Lana by the upper arms, pinning them to her side. He shouted in her face.

"We sell drugs, we sell whores, and we sell guns and ammunition, Lana."

Lana looked stunned, as if she had been slapped. Malik had his face inches away from hers; she could smell chilli and tobacco on his breath. His words echoed around her brain, drugs, whores and guns. Her husband imported drugs, whores, and guns. They were gangsters. Ashwan Pindar, the father of her child was a drug runner, people trafficker, and arms dealer. She went weak at the knees, only Malik's grip held her up.

"We work in a dangerous world, our enemies are always trying to steal our products, and take our business. When they do, we kill people and take all their money and drugs from them. It's the survival of the fittest, Lana. Dog eat dog." Malik let go of one of her arms, and grabbed her chin. For one awful moment, she thought he was going to kiss her. She felt bile rising in her throat. "Someone has taken your son, and I'll find them. When I do I will cut his fucking heart out and bring it to you cooked and stuffed with cheese. The police cannot help you, Lana, but I can."

Lana slid down the wall slowly as he her knees finally gave way. Spittle dribbled down her chin and her lips quivered.

She stared at her husband.

"You are a liar!" she shouted to Malik. He stood over her like a boxer stalking his injured opponent. "Tell me that he's a liar, Ash."

Ash couldn't look at her in the eye. He rolled his eyes skyward and wished the ground would open up and swallow him.

"Tell me!" she screamed. "Tell me he's lying!"

Ash walked over to her and moved Malik away with his forearm.

"He's not lying, Lana, but it's not as bad as it sounds," Ash could hear his own words, and he thought they sounded like the words of a desperate man; a drowning, man clutching at fresh air.

"It's not as bad as it seems?" Lana wiped saliva from her face and tried to gather herself together. "There was a dead teenager on my lawn tonight. My husband dragged the body of a dead teenager into my garage, and then telephoned his business partner to come and take it away." She glared at Malik.

"That's what you did, isn't it, Malik?" She stood on shaky legs and looked from Malik to Ash incredulously. "You made the body disappear didn't you?"

"We have to do what they say, no police." Ash pleaded with her. She stared at him wide eyed, shocked and devastated at the revelations that she had heard tonight. She walked over to Malik Shah and looked up into his face.

"Do you know who has my son?"

"Not yet."

"The men that killed that boy, have Mamood?"

"Yes, it looks that way."

"Get my son back."

"We will, but no police, Lana," Malik half smiled. "You must let me do what I need to do to get him back. The police will get in the way."

Ashwan needed to sit down and walked across to the wide sweeping staircase. He plonked his weary body down on the bottom step.

Lana leaned closer to Malik. She whispered in his ear. "You make me sick." Malik frowned. He didn't do insults well at all. "I see the way you look at me, Malik. Get my son back and you can have what you want. I'm not sure who disgusts me the most you or them."

Malik nodded and an evil smile crossed his lips as she walked away. He would enjoy doing that bitch, whether Mamood lived or not, and he would make sure that she regretted that remark many times over.

"Take your things and get out of my house," Lana said as she walked by Ashwan.

"What?" Ash stood up and grabbed her arm. "This is a shock, but we'll fix it."

"Get your hands off me," she hissed in his face. "I don't even know who you are. Get out of my home. Get my son back, you owe me that."

19

Sarah

SCHOOL DAYS

The court usher seemed to glide as he walked into the Crown Prosecution chambers, his cloak floated behind him. At the door, he turned and waved his skeletal arm to guide Mr Bernstein and his daughter into the meeting room. They stepped in nervously.

"Take a seat at the back please, Mr Bernstein." The prosecution lawyer, Carol Smythe, smiled and tried to make them feel more comfortable. "Sarah, if you could sit here next to me please."

Sarah shuffled toward a long wooden bench piled high with manila files and lever arch boxes. Her hands were pulled up inside her coat sleeves, just the tips of her fingers showed. Her face blushed pink and her head was down, shoulders stooped. The lawyer pulled out a pine chair and patted the red seat pad, indicating to Sarah to sit down. The young girl flopped into the chair and stared at her nails. She looked like a frightened young girl.

"Could we introduce everyone please, so that Sarah knows what is going to happen today," a grey haired woman spoke. Her hair was pulled tightly back into a bun on the back of her head, and rimless spectacles perched on the end of her nose. She peered over the lenses as she spoke. "I'm Louise, and I represent the Crown Prosecution Service." Her thin lips formed a smile, but there was no warmth in it.

"Margaret Bangor-Jones, representing the defence," a crisp, assertive, female voice came from the right hand side of the solicitors bench. Sarah stole a glance in that direction. The defence lawyer had jet-black hair tied into a ponytail; it shined as the electric lights reflected from it. She was early thirties, stunning, with high cheekbones and full lips. Sarah looked away when she caught her eye. Her eyes seemed to look inside her and read her mind.

"Mr Bernstein. For your benefit I will explain what will happen," the clerk removed her glasses and spoke to the victim's father at the back of the room. He was ten yards away from her, at the most. The room was no bigger than a large living room. There was no dark wood panelling in there. The room was windowless but well lit; the austerity of the court building had been omitted purposely, because of the nature of the cases dealt with here. "We will gather the details of the prosecution's case, and Sarah's statement. Then the defence's representative will ask questions based on the statements from the accused." The thin smile returned. "Is that clear to you, Sarah?"

"Yes," Sarah nodded mutely and stared at her fingernails again.

"This is not a trial, Sarah. We want to establish the facts so that we can make a decision to prosecute your attackers."

Mr Bernstein shifted uncomfortably in his chair. He had not been given access to Sarah's evidence, and as such he had a gut wrenching feeling inside. He couldn't help but feel anger and revulsion toward his daughter. Sarah had been the apple of his eye when she was younger, and he struggled to remember at which point she had grown up. One minute she was playing with dolls, the next she was having consensual sex with one boy, and accusing several others of drug-induced rape.

He wanted to feel sympathy for his little girl, but he had nothing inside but disgust. As for the pregnancy, it had caused blazing rows in the Bernstein home. Sarah was adamant that she loved Malik, and the child was his. There was no talking to her about abortion. The shame she had brought on the family amongst the Jewish community was too much to bear. Mr Bernstein was struggling to cope with the situation. It was a never-ending nightmare.

"Ms Smythe, if you could begin please," the clerk placed her spectacles on, and pushed them up her nose with her index finger.

Carol Smythe shuffled her papers and remained seated as she spoke. "The outline of the case is as follows. Sarah Bernstein is fourteen years old, and pregnant. She was involved in a relationship with her boyfriend, Malik Shah. Malik is a sixteen year old male, from the same school." The clerk looked down her nose at Sarah as her lawyer detailed the basis of the accusations. "Sarah attended several parties with her boyfriend, and over a period of a few months a sexual relationship between them ensued."

The clerk and the defence lawyer scribbled notes as Carol Smythe spoke. Mr Bernstein felt physically sick listening to her. He wished that there was a window in the room, so that he could look out of it and pretend that this wasn't happening. After everything he had done to educate his daughter, this was how she repaid him. She gave her body to a Muslim boy, at the tender age of fourteen. Her grandparents would be turning in their graves.

"It was at one of these parties, February the second, to be precise, that Malik Shah gave drugs to Sarah. Cannabis and an acid tablet. They went into a bedroom and had consensual sexual intercourse. Later on Malik gave her tequila shots. Sarah took them willingly; however, on this occasion she believes that she was spiked; drugged with a sedative such as Rohypnol.

The drug is used as a sedative. It can affect both the motor functions, and the memory."

"I think we can skip the medical blurb, Ms Smythe. We are all familiar with this drug, unfortunately," the clerk interrupted.

"Later Sarah remembers waking up in the bedroom again. There were several males there, and they were carrying out various sexual acts on her, including non-consensual intercourse. Sarah has memories of what happened, but she couldn't do anything to stop it. The names of the accused are noted in the records. Although we admit that the prior sex with Malik Shah was consensual, he was complicit in the rape because he administered the drug."

Mr Bernstein wiped his hands against his pinstripe trousers. It was his best suit, and under normal circumstances he wouldn't dream of doing such a thing. His hands were sweaty, and his stomach felt knotted. The thought of his daughter having sex at fourteen was sickening. Worse still was the fact that she had been drugged and abused by a group of men. He wanted to throw up, scream and kill them all at the same time.

"Is there any evidence of the use of Rohypnol Ms Smythe?" the clerk asked. She raised her eyebrows quizzically.

"No. There was too much time elapsed between the rape and the reporting of it."

"Alleged rape," Margaret Bangor-Jones objected.

"We're not in court yet!" Carol Smythe retorted.

"Quite, save the legal jousting for the trial please Ms Bangor-Jones," the clerk looked over her glasses like a headmistress scolding her class.

"Then I think we must have more robust evidence to include it in the case," the clerk looked concerned. It seemed the entire allegation hinged on proving that Sarah had been drugged against her will, and then abused.

"Bottles of Rohypnol were found in the possession of Malik Shah, Ashwan Pindar, and Amir Patel," the prosecutor pointed out the evidence gathered by the police, upon the arrest of the accused boys.

"I see. Okay we'll allow it for now," the thin smile flashed briefly across her lips. "Ms Bangor-Jones, your questions please."

Sarah felt a chill run down her spine as the defence lawyer turned half toward her, so that she could address the clerk and Sarah simultaneously. Her face blushed red and she pulled her hands back into her sleeves as a tortoise would its head. Her father put his elbows on his knees and leaned forward protectively.

"How long had you been seeing Malik before you had sex with him?" The defence lawyer asked. Her black hair shone. She smiled warmly at Sarah, disarmingly.

"I can't remember," Sarah mumbled.

"I'm sure you can remember, Sarah, if you try."

"I can't."

"Sarah has answered the question twice," Carol Smythe interrupted.

"Make your point please," the clerk said without looking up.

"It was your first date with him, Sarah."

"How can you possibly know that?" Mr Bernstein was outraged. He stood up and folded his arms defiantly.

"Mr Bernstein, while I realise that this is difficult to listen to as a parent and guardian of a young girl, you must understand that we are trying to save your daughter the trauma of doing this in open court," the defence lawyer spoke calmly and with sympathy in her tone.

"Mr Bernstein, my honourable colleague is right, however I do need you to justify that statement Ms Bangor-Jones," the clerk said. "How exactly can you know that?"

"I have statements from witnesses who saw Malik Shah coming out of the bedroom waving a used condom over his head and bragging that, 'I took her cherry on the first date, a hole in one.'" Ms Bangor-Jones looked embarrassed as she glanced at

Mr Bernstein and his daughter. Mr Bernstein crumpled into his chair, broken and confused. "If I may continue?"

"Please do," the clerk said looking down at her notes. Her face had darkened to a scowl. Nobody enjoyed watching a young girl being dissected publicly, but this had to be done.

"Do you remember the night when Malik and Ashwan drove you home after a party?"

Sarah's head stooped lower. She stared at her fingers and bit her lip. Mr Bernstein could tell by her posture and body language that Sarah knew what was coming.

"Sarah?" the clerk prompted her.

"Yes I remember," she whispered.

"They stopped the car near to your house and you performed oral sex on both of them," Margaret Bangor-Jones spoke calmly. "Is that true?"

"Yes," Sarah whispered. Tears rolled down her cheeks and her chin sunk to her chest. "Malik told me it was to prove how much I loved him, making his friend feel good. I didn't want to."

"Oh my god!" Mr Bernstein took a deep intake of breath as she spoke. He couldn't get the sickening images out of his mind. Tears of anger leaked from the corners of his eyes and he wiped them away quickly.

"I do not want to make this any more painful than it is already, Sarah, but you had performed sexual acts on all of the boys that you have accused of raping you, at one time or another, prior to this allegation, had you not?"

The prosecution lawyer was aghast, as was the clerk. This revelation had come unexpectedly. Mr Bernstein sat open mouthed as he digested the information.

"Is this true, Sarah? A simple yes or no will suffice," the clerk removed her glasses. She had heard enough in five short minutes to realise that this case was going nowhere.

"Yes, it's true, but not that night. They drugged me, and

they raped me, all of them did." Her voice was monotone, defeated.

The legal representatives looked at each other, and a silent communication passed between them. Raped or not, Sarah would never be believed in a court of law by a jury of ordinary people. The prosecution had to prove beyond all reasonable doubt that guilty was the only verdict. Sarah's prior behaviour would make that impossible.

"I can see no point in proceeding any further with this. I'll submit my findings to your offices and the police by finish of work tomorrow. Thank you both for your time, and thank you Mr Bernstein. This cannot have been easy for you. I would thank your lawyer to recommend some counselling for Sarah, and your family."

"You don't believe her do you?" Mr Bernstein was livid. He wasn't sure who he was angry at. Sarah? The Crown Prosecution? Himself? How had he allowed this to happen?

"Whether I believe Sarah or not, Mr Bernstein, is irrelevant. I have to assess the evidence from both parties and gauge the probability of gaining a conviction," the clerk removed her glasses and looked at him with a stern face. He had to face the truth, like it or not. "Sarah has given her evidence, as have the accused. You have heard some of it yourself, Mr Bernstein. If you were on a jury could you convict, beyond all reasonable doubt?"

"These animals put my son in intensive care, they cut him with a knife, and now they have raped my fourteen-year old daughter. She is fourteen!" Mr Bernstein's face was purple, and his jowls shook as he spoke. The veins at his temple throbbed angrily. "Are they going to get away with this?"

The room was silent. The lawyers began to pack away their files into briefcases. The clerk shook her head and stood up from her chair. She looked as if she was going to speak again, but then she thought better of it and walked hurriedly toward a door at the back of the chamber. Carol Smythe led Sarah away from the bench toward her father. The young girl looked pallid and drawn. She couldn't look her father in the eye. Sarah kept her head down and walked past him, heading for the doors. Mr Bernstein followed her with a look of disdain on his face.

"Don't be too hard on her, Mr Bernstein. For what it's worth, I believe that she was drugged and abused. If it means anything to you," Carol Smyth tried to smile.

"Your opinion is of no importance to me. It doesn't mean anything to me at all, absolutely nothing," Mr Bernstein turned and walked out of the courtroom. He felt like his daughter had died. He felt like he was a grieving father, pining for his innocent little girl that had somehow been lost. As they left the antechamber, the two detectives turned to face them. Mr Bernstein's face flushed with anger. His face was like thunder.

"It didn't go well?" Detective Sergeant Aspel asked sheepishly.

"You knew what evidence they had, contrary to Sarah's statement?" Mr Bernstein's voice was hushed, almost a whisper.

"We interviewed the attackers, Mr Bernstein," Detective Wallace nodded solemnly.

"Then you knew what they would do to her in there, and yet you allowed me to take my daughter into that room, and made me sit there and listen to that?"

The detectives looked at the floor, disappointed, guilty and embarrassed all at the same time. "Mr Bernstein, we interviewed your daughter, and we interviewed her attackers. We believed Sarah's version of events. That's why we proceeded."

"We're leaving," Mr Bernstein walked away from them and spoke to his wife. She was holding Sarah in her arms, the young girl sobbing uncontrollably. "We're leaving now."

"Mr Bernstein, this was always going to be difficult...." Detective Sergeant Aspel began, but he was cut short.

"Difficult?" Mr Bernstein turned to face them, his voice boomed across the waiting area. "Difficult?"

The people in close proximity fell silent and all eyes watched the drama unfolding before them. The detectives were fully aware that the eyes of the public were on them. Some of their old criminal adversaries were present, and they sniggered as they watched the officers cringing.

"Mr Bernstein, we acted with Sarah's best interests at heart."

"You raped her again in public. You put her in that room knowing full well what would happen." Mr Bernstein began to shake. His voice cracked with emotion. He pointed a shaking finger toward the courtroom. "You let me take her in there, knowing she would be humiliated in front of me, her father."

"Mr Bernstein," Aspel tried to placate him, but he took his wife by the arm, and guided his daughter through the watching crowd.

The waiting area remained silent for long minutes as the embarrassed detectives followed them at a distance.

20

Malik Shah

"Do you think we endear ourselves to the people we do business with?" Malik turned angrily and waved a gloved hand around the hallway as Lana ran up the stairs. She was hysterical.

"Do you think I care?" she screamed. "Get out of my house, you animals, and if Mamood isn't back here tomorrow, I'm calling the police, and to hell with the both of you!" The bedroom door slammed closed.

"Get changed, Ash. We need to find out who is doing this."

An hour later, they were driving along the dock road, heading north. To their left were acres of unused dockland, silted up canals and rusted anchor rings. On the right towered ancient warehouses, once the centre of international trade, now derelict and deserted. Malik indicated, and turned his BMW off the main road, steering it between two giant grain stores. The buildings were twelve storeys high, built from chocolate brown brick. He slowed the vehicle and turned off the headlights. As their eyes adjusted to the darkness, they saw two Asian men sat in a Mercedes a few hundred yards away, down an alleyway. The driver flashed the headlights and pulled the vehicle away from the kerb, driving toward them slowly.

"We'll find out who is fucking with us, and we'll wipe them off the planet. Do you have the balls to do this, Ash?"

Ash looked at the approaching vehicle and swallowed hard. He recognised the two men inside it. They'd been with them since their school days. They didn't have the IQ to help run the organisation, but they were loyal to Malik. They used them as hired muscle, stone cold killers that they employed when they needed to 'disappear' somebody. Ashwan was tired of the killing. He was tired of being on the wrong side of the law, and he was tired of Malik Shah. They were no better than the men that had killed his dealers in the blink of an eye, and kidnapped his son. He chose to live in this world, and financially it had been kind to him, but when you work with vicious animals, it is easy to be bitten. For the first time in his life he wished he'd chosen a different path. Lana would never be the same again, how could she be?

"What are you going to do with Abdul's body?" Ash was shaking as he replayed the night's events in his mind. "I cannot involve the police. They said they would kill Mamood if I didn't do as they say."

"You know how it works, he's on his way to feed the fishes tonight." Malik replied. They disposed of bodies the same way every time. The corpses were strapped to gym weights with duct tape and then wrapped tightly in several rolls of chicken wire. The wire ensured that the weights never dropped of the body, no matter how rotten it became, and it allowed bottom feeders and crustaceans to devour the corpse through the mesh. The body of Abdul Salim would be gone in less than a month.

"You don't know who has your son, Ashwan. I'm going to find out who they are, and then we'll get Mamood back."

"How can we find out who they are?"

"We'll ask some of your enemies, first hand," Malik turned to the road. The Mercedes was nearing.

"I don't know what you have in mind, Malik. I'm so confused, and they said they will kill him if we don't follow their orders. Where do we start?"

"Shut up, you tart! I follow no one's orders." Malik was fuming. This wasn't the first incident of this kind. Although he hadn't realised at the time, some of the trouble that his bookkeeper experienced had been the beginning of something bigger, but Ashwan didn't know that yet. Amir Patel received blackmail demands, death threats, and his haulage company was attacked. Malik kept it a closely guarded secret. Any sign of weakness in this business could be fatal. Rival gangs in the city would smell blood a mile away, and they would circle his empire like vultures, waiting for it to become weak enough to devour. Amir asked Malik to help him, and he had made some enquiries, but his enquiries drew a blank. Demands for money were made, and three tractor units were torched as a warning. Malik ordered Amir not to pay any monies under any circumstances. He was convinced that the blackmailers would make a mistake, sooner, or later. A week later Amir and his wife were blown to bits at the opening day of the Mosque, coincidence? Malik didn't believe in coincidence. Now Ashwan was being attacked. The level of violence being used was escalating, and they'd kidnapped his son. Someone was playing with fire, and people that play with fire get burnt. Malik was going to burn them himself. "Who was the last person you had an issue with?"

"What do you mean an issue?"

"Fucking hell, Ash! Who did you last have trouble with?" Malik was becoming frustrated with Ashwan. Over the years, he had been his right hand man, ever since school. Ash had been handy with a knife as a youth, and was quick to use one if there was trouble. As Ashwan aged, he mellowed and avoided violence. He was becoming squeamish, and that made him a liability. Malik on the other hand had not tired of the violence.

"I've had no trouble for months, what are you getting at, Malik?"

"Listen to me. You repeat this to no one, do you understand?"

"Yes, of course I understand."

"Amir was being blackmailed."

"What?"

"He was blackmailed. Someone torched his lorries and demanded money. Then he received death threats, about two weeks before the bombing at the Mosque."

"I thought it was a terrorist attack?" Ashwan was stunned as he tried to process the information.

"I think someone made it look like one, to send a message to us. At least that is what I suspected, until Mamood was kidnapped and Abdul Salim was shot and dumped on your lawn. Now I'm sure that we're being targeted. Somebody is coming after us, Ash, and they're very clever people. "

"I can't think straight."

"You need to think, Ash."

"Nobody comes to mind that would have the audacity to attack Amir, and then kidnap my son."

"What about that trouble in the Eagle and Child?" Malik was making reference to a minor dealer that had strayed into a pub that was in Ashwan's area a few month earlier. Dealing on Ashwan's turf was a dangerous game. Ash sent his heavies to wait for him. He was given a good beating, robbed of his drugs and his money, and then sent to hospital with his thumbs in his coat pocket. Ash's men used a carpet blade to remove his digits.

"Bruce Mann?" Ash said thinking about what Malik had said. "He wouldn't do this. He wouldn't dare."

"You had his thumbs cut off, Ash. He might be coming after us."

"He is stupid enough to have a pop at us, but this takes planning and a level of intelligence." Ashwan whispered to his himself as he thought about it. "Do you think he would be capable of this?"

Malik smirked and shrugged his shoulders. "If you cut my thumbs off, I'd kill your kids and make you watch, just for a starter."

"He is well connected, and he knows most of the shit that happens in the city," Ash could see possibilities. Bruce Mann was a freelance gangster, never affiliated to any of the city's crime families, but always around the periphery. He sold drugs and guns to teenagers, his reputation as a scumbag was well established. If he hooked up with a one of the big families, then it was a possibility that he could be responsible.

"Do you think it's worth talking to him?" Malik smiled. There was a twinkle in his eye. Ash knew that look; it meant that Malik had a surprise up his sleeve.

"Yes, definitely, It's worth talking to him." Ash nodded his head repeatedly. "He may not be involved, but he may have heard who is."

The black Mercedes pulled up next to them. Malik walked to the boot of the car and popped the lid. "Let's ask him then."

Ash looked inside the trunk at the bloodied, gagged face of Bruce Mann. He was trussed up like a chicken in a roasting tin, and from the state of his face, he had already been asked some questions. "Get in."

Malik closed the boot and walked around to the rear passenger door. Ashwan followed him and climbed in behind his boss. It seemed obvious that Malik was already one-step ahead of the game, for now anyway. Ashwan would have to trust his instincts.

2 1

The Major Incident Team
PRESENT DAY

Superintendent Alec Ramsey frowned as he headed away from his desk. He checked his appearance in a cracked mirror, which clung perilously to the back of the office door. His slate grey suit was crisp and sharp, two buttoned with narrow lapels. He wore a fresh grey shirt, open at the neck, and he took a dark silver tie from a hook above the mirror, and he placed it through the collar before knotting it neatly. There was a rap at the door and he had to step back to avoid being hit in the face as it opened. Detective Inspector Will Naylor poked his handsome head around the door. His short black hair was styled and gelled into spikes.

"Nice suit, Guv," Will smiled.

"Are you taking the piss?" Alec straightened the knot and pushed his hair off his face. He wasn't sure if his younger colleague was passing a genuine compliment, or having one of his sarcastic moments. DI Naylor was his own worst enemy; his cutting wit was sometimes too acidic for those around him. Alec Ramsey thought he was amusing at times, and hilarious others. They had the same sense of humour.

"Giorgio Armani?"

"Giorgio ASDA, more like. Twenty-five quid for the suit and a fiver for the shirt and tie set."

"Bargain, never would have guessed," Will smiled again.

"Piss off!" The Superintendent laughed as he stepped toward the door. "The wife bought it."

"That's why it looks alright, Guv, cheap and cheerful."

"I can't get anything in the pockets," Alec slid his hands toward the side pockets, which were still stitched closed.

"You get what you pay for, Guv."

"Have you had the lowdown on this meeting?" Will asked as they walked through the open office space, which housed the Major Investigation Team. The team had been increased to nearly fifty experienced detectives working a mixture of ongoing cases, but the majority of them were investigating the Mosque bomb.

"I've had bits and pieces, but nothing solid. Chief Carlton is strutting about the station like a cat on hot bricks, something is going on."

"What's all the fuss about?"

"The uniformed division have been talking to MI5, and it seems that they have come up with a lead on the Mosque bombing, they want to bring us up to speed."

Alec straightened his tie tight against his collar. He hated wearing neckties, but they were mandatory at joint department briefings, unless uniform was stipulated.

"MI5 are sharing information with the police department? Wonders will never cease," Will smiled widely. His teeth were straight and white, and his green eyes sparkled when he laughed. Superintendent Ramsey was aware of the rumours about his young Detective Inspector's sexual conquests. It seemed that he was a big hit with his female colleagues, both the single women and the married ones too. All that, aside he was the best detective on the force, and Alec knew he would mellow with age, providing he didn't fall foul of the senior hierarchy beforehand.

Alec shrugged the comment off, and opened the door to

the conference room with his swipe card. Only officers with security clearance could gain access. Inside was an unusual mix of military uniforms, police top brass, and Secret Service personnel. Chief Carlton was talking to the joint taskforce personnel, and the divisional Commander. He saw them enter and signalled them to come over, pointing to two empty seats next to him.

"We're just along for the ride today," the Chief smiled at Alec as they sat down. He blanked DI Naylor completely, and couldn't hide the look of contempt on his face. "The Agency director has got the bit between his teeth about something, let's hope it's important."

"Any whispers from the spooks?" Alec asked, referring to the intelligence agencies.

"They have some snippets of information, but nothing that they want to divulge. The want to hold on to it for themselves, so I'm not holding my breath that we're going to hear anything spectacular," the Chief said sarcastically.

"I can't wait," Will grinned as he looked around the room. He had a low tolerance level for these formal gatherings.

"Ladies and gentlemen," the Intelligence Agencies' director called out over the buzz of voices. "We are ready to begin."

The general din died away as the attendees took their seats. The picture of the wreckage from the Mosque bombing appeared on the main screen. Six smaller screens displayed more of the crime scene images, taken in the aftermath of the atrocity.

"I'm sure that you're all familiar with the crime scene pictures however I'd like to recap the findings as they stand at the moment." The director glanced around the meeting room to gauge the mood of his captive audience. Careers could be ruined by boring the pants off everyone at the joint department briefings. "The device was a very sophisticated fertiliser bomb, placed into a stolen vehicle, which had been customised to purpose."

The screen changed to a close up picture of the wrecked van's interior. Two pictures, taken from different angles, flicked on, and then moved to the smaller screens.

"The pictures show that steel plates had been welded into the interior of the vehicle, one against the driver's side here, and one to the floor here, directing the blast toward the front of the Mosque here."

The director removed his blue suit jacket, and pushed his shirtsleeves off his wrists as he pointed to the parts of the picture that he was referring to. The vehicle chassis beneath the plates was virtually intact; the rest of it shredded into metal ribbons. Welding plates into a car bomb allowed the bombers to 'aim' the shrapnel at a specific area to maximise the damage.

"Witness statements indicate that the majority of the attendees had left the building before the device was detonated," the director paused for effect. "First impressions are that the bombers timing was off and they missed the bulk of the crowd. Originally we thought the four fatalities were unfortunate victims of a terrorist attack which was aimed at the Mosque itself."

"This sounds like there is a 'but' coming," Alec whispered to Will.

"Maybe he's not as stupid as I think he is," Will replied. Chief Carlton smirked at the comment, although he didn't want to acknowledge that he found the young detective's comment amusing.

"After thorough investigation we discovered some anomalies, which may shine a different light on things," the director switched the picture on the main screen. The image of two unrecognisable corpses appeared. "The two victims here are Mr and Mrs Amir Patel. They took the full force of the blast."

The image changed again, three burnt out tractor units

appeared. "This picture was taken by Amir Patel's insurance company, two weeks before his untimely death. The lorries were deliberately set on fire, at first the local police force were open minded, considering both arson, and insurance fraud."

The picture changed again, this time the image of Mina Patel appeared. She was dressed in traditional Pakistani wedding attire, her eyes were dark and beautiful, and her smile was enchanting. It was a stark contrast to the crime scene pictures of her broken body.

"A quick look at the finances of Patel's haulage company showed that the business is in good shape, very good shape, and so fraud was ruled out. Further investigation following the bombing led the team to interview the mother of Mina Patel. She revealed that in the weeks running up to the bombing, Mina was worried about Amir's behaviour. She said that he had been secretive lately, and during one domestic argument he told Mina that he was being blackmailed."

Alec raised his eyebrows in mock surprise. "The plot thickens, why don't we know this?" he whispered.

"We do, Guv."

"I know we do, Will. What do they think we have been doing for the last three days?"

"Sharpening our pencils, and scribbling in our little notebooks, like good coppers are supposed to do," Will whispered sarcastically. The Chief turned away pretending that he wasn't smiling.

"With the help of our colleagues in MI6, we explored the right wing extremist theory for the bombing, and we turned up nothing irregular. We have undercover operatives in most of the far right organisations. All the usual suspects can account for their whereabouts. So we have to look for another motive for the bomb, and we started to look at the four victims as possible targets for the attack, not the Mosque." The director shrugged his shoulders.

"Apart from the lack of an extremist motive, do you have anything else to indicate the Patels were the target?" Chief Carlton asked.

"We have Patel's laptop. It's being analysed as we speak. That may reveal something concrete that we can work on. What we do have though is this," the director changed the images again. The image of a dead Asian teenager appeared on the screen.

"This is Ali Rasim, known to his friends as Rozzo. Rasim was a teenager, shot dead near the city centre shortly after the bomb. We believe he was a lookout, a drug runner for a local dealer. Following an anonymous phone call, when his body was found, there was a note stuck to his forehead. The dealer that he worked for is one, Abdul Salim. He's been reported as missing by his father."

The screen changed again, and a close up of the note appeared. The message had been scrawled in biro, and then stuck to the dead teenager's head with chewing gum.

'THIS SCUMBAG WORKED FOR MALIK SHAH AND ASHWAN PINDAR. IF YOU DONT TAKE THEM OFF THE STREETS, THEN WE WILL'

"Malik Shah and Ashwan Pindar are known to us. They are business associates of the Patels. We have been investigating them and their businesses for some time, but on the surface, they are clean as a whistle. We have whispers of information that they finance organised crime, but we can't pin anything on them. Our colleagues at MI6 have been tracking them for some time too." The director gestured to his representative from the intelligence service. The MI5 man was dressed in a blue tailored suit, with a blue silk tie to match. His silver hair was gelled back from his face. Agent Spence coughed before speaking.

"Assuming the Patels were the target, and that their links with Malik Shah were the motive for the attack, then we need to share our information on him with you."

"Well I never, information sharing, Guv, what's all that about?"

"It's the future."

"Mind blowing, wish I'd have thought of it before."

"Shut up, Will, this is getting interesting."

"We have two lines of enquiry open on Malik Shah at present," he began. "We believe that he finances the shipment of reactivated weapons from Pakistan into Europe, the African continent and the United Kingdom. We also believe that he imports heroin and crack cocaine, using some of the more unfortunate members of the Asian community as human mules." The agent left the sentence hanging, not wanting to go into too much detail at this point. MI5 were reluctant to share all their information with the uniformed police divisions. "We believe that if you concentrate your investigations on Shah's local drug activities, then you will stumble across his enemies."

"Stumble?"

"Shut up, Will."

"Fucking stumble?" Will muttered under his breath. "So far they have told us nothing that we don't already know, and we might stumble across the bombers?"

"How far have your enquiries into Shah progressed?" the Chief prompted. He tapped his index finger on the desk irritated. The flippant comment had annoyed him too. MI5 rarely shared all their intelligence with the other departments, much to the detriment of good working relationships between the agencies. Their arrogance was infuriating the police officers in the room.

"They're still in their early stages," the agent straightened his tie uncomfortably. He didn't make eye contact with the Chief.

"You mean you've got Jack Shit, or you're waist deep in this already, and you don't want a police investigation to interfere in your operation," Will said tactfully.

Agent Spence turned angrily toward the young Detective. There was a mixture of anger and amusement on the faces around the room. Will Naylor had said aloud what most of the senior detectives in the room were thinking.

"I beg your pardon?" the agent sneered.

Alec Ramsey tapped his DI on the wrist, a signal to keep quiet for the moment.

"I think my DI is questioning your motives, Agent Spence," Alec raised his eyebrows as he spoke. "It's most unusual for you to call a joint department meeting, and then tell us which direction we should be steering our investigations."

"We are sharing information, that's all."

"You have told us nothing that we don't already know. Why steer us toward Malik Shah's drug enterprise?" Alec pushed the point. He had been around to many years to believe that MI5 were cooperating and sharing information, without an ulterior motive.

Agent Spence looked uncomfortable. Beads of sweat formed on his forehead. He looked to his director for help. None was forthcoming at this point.

"As Director Leigh alluded to earlier, on the surface, Shah is squeaky clean. He covers his tracks very well indeed," the agent reddened as he spoke. He glared at Alec. There was no love lost between Superintendent Ramsey and the intelligence agencies, he couldn't stand their bullshit. Alec called a spade a spade, MI5 would call it a shovel, a gardening tool or a cultivating implement, whatever suited them at the time. Experience gleaned during previous operations taught Alec that Agent Spence was neck deep in manure every time he opened his mouth.

"Like I said, you've got nothing, or you're covering something up," Will sat back in his chair and folded his arms. "Let's not waste time here, have you got anything concrete to link Shah with the bombing?"

"We think that he has enough enemies to constitute him being a legitimate target," the director interrupted. "Ashwan Pindar, Malik Shah, Amir Patel, and half a dozen others are all linked by a group of limited companies."

"Why blow up the Patels?" Alec shrugged. The theory was identical to his, but he was fishing. "Why not go straight for Malik Shah?"

"We don't know the answer to that yet."

"What do you know, Director?" Alec pressed the issue. Something was missing. He pointed to the screen, and the picture of the dead teenager. "This looks more like a turf war, drug dealers flexing their muscles, in which case the investigation should stay with us."

The Police Chief nodded in agreement, but he didn't realise that the Superintendent was trying to provoke a response from Agent Spence. If MI5 had an ongoing operation, the last thing they would want was a uniformed division and police detectives trampling all over it. If there was an MI5 operation going on, then Alec wanted to know about it.

The director sighed. He had anticipated detailed scrutiny from Alec, his reputation as a good detective was legendary. The director picked up a silver camera case and placed it on the table. He undid the metal clasps and opened it, to reveal a Mac 10 machinegun. "This is a reactivated Mac 10, one of a cache of twenty that we recovered from an address on the Bullring estate, Netherley, near to the outskirts of the city. The address was subject to a raid by your drugs squad, and as well as the weapons, a substantial quantity of crack cocaine was seized."

"We're aware of the raid, Director. Why would you be interested in that?" Alec asked.

The weapon passed around the table until it reached Alec. Alec was aware that drugs and weapons had been recovered by the drugs squad, however MI5's interest worried him. He held the weapon like it was a baby, gently testing the weight and the balance. He slid the magazine out of the pistol and then clicked it back into its place. It clicked as it locked. Alec looked down the barrel, inspecting the rifling grooves. He had spent five years in armed response units, and he knew weapons inside out and back to front.

"This has been reactivated by a butcher. It's more likely to jam, or blow your hand off, than it is to fire," Alec shook his head. There was more to reactivating an automatic weapon than meets the eye. "This is definitely a foreign import. What is your intelligence telling you about these weapons?" Alec looked at the director.

"We think that he's purchasing replicas, and deactivated weapons from the USA, and Russia, and then shipping them to sweatshops in Pakistan for reactivation. We know he's selling them in the Middle East, Africa, Spain, and here, but we can't catch him at it, yet."

The room fell quiet for a moment. Arms dealing is a risky business at the best of times, but if Malik Shah was selling reactivated weapons as new, then he would be crossing some very dangerous people.

"What are your thoughts?" Agent Spence threw the question open to the room. He was basking in the glory of the moment. A terrorist attack generally summoned the presence of the most experienced investigators in the service of the realm, but this time, it was he, that held centre stage, for the time being. He was going to milk it for all its worth.

"If Malik Shah is selling weapons like this, then he will be making plenty of enemies," Alec said, handing the weapon to Will. "Sooner or later, this weapon will jam, and the buyers will be looking for their money back."

Agent Spence felt smug as he looked around the room, inviting comments. What he didn't realise were the wider ramifications of the issue. It was becoming clear that MI5 knew more about the Patels than was originally thought. Chief

Carlton looked at Alec, and his face had darkened. He looked like thunder was about to erupt from his ears.

"I think we're being fed a line," Alec looked up from the weapon and stared at the MI5 man's face. "How long have you been following these reactivated weapons?"

Agent Spence fiddled with his tie nervously. He ran his hand across his chin, thinking of the correct words to use as an acceptable reply. "That's classified information and not for general release at the moment."

"What?" Chief Carlton was flabbergasted. "I thought this was a multijurisdictional investigation?"

Agent Spence sneered and shook his head. He looked at the uniformed police officer as if he were from a different planet. "We have no problem sharing relevant information with you, providing it is not of a confidential nature, or if it could endanger any ongoing investigations."

"They have been following the weapons from day one, Chief Carlton," Alec interrupted. "The sale of unreliable, positively dangerous weapons, to criminals across the globe is not something MI5 would want to discourage." He tossed the Mac 10 across the table toward Agent Spence, and it clattered across the polished wood veneer before stopping with a loud clunk against a water jug. "Why would you want to stop the sale of unreliable weapons? I'd be surprised if they're not actively encouraging them."

"Have you got anything solid to link Malik Shah to the sale of these weapons?" Chief Carlton asked calmly. His voice belied the anger inside him.

Agent Spence rolled his eyes skyward and let out a loud sigh. The police officers were not about to be fobbed off with half the truth. The director stood up and walked a few paces toward the wall before turning to speak.

"We had an informer in the witness protection scheme, about two years ago. He was arrested by customs officers, driving an articulated lorry onto a ferry sailing from Rotterdam to Hull."

"You had an informer?" Alec prompted.

"Yes, he disappeared."

"Disappeared?"

"Yes."

"Is this like, give us a clue? We ask questions and you give us one word answers until we guess the truth?" Will chirped in.

Agent Spence coughed and looked into Alec's steely blue eyes, ignoring the comment from Will.

"The lorry was loaded with crates of coffee grounds, and customs searched several of them. They impounded it when crack cocaine was discovered. An initial search of one of the crates uncovered ammunition, and the resulting searches found twenty kilos of crack, and eighteen Mac 10's."

"The driver turned informer in return for what?" Alec pushed.

"Protection and a lighter sentence. He was terrified that his employers would kill him and his family," Spence continued. "The driver was Asian, Pakistani origin, and he fingered Malik Shah as the brains behind the operation."

"So what happened?" Will asked.

"We lost him."

"How did you lose him?" Alec looked at Will. They swapped glances and then glared at the intelligence agent.

"We took his wife and two children into protective custody, and placed them into the witness programme. They were labelled Blogs 18 and 19. Two weeks into the programme the parents of Blogs 18, and the parents of Blogs 19 disappeared. Their homes were searched and we came up with nothing, two days later Blog 18 and his family disappeared. We haven't been able to trace them since."

"How could they disappear?" Alec asked frowning. He knew that Blogs were kept under strict supervision. They were virtually prisoners. "You said they were in custody."

"Our operation was compromised," Agent Spence folded his arms and sat back in his chair.

"Compromised?"

"Yes, compromised."

"Would you like to elaborate on that, or do we have to speculate how you can lose a witness, his wife, his kids and his extended family."

"The safe house was penetrated, and our agents were immobilised. The Blogs were kidnapped, assumed murdered."

Alec and Will swapped glances again. Locating an informer in the witness protection programme, and then having the gall and knowhow to kidnap them, was not the work of amateurs. There were murmurs and hushed comments passed between the attendees around the table.

"How could their whereabouts be discovered?" Chief Carlton asked. He could feel his investigation slipping away from him with every new revelation. It was obvious that MI5 had been withholding vital information from them. He couldn't decide whether it was now more likely that the Patels had been the target, or not. "Surely their whereabouts would be confidential information and not for, 'general release', as you so eloquently put it."

The police officer's sarcasm brought a smile to Alec's lips, but it brought a look of disdain from the MI5 agent. There had been a serious breach of security within the agency, and it was a sore subject. Now it was out in the open, questions would be asked.

"We think that the driver, or his wife may have contacted a family member by telephone, and they in turn gave their whereabouts to Shah's gang."

Alec looked at Will and he grimaced. The parents of Blog 18, and his in-laws had disappeared from their homes. It was simple to conclude that they'd been kidnapped and tortured, before they finally parted with the whereabouts of their children, and grandchildren. Malik Shah had a dreadful reputation amongst the Asian communities, and they would have been under no illusions as to what he would do to them if he found them. How much pain would a parent suffer before they could bear no more, and reveal the location of their children? It was impossible to imagine.

"We're wasting our time here," Superintendent Alec Ramsey stood up from the table and grinned at Agent Spence. He looked to the director.

"You knew we would be all over Malik Shah sooner rather than later, and you don't want us spoiling your arms investigations, right?"

"Right," the director knew better than to backtrack now. The cat was out of the bag.

"Why waste our time and insult our intelligence with this bullshit?"

"We have thousands of man hours invested in this."

"Fine, send us whatever files you're willing to share and leave it alone. We are looking for perpetrators of a bombing. Malik Shah's machineguns don't interest me for now, they're your problem." Alec turned to the Police Chief. "This information changes the dynamics of the bombing completely. It is now more likely that the perpetrators are targeting Shah's foreign activities, which makes it an international incident, rather than a domestic one. We'll need all the information that you have on Shah, and we'll take it from here."

The room remained in shocked silence as Alec and Will left the room. The Major Investigation Team's investigation into the bombing took precedence over all other departments. Chief Carlton knew that there was little point in protesting, he glared at Agent Spence with contempt. The MI5 agent smoothed his hand over his grey hair and shrugged his shoulders. Following the bombing, it was only a matter of time before the truth came out. Now they would have to hand over all their information for the MIT to investigate, and that would mean that heads would roll somewhere within the agency. He just hoped that when the axe fell, it would be way above him.

22

Sarah

SCHOOL DAYS

Sarah Bernstein was six months pregnant, and feeling like a beached whale. None of her trendy clothes would go near her anymore, and the ones that did only emphasised the growing bump at her middle. Her father hadn't looked her in the eye, never mind spoken to her, since the pre-trial hearing, and her mother just cried all the time. To make matters worse her hormones were all over the place, she was vomiting every day, and she felt like screaming. Sarah's allegations of sexual assault weren't taken seriously when her sexual history came to the fore, and the rape charges were eventually dropped. The police and the Crown Prosecution Services decided that the timing of Richard Bernstein remarkably remembering who attacked him was no coincidence, and the charges of grievous bodily harm, and malicious wounding with intent, against Malik Shah and his gang were thrown out of court. The defence lawyers argued that he was accusing them because of what had happened to his sister, and the Crown Prosecution Service decided that a jury would never give a guilty verdict.

The police investigations came to nothing, causing the Bernstein family more embarrassment and shame in the Jewish community. Mr Bernstein couldn't cope. Behind the scene, he was arranging for Sarah to be taken to Israel to give birth to her child. He planned to place her with extended family in the homeland, until Sarah and the baby were old enough not to cause raised eyebrows and fuel wagging tongues. That was the reason for her mother's tears. She would lose her daughter, and her granddaughter in one sweep. Sarah had gotten wind of the plan, and she was feeling as low as she had ever been. Israel was not her home, and it never would be. She was Jewish, not Israeli. The school decided that it was best if she and Richard didn't attend, and social services tried to locate places at neighbouring schools for them, until the whole thing had blown over, whenever that would be. Sarah didn't think it would be anytime soon. A couple of her old friends kept in contact, but their phone calls were becoming less frequent as pressure from their parents to cut ties with her began to bite. The rest of her friends cut contact completely, some because she was pregnant, the others because she had made the rape allegations against the coolest guys at school. The majority of her friends and acquaintances knew full well that she was sleeping with Malik, and that she had done sexual favours for the others. No one believed that she had been drugged and raped by the gang. She felt lost and alone.

Sarah was alone in her room, sat on her Holly Hobbie quilt, writing down her feelings in her padded diary. The diary had the same character on the front of it as her bed covers. Beatrix Potter characters stared down from the pine-framed pictures that had suddenly reappeared on her wall. Her father ripped her Duran Duran and Spandau Ballet posters down, and replaced them with her childhood favourites, as if it might bring back her innocence. She felt like she was in a bad dream. Sarah felt isolated and afraid, afraid that things would never be the same again. Her unborn baby kicked, and reminded her that this was no dream. She placed her hand on her belly and a tear ran from her eye. She wondered what was to become of her and her baby when a pebble rattled her window.

The noise made her jump and she held her breath and waited. Five seconds went by before another clunk sounded. She held her breath again and looked at the door, waiting for her father to burst in, but he didn't. She tiptoed to the window and peered around the curtain, her heart was beating like a drum in her chest. It took a few seconds for her eyes to adjust to the darkness outside, and she cupped her hand against the glass so that she could see who was there. There was a black Ford Capri parked across the road from her house. The lights were switched off but she could see that the engine was running, fumes were pumping from the exhaust pipe. A movement closer to the house caught her eye.

"Malik!" she exclaimed under her breath. Her heart fluttered like a butterfly. She had missed him so much, despite all that had happened; she loved him. She worshiped him. She would do anything that he asked her to do, and there in lay the problem. He waved from behind a Weeping Willow tree and pointed to the trunk. She could make out a white oblong against the bark, and she realised that it was an envelope. He had written her a letter, and pinned it to the tree, how romantic, after everything that had gone on. Sarah could barely contain herself. She wanted to run outside and hold him, but she knew that it was impossible. Her father had placed her on a strict curfew, and she dare not provoke his wrath any further. The front door was locked and barred by seven-thirty every night. Malik waved again and ran down the drive to the waiting Capri. He climbed into the passenger seat, and the Ford screeched away. It travelled a hundred yards before the headlights came on, and then it disappeared around a bend and the road was silent once more.

Sarah stared at the envelope, and she dreamed of the wonderful things that it would contain. Her imagination went wild as she climbed back onto her bed. She clutched her diary to her chest and smiled. Malik had written her a letter and risked being confronted by her brothers, and father to bring it to her. She loved him so much that it hurt inside, and yet she felt a warm glow deep in the pit of her stomach when she thought of him. Sarah opened her diary and slid the pen from the spine. 'I LOVE MALIK, AND WOULD RATHER DIE THAN BE SENT TO ISRAEL.' She wrote in capital letters, as if they would be more significant that way. She spent that night tossing and turning in fitful sleep, desperate to get her hands on the letter, never once thinking that it would be the last time she ever wrote in her diary. In fact, it was the last thing that she would ever write.

23

Bruce Mann
PRESENT DAY

Bruce Mann was more frightened than he had ever been before, and with good reason too. He was naked, and tied to a wooden chair on the third floor of an old leather hide warehouse, somewhere near the river Mersey. He wasn't sure exactly where, but he could smell the sea, and the sound of seagulls squawking drifted through the iron framed windows. The windows were at least ten feet tall, and divided into eighteen squares by metal frames; much of the glass was missing and the stars twinkled against the inky black sky. The walls were rendered with thick grey plaster, big chunks of it missing, and the floors were bare wood planks, cracked and splintered by age. There was a dank stale odour about the place. The stench of rotting animal flesh still lingered in the floorboards.

Bruce looked around and tried to fathom why he had been abducted and beaten. He remembered being hit hard from behind, and his attackers punched and kicked him unconscious, all the time asking questions about Malik Shah. His next recollection was being dragged roughly from the boot of a car, and then being manhandled up six sets of stairs separated by wide landings. He guessed two staircases joined each floor, hence, he concluded that he was three floors up. Despite kicking and screaming for help all the way, no one had come to his aid. The building was empty. He knew that he was at the mercy of Malik Shah, alone, and devoid of any hope of rescue. Bruce didn't know what he had done wrong, but he knew that he was in big trouble.

Bruce flexed his wrist painfully, a thick plastic cable tie cut into his flesh and his fingers felt swollen and numb. His thumbs ached badly, but they always did, ever since they'd been sliced off with a box cutter blade. That episode of his life was one that he promised himself he wouldn't repeat, and yet here he was, up to his eyes in shit again. He had done his level best to avoid Ashwan Pindar and his boss, Malik Shah, and he had no conceivable idea what he had done to offend them this time.

'Hadn't he kept a low profile since? Obviously not low enough', he thought. His head ached from a combination of inhaling exhaust fumes in the boot of the car, and because of the beating, he had taken. There was congealed blood in his nostrils, and his bottom lip was swollen and bloody. Through the windows on the east, he could see the night sky was lighting up slowly on the horizon. The sun was coming up but it made little difference to the temperature inside the warehouse. He was shivering from the cold. Bruce knew that he had been left alone, bound and naked, so that he would have time to dwell on what was about to happen to him. He was going to be tortured, no doubt about that. What, exactly, it was that he was supposed to know was beyond him. Footsteps began to echo up the staircase from somewhere below. He took a deep breath and prayed that it would be quick.

It took a full five minutes for the footsteps to reach the third floor. There were no voices, just the sound of multiple footfall approaching. It felt like an eternity to Bruce, and he screwed his eyes closed tight as warm urine ran down his legs, fear held him in its merciless grip. There was a screech as a metal door opened. The door clanged shut and the noise echoed through the cavernous building. The footsteps were in the room and a stinging tear ran down Bruce's cheek. He was more frightened than he had ever been.

24

Sarah Bernstein
SCHOOL DAYS

Sarah waited patiently at the bus stop after school. It was cold and wet, and the wooden shelter smelled of stale urine inside. The other students had all gone, their number dwindling as a series of green double-deckers buses came and went. Her father would be livid that she had purposely missed her school bus, but she would cross that bridge when she came to it. She had to see Malik. The red public telephone box next to the bus shelter was smashed and vandalised, not that she could call Malik at his parent's home anyway. He was an hour late.

Sarah sneaked out of the house that morning to retrieve his letter from the tree while the rest of her family ate breakfast. Crumpled up in her school blazer, she had to wait until she arrived at school to read it. Sarah hoped that it would be full of romance and kisses, but it was not. The letter was short, and to the point. Malik said that he needed to see her, and that he would pick her up from the stipulated bus stop at four o'clock. It was ten minutes past five when his cousin's black Capri pulled up. Rainwater sprayed from the tyres as it screeched to a halt. 'The Jam' were blaring a track through the speakers as Malik opened the passenger door and climbed out. He smiled, but there was no warmth in it. His eyes appeared sullen and dark, his pupils dilated. Sarah knew that he was stoned before she said hello to him, and his cousin leered at her from the driver's seat. Her heart sank.

"What you waiting for? Get in," Malik tipped the passenger seat forward to allow her to climb in. His voice was thick and slurred. Sarah wasn't convinced that it was a good idea. This was not what she had envisaged their meeting would be like in her mind. Sarah was hoping for hearts and flowers, promises of undying love but that wasn't forthcoming. "Get in."

The rain intensified, and the wind blew through her school blazer and chilled her to the bone. That chill blast swayed her, and she decided to get in the car. She swallowed her pride and climbed into the Capri. Instead of climbing into the back with her Malik reset the front seat and climbed into it, leaving her in the back alone and confused. His cousin eyed her in the rear view mirror. He made her flesh crawl.

"I thought you wanted to talk," Sarah sat forward so that she could see Malik's face.

Malik lit a joint as he turned to face her. He blew the smoke toward her and the sickly smell of cannabis filled her nostrils. She had smoked it with Malik many times, enjoying the mellow high it gave them. He held it up to her. This was the last thing that she wanted, but life had been so constrictive lately, maybe a little fun was what she needed.

"Here, chill out, bitch."

Sarah hated it when he called her that. He said it was a term of endearment, and that she should be grateful to be his bitch. She didn't feel grateful right now, that was for sure. Sarah took the reefer and inhaled deeply as she slumped into the back seat. She looked out of the window and tears filled her eyes as she watched the rain run across the glass. How did things get so bad? Malik turned around to face her.

"Here," he handed her an open tin of Coca Cola. The cannabis resin mix was burning hot and drying her throat. She took the tin and gulped. It was warm and flat but it took the edge off her thirst. By the time she had finished the joint, the Rohypnol in the coke was starting to take effect. Her head felt thick and her limbs were beginning to numb. Sarah looked at Malik and he smiled. It turned into a sneer. Sarah remembered the feeling well, from the night she had been gang raped. Malik had slipped her the drug then, and he had done it again. Why would he do that to her now, after everything she had been through? She asked herself. She loved him, and his baby inside her, and she thought he loved her, in his own way. Sarah opened her mouth to scream but no sound came out. Her face contorted as the muscles tried to contract, but the drug was taking a hold. The Capri stopped at a red light and Sarah looked at the driver in the car next to her. She tried to plead for help with her eyes because her mouth wouldn't work. The driver turned his attention back to the road as the lights changed to green, and she closed her eyes as her consciousness slipped away.

"Do you have any idea how much shit you have caused me?" Malik's voice drifted in her ear. "It's payback you fucking slut."

It was dark when Sarah began to come round. She was confused and disorientated, alien sights and sounds flashed through her mind. Above her was a gigantic steel arch, illuminated by hundreds of halogen lamps. Yellow streetlights stretched away from her into the distance, and the air was thick with choking diesel exhaust fumes. The suspension bridge above her was enormous, spanning the River Mersey between the industrial towns of Widnes and Runcorn. It's a landmark that could be seen from miles away. Sarah recognised it somewhere in her befuddled brain. She was sitting upright against the safety railings that lined the pedestrian walkway, out of sight of the passing vehicles. Four lanes of traffic streamed past her in a blur of bright lights, steel and noise.

Her memory began to piece together the last few hours. She was sore and wet between her legs, her face was sticky, and she could recall Malik and his cousin taking turns to have sex with her in the back of the Capri. Their voices echoed in her mind, and the smell of their sex and sweat clung to her. She had no idea how many times they'd used her. She had let it happen again. Sarah stood on shaky legs, gripping the railings to help her stand. Her father would be going out of his mind looking for her by now, and what was he going to find? His slut of daughter stoned and raped....again. No one would believe her. They didn't the first time why would they now? She got into the car of her own free will. She took the cannabis willingly, and drank the coke that Malik gave her, despite the previous allegations that she had made. Sarah leaned over the rail and vomited into the black abyss, which separated the road bridge and the river, far below.

Sarah was traumatised emotionally and still reeling from the drugs in her system when she felt warm fluid running down her thighs. She lifted her crumpled skirt and saw liquid streaked heavily with blood running from her. Sarah knew she was miscarrying, and she screamed into the darkness, her waters had broken, brought on by the physical trauma. Her father would never speak to her again, her brothers would be ridiculed at school and she would be banished to Israel forever this time. Saliva dribbled from her lips as she cried hysterically, and her vision blurred by her tears. She had ruined her own life, and was now responsible for the death of her unborn child. Sarah leaned forward, calming suddenly. There was a way to stop it all right now. She gripped the railings low down and tipped her body weight onto the rail. The world seemed to be spinning very slowly as she paused for a few seconds. The traffic became silent while she thought about it all one more time. Could she face her family? Sarah could see her father's face in her mind's eye, his shame and disgust etched deep into every wrinkle. When she let go there was no peace as she tumbled in the blackness. The pain inside her heart didn't fade as she hurtled toward the icy river. Hitting the water from that height was like hitting concrete. Sarah didn't live long enough to feel how cold the water was, and the impact mercifully ended her torment.

25

Bruce Mann
PRESENT DAY

Bruce Mann looked at the faces of the four men in front of him. He recognised Malik Shah and his lieutenant Ashwan Pindar. The other two were strangers to him, up until they hit him on the head and stuffed him in the boot of their Mercedes. Malik and Ashwan were suited, smartly dressed. Their associates had long rubber aprons, gauntlets and wellington boots, slaughterhouse uniforms.

"Hello, Bruce," Ashwan said.

"Ash," Bruce swallowed hard, trying to maintain his composure. "What am I doing here, Ash?"

"We need to ask you some questions about Mamood."

"Mamood?"

"My son," Ash bent level with his face and stared into his eyes.

"I don't know your son, Ash," Bruce shook his head rapidly. He was beginning to think that maybe he had sold him some drugs, or an illegal firearm without realising who he was related to. "Honestly, I don't know your son."

"Maybe you do and maybe you don't, but how can I believe a scumbag like you?"

"What do you think I know about your son, Ash?"

"You know where he is."

"What?"

"We think you might know where he is, or you'll know someone that does know."

"Is he lost?" It was an instinctive question from Bruce's point of view, but Ashwan took it as arrogance. He punched Bruce hard in the mouth. Pain flashed from the exposed nerves in his broken teeth, and he spat blood and enamel onto the ancient floorboards.

"He isn't lost, he's been kidnapped!" Ashwan spat the words.

"Fucking hell, Ash!" Bruce breathed deeply and shook his head again. "You cut off my thumbs for selling a bit of smack on your turf. Do you think I'd still be around if I was holding your son for Christ's sake?"

"You have your ear to the ground." Ash nodded to the two men in aprons. One of them wheeled a metal trolley from somewhere out of Bruce's field of vision. He couldn't see what was on it, but he could hazard a guess that it wasn't tea and biscuits. "Who has my son?"

"I haven't got a clue, but I have nothing to do with it, I swear."

"What do you know about the bombing?"

"What bombing?" Bruce wracked his brains. "You mean the Mosque?"

"Yes, the Mosque."

"Why would I know anything about that?"

"We think someone is having a pop at us," Malik spoke. "Who has got it in for us?"

Bruce stared at the floor, shaking like a leaf inside. His mind processed information at a million miles an hour, trying to think of anything that might be significant. One snippet of information could save his life, but nothing sprang to mind. The whirring noise of a power drill echoed in the darkness. A tungsten drill bit glinted in the darkness as it turned at high speed. Bruce opened and closed his mouth and he struggled against the restraints.

"Where is my son?" Ashwan removed a photograph from his suit pocket. He held it up to Bruce's face. Bruce looked at the picture through his tears, his vision blurred. Mamood was a handsome teenage boy, naked, tied up and terrified. Tears streaked his face and there was terror in his eyes. "Where is my son?" Ash repeated. The man with the drill approached.

"Please, Ash!" Bruce dribbled and screwed his eyes tight shut. The memory of having his thumbs cut off was still raw. He couldn't stand the thought of prolonged torture, his heart would explode with fear. "Believe me, if I knew where he was I'd tell you. I don't know where he is, Ash."

"Maybe Mr Drill can convince you to remember." Ashwan nodded to the man with the drill. He stepped closer and then kneeled down on one knee. He held the spinning drill bit six inches from Bruce's foot. "I once watched a man being questioned by my colleague and Mr Drill for nearly four hours."

"Ash, I don't know anything," Bruce was gibbering, dribbling and shaking his head in panic. "I could help you to find him, Ash!"

Ashwan waved and the drill was withdrawn, although the bit kept spinning as a reminder that it hadn't gone away. He could smell the fear coming from Bruce, and the offer of cooperation was worth exploring before the screaming started.

"How can you help?" Ashwan asked. "One chance, Bruce, think carefully."

"I know people, Ash," Bruce took short sharp breath in between his words. "I'll spend every minute of the day asking people about your son, I'll look under every rock and stone to help......."

"What people?" Ash interrupted.

"You know what I mean, Ash. I'll ask around."

"No, I don't. Enlighten me, Bruce."

Bruce swallowed hard. His mouth was dry and caked in congealing blood. "I figure if someone is stupid enough to kidnap your son, then they either want money, or they're doing it to hurt you, right?"

Ash took a bottle of mineral water from his overcoat pocket. He twisted the top off it and placed it to Bruce's lips. Bruce swallowed greedily and then began to cough and splutter.

"Which category would you fit into, Bruce?" Malik interrupted.

"Which category?"

"Yes, would you do it for money, or revenge?"

"Neither, Malik." Bruce coughed again before he spoke. "I fucked up once, and I paid for it, right?"

"So you're in the second group then?" Ash said.

"No!" Bruce shook his head from side to side. "I sold a bit of smack in one of your pubs, and I paid dearly for the privilege. I know the score, you fuck up, you pay for it. I have made a real effort to stay out of your turf, Ash."

"Okay let's say I believe you," Ash said. "Who would fit your profile?"

"I can think of a dozen of your rivals, any one of them could pull a stunt like this," Bruce struggled to say what he really thought. Malik Shah and his henchmen were spectacularly unpopular. Most of their rivals wouldn't think twice about killing Malik's men or their families. "Have they asked for money?"

"Not yet," Ashwan frowned. "Why do you ask that?"

"If they were amateurs then they would have asked for the money by now," Bruce said shakily. "The chances are if they haven't asked for money yet then it's personal."

"The chances are it's someone we've had issues with in the past, Bruce," Malik said. "Someone we've hurt, like you."

"I'm a one man band." Bruce was trying to think on his feet. The kidnap was baffling, but to think that he was a suspect didn't make any sense. "I'm under no illusions what people think of me, I work alone because nobody trusts me, nobody likes me. I make a few quid here and there, selling smack and the odd shooter to junkies. This is way out of my league."

"Who's league is it in, Bruce?"

"Fucking hell, Ash, kidnap? What about the Richards family?"

"What about them?"

"You remember when they fell out big time with the Burgess Brothers?" Bruce was gibbering at a hundred miles an hour.

"Yes I remember," Malik screwed up his face as if he were getting annoyed. "What about it?"

"Well, if you remember the Richards family blamed the Burgess Brothers for whacking one of their drug deals, right." He nodded his head to reinforce his story. "One of their heavies was shot, and the drugs and the money were lifted, remember?"

"Get to the point, Bruce," Ashwan snarled.

"The Burgess Brothers paid the Richards off, over half a million from what I heard!" Bruce thought this information was buying him some time.

"Why, what happened?" Malik was curious. He heard the same story via the rumour mill, but he never found out why one of the families had backed down.

"The Richards took old mother Burgess from outside the hairdressers in Page Moss, kidnapped her in broad daylight."

"Carry on," Ash listened intently.

"They held her in a unit, and they sent pictures of her in a coffin holding a wreath, cheeky bastards!" Bruce tried a smile. Malik looked to Ash while he mulled over the information. "The Richards were a smaller outfit, but the Burgess Brothers paid up, and they paid compensation for the drugs on top," Bruce nodded emphatically as he finished his story. "No one would fuck with them ever again after that. It sent a message across the city that no one could ignore."

"I think you're right, Bruce." Malik stroked his chin as he spoke. He looked at Ash, but Ash couldn't read his thoughts. "I think it's way above your head."

"Thank god!" Bruce gasped. He smiled through swollen bloody lips. "I'll help you find him, I promise I will."

"You are also right about the message, and we need to send one too. Kill him," Malik said to the man with the drill. "Mess him up first, and then kill him."

The drill whined louder as it approached Bruce's foot. Bruce twitched violently as the tungsten bit ripped through his skin, before tearing bone and cartilage and spraying blood in a wide arc. Bruce screamed and he bit down on his lip hard, but he couldn't escape the pain.

"I'm confused," Ashwan said as they stepped clear of the blood splatter. Their suits were expensive to clean. "Why kill him?"

"Tell them to cut him up and dump his body on the town hall steps. I want every scumbag in this city to know what happens when they fuck with us. We'll send out a message that no one will ignore. I want his body on the front pages of every newspaper. Whoever has Mamood will think twice, and we hit the Richards gang tonight."

Ashwan took a last look at Bruce Mann. Both men were drilling and cutting, pulling and tearing and the screams were deafening. Ash almost felt pity for him but then the visions of his son restrained and terrified came to the forefront of his mind, and his pity vanished. The screaming echoed through the empty warehouse for nearly forty minutes before they were finally silenced.

2 6

The Bernstein Family
School Days

Two weeks after Sarah's inquest Nick waited for David Bernstein to finish rugby training. David was struggling to deal with the death of his baby sister, especially as he had to see Malik Shah every day. The coroner signed a verdict of suicide, much to the distaste of the Bernstein family and the police. Witnesses reported seeing Sarah getting into a black Capri, and it didn't take the police long to connect the vehicle with Malik Shah and his cousin. The witnesses also said she climbed in of her own accord, she wasn't forced in anyway. The police interrogated Malik and his cousin, and they confirmed that they'd picked her up after school. They admitted driving to a park, getting drunk and smoking cannabis, and having sex with her, but they were adamant that it was consensual sex. Malik's cousin told the police that he had dropped her off at Runcorn train station about ten o'clock that night, and that was the last that they saw of her.

Sarah died on impact with the river. Her body was travelling at over seventy miles an hour when she hit the water, although the water stopped her body dead, her internal organs carried on travelling, ripping free of their surrounding muscles and tissues, and causing death instantaneously. She drifted down the river for four days before her bloated body, spotted by a passing tanker at the Stanlow oil refinery, was pulled from the water. The polluted river had washed away any useful evidence from her body, and at first, the police were baffled. News bulletins appealed for witnesses, and a lorry driver reported seeing a young girl being sick over the safety rail on the Runcorn Bridge; his elevated position in the cab offered him a narrow field of vision of the pedestrian walk-way which ran parallel to the road platform.

The police were open-minded as they investigated her death, never ruling out foul play, misadventure, or suicide. It was Sarah's diary which swung the coroner in the end. He took her final entry as a gauge of her mental state of mind, and she said that she would rather be dead than be sent to Israel. She also said that she loved Malik, so it didn't appear too odd that she had secretly met him, or that she had sex with both Malik, and his cousin. Her reputation for being promiscuous was already on record.

Mr Bernstein refused to attend the inquest, driving a wedge between himself and his distraught wife. She blamed him for being too hard on Sarah, pushing her to jump from the bridge, and she would never forgive him for that. Mr Bernstein couldn't listen to the reports that his pregnant daughter took drugs and had sex with two men in a car, after the trauma the family had already been through with the failed rape case, and Richard's assault. It was too much for him to swallow. David Bernstein escorted his mother to the inquest, everyday for a week, until the final verdict was decreed. The details were sickening to him, and they began to eat away at him inside. Every night after the inquest, when his mother had gone to bed, he shared his feelings with his friend Nick, and his brother Richard, and the three agreed that Malik Shah was to blame for Sarah's death. Mr Bernstein spent most of the week in his study, drunk on whisky, rarely coming out, and never sharing his wife's bed. They never shared one again.

David was fast approaching his final exams, so changing schools was not an option. His parents were so shattered and disorientated that they never once considered that David would see Malik Shah at school. The pain inside was eating him away, and the pressure was building to critical. Not only had he lost his beautiful sister, but also he had to watch his parents' marriage falling to pieces. Richard asked Nick to keep an eye on his older brother, knowing from past experience how Malik and his gang settled disputes. He didn't want his older brother doing something stupid, and becoming a target. He was tough, and so was Nick, but they were two teenage boys, and no match for an armed gang. Nick knew that David had rugby practice on a Tuesday, and so he waited by the playing fields for him to finish, so that they could walk home together.

"Hey, Bernstein," Nick called as he spotted David crossing the road. David smiled, pleased to see his big friend.

"Hey, Nick," David bumped fists with him. He laughed. Nick's fists were huge, far too big for a teenage boy, more suited to a gorilla.

"How was training?"

"Shut up! What do you care about rugby practice?" David laughed. It was obvious that his clumsy friend was concerned about him, and while he appreciated that, he didn't want their friendship changed by it all.

"I was just asking, you freak!" Nick punched David's arm, deadening it with his heavy blow.

"Ahh, you big monkey! That hurt," David kicked Nick in the shin in retaliation and then ran off out of reach. Nick jogged slowly after his friend, never having a hope of catching him. They laughed and joked as they ran toward the park, on their way home.

Sefton Park is made up of wide grassy areas, wooded areas, and two boating lakes. A two-lane road, which is a kidney shape, surrounds it and footpaths crisscross it. They reached the perimeter of the park, crossed the road and walked through a wide car park that serviced the facilities. The sun was shining and David felt more relaxed as the smell of freshly cut grass became stronger, the closer they got to the park. The car park was full. Halfway across the parking lot Nick spotted the black Capri, that belonged to Saj Shah, Malik's cousin. It was the last vehicle that Sarah had ever travelled in. His stomach tensed as he thought about the impact it would have on David, should he see it. David noticed that Nick's expression had changed to one of concern, and he followed Nick's gaze. David recognised the vehicle, and his face darkened with anger. The Capri was empty, and there was no one around. The temptation was too great. David Bernstein picked up a half brick and ran toward it.

"David, don't!" Nick hissed, not wanting to attract attention. He stretched out his long arms to grab him, but David shrugged him off and ran onwards.

It was a futile attempt to stop him. David launched the brick with venom and it shattered the windscreen into a million pieces. Nick caught up with his friend and he pulled him roughly onto a footpath that led away from the car park into a wooded area. They ran for a short distance and then began walking as they cleared the trees, deciding that it was less conspicuous to walk than run.

"Bloody hell! David. We need to get away from here."

David turned reluctantly, and they ran toward the path network.

"That was fun," Nick panted sarcastically as they put distance between them and the damaged Capri. He watched his friend's face. There was no humour in his expression, just hate.

A grassy slope stretched gently away to their right, ending where it met the edge of the largest lake in the park. In the centre of the lake was a mock pirate ship, complete with tall masts, crow's nest and fake cannons. The lake attracted groups of youngsters and families with toddlers. The pirate ship appealed to the imagination of old and young, and it was a popular picnic site. There were a handful of people milling about near the water. To the left of them was a huge arboretum built in Victorian times from arched wood frames and huge glass panels. It was being refurbished and there were a dozen or so workers fetching and carrying rubbish. Discarded pipes, and timber struts, were tossed into two overflowing skips. David and Nick were catching their breath when a voice shouted at them from behind.

"Hey!"

David and Nick turned and looked over their shoulder. Saj Shah was sprinting through the wooded area, fifty yards behind them, and gaining fast. There were two others with him, following behind. Saj Shah was eighteen, two years older than Nick and David. He was also a bad egg, a dealer and all round bad boy with a reputation for violence.

"Run," Nick shouted. He began to sprint as fast as he could, but to his amazement, David had turned to face Saj as he neared. "Run, David!" Nick called again, trying to spur David into action.

"Fuck them," David growled. He readied himself to face his pursuer. The anger inside him had fuelled his bloodstream with adrenalin. The hatred inside him gave him strength. "I'm not running from these bastards."

Nick stopped running and turned back. He couldn't leave his best friend to face three attackers alone, especially not Saj Shah. A loud clang drew his attention. A workman had flung some lead piping into the skip and it bounced off the metal and landed on the grass nearby. Nick looked at the pipe, and picked it up without thinking about it. The lead pipe would even things up a little.

"You smashed my windscreen, you prick!" Saj stopped five yards from David. His face twisted with anger and spittle flew from his mouth as he shouted his words. "You're fucking dead, Bernstein!"

"I think you'll find me a bit tougher than my little brother, or my little sister, you fucking coward," David spoke clearly but there was a look in his eye that stopped Saj Shah and his colleagues in their tracks. David was a competent fighter, and he knew that he could hold his own against most other youths his size. Saj Shah was smaller than he was, older but not as athletic. David also knew that Saj, Malik and the rest of the gang were pack animals. They fought as a group, never one on one. They'd not beaten anyone of any significance singlehanded. "Come on, let's see how hard you are against someone closer to your own age, Shah, you're fucking scared aren't you?"

Saj hesitated. He laughed and shook his head in disbelief. David was correct, he was scared, especially when he saw Nick approaching with a two foot length of lead pipe in his hand. Nick was tall and well built, and he looked like he would be a handful. His exaggerated facial features made him look mean. Saj stood his ground and goaded David. "You're nothing, Bernstein, Jewish scum, and your sister was a slut!"

David closed the gap between them in flash, and his hand speed surprised Saj. A stinging left jab hit him square on the nose, making his eyes water, blurring his vision, and the coppery taste of his own warm blood filled the back of his throat. Saj wiped blood from his nose with his sleeve, and his eyes widened in shock. He threw a wild swinging punch at his younger opponent, but David ducked beneath it easily and hit him again in the ribs.

David Bernstein could see the fear in Saj's eyes, and he unleashed the anger that had been burning inside him for months. He hit Saj Shah four times in the face before his knees buckled beneath him. His front teeth smashed, and his top lip split apart like a squashed caterpillar. Saj put his hands over his face to protect himself, but the blows rained down on him in a relentless tirade. He fell flat on his back and curled up, battered and bloodied.

"Get up, Saj," David stepped back.

"Fuck you," Saj spat blood and got to his knees. He looked to his friends. They were poised waiting to join the fray at the earliest opportunity, but the presence of Nick carrying a lead pipe was a deterrent for now.

"Come on, Saj, batter him," one of his friends offered some encouragement, despite the fact David was totally overwhelming him.

"Yes, do him, Saj."

"Yes, come on, Saj, what's the problem?" David said. There was madness in his eyes now. One of the men that abused his beautiful sister, pretty little Sarah, was here in front of him, and he was bleeding. It felt good, but not nearly good enough.

Saj tried to stand up. His legs were shaky, but he stood erect and spat toward David again. Blood and phlegm spattered on the path.

"Come on, Saj, get up, or are you scared?"

Saj put his fists up and moved hesitantly toward David. There was fear in his eyes, and David could sense it. He felt anger inside him like never before, pure rage. Saj moved within striking distance and David launched at him, fists flying. Three powerful punches landed in quick succession, cracking Saj's jaw and shattering three teeth. He fell back down onto the path heavily, landing in a sitting position, his head and face exposed.

David Bernstein wasn't ready to stop his attack, and he kicked Saj in the face. His eyes rolled back into his head and he hit the concrete path hard, cracking the back of his skull like an egg.

"That's for Sarah." David spat the words as he kicked Saj in the side of the head. His skull was exposed. He kicked him again. "That's for my brother."

Nick could tell that Saj was seriously injured, blood was pooling from the back of his skull, and more ran from his ears, but David was like a wild animal, and he stamped on the prone man's ribcage. There was a loud snapping sound as his sternum cracked. Blood and phlegm squirted from Saj's mouth. It was then that Saj's associates jumped into the fray.

David was punched in the side of the head, stunning him. He dropped his hands and a right hook landed on his jaw, cracking the bone and whipping his head sideways violently. A third blow smashed into his nose and his brain went into momentary shut down. He buckled and collapsed into a heap on the path. As David hit the floor, Nick swung the pipe and connected with the cheekbone of one attacker. His face imploded as if made from papier-mâché. A huge purple swelling formed in seconds and the man took a few steps sideways before falling onto the grass face first. His associate looked at the carnage around him, thought about fighting on, and then thought again. He bolted.

Saj was dead or dying. Nick was in no doubt about it. Workers from the arboretum, and shocked day-trippers started to approach the scene cautiously. Some of the braver members of the public called out for the violence to stop. Nick knew his friend was in trouble for what he had done to Saj Shah. The police would be on their way. David would be charged with grievous bodily harm at best, but looking at Saj, manslaughter or murder was more likely. Nick thought about Mr and Mrs Bernstein, Richard, who idolised his older brother, and beautiful Sarah. He couldn't let the family suffer anymore. Nick raised the pipe and brought it down hard on Saj's skull. The slushy thud was sickening to hear. A second heavy swing split the skull open like a melon, and his brains spilled out across the concrete. He looked at the shocked faces around him, and tears of anger ran down his face. Women shrieked, children, their faces covered from the horror by their parents, screamed. Nick clung to the pipe and sat down on the grass. The sound of sirens grew louder as he lay back and closed his eyes, wishing that this nightmare would be gone when he opened them.

27

The aftermath
School days

David Bernstein and Nick Cross were arrested at the scene of
the fracas in the park, and a lengthy investigation commenced.
Witnesses reported seeing Saj Shah and his friends chasing
across the park, shouting abuse before the fight started. Initial
thoughts were that it was a feud between young drug dealers,
however as the history of the youths involved came to the
fore, the waters became very cloudy. David Bernstein had
motive to kill Saj Shah, but witnesses said the fatal blows were
struck by his friend Nick, and they confirmed that David was
unconscious when it happened. It also appeared that David
was chased, and attacked by Saj and two others, and that he
had defended himself. A month into the investigation, David
was charged with affray and given a six month suspended
sentence. Nick Cross was charged with murder. Manslaughter
was thrown out as witnesses were unanimous that Saj Shah was
prone when the final blows were struck. He was sentenced to
life with a recommendation that he served fifteen years.

The court case was the final nail in the Bernstein family
coffin. Mrs Bernstein moved away to live with her elderly
mother in Scotland, claiming that she needed to be nursed
because of the onset of dementia. The truth was that she
was ashamed of her husband, and the way he dealt with the

ongoing crisis. Mr Bernstein spiralled into alcoholism, and his liver packed up by the end of 1986. He never recovered from his daughter's fall from grace, and subsequent suicide. Richard was well looked after by a trust fund that his parents had set up for him, and by the time his father died, he was off to university and the beginning of his adult life. Malik Shah, his family, and his gang had shattered Richard's family life into pieces, killed his sister, and his father, and made his mother run away. Nick was given a life sentence, with a view to be eligible for parole after fifteen years. He served twelve, and Richard went to see him every month without fail. Their bond was strong, etched in blood, and it would remain so forever. They talked for hours about revenge during their visits; Richard never lost sight of his goal.

David left school and went to university in Israel. He needed a fresh start. After his academic studies, he joined the military and focused his hatred for Malik Shah, and the young Muslims that had ruined his life, into the Israeli struggle against the surrounding Arab governments. Richard lost everyone important to him in the space of two years. The hatred and the sense of loss remained inside him, burning slowly, always hurting. The slow burn evolved into a living, breathing monster, a life-long plot for revenge. David loved the military, and within two years he joined the Israeli Special Forces. He waited patiently for Nick to be released, and when David left his military career, he had reached the rank of Captain. Richard Bernstein was waiting outside the prison gates when Nick was released, and they headed for the farm, stopping off at McDonalds on the way, so that Nick could buy a chocolate milkshake. One week later, David Bernstein, boarded a plane at Tel Aviv airport. He was ready to join them on their bitter quest.

28

Present day
LIVERPOOL

Liverpool Town Hall stands in High Street at its junction with Dale Street, Castle Street, and Water Street. It's a grey stone building with a huge bronze dome on the top. Tall Roman columns stand guard either side of the wide doorway. When Alec and DI Will Naylor arrived, the historic facade had been sealed off from the public by yellow crime scene tape, which flapped noisily as the wind blew in off the River Mersey. Chief Carlton waited patiently for Alec and Will to arrive. The Chief felt that the mutilated body that had been dumped on the Town Hall steps was linked to the Malik Shah investigation. The cause of death was not obvious, because the victim was so badly tortured.

"Alec, Detective Inspector Naylor," the Chief acknowledged their arrival. A blast of wind brought a smell of the ocean with it.

"Chief." Alec responded. He looked toward the naked corpse and grimaced. "This looks personal."

"You could say that. Or someone wanted information from him."

"I'm guessing that he told them everything he knew. No one could withstand that amount of torture." Alec stepped closer to the body. There were dozens of deep ragged holes all over the body, but the highest concentration of them was on the feet and shins. It appeared that the victim was subjected to a prolonged attack with a power tool of some description. "Why call us?"

"I think this is connected to Malik Shah," the chief replied, pointing to the battered corpse. Lividity was setting in and the body was turning blue were it touched the stone steps. "We don't know who he is yet, but he was dumped here as a warning to someone. I'm guessing it's a revenge attack."

Alec thought about it in silence. There was no doubt that the body was dumped in a public place for a reason, and the level of violence used was disproportionate to an interrogation. The victim had been systematically tortured, but the perpetrators had targeted the limbs heavily in order to keep the victim alive as long as possible. Any man, no matter how tough would have parted with whatever information they had a long time before most of the wounds were inflicted. He had to agree that the level of violence used, and the site of the body dump, was probably a message to someone.

"It could be a gangland murder?" Alec thought the link to Malik Shah was tenuous at best, unless the Chief knew something that he didn't.

"Can you see the scars on the thumbs?" the Chief said.

Alec leaned closer to the body. The smell of blood and excrement became heavier, the closer he got. There were scars around the bottom of each digit.

"I see them."

"I can't be sure yet, but a couple of years ago, there was a small time gangster sent to hospital with his thumbs in his pockets. I remember the case well. He wouldn't speak to us at all, but informers told us that he had crossed another dealer. Ashwan Pindar's name cropped up."

"Malik Shah's sidekick?"

"Bingo," the Chief nodded.

"He would have a motive to bomb Shah's people," Alec mused. It was a possibility, but he didn't buy into it yet. Having your thumbs cut off was extreme, but not uncommon in the drug world. Jumping from there, to a well organised assassination, using a van bomb, was too much for a small time crook to pull off.

"Maybe you're right. Until I'm sure it's the same man I can't say, but I wanted you to see it before we move in and search his home etcetera."

Alec nodded in agreement. "Thanks, when you know for sure if it's the same guy, let us know."

"Do you want in on the search?"

"I think we should be there, Chief. You run with it here, and we'll concentrate on the Shah links. We're trying to track down the relatives of the informer that went missing in the witness protection programme."

The Chief smiled and held out his hand. Alec shook it. He turned and walked away from the mutilated victim, the smell of the sea filled his senses and the air seemed fresher the further away from the body he was. Seagulls squawked in the distance as they floated on the wind above the Irish Sea. It was time to turn up the heat on Malik Shah.

29

Alec Ramsey
PRESENT DAY

"Superintendant," Graham Libby greeted Alec. He nodded to his younger colleague. "DI Naylor, are you still working your way through the female population?" Dr Libby was the crime scene specialist, head of SOCO. He'd lost a valued member of his team when her affair with the young DI became public knowledge, much to the angst of her husband.

"So many women, and only one life," Will sighed sarcastically.

"Quite" the doctor replied in an acid tone. "We have the early results back. The blood in the alleyway matches the missing boy, Abdul Salim, but we don't have DNA yet."

Graham Libby turned, and walked down the alleyway. He waved his hand beckoning the detectives to follow him. Yellow tabs made a trail between the two tower blocks, each one numbered, marking a vital piece of evidence.

"They were shot out there, and then dragged down here toward the loading bay at the rear of the buildings."

The air became chill as they walked deeper, out of the reaches of the sunlight. Chewing gum splodges littered the pavement, and the stench of urine clawed at their throats. Dark trails of congealed blood reached off into the distance.

"The bullets were nine millimetre rounds, hollow points, fired with uncanny accuracy."

The detectives looked at each other with concern. Hollow points were manufactured for one reason and one reason only, to decimate the interior skeletal structure, and internal organs of a human target. Accuracy with a pistol can only be developed by practice, which hinted at a military career, perhaps a law enforcement background. They emerged at the rear of the buildings, cast in shadows. The air was just as rank, if not worse.

"The bodies and the mountain bikes were here, and here."

"Have you seen anything like this recently?" Alec asked. Dr Libby attended most of the violent deaths in the city.

"Dead drug dealers, yes," he frowned and shook his head. "This is a new one on me."

"What makes you say that?" Will asked. He was completely unfazed by the Dr's dislike of him. The technician he'd been sleeping with resigned because her husband forced her to. He wouldn't allow her to return to work, where she could come into contact with Will. How was that his fault?

"The accuracy of the shots. They were centre of the forehead, and the ammunition." He counted the reasons on his fingers as he talked. "The drugs and the money were left at the scene."

Will looked around the crime scene while he thought about it. The note left on the victim specified that the young dealers worked for Malik Shah. Initial investigations supported that, although it was mostly rumour and speculation.

"Why leave the money and the drugs behind?" Will said.

"I don't think that is why they came here," Alec replied. "They didn't kill them to rob them." He crossed the delivery bay to a recess in the towering building. There was a double delivery door padlocked and barred with a rusty chain. On the floor, a cardboard box looked out of place. It was clean and dry. "Have we had officers here at night?"

"No, Guv, why?"

"Someone's been sleeping in this doorway, recently." Alec kneeled down and looked back to where his colleagues stood. "Will, have a look around. I can't see you from here. We may have found a witness."

30

The MIT

PRESENT DAY

Agent Spence reluctantly handed over two computer disks. The Commander took them and placed them on the desk in front of him. He gestured to a chair and the agent smoothed his grey suit before sitting down.

"Where's Alec?" the Commander clicked the intercom on his desk.

"He's gone to meet the Chief at the town hall, Commander. Something to do with a body found there, sir."

"Well it's just you and me for now," the Commander picked up the disks. "What are these going to tell us?"

"Where do you want me to start?" Spence shrugged. "There's information going back years on there. The paper files will be with you this afternoon."

"I want to know why Malik Shah is still at liberty if you have been watching him for so long."

"He's smart, that's why. Every time we have got near him he's onto us immediately, and you know about the witness that we had. Malik Shah made him disappear from under our noses."

There was a knock at the door and Alec walked in, closing the door behind him. He nodded a greeting to the Commander and sat down without acknowledging Agent Spence at all.

"Agent Spence was just about to explain why Shah has not been neutralised yet," the Commander smiled.

"Should be enlightening, I'm glad I didn't miss it," Alec replied deadpan. He looked at the agent for the first time, and Spence shifted uncomfortably. Alec's eyes were icy blue and they seemed to look inside you.

"Shah is slippery. All our investigations have hit brick walls before we can get close to him," the agent pointed to the disks. "He doesn't have a hair out of place, never gets physically involved in anything illegal, and neither do his partners. They hire people to work for them, and so they're expendable. If any one does get caught, and that's rare, then there are no direct links back to Shah."

"Have you had any infiltrators in his organisation?" the Commander raised an eyebrow. It was an obvious question, but it needed asking.

"We looked at it, but he doesn't have any outsiders on the team. Not a single person, his close associates are all family or old friends going back years. Nobody else gets close to them. An outsider would be spotted immediately."

"What about the drugs smuggling?" Alec asked. There was always a link between drugs and drug dealers, and they usually leave a trail leading back to the kingpin.

"We know the Shah family made their fortune in the eighties, bringing heroine in from Pakistan and Afghanistan. Later on, they pioneered ecstasy smuggling from Amsterdam. Malik worked his way through the ranks, and as he progressed several of his older cousins met sticky endings, if you know what I mean."

"Why have they never been busted, if you know where and what they were trafficking?" Alec pushed.

"They target poor Asian families, both here and in Pakistan. They lend them money or drugs, and then they whack the interest sky high. Their enforcers are brutal, and they start applying pressure. The next thing they offer them an easy way out of the debt."

"Mules," Alec mused.

"Exactly, and they never know who they are working for, so they couldn't tell us even if we catch them at it. If the drugs are seized the debt passes back to the family with the cost of the drugs on top. They never escape the cycle and there is an endless supply of people desperate to clear the debts."

"What information did the informer have that made him such a target for Shah to risk attacking a safe house?" Alec asked. He wanted to ask a number of questions about the loss of a witness from the protection programme, but he had to take it softly to glean the information from the MI5 agent. MI5 were not his favourite agency, but he respected the ability of their agents. To snatch a witness from a safe house was incredibly daring.

Agent Spence paused a moment. He smoothed his gelled grey hair back from his face with his hand. Alec noticed that he did this when he was under pressure. He looked at the floor in front of him for a second, thinking about what he was about to say and then met Alec's gaze.

"The informer was arrested in Amsterdam, driving a truck onto a ferry. The truck was supposed to be empty, but the driver screwed up. Over a period of a week or so, he was supposed to find the vehicle waiting areas, choose a British car, break into it and stash some of the drugs, and a couple of weapons in the door panels. He would then note down the registration and leave it, so that the owners were completely unaware. Then he had move onto another one, and another one until the contraband was gone."

"You have to admire their thinking," Alec looked at the Commander.

"It's brilliant," the Commander agreed.

"It's simple, they trace the number plates and a couple of

weeks later they find the vehicle and break into it again, this time to recover their contraband. No one is near the gear when it comes through customs." Agent Spence was talking freely now. He had relaxed a little.

"So what went wrong?" Alec encouraged him to keep talking.

"The driver got cold feet. He was rumbled breaking into a car and panicked. He was terrified of failing and attracting the wrath of the dealers, and so he chose to drive the truck with the contraband still onboard."

"Okay, that makes sense, but what did he have on Malik Shah?" the Commander asked.

"He saw Shah in Pakistan, shaking hands with the men that handed over the truck to him. Shah didn't know that the driver was from here. It became apparent that he had been at the same school, a few years below him. It's the only time we've been able to place Shah at any operation."

"Not a lot to go on in court," Alec said.

"We had a witness, willing to testify against Malik Shah. We slipped him into the programme while we tried to build a case. We were in no hurry."

"Has there ever been any trace of the witnesses?" Alec asked.

"Nothing, the witness's family and both sets of in-laws disappeared. We can only assume that they're dead."

"You're sure that the leak came from the family themselves?" Alec said thoughtfully.

"We're sure that it didn't come from our agents. Therefore we think that the witness contacted a member of his family, and Shah had them captured and probably tortured the information out of them."

"How did they get to them?" Alec asked.

Agent Spence smoothed his hair back again before speaking. Alec thought that he would be easy to read in a poker game.

"The property we used was a semi-detached, built in the

fifties. We used one side, and the other was rented to an elderly man. Shah's men broke in, tied him up and then gained access to the attic."

"A fifties built house, conjoined loft space, right?" The Commander shook his head. It was a basic oversight.

"I think we have a way to get to Shah, and it's staring us in the face," Alec said.

"I'm sorry, I'm not following," Agent Spence looked confused.

"You said earlier that if drugs were seized when a mule gets caught, then Shah's heavies passed the debt back to the family, correct?"

"Yes."

"Then your informer lost a large consignment of drugs and weapons when he was arrested, yes?"

"Yes."

"Then someone is being forced to pay back that debt," Alec raised his shoulders. "We need to find out who that is, and start digging from there."

"What will we find? A loan shark ring at best?" the Commander said slowly, shaking his head.

"If we can pin something on him, then we can start pulling his operations apart. Don't forget why we're after Shah, we want the bombers that targeted the Patels. We get Shah and we'll have a clear view of his enemies."

The Commander handed the computer disks to Alec. "I'll get these analysed straight away." Alec stood up and left the room without another word.

31

The Richards gang

Kenny Richards smiled at the waitress as she delivered another round of drinks to the table. It was getting on for two o'clock in the morning, and she was tired. Kenny Richards, his three brothers, and two senior lieutenants were getting drunk, becoming more obnoxious with every round. They behaved as if they owned the place, which they did to be fair. Well as good as. The owner lost to Kenny in a poker game, and he was holding the deeds against a fifty thousand pound debt, which was gaining interest daily. Now Richards and his dragoons ate and drank for free, taking over the restaurant most nights from eleven o'clock until they were plastered. The last customers left the Chinese restaurant hours ago. The manager locked them in and pulled the roller shutters down to avoid unwanted attention from the police.

"Thanks, darling!" Kenny slapped her shapely behind as she placed the drinks down. His thick gold bracelet rattled when he spanked her, and his snake like grin revealed more of the precious metal in his yellowed teeth. "You know, Wendy, I've been looking for a princess like you all my life."

"Princess?" his brother slurred. "Take no notice of him, Wendy. He wants to bend you over the table." The men laughed in unison, their eyes becoming bleary, and there expressions idiot like.

Wendy tried to smile again, even though her buttocks stung to the point her eyes were watering. She grimaced and walked away without speaking, embarrassed and annoyed. The sound of the men's raucous laughter faded as she entered the kitchens.

"God, I hate that man!" she complained to the manager. A tear leaked from the corner of her eye, tiredness was catching up with her. "I really don't need this job that much."

"Don't be hasty, Wendy, it pays your way through college remember," the manager couldn't afford to lose anymore staff, especially a good one like Wendy. China Town was a rough area to work in late at night, frequented by drunks and clubbers. "Ignore them, they're drunk."

"They're always drunk!" Wendy choked back a sob and tried to smile. Things weren't going well at college either. She had flunked her exams, was behind with her course work, and her boyfriend ditched her for her best friend. "I've had enough, I'm going home." The last bus had gone, and it would cost her two hours graft to get back to her damp ridden bedsit. Coming to the big city to complete a university degree wasn't all that it was cracked up to be. She was thousands in debt already, and had nothing to show for it if she was kicked off the course.

"Get a good night's sleep, and I'll see you tomorrow," the manger said considerately. She took off her apron and he handed her coat. "I'll sort this lot out, they're the only customers left now anyway."

"That's because they've insulted the rest, and made them leave. Three complaints I had about them tonight." She wined, still sobbing. "At this rate you won't have any other customers to worry about." Wendy turned and pushed her way through the chain fly-curtain at the back of the kitchen. It jingled as she went out into the night. The manager sighed and looked up at the strip lights on the ceiling. They were being dive bombed by a squadron of flying insects, testament to how well the fly-curtain worked.

"Fucking marvellous, now I've got to clean up on my own," the manager pulled a pack of menthol cigarettes from his apron pocket. There was no one left in the restaurant to complain if he lit up. He sparked his lighter and inhaled deeply as Wendy came back through the metal curtain. He frowned, as she looked terrified. "You forgotten something?" He laughed, drawing on the cigarette again. "You've caught me puffing away in the kitchen! Don't tell anyone!"

The chain links rattled again as first one masked man, and then a second followed Wendy into the kitchen. The first man had an Uzi pressed into the small of her back. The second had one aimed directly at the manager's face, his index finger was to his lips, indicating that he should be silent. The manger nodded his compliance and raised his hands in the air. The menthol still burned in his hand. Wendy was shoved toward a backroom area where the sink tubs where situated, and the gunman beckoned the manager to them. Reluctantly he edged toward the backroom. The Uzis looked dull but deadly. They had been adapted to take a fat suppressor on the barrel, homemade silencers.

"Kenny Richards is in the restaurant, right?" the gunman whispered. Wendy and the manager looked at each other, and then nodded. "How many of his goons are with him?"

The gunmen were dressed in black, and the ski-masks they wore revealed only their eyes. Wendy couldn't be certain, but she thought the men had dark skin. Not African, Asian. The manger looked at Wendy to answer the question. She had been serving them all night, and he hadn't really noticed how many of them there were. He'd stayed in the kitchen area, out of the way. Wendy made a mental note of where they sat around the table, and how many drinks she poured each round. She held up five digits.

"Five including him, or five plus him?"

Wendy thought for a second, and then held up six digits. The gunman opened a steel door, which led into a walk-in refrigerator. He hustled the terrified employees inside.

"Get in there, keep quiet and you won't get hurt, understand?"

The door closed and Wendy heard a metal clunk as the bolt was thrown. It wasn't long before the shooting started.

32

Witness

Ronald Theakston pushed his belongings along the pavement in a shopping trolley. The front wheels were wonky, but it was his shopping trolley. The sun was going down, and night was closing in. It was time to head home to his box. A quick trundle to the local bargain booze stop, and he was set for the night, six litres of strong cider, dry roasted peanuts, and for dessert, vodka. He could hardly contain his excitement. Drinking to oblivion was his only pleasure now. As he turned the corner to reach the delivery bay, which had become his latest home, his heart stopped beating for a second.

"Hello," DI Will Naylor said. "You come around here often?"

"Piss off!" Ronald put his head down and pushed his trolley faster. The man in the suit looked like trouble. In fact, most people looked like trouble. He wanted to get to his doorway, and drink.

"Can't do that I'm afraid, I need a word with you." Will grabbed the homeless man's arm, and then immediately wished that he hadn't. His sleeve was encrusted with god only knows what bodily fluids. "What's your name?"

"What's it to you?" Ronald tried to break free, but his wasted muscles were no match for the young detective. "Get off me!"

"Look, I'm a police officer," Will showed him his identity card, still maintaining his grip on the man. "I think you can help me, and there's a few quid in it for you."

Ronald stopped struggling. He'd spent all of his money at the booze station, and there was two full days until he could claim his pension again. He eyed the detective suspiciously. There had been lots of funny goings on the last few days, mostly blurred memories now, almost dreams, but not good ones. There were police officers all over the place, but none of them had shown any interest in Ronald. He stayed away from the loading bay until night-time when they had gone.

"Do you sleep here?" Will relaxed his grip.

"I might do, it depends."

"Is that your cardboard in the loading bay?"

"Might be."

"We can always have this conversation at the station, but that would take a few hours, and I'm not sure your booze would still be here when you get back, are you?"

"Alright!" Ronald frowned at the thought of his alcohol left unattended. He needed it. "What do you want?"

"Have you seen or heard any shooting last few days?" Will pulled out a ten-pound note, and waved it in front of his face. "Anything unusual?"

Ronald snatched at the money, but Will pulled it away from his grasp. "What's your name?"

"Ronald Theakston."

"Okay, Ronald, nice to meet you." Will let him take the money. "Have you seen or heard anything unusual?"

"Yes, I know the sound of a nine-milli anywhere," Ronald slurred. Will raised his eyebrows in surprise.

"You an old soldier, Ronald?"

"Royal Marines, did the first Gulf gig," Ronald felt a twinge of pride deep inside somewhere. It was an alien feeling to him nowadays.

"You heard shooting?"

"Yes, nine millimetre pistol, probably a Glock."

"Did you see anything?"

"No, move fast, and keep low, that's my motto. I kept my head down."

"So you heard the shots, and then what?"

"Heard one of those kids fucking and blinding, must have been hit because he was moaning like I don't know what."

"Did you hear him say anything specific?"

Ronald thought about it, "something about money and drugs, can't be sure though."

"You hear anything else?" Will asked.

"Maybe a diesel engine, can't be sure, doors opening and closing. It's all a bit hazy," Ronald needed a drink.

"If you think of anything else, you call me, Ronald," Will pulled out another tenner and slipped it into the old marine's grimy hand along with his card. "Anything at all, okay?"

"Thanks," Ronald stuffed the money into his pocket and aimed his trolley toward the loading bay. Will watched him wobble down the road, a mixture of sadness and pity inside him as the old soldier headed to his makeshift bed. He was about to leave when the tramp turned and looked thoughtful for a moment. "Einstein!"

"What did you say?" Will asked confused.

"Einstein," Ronald smiled at the memory, pleased that his mind wasn't totally useless. "One of them was called Einstein."

33

The Bernsteins

Richard Bernstein read the list for the millionth time, Malik Shah, Ashwan Pindar, Rasim Shah, Omar Patel, Shah Shah, Mustapha Shah and Saj Rajesh. He flicked the paper with his finger as his mind replayed his past. The assault in the park; the months of hospital treatment; the scars; the pain and suffering; the embarrassment of wetting his pants as they kicked him senseless. It was all so fresh in his mind, and then there was Sarah. Beautiful Sarah. Nick serving over a decade in prison, David's self imposed exile in the Israeli military and the destruction of his parents' relationship. His sister killed herself to avoid the shame she was causing, and his father killed himself with whisky for the same reason. That's why they were here, doing what they were doing. They had to pay for what they'd done, and tonight the debt was due. He munched on salt and vinegar crisps as he waited in the van for his brother and Nick. They were in an expensive neighbourhood near the edge of the city. The houses were huge, surrounded by high walls, and set back from the tree-lined roads. Malik Shah's men had done well from their chosen profession, but all the money in the world couldn't protect them now.

*   *   *

Nick dropped over the wall and landed heavily, ankle deep in dead leaves and undergrowth. The ground covering crunched as he moved slowly toward the building. It was L-shaped, one part elongated with a long slanted roof, making it look cheese like. The nearer section was oblong with a high vaulted ceiling. The roof was clear plastic, which allowed the sun to warm the pool beneath it. Nick approached the pool block, and crouched low as he reached a set of sliding glass doors. He slid a metal file into the keyhole and twisted it twice, click, click. He tiptoed through the patio doors, quiet as a mouse. The lock was a doddle to pick, a trick he'd learned during his long stay at Her Majesty's pleasure. Prison was a university of crime, the longer you stay the more you learn. The smell of chlorine was strong, and he could hear the gentle hum of the filter pumps. There was a half-moon, and it reflected off the surface of the water. He navigated his way up the poolside to the door that accessed the house. Nick grabbed the handle, and twisted it slowly.

He breathed out as the unlocked door opened, and headed into the living area. Nick moved like a ghostly whisper across the laminate flooring, heading for the green dot of light, which glowed in the corner of the room. He kneeled down and picked up the i-phone, that was on charge. Rasim Shah plugged it in two hours earlier on his way to bed. The battery life was a major issue for him, constantly running low when he needed to be contactable at all times. His cousin Malik flipped his lid if they didn't answer when he called them, so now he plugged it in every night. Richard Bernstein hacked Shah's company mobile contracts, and he knew the make and model they used for business. Nick slid the back off the mobile and removed the SIM card. He slid it into a replacement i-phone, a specially prepared i-phone. It was unlike any other, as it contained enough Tovex liquid explosive to blow the user's head clean off.

*　　*　　*

Half a mile away, Omar Patel paced his living room. He was worried that Malik was taking them to war with the city's other crime families. Omar had control of the undertaker business, and he'd organised the disposal of Abdul Salim. Abdul worked for Ashwan, yet the body had been dumped on Ashwan's lawn. That had to be a warning from someone, but who? He spoke to Malik but he wouldn't give anything away. He always kept his men in the dark as much as possible, what they didn't know, they couldn't tell. Malik didn't trust any of them completely, even though they had been together since their school days. He was a paranoid schizophrenic, no doubt about it, and Omar was getting sick of him and his tantrums.

Omar guessed that a rival gang had killed Abdul, and Malik was pointing the finger at the Richards crew. Two of Malik's hit men were dispatched to take out as many of the Richards crew as possible. One of them had called Omar and told him that much, but he wouldn't say anymore. They were to keep one alive until the last minute, and question him about something, but they wouldn't tell him what. What could the Richards gang know that was important enough to start a war over?

Sending out the hit men was a blatant act of war against a rival gang, and it would have repercussions that would echo through the foreseeable future. Malik was angry, that was obvious, but there was more to this than met the eye. Omar had the feeling that he was keeping something from them. His cousin Amir was his closest friend, and they confided in each other. Now he was gone, blown to bits, and Malik had lost the plot. Was there a coincidence, a connection between his death, and what was happening tonight? Ashwan wasn't answering his mobile, which was unusual, and he felt that they knew something that the rest of them didn't. If they were going to war, then it was only right that they were made aware of the reason why. He continued to pace up and down the room. David Bernstein watched Omar's shadow on the curtains as he attached a mercury triggered bomb to his Lexus.

34

The Richards

Kenny Richards swallowed the remaining half of his pint in one go and slammed it down on the table loudly. He was a big, red-faced man, with a grey flattop haircut and too many gold chains and sovereigns. Steroids made his face bloated, and caused acne on the back of his neck and shoulders. There were always half a dozen yellow heads lurking un-squeezed above his collar. No one mentioned them of course, because the steroids also made him temperamental at best, violently unstable at worst. His younger brothers, Jimmy and Billy, were smaller versions of him.

The Richards started their careers working on the doors of the city's nightclubs. They began taxing the drug dealers, and eventually started to supply them with wholesale gear themselves. The brothers set up a construction company, working on civil engineering projects for the highways agencies. It was a perfect way to launder their income. Kenny was known as a hard man, with a granite jaw and fists like bowling balls. His brothers were always armed with knuckledusters or blades. Anyone stupid enough to tackle them was dispatched to accident and emergency at high speed. Repeat offenders found themselves surrounded by quick drying concrete, entombed in the foundations of a motorway bridge.

The men were talking, when Kenny slammed down his glass, and shouted for another round. "Wendy! Get us the same again, sexy." He looked toward the kitchen and saw shadows approaching the swing doors. There were round porthole windows in them, allowing the waiting to staff to see their colleagues coming the opposite way, loaded with plates of food.

"Wendy, you sexy bitch, get over here with the beer!"

His face reddened when two masked gunmen entered the dining room. "Shut up!" He said to his party. They were listening to a succession of dirty jokes, and unaware of what was happening. One by one the Richards gang became silent. The masked men approached the table, their silenced Uzis raised.

"What the fuck is this all about?" Kenny snarled. His face had turned purple with outrage.

"Get over there against the wall, hands on your heads." The gunmen waved the muzzles in the direction of the wall. "Move it!"

The Richards stood slowly, hands in the air.

"You're fucking dead men walking," Kenny snarled.

"Not you," the masked man indicated that Kenny should remain seated. "You stay there, fatty."

"Fuck you!"

"Shut up, Kenny, or I'll blow your face off now." The gunman was ice cool, no emotion in his voice. This was another day at the office, and Kenny could sense it too. They were in big trouble.

"What do you want?" Kenny asked. His brothers and the others moved away from the table.

"Kneel down and face the wall."

"Whatever they're paying you I'll triple it," Kenny said.

"Shut your mouth." As the men kneeled, one of the gunmen opened fire, emptying his clip in seconds. A Chinese mural became a grizzly freeze of blood and gore. It changed shape slowly as the mush began to dribble down it. Kenny's brothers and his men twitched momentarily, and then lay still. The second man covered Kenny with his weapon.

"You have no idea what you have done," Kenny growled. Self-preservation stopped him bolting for the door, or rushing at the gunmen in a desperate last effort to save his own life. The kitchen was the only viable exit, as the manger had locked and shuttered the front of the restaurant hours before. Keeping his liquor license was more of a priority than letting the Richards out of the front entrance in the early hours of the morning.

"I'll ask you once, and once only." The gunman speaking slid a sawn-off shotgun from his belt. He walked around the table and stuck the gun against his temple. The second man slid a wire noose over his head and a simple pull of the wrist tightened it to choking point. Kenny tried to place his fingers between the cutting wire and his throat, but the man was too quick. He clawed at it desperately with his fingernails, but the wire sliced into his flesh.

"Do you have Mamood Pindar?"

Kenny's eyes widened. Pindar. The only Pindar he knew was Malik Shah's side-kick, and he was sure his first name wasn't Mamood. The wire tightened and his eyes bulged as his air supply was restricted. He shook his head in the negative.

"Last chance, do you know where Mamood Pindar is, or who has him?" The gunman could tell by the confusion on Kenny's face that he didn't know what he was talking about. He'd questioned enough men in his time to see past the fear and spot the truth or a lie.

Kenny Richards croaked and blood began to pour from the vicious wound on his throat. His larynx was sliced and air hissed into the gash. Kenny shook his head.

"He doesn't know anything, step back." The sawn-off kicked in the gunman's hand as both barrels fired. The twelve gauge shot ripped the side of Kenny's skull away exposing his teeth, and covered the mirrored wall in grey matter.

35

Major Investigation Team

CHINA TOWN

DS Alec Ramsey yawned as he drove toward China Town. The news of a multiple homicide reached him shortly after six that morning. He stopped at the traffic lights, and looked at the empty shell of a bombed out church, a reminder of how the city suffered during World War II; it marked the start of the Chinese quarter. He indicated right and pulled off the main road into the maze of streets that serviced that area of the city. An ornate Chinese archway covered the road and he parked up beneath it, next to a row of marked police cars, and two ambulances. The streets were beginning to fill up with early morning commuters, and uniformed officers were building a cordon to keep curious onlookers back from the scene.

"Where's DI Naylor?" Alec asked a uniformed sergeant that he recognised from his early career. The portly sergeant nodded a greeting and shook his head, wobbling his jowls as he did so.

"Round the back of the Lucky Dragon, Guv," he leaned closer and lowered his voice as he lifted the crime scene tape to allow him in. "It's the Richards crew, Guv, I've known them for years."

Alec patted him on the shoulder and ducked beneath the tape. "Lucky Dragon indeed?" he mused to himself.

The restaurant looked peaceful enough from here. The roller shutters were locked down, but the main signage was still lit, as if someone had forgotten to turn it off when they went home. He headed round the back via a narrow cobbled lane.

A uniformed officer staggered out of the backyard; his hand covered his mouth, but didn't stop the vomit from coming up. It sprayed through his fingers across the cobbles and up the wall. Alec skirted around the officer at a safe distance and entered a small backyard. The smell of rotting vegetables mingled with cooking odours and rancid refuse hit him. The yard was untidy. There were empty cooking oil drums stacked on top of each other next to an over flowing skip. Flattened cardboard boxes strewn across the yard by the wind, and never tidied up. Next to the door a bun tray of frozen chickens sat defrosting on an upturned peddle bin.

"Morning, Guv," Will Naylor stepped through the chain fly-curtain. "Just getting a breath of fresh air, whiffs a bit in there."

"Whiffs a bit out here too," Alec replied, pointing to the defrosting meat.

"I don't think food hygiene was number one priority," Will replied. He held open a gap in the chains and gestured the Superintendent through it. "The milkman found the backdoor open like this, about five o'clock this morning. He went into the kitchen and shouted 'hello', and heard the manager and the waitress calling for help. They'd been locked in the fridge there."

Will pointed to a wash up room. Stainless steel tub sinks lined the walls, and spring-loaded spray heads hung from the walls above them. At the far end was the walk-in.

"Were they locked in?"

"Yes, Guv, the bolt was thrown."

"Are they hurt?"

"No, Guv. The waitress went out the backdoor to go home at about two o'clock, and encountered two masked men in the backyard. They pointed machineguns at her and the manager, asked them how many of the Richards crew were in there, and then locked them in the fridge."

"The gunmen knew the Richards were in there?"

"Yes, Guv, they knew Kenny Richards by his first name."

Alec scanned the kitchen but there was nothing out of the ordinary there. The gunmen had entered by the most obvious route, the only route available at the time, because the front was locked up. He walked toward the swing doors and pushed through them into the dining room. The sickening smell of death met him as he entered, blood, urine and faeces, mingled with the cooking odours of ginger and satay oil. Will was close behind him.

"First glance indicates that Kenny was garrotted in his chair, while his men were executed, and then he was given both barrels close up."

"Why?"

"Why what, Guv?"

"Why not just blow him away with his men, if it was a hit that is?"

Will looked back at the bodies and studied the scene. It looked like a hit to him. Alec moved closer to Kenny's body, careful not to stand on any evidence. A forensic team was en route.

"Why bother to garrotte him, and blow his head off?" Alec asked himself aloud. "If it was a hit he'd be over there with his men."

"Maybe they wanted to make him watch," Will suggested.

"Or maybe they wanted to ask him some questions."

"It doesn't look like he gave them the right answers," Will said nodding.

"Maybe he didn't know the answer, Will," Alec stepped away from the bodies and walked back toward the kitchen. They would have to wait for the forensics reports before they could hazard an educated guess as to what went down.

"Have you got any theories, Guv?"

"We have two dead dealers linked to Malik Shah, and then a small time gangster is tortured to death, and dumped on the town hall steps. Shah's bookkeeper is assassinated, and now the head of a major crime family and his men are wiped out. I think somebody is looking for answers or revenge, and my guess would be that it's Malik Shah," Alec pushed open the kitchen doors and came face to face with Graham Libby. "Morning, Doc."

"Ah, Superintendent, I hope you haven't contaminated my crime scene," he said sarcastically. Will came through the doors and he ignored him.

"I need whatever you can give me, as soon as you can," Alec carried on walking.

"Charming," Dr Libby muttered as he entered the dining room.

The detectives walked back to their cars in silence, mulling over what they had seen, and trying to put the pieces together. Will recalled the events of the previous evening, and he hadn't had chance to speak to Alec about them yet. It wasn't significant enough to bother him at home, but it needed to be told.

"I found our homeless guy last night, Guv."

"What?" Alec was deep in thought.

"I found the homeless guy that lived at the back of the shops, where we found the dealers."

"Oh, right," the cardboard box sprung into his mind.

"His name is Ronald Theakston, an ex-marine turned wino."

"Did he have anything useful?"

"He was there when the shooting happened, and he recognised the weapon as a nine millimetre handgun from his army days." Will paused, and thought about how to explain the rest of the conversation. "He didn't see anything, but he heard a diesel engine."

"That it?" Alec thought there was more.

"He said one of the men was called, Einstein, Guv."

"Einstein? Was he drunk?"

"Wasted, Guv."

"Okay, we'll park that for now." Alec couldn't make any sense of it. "Get the team together, and bring in Malik Shah and Ashwan Pindar. It's time we had a little chat with them."

36

Rasim Shah

Rasim Shah woke early. He was still weary, as he hadn't slept well. The events of the last few days played on his mind. Omar told him that Malik had set the dogs onto the Richards gang, but he didn't know why. He called Malik to ask him what was happening, but he told him to sit tight and wait, nothing more. Rasim hated Malik with a passion. If he wasn't so scared of him, he'd have left the organisation years ago. He had enough money now, and didn't need the bullshit that came with working for Malik, however no one that had walked away lived very long afterward. Shah and his organisation operated in the city with relative impunity from the other crime families. They didn't bully the smaller gangs, and they had enough firepower to ensure that none messed with them. The Richards weren't as big by any stretch of the imagination, but they were popular, Malik and his men were despised by everyone. Attacking the Richards could encourage the smaller organisations to unite against them, and then things would get messy. Rasim didn't have the stomach for a turf war of that scale. He had too much to lose.

"Are you okay, Ras?" Shelpa reached out and touched her husband's cheek with the back of her hand. "You've been twisting and turning all night long, darling."

"Indigestion," Rasim turned to her and kissed her forehead. "It's your cooking, I'm sure."

"Well if it's that bad, I'll stop cooking, cheeky boy," Shelpa moved closer to him and she pointed her finger playfully at his nose. Her other hand stroked the thick hair on his chest. Rasim was in good shape for his age. He swam fifty lengths every morning, which kept his muscles toned.

"If you stop cooking, I'll file for divorce," Rasim kissed her lips gently. Shelpa responded, opening her mouth and probing gently with the tip of her tongue. "What's the point in having a wife if she doesn't cook?" He whispered.

"Is that all I'm good for?" Shelpa pulled away and kissed his chin, running her tongue across his neck, stopping momentarily to nibble his earlobe. She could feel him growing hard against her stomach. Her hand slid down, teasing the skin on his stomach. She wrapped her fingers around his erection and began to stroke him up and down. "Well, is that all I'm good for?"

"I'm thinking about it," Rasim whispered playfully. He put his hand on the back of her head and pushed her down gently toward him. Shelpa took him deep into her mouth, and she rocked her head back and forth until he cried out in ecstasy.

"I remembered why I married you," Rasim gasped. She held him tight while his head returned to planet Earth. "It wasn't your cooking."

"Do you feel better?"

"Much better."

"Go for your swim," Shelpa kissed his cheek.

"I'm going, bossy boots," he kissed her back.

"Are you hungry?"

"Starving."

"Do you want eggs?" Shelpa sat up and gathered her long black hair into a ponytail as she spoke.

"You are beautiful, you know?" Rasim touched her neck

with the back of his hand.

"Thank you," she took his hand and kissed it. "I love you."

"I love you too," he leaned over and kissed her lips. "Even though you give me indigestion!"

"Ras!" she punched his arm gently. They held each other for a precious moment, kissed and then moved to the end of the bed.

Rasim pulled on a towelling bathrobe, and tied the belt at the front. He grabbed a towel and padded down the stairs toward the swimming pool. The laminate floor was cold as he stepped off the carpeted staircase and headed through the wide split-level living room. In the corner of the room was a white marble coffee table. A black onyx table lamp stood proudly in the centre, guarding three remote control pads, and his mobile phone. Rasim picked up a remote and switched on the music system. David Bowie started to sing, Heroes, and Rasim turned the volume up in the pool area. He eyed his mobile as he walked by, checking the battery was fully charged. It was. Rasim put it back down and walked toward the pool block. The phone began ringing and he stopped in his tracks. It was early, and the call would be trouble, he was sure of that. He sighed and thought about ignoring it. If it was Malik then he would be furious it wasn't answered, it was his pet hate. The Richards crew had been attacked last night, so he guessed Malik would be ringing to bring him up to date. He walked back and looked at the screen. The caller's number was withheld.

"Who is that at this time in the morning?" Shelpa called through from the kitchen. Pots and pans clanged as she prepared to make their favourite breakfast. It was omelette with onions and peppers fried in sunflower oil.

"The number is withheld, it will be Malik."

"I hate that man, he makes my skin crawl, ignore him."

"He's my boss, Shelpa, you know how he is."

"He's a creep, he stares at me."

"I stare at you."

"You're allowed to."

Rasim smiled as he placed the phone to his ear and accepted the call. The fingers on his right hand were blown clean across the room, and his skull exploded like an egg being hit with a sledgehammer. Crimson fluid splattered the wall and ceiling and his body stayed vertical for a few seconds, as if it could function without its head, then it fell forward and knocked the onyx lamp across the room.

3 7

OMAR

Omar woke from a dark dream. He was stuck fast in a muddy field, no matter how hard he tried to free his legs he couldn't get out of it. As soon as he freed one, the other became trapped. The more he struggled the deeper the mud was. He needed help but he couldn't find his phone to call anyone. Then it started to ring, but he couldn't see it. The ringing became louder and more real as he drifted back from sleep land to reality.

"Will you answer the fucking telephone," Lindsay Morgan nudged him hard in the back with her knee. "Omar, answer the phone, for fuck's sake!"

"Do you have to moan from morning until night, have a day off will you?" Omar rubbed his eyes and yawned. He was sick of Lindsay and her foul mouth. She did nothing but whinge, morning noon and night. The only time she was happy was when she bought shoes or handbags with his money. He put up with her bad attitude because she was a looker, and the sex had been good at first. It was still good, but she rarely wanted it now. Omar had the feeling that she was getting it somewhere else, but Malik told him to stop being paranoid. When they first met, she bought red satin sheets and she would dress sexy for him, suspenders, and fishnet stockings, whatever he wanted. Now she came to bed in a tracksuit. What he didn't know was that she had been sleeping with Malik for nearly six months. She enjoyed his dominant rough bedroom manner. He used and abused her body in ways that Omar would never think of, and she enjoyed the thrill of feeling like a hooker. They met at hotels, had rough sex, and Malik would chuck two hundred pounds at her as he left, more shoes, happy days, sex and shopping in one afternoon.

"I will stop moaning when you answer the phone!" Lindsay shouted at the top of her voice. She pulled the quilt violently over her head and turned away from him.

Omar paused a moment before picking it up. The landline was ex-directory, only his close friends and family used the number, and that was usually if his mobile was switched off. He opened his bedside drawer and looked at his mobile. It was on silent, and he had twelve missed calls.

"Shit," he muttered as he answered the landline, hoping the missed calls weren't from Malik. "Hello."

"Omar, Ras is dead!" Shelpa was hysterical. She could hardly speak for sobbing. He heard her wretch and cough, almost choking. "He's dead, Omar, help me please!"

"Shelpa, what are you saying?" he shot out of bed and grabbed for the trousers he'd discarded the night before. "Shelpa, have you phoned an ambulance?"

"Yes, but his head is gone, and there's blood everywhere. Omar, please help me!" She wailed like a banshee, and her words were almost inaudible. She didn't make any sense. "Have you phoned an ambulance?" he repeated.

The telephone clattered at the other end, as if she had dropped it on the floor. Omar thought that she might have fainted. "Shelpa, Shelpa are you okay?"

"What does that silly bitch want at this time in the morning?" Lindsay moaned from under the quilt.

"Shut your mouth, Lindsay, she's hysterical."

"She's always fucking hysterical."

"Shut your mouth, you stupid bitch!" Omar yelled. He was struggling into his clothes as fast as he could. He grabbed his mobile and forced his feet into his shoes without undoing the laces. The backs collapsed and clung to his heels.

"Where are you going?" Lindsay poked her head from under the cover. "You're not running to their house because that fucking drama queen is having an episode are you?"

Omar couldn't think of a response worthy of delivering, although if he'd had a gun at hand he would have shot her right there. He slammed the bedroom door as he left, and hurtled down the stairs at a million miles an hour. He reached the hallway where a key rack hung above an overflowing shoe rack. His car keys weren't there.

"Keys, keys keys," he turned full circle checking the furniture nearby, in case he had plonked them down somewhere. Nothing.

"Where are my car keys?" he shouted up the stairs.

"How the fucking hell should I know?" Lindsay shouted back.

"Have you moved them?"

"Fuck off!"

"Lindsay, this is an emergency!" He screamed. His face was flushed red and his blood was reaching boiling point.

"Fuck off!"

Omar ran into the kitchen and searched frantically along the worktops. He moved his diary, nothing, on top of the microwave, nothing, under the newspaper, nothing. His coat hung on the back of the kitchen door. Omar squeezed the pocket and his keys were there. He sighed loudly, snatched them out and ran for the front door. The chain was fixed, and the bolts were thrown, and it took him what felt like an age to open the door. He stepped outside onto a gravel driveway, and it crunched as he ran to the silver Lexus. The indicator lights flashed as he opened the door with the key card.

He climbed in and slipped it into the dash. The supercharged engine roared into life, and the rev counter flicked into the red zone. Omar clicked his mobile into its cradle, and pressed the number two as he selected first gear. The mobile searched its speed dial memory and found the number for Malik Shah. Omar pressed dial and released the handbrake. He heard the line click as it began to dial, and he heard the gravel crunch beneath the wheels as the vehicle surged forward at speed. What he didn't hear was the mercury slosh in a glass vile as it made the connection between the detonator and the explosive that was packed around his fuel tank. The Lexus was lifted three yards into the air by the force of the blast and the interior became a blazing inferno in a millisecond. Omar didn't have time to be confused, or to contemplate what was happening to him. His brain registered the dreadful pain as his skin was peeled from his body by the intense heat. He felt his lungs sizzle as he breathed in the flames. Mercifully, death came for him quickly.

38

MIT

Will Naylor sat at his desk and ploughed through the information that he had for the fifth time in as many hours. He had the police and MI5 files on Malik Shah stretching back to his late teens. It was like looking for a needle in a haystack. Many of his business associates, including members of his family, had died in mysterious circumstances. He'd been investigated numerous times, but nothing stuck to him. He was like Teflon. His businesses were legitimate, and profitable, even the overseas ventures looked genuine. Finding an obvious suspect was impossible. The Superintendent acquired arrest warrants for Ashwan and Malik, on the back of the Lucky Dragon murders. He also brought in two of the other known crime lords from the city, hoping someone would have the information that would give them a lead.

"You still staring at that?"

"Yes, Guv." Will smiled and pushed his chair back from the desk. "Do you want a brew?"

"Why not," Alec looked at the screen thoughtfully. "You found anything useful in this lot?"

Will disappeared into the small kitchen area, which consisted of two cupboards, a sink, a microwave and coffee machine. The coffee pot was half-full or was it half-empty,

Will couldn't decide. He filled two cups with black liquid and the aroma of stewed coffee drifted up to him.

"I can't see anything in there that is relevant to our investigation," he passed the cup to his boss as he walked back to his desk. "There's plenty of accusation and speculation, but nothing we can use to hold him."

"Smithy and his team are trawling through his finances, but there's nothing untoward there either," Alec sipped the stale coffee and grimaced. "Uniform have picked them up, they were both at Shah's residence. When they knocked at Pindar's home the wife was very cagey, said he'd gone away. The officer said she looked like she'd been crying."

"Domestic maybe?" Will smoothed the creases in his trousers. His navy blue suit looked immaculate, and his shirt was crisp and white.

"I'm not sure what to think, Will," Alec sensed that there was an undercurrent somewhere beneath the recent events. Something that they didn't know about yet, something that would explain what was going on. "We're going to question Shah, and then you take lead with Pindar. We might get lucky."

"Have they asked for lawyers?"

"Oh yes."

"Who?"

"Grenade and associates," Alec used the force nickname for Grenace and Associates. They had a formidable reputation for representing bad guys, and getting them off. The force detectives called them 'Grenade' for obvious reasons.

"Great, I love a challenge," Will crossed his legs and put his feet up on the desk, sipping his coffee loudly. His trousers rode up above his ankles to reveal shiny black Chelsea boots.

"Nice boots," Alec smiled sarcastically.

"You wouldn't understand, Guv, fashion you see?"

"I had a pair just like them when I left school."

"Really?" Will looked concerned.

"Exactly the same."

"Retro, Guv," Will scrabbled for some credibility. "Vintage clothing, it's all the rage."

"Vintage?" Alec teased. "You mean second-hand."

The telephone on Will's desk rang. He picked it up. "DI Will Naylor."

His face darkened immediately, and he grabbed a pen and began to scribble notes. Alec could see the shocked look on his face.

"When was this?" Will put his hand to his forehead. "Unexplained?"

"Jesus Christ! Okay, keep me up to date."

Alec raised his eyebrows as he looked at the scribbles. He could make neither head nor tale of it. "What is it?"

"I don't believe this," Will put the phone down and shook his head in disbelief. "There has been two emergency calls made in the last thirty minutes, a Lexus exploded which belongs to one Omar Patel, and the other is the unexplained death of Rasim Shah."

"Unexplained, why?"

"The ambulance crew that responded couldn't be specific as to the cause of death, but the first officer on the scene said his head had been blown off."

"By what?"

"We don't know yet, could be a high velocity bullet?"

"Maybe, and the Lexus?"

"He was dead before his girlfriend made the call." Will chewed his index fingernail nervously. He was thinking over the shocking information that they had just received. "They are both on the list of Malik Shah's directors, right?"

"Yes," Alec replied. Someone was upping the stakes, but why. "Could this be a retaliatory strike for the Richards murders?"

"What about the rest of Shah's business associates?"

"Get the team onto it now. Warn them not to use their cars

and to stay away from their windows, there could be a sniper out there."

"I'm on it, Guv." Will dashed across the office barking orders as he went. They could be too late already.

Alec called the armed response unit, and communicated the name and addresses of the other directors on the list. "Get me a response team to each address, and dispatch the bomb squad to check every vehicle they own."

"Guv!" Smithy shouted across the office. Alec put his hand over the mouthpiece to block the office noise. "Graham Libby on the telephone, Guv, says it's urgent."

"Thanks, Smithy, put him through." Alec turned back to the first call. "I'll keep you informed of any developments, let me know if anyone is unaccounted for," he switched the line from the armed response unit to Graham Libby. "Doc?"

"Superintendent," he sounded out of breath. "Look, the crime scene at the Shah fatality is like something from a Bourne movie."

"What do you mean?"

"The victim has no fingers on his right hand, and his head has been blown off his shoulders, completely. I couldn't understand what had happened until his wife said that he was taking a phone call."

"I don't understand, Doc?"

"I think his mobile exploded, Alec."

"You think someone put a bomb into a mobile phone?"

"There is no other way to explain the injuries, until we begin to recover pieces of the bomb, but for now that's my theory."

"Shit!" Alec realised what Will and the team were doing, calling the potential targets, on their telephones. "Will!" he bellowed across the office.

"Guv?"

"Don't call any of them, one of the bombs was in a mobile phone!"

39

Ambush

"My client and I have been waiting here for nearly two hours, Superintendent Ramsay," Nigella Nielsen removed her glasses and greeted Alec with an icy glare.

The Superintendent ignored the remark and slotted two cassettes into a battered recorder, which perched on a shelf above the only table in the square room. The table and chairs were screwed to the floor through metal brackets, to prevent them being thrown by violent suspects. Will Naylor stepped into the room behind him and Alec pressed the machine into life.

"Detective Superintendent Ramsay, conducting an interview with Malik Shah, represented by," Alec remained silent to allow the brief to respond.

"Nigella Nielsen," she tapped her fingers on the table angrily. The table was scored with scratches and doodles. Someone had carved a love heart with an arrow through it, declaring their love for 'Soggy'.

"Also present," he remained silent again.

"Detective Inspector Will Naylor."

"Interview commencing at eleven fifteen AM," the detectives took their places at the table. The room was small, almost claustrophobic, and the walls were scared with graffiti. "Malik,

I can call you Malik can't I?"

"Could you tell me why my client is here, Superintendent?" Nigella put her glasses back and opened a notebook. Malik didn't respond to the question, but he met the Superintendent's gaze and held it.

"Do you know this man?" Alec flipped a mug shot of Kenny Richards out of his file. The black and white picture had been taken years before when Kenny was lifted for a vicious assault. Alec knew they had nothing on Shah, but he was hoping that he might be able to give them a lead.

"That is Kenny Richards," Malik sneered. "How is Kenny?"

"Oh, he's dead, Malik, but then you know that don't you?" Alec placed a second picture onto the table. Kenny's body was sat upright in a chair, garrotted and shot through the head. His cheekbone and jaw were exposed, and the top of his skull was blown away.

"That's not his good side, is it?" Malik looked at the picture and then looked at Alec in the eye. He was stone cold. There was no reaction to the picture at all. Alec had dealt with more killers than he cared to remember, and Malik Shah had the same dead look in his eyes. There was no emotion in them.

"He was shot dead last night, along with his brothers, and two of his business associates," Alec maintained the eye contact. Malik hadn't blinked yet. "Can you see the garrotte?"

Malik looked down at the picture, but he didn't reply. He smiled at the Superintendent, but it was an evil smile. There was malice behind it.

"All the other victims were shot in the back. Why do you think they garrotted Kenny?"

Malik yawned and put his hand over his mouth. Alec could see why nobody had broken through the ice cool exterior. He pressed on with the questioning, hoping that something would press the right button.

"You see I think somebody wanted to ask Kenny some

questions, before they killed him obviously. So they shot his men, and then strangled him while they asked him questions."

"I really don't have time for this," Malik turned to his lawyer.

"Are you actually going to question my client, Superintendent, because if you're not then let him go," Nigella looked over her glasses as she spoke.

"I think someone wanted information from Kenny Richards, and I think it was you, Malik," Alec tilted his head and waited for a response. He ignored the protestations of Nigella Nielsen for now, but he knew that he would have to let Malik walk very soon. They had nothing, and he was giving nothing away.

"My client has an alibi for last night."

"Oh yes, I'm sure he does," Alec replied, turning to the brief. "I don't think for one minute that he did this with his own hands, because that's not how you work, Malik, is it?"

"No comment," Malik smiled.

"I think you want to know who is attacking your organisation, because it's obvious now that somebody is, and you think that too, don't you?"

"No comment." There was a flicker of acknowledgment. He did think that his organisation was under attack. Alec saw a momentary dilation of his pupils. It wasn't evidence, but it was an indication that he was driving down the right road.

"Did you ask Bruce Mann questions too?"

"Who?" Malik grinned again. Alec could see that this man was ice cold inside. He thought the whole process was a game, and he showed no fear or concern whatsoever. The mention of Kenny Richards and Bruce Mann brought no visible response from Shah, but when he mentioned his organisation, there was a flicker. It was more evidence that Malik Shah didn't care a dot about who was hurt, but his business was important to him. It may be the only thing that he cared about.

"Bruce Mann," Alec put a photo of the tortured body onto the table. Nigella recoiled visibly and she glanced sideways at Malik. Alec was happy with the response from the Grenade representative. It was about time she realised what the scumbags she defended were capable of. "He was tortured with power tools, and then dumped on the steps of the town hall."

"No comment." The dead glaze returned to Malik's eyes. The torture of Bruce Mann meant nothing to him. He shut down again.

"Have you spoken to Rasim Shah today?" Alec looked in his eye. There was a flash of a response, but it was gone in a second. "This is his Lexus." The image was shocking. The Lexus was nothing more than a twisted burnt out shell. The charred remains of the driver were still in situ nothing remained but blackened bones, and a grinning skull. "Rasim Shah was in it when it exploded this morning. See? That is one of your partners."

The glaze shifted and a sharpness came to Malik's eyes as he took in the detail. Alec couldn't gauge his response, but he knew that Malik was shocked. He could see anger in his eyes too. Malik Shah folded his arms, and turned to his lawyer. "Get me out of here, do it now. I'm saying nothing else to this idiot."

"We will make a 'no comment' statement from here on in, Superintendent." She looked at her watch and wrote down the time in her notes. "Charge my client, or release him."

"Charge him with what exactly?" Alec responded. He looked at the lawyer.

"Exactly, Detective, you have nothing to charge him with." She removed her glasses and twisted them between her finger and thumb. There was concern on her face. Alec could tell that she wasn't comfortable sitting next to Malik anymore. She couldn't wait to get out of there, and he'd hazard a guess that she wouldn't represent him again.

"Omar Patel is dead too," Alec threw in another grenade of his own.

"Yes, he had his head blown clean off minutes before Rasim was hit," Will spoke for the first time. The detectives planned their moves before the interview to measure Malik's reaction when he heard about the morning's events. It was an ambush. "The bomb squad are on their way to three addresses, all belonging to your business partners, just in case they have been targeted too."

"No comment," Malik snarled. There was real anger on his face now. The death of his partners was news to him that was certain. He showed no fear though, only anger.

"Who did you think was attacking you?" Alec asked. "Amir Patel was the first target, wasn't he?"

"No comment." Malik looked at the ceiling. He was seething, Will could almost feel the blood boiling from across the table.

"Was it you that questioned, Bruce Mann?"

"No comment."

"He didn't know anything, so you dumped his body in a public place, as a message," Alec continued. "Then your dealers were whacked, so you attacked the Richards, hoping Kenny would have some answers, right?"

"No comment."

"You must have upset someone, Malik?"

"No comment."

"Does the name, Einstein mean anything to you?" There was no recognition in Shah's eyes.

"No comment."

"I think that you're under attack, angry crack suppliers, rival arms dealers, who knows?" Alec crossed the line mentioning guns, but he had to push home the advantage that they had. Shah was steaming, and angry men make mistakes.

"No comment," Malik looked Alec up and down with hatred in his eyes this time, real hatred. Alec could feel the loathing coming across the table from him. The mention of drugs and guns had offended him. "Are you going to charge me, or release me?"

"Do you have any evidence that my client handles drugs of arms, Superintendent?" Nigella asked. Her face had turned visibly pale. She wanted no part in this. That was becoming more obvious.

"No, I don't." Alec leaned back in his chair and sighed. "I do have evidence that someone built an explosive device into a mobile phone, and blew your partner's head clean off his shoulders. What kind of people can do that?"

"No comment."

"The skill and technology and sheer determination that is required to pull that off is frightening. I would be very concerned if I were you, Malik."

"You could be next," Will closed his file and leaned forward, placing his elbows onto the table. Malik leaned forward too, and glared at Will.

"Read my lips, no comment."

"Are you going to charge my client, or not?"

Alec closed his file; they were getting nowhere fast. "Interview terminated. You're free to leave, Malik, but I'd keep my head down if I were you." He stood up, frustrated, and annoyed. They had nothing. Nothing to charge him with, and not a clue what was going on. A knock on the door stopped everyone from leaving. Smithy popped his head around the door. "Can I have a word, Guv?"

"Does it concern Mr Shah?" Alec asked sarcastically. "He's just leaving. Am I to assume that Mr Pindar will be making a no comment statement too?"

"Yes," Nigella picked up her briefcase.

"What is it, Smithy?"

"Ahmed Shah, Mustapha Shah and Saj Rajesh, Guv. All dead, Guv."

Malik looked physically shocked. Will was pleased that the grin had been wiped off his face, but he was worried by the expression that replaced it. Shah looked furious. Furious gangsters are dangerous people. Someone would be on the receiving end of violent retribution.

"What happened to them?" Alec sat on the edge of the table.

"Letter bombs, Guv. At least that's the bomb squad's initial assessment."

"Thanks Smithy."

"Guv," the ginger detective backed out of the room and closed the door.

"Have you got anything to say, Malik?" Alec stroked the deep dimple on his chin. The lines around his eyes creased as he looked at him intensely. "Every one of your business partners except Aswan Pindar has been murdered. You could be next Malik."

"No comment," Malik hissed as he pushed by him. The door slammed loudly behind him as he left the room.

40

Lenny Mcvitie

Lenny Mcvitie was a sixty-year-old Irishman, and he was a legend in the underworld of crime. A onetime bare-knuckle champion, Lenny was feared and respected by people on both sides of the law. Alec had dealt with Lenny many times, never as a suspect though. Lenny had been a vital source of information over the years. He was an old-fashioned criminal, and he didn't like the influx of foreign gangs or the way they operated. He had manners and he liked to think that he had some morals.

"Detective Naylor, how the devil are you?" Lenny stood up and towered over the table. He held out a giant gnarled hand and greeted the young DI with a genuine enthusiasm. His ruddy face parted in a toothless grin. "Where's Alec?"

"He's on his way, Lenny," Will tried to free his hand from the giant Irishman's grip, but he wasn't finished shaking it yet. It would be a huge mistake to disrespect Lenny. He was the type of man that would go out of his way help the people he liked, but woe betides those that crossed him.

"Now then, are you still seeing that little darling from the forensic unit?" Lenny released Will's hand. The question hit Will in the guts. He thought that his private life was relatively private, especially when the city's biggest villains were concerned.

"No, Lenny, it finished a while ago," Will was embarrassed. Lenny had eyes and ears all over the city, and he liked to keep a track of what was going on around him. Keeping up with a police detective's extramarital affairs could be used to his own advantage one day. It was also fun too.

"Did her husband find out?" Lenny chuckled at Will's discomfort. He tipped him a cheeky wink of the eye. "Shame, she was a diamond so she was."

Will was rescued from the unwelcome questioning when Alec entered the room.

"Lenny," Alec said. "How are you?"

"Damn fine, Superintendent," Lenny shook his hand with the same enthusiasm as before. "Now then, will I be needing a lawyer?"

"I doubt it, Lenny," Alec sat down and gestured for the big man to do the same. Lenny smiled. His front teeth were missing, a result of a bare-knuckle bout years ago. "We just want a chat."

"About Kenny Richards, I bet?" Lenny wiped his flattened nose with the back of his hand and sniffed. "Good man, Kenny Richards, god bless his soul." Lenny made the sign of the cross and kissed an invisible crucifix. He wasn't a religious man. He had a catholic upbringing though, and some old habits die-hard. He crossed himself more out of superstition than his religious beliefs.

"You've heard then," Alec smiled, putting the gangster at ease. They went back years. They met first a charity ball. They are strange events frequented by high-ranking officials, celebrities, and criminals alike. Within minutes they were chatting about Alec's time in Ireland, the troubles and some of the characters that they both knew. It was the start of an unusual relationship where they shared information, and a mutual respect.

"Who hasn't heard that?" Lenny shook his head and frowned. "Bad news travels fast, Superintendent." Lenny had a habit of switching from addressing him with his Christian name, and his rank, depending on how comfortable he was with the subject matter. He obviously had a problem with talking about Kenny Richards.

"What have you heard on the grape vine?"

Lenny looked thoughtful for a moment. He was selecting his next words carefully. Lenny wasn't the brightest bulb on the tree, but he wasn't stupid either. Some things were best unsaid.

"The funny thing is, Alec, I haven't heard a thing," Lenny tapped his bent nose with his index finger. "Now that is all wrong because I hear everything. Your randy young DI can verify that, cant you, Will? "

Alec looked at Will and frowned. Will shrugged, not wanting to go into any detail about their earlier conversation. He waited for the Irishman to expand.

"Kenny Richards was a very good friend of mine, Alec, if someone were to put out a hit on him, then I'd know about it."

"What if it was someone from out of town?"

"I'd know about it," Lenny looked deadly serious.

"We know that Kenny was targeted, the gunmen mentioned his name to the staff that they locked up," Will said.

"I'm talking hypothetically, of course," Lenny put his huge hands palms down on the table. His knuckles were crisscrossed with scar tissue, and a heavy gold bracelet hung from his left wrist.

"Of course," Alec replied.

"Kenny was a popular man. He had many influential friends in the city, and across the country. Now if he'd upset someone to the point that they wanted him dead, then whoever it was would have to seriously consider who else would be offended by his death. Me for instance, and if I hadn't been consulted then there could be severe consequences, you understand." Lenny looked annoyed as he spoke about his friend.

"Who would put a hit out on him?" Will asked.

"Everybody knows that me and Kenny were good friends. Now if someone knew that a hit was going down then someone would have warned me, and I would have stopped it. He was one of the lads, everyone's buddy, unless you pissed him off, of course."

"Of course," Alec humoured the old lag. "Has he pissed anyone off lately?"

"No, Alec, I would have heard about it."

"Kenny was tortured," Alec put the picture of Kenny garrotted on the table. Lenny picked it up with trembling hands. His face reddened and his eyes looked watery for a moment. "I think someone questioned him before he died."

"Looks that way," Lenny grimaced and handed the picture back.

"What could he possibly know that would result in his entire crew being assassinated?"

"Most of us do business together in a relatively civilised manner, only the foreigners keep themselves to themselves, and they cross the line more often than not." Lenny didn't see himself as foreign.

"Foreigners?"

"The Russians, Polish, Pakistanis, Somalis, you name it they're all out there, and they're nasty bastards the lot of them," Lenny ranted. "They have no respect for anybody, especially Shah and his mob, bastards the lot of them."

"What makes you mention his name?" Alec asked.

"Bruce Mann, poor bastard," Lenny tutted.

"What about him?"

"Come on, Superintendent," Lenny sat back in his chair. "Everyone knows it was Shah that did for him. They dumped the poor bastard on the town hall steps as a message to someone."

"Unless anyone can come up with any evidence, then we can't pin a thing on him, Lenny."

"He is a slippery bastard that Shah character. Bruce was no friend of mine, but he didn't deserve that. They did him the first time round, cut off his thumbs the evil bastards," Lenny was getting angry. "Look what they did to him and then look at that picture of Kenny, see any similarities?"

"You think Shah hit Kenny Richards?"

"I do," Lenny clenched his fists. He regretted saying that as soon as he spoke, but it was the truth. Shah's mob were the only ones that could put out a hit without him knowing about it, and that was because they kept everything in house, never using outsiders.

"Why would Shah hit Richards and risk a turf war?"

"That, I don't know," Lenny breathed out loudly. "I have been asking questions all over town but I'm none the wiser for my troubles."

"We think someone is targeting Shah and his partners, Lenny," Alec decided it was time to share information in an effort to gain some in return. The news would be out in the public domain by now anyway. The press would be having a field day when they put the names of Shah's associates together. It wouldn't take them long. They would link it to the Mosque bombing, and invent a right-wing bombing campaign against Asian owned businesses and properties.

"Why would you think that?"

"A couple of their dealers were murdered, and his business partners were killed this morning," Alec kept the details to himself for now.

"I heard about a couple of his runners being killed, but that could have been any smackhead in the city."

"We don't think so, Lenny. The shots were too clean and nothing was stolen."

"Well I didn't know that, and that sheds a completely different light on things, so it does."

"Can you think who would attack his people?"

"Who would?" Lenny frowned. Alec could see the cogs turning in his head. "It would be easier to give you a list of people that wouldn't kill the bastards, Alec. They're despised."

"Rasim Shah and Omar Patel were killed early on this morning."

"How?"

"We're not sure yet, but it looks like bombs. One device was placed in a car and the other one, we think was in a mobile phone."

"Jesus Christ," Lenny shook his head and stared at the table. His mind drifted as he digested the news. The world was changing fast, and different methods were used by different organisations, but this was hardcore military technology. "I'll tell you something for certain, Alec."

"Go on."

"If someone was gunning for Malik Shah, I'd have heard about it. There's nobody that I know in this city that could pull off a stunt like that."

"What about his gun running business?" Will asked. If it wasn't a local crew then it could be a foreign entity attacking Shah.

"I don't know enough about those people to comment, Will. He sells reactivated shit, and everyone knows it. It's possible that he's made enemies abroad but would they bother with his partners?"

"You don't think that they would?" Alec asked.

"I can't see it Alec. Those people have mega-bucks, and they can reach out across the globe. Nowhere would be safe to hide if they wanted you dead. I think they would put Shah's head on a stick if they wanted him."

"Does the name, Einstein mean anything to you?" Will knew it was a long shot.

"Einstein? That means nothing to me, Will."

"Have you got any plans to revenge Kenny Richards,

Lenny?" Alec sat forward. The last thing they wanted now was a turf war in the city. It was clear that Shah had made enemies outside of the city's crime world.

"I am too long in the tooth to be playing games like that, Superintendent. If someone out there is taking on Malik Shah, then it would be advisable to keep out of the way. I'll let them blow the shit out of each other and see what bits and pieces are worth picking up when they've finished."

"Thank you for your time, Lenny, and if you hear anything give me a call?"

"Oh, you'll be the first to know, Alec," Lenny raised his hand as he stood up. They shook hands. A mischievous grin crossed his face. "There is one other thing."

"What is it?" Alec raised his eyebrows.

"There's an old leather warehouse on the docks, near Panama street," Lenny nodded. "You might want to have a look at it. Rumour has it Shah's lot use it for interviewing clients, if you know what I mean."

"Thanks, Lenny, we'll do that."

41

Present day
RANSOM

Ashwan Pindar packed three kilos of crack cocaine into a small holdall. He placed the holdall into a black suitcase and zipped it up. The smell of eight hundred thousand pounds in mixed notes wafted up to him. The odour was a mixture of paper and sweat. His hands were shaking as he stood the case on its wheels. He checked the screen of the mobile phone that had been sent to him that morning. He was released from the cells without questioning, and he returned home for a change of clothes and to smooth things over with his wife. She wasn't returning his calls or replying to his text messages. The police swooped on his home and checked out all their vehicles and phones for explosive devices. Malik was going ballistic. Omar, Rasim and the others were assassinated and he was feeling vulnerable.

Ash switched on his laptop and checked his e-mails and the kidnappers had made contact. He followed their orders and drove to a lay-by a few miles from his home. In a litter bin he found the mobile phone and a set of instructions. The signal bar was full, as was the battery power, but there was no message yet.

"Anything?" Malik Shah asked angrily. His face was like thunder. He was sitting on the edge of long pine table, swinging his legs back and forth. A Mac-10 machinegun lay on the tabletop, next to him. He picked it up and stared at it in his hand. The weapon was compact, but deadly. Its matt black finish belied its lethal potential, making it look toy-like. Far from a toy, it was capable of firing nine hundred, nine millimetre bullets a minute.

"Nothing," Ashwan shook his head. He felt his trouser pocket through the material, wallet, keys, and phone. He had checked them every five minutes for the last two hours. They hadn't moved, but he checked them anyway. "I'm nervous, Malik. Who is doing this to us? It must be someone that we know. Who would ask for three kilos of gear unless they knew us?"

"We'll be behind you every step of the way. There is no way they'll get their hands on that money or the drugs until Mamood is safe, and sound. Once he is, they're fucking fish food."

"What if they spot you tailing me?"

"They will not."

"What if they do?"

"Shut the fuck up, Ashwan!" Malik was on the edge. The sustained attack on his business interests had him seriously rattled. He was clueless as to who the perpetrators were. Someone was stalking him and Ashwan, someone dangerous and deadly.

Ashwan looked down at the suitcase and frowned. Eight hundred thousand pounds was not a substantial amount of money, compared to the safe return of his only son. Malik had put up the money, and he had acquired the drugs from their own dealers. He had taken over the whole ransom operation, much to Ashwan's concern. Malik was making this a personal vendetta. Ash just wanted his son back unharmed. It was rare for Malik to become physically involved, but the murders of Rasim and the other directors forced his hand. They had worked together since their school days, and now there was only Ashwan and himself left alive. He wasn't going to wait around for the killers to get them. It was time to take this war to them. They had demanded money and drugs for the safe return of Mamood, and that required them collecting the ransom. When they did his men would be there waiting.

The kidnappers had told Ash to drive his Porsche until they contacted him. Malik and a small army of their men would take it in turn to follow him, reducing the risk of being spotted. Ashwan had no idea who had taken his son, or how many of them there would be at the ransom drop. What he did know, was there weren't many outfits with the men and machineguns that Malik's gang had. The kidnappers would be outnumbered, out gunned, surrounded, and dead five seconds after Mamood was released. At least that was Malik's plan.

Malik Shah was a cold man. His brutality stemmed from his contempt for humanity itself. As a teenager he systematically used and abused anyone that came near to him, girls, family and his friends. He surrounded himself with the strongest characters, and used them as a shield. Anyone who crossed him felt the wrath of his close-knit unit. Malik Shah and his gang left school at the time of one of the worst periods of recession and unemployment, to hit post war Britain. His older cousins, Imran and Ishmael, were already importing heroin into the country, via extended family in Pakistan. The cities of Manchester and Liverpool became battlegrounds as feuding crime families battled for turf. The eighties was the decade of the chemical generation as ecstasy became the social drug of choice, and drug taking became part of the club scene, and socially acceptable. Drug dealers became millionaires almost overnight. Malik was a natural leader, and as he matured, he rose through the ranks and took control of the business. He was brutal, and ruthless, taking out several of his older family members on his way to the top. As his wealth grew, so did the number of his enemies, although few dared to cross him.

At the age of twenty-four, Malik and his cousins boarded a North Sea Ferry, headed for the Dutch port of Rotterdam. Imran carried a sports bag, which contained seventy five thousand pounds. They were planning to exchange it for tablets, at seventy- five pence each, which would be resold at twenty pounds a pop. The demand was enormous, and this deal would make them one of the richest crime syndicates in the country. Imran liked Malik because he was sharp. If given an area to look after, then he did it with an iron hand. Other drug dealers were dispatched without mercy and his profit margins were always top drawer. He demanded the respect of all those that worked with him, and he was feared by his enemies. With that in mind, Imran decided to take him on the trip to Holland, and Malik jumped at the opportunity. They travelled as foot passengers and the voyage was uneventful. Imran and Ishmael talked openly with their young cousin about their plans to offload the drugs when they returned to Britain. Half the haul was to be sold wholesale to two big crime families in London, and the remainder would be sold at hugely inflated prices to local dealers in the Liverpool and Manchester areas. They had no plans to retail the drugs themselves, which meant that Malik had no way of taking any profit from the deal. He raised the issue, and offered to take personal control of the resale of the tablets, but his cousins wanted the drugs gone quickly. Malik was both gutted, and offended by the plan. He began to think that his cousins were losing their backbones, and missing the opportunity to maximise the potential profit from the deal, by selling it on the streets themselves. Malik spent the rest of the crossing coming up with his own plan.

The trio travelled in a hire car to a service station on the outskirts of Rotterdam, where they met a Hell's Angel who went by the name of Grizzly. Malik could see why he was called that. He was a monster of a man, muscular arms completely sleeved in tattoos, and his hands were the size of a gorilla's. He wore a red bandana and mirrored sunglasses, black leather pants and a biker jacket with the Angel's crest embroidered on the back. Imran handed the biker a brown envelope full of money, and in return, he received a leather satchel. Imran handed the satchel to Malik while the Hell's Angel counted the cash. He opened the bag. Inside was an Uzi nine millimetre machine pistol, and three full clips of ammunition. Imran was taking out some insurance. It made sense, and it took away the hassle of smuggling weapons onto the ferry. Grizzly slipped the envelope into his scuffed leather jeans, and walked away without saying a word. The huge Dutch biker had Swastikas tattooed on his hands. He hated Asians, but he put his prejudice aside, as their money was the same colour as his and business was business.

They drove on twenty miles in silence. The reality of their predicament was sinking in. They were far from home, carrying a huge bundle of money, and looking to do a drug deal with people that they didn't know, and couldn't trust. The Uzi offered some reassurance, but not a lot. The meeting place was the exit road of another service station. Ishmael indicated and looked at Malik in the mirror.

"We're here, game on," he said, trying to sound aloof, but failing miserably.

Two men in a dark green Range Rover waited for them on the far corner of a large car park. Imran pulled the vehicle behind them, but before he could get out the driver signalled for them to follow the vehicle. The Range Rover drove at a steady pace for over half an hour, before turning onto a deserted farm track. The track was rutted and the vehicles bumped their way along it until they reached the farmhouse and outbuildings. The property was ramshackle and in disrepair, the windows were gaping black holes in a crumbling facade. Imran took a packet of Marlborough from his shirt pocket. He removed three, and handed them out to

225

his cousins. Malik felt a rush of adrenalin as he inhaled the soothing smoke deep into his lungs.

"Wait here," Imran instructed, as he and Ishmael climbed out of the vehicle. "Keep the gun loaded and cover our backs."

Malik slammed a full clip into the breach, and it clicked home. He slipped the spares into his jacket pocket. Imran and Ishmael waited nervously for the men to exit their vehicle. When they did, Malik thought that they were Turks. Both men were dark haired and unshaven. They looked alike, and Malik thought that they could have been brothers. One of the men walked to the tailgate of the Range Rover, and opened it slowly. He took out a large rucksack and a silver twelve gauge Mossberg pump action shotgun. Malik was surprised that they didn't have backup with them, and that the only weapon he could see was a weapon limited to five shots, before it needed to be reloaded. The Mossberg would do terrible damage to a human target with five shells, but it would be limited against multiple moving targets. The Uzi would fire a full clip in under four seconds, spraying a wide area and increasing the chances of a kill.

The Turks approached his cousins, and they met cautiously halfway between their respective vehicles. Malik edged out of the hire car and stood behind the rear passenger door. Words were exchanged, but Malik couldn't make out what was said. Imran opened the sports bag and showed the Turks the cash. The Turks responded by opening the rucksack. The man with the Mossberg looked nervous, and sweat was trickling from his temples, running down the side of his face. Malik could smell his fear. He stepped from behind the car door, raised the Uzi and pulled the trigger. The nine-millimetre machinegun bucked in his hand as it released its lethal load. Imran and Ishmael never knew who shot them. Bullets slammed into their backs smashing bones and tearing organs to shreds as they ricocheted around inside their ribcage. They dropped dead where they stood. One of the Turks took two rounds in the face, blasting the lower jaw and cheekbone from his skull. The other man was hit in the shoulder, and he tried to crawl away from the scene, digging his heels into the ground, his breaths coming in short gasps. Malik released the empty clip and slammed a full one into the Uzi. Malik walked over to the wounded Turk. He stood over him, looking into his eyes. His mouth opened, but no words came out. Malik pulled the trigger and emptied the magazine into his twitching body.

The Uzi was red hot. Malik kneeled down next to Imran's dead body. His eyes were wide open but there was no life in them. The light inside had been extinguished. Malik took the cigarettes from his cousin's shirt pocket, and lit one as he surveyed the carnage around him. It took him ten minutes to strip the bodies of any valuables or identification, and he removed his jacket and tee shirt, leaving them on the front seat of the hire car while he worked. He put the bodies into the Range Rover, his cousins in the front, and the Turks in the back. Dragging them across the farmyard was difficult, and lifting them up into the vehicle was backbreaking but he managed to complete his gory task. When he finished, he was covered in blood and gore from head to toe. Malik tossed the weapons into the back seat with the dead Turks, and then he ripped the shirt from one of the bodies, stuffing it into the petrol filler pipe. He set fire to it and jogged back to his hire car.

Malik smoked another cigarette as he watched the material burn. It wasn't long before the petrol tank exploded and the vehicle became a raging inferno. He had seventy five thousand pounds in cash, plus the drugs, and a selection of credit cards that he had found on the bodies. It would be the financial rock, upon which he would build his empire. Malik posted the drugs in several packages to himself, and he returned home as a foot passenger on another ferry. Within a month of returning home, he was the richest, most powerful drug dealer in the north of England. Ashwan and the others stayed loyal to him, and they prospered as the business grew.

A knock on the kitchen door snapped Ashwan back to reality.

"We've got a problem." A huge fat man filled the doorway. His cheeks were flabby jowls, which joined his neck without the need for a chin. Indi Pindar was a cousin to Ashwan. He had a black sweater stretched over his massive bulk, dark sweat patches were spreading from beneath his armpits.

"What is it?" Malik stood up from the table. He held the Mac-10 in both hands ready for action. Ashwan could see how tense his boss was, and that worried him.

"We've got company outside," Imran nodded toward the window. "We're under surveillance."

Malik walked to the doorway and switched off the kitchen light. He went to the window and parted the venetian blinds with his fingers. Across the road, one hundred yards away, was a white transit van. Two men sat low in the front seats, and there was a dull glow from the rear of the vehicle. It was a surveillance unit with a sophisticated listening capability fitted to the back.

Malik reached for the sink and put the plug into the hole, turning both taps full on. The he switched on the radio and turned it up full blast. Indi followed suit by waddling through every room in the house, switching on every television set and turning the volume up full on. Malik laughed as he looked through the blinds again. The two policemen in the front seats of the van were sat bolt upright. They twisted round to face the men in the rear of the vehicle, and a heated conversation was going on. The driver slammed the steering wheel with his fist, furious that they'd been spotted. There was little point in remaining there anymore, and he started the engine, switched on the lights and drove toward the house. The vehicle slowed slightly as it neared. Malik flicked on the light and waved through the blinds sarcastically. The surveillance officer returned the gesture by raising his middle finger. Malik Shah was too clever to be caught out by a clumsy operation like that, MI5 had been trying to catch him for years, and they couldn't find a shred of evidence against him. His men were sharp, and on the ball. He had Electric Counter Measures in every house, and every vehicle. As soon as a listening device was aimed at them, they were informed of the fact.

"What are those fuckers doing here tonight?" Ashwan hissed.

"Probably looking for whoever dumped Bruce Mann on the town hall steps," Malik laughed. Indi came back into the room, bringing the sickly sweet smell of body odour with him. "Have you checked everything?"

"Yes, they're gone," Indi replied. His neck rippled as he spoke.

"Are you sure?" Ash was flapping, rattled by the police presence. He didn't want anything to interfere in getting Mamood back safely.

The mobile phone beeped loudly, silencing the conversation. There was a message on the screen.

HEAD EAST ON THE M62. ANYONE FOLLOWS YOU MAMOOD DIES. GOOD JOB THE POLICE SURVELLANCE TEAM LEFT OR HE WOULD ALREADY BE DEAD.

"The bastards must be watching us!" Ash gasped. "They know about the police surveillance van being here."

Malik snatched the mobile phone from Ash and glared at the screen. It was becoming obvious that people they were dealing with were not amateurs. Malik wanted them dead, whatever the cost, and if that included Mamood being sacrificed then so be it.

42

The Dream

Ashwan Pindar wiped sweat from his forehead. He clicked the windscreen wipers on as rain began to fall, blurring his vision. The headlights of oncoming vehicles were dazzling as he drove his Porsche. The radio was switched off, and engine noise filled the vehicle. The mobile phone in his hand beeped. Another set of instructions had arrived. He had been driving around in circles for nearly forty minutes now. Malik and his men were trying to second-guess where the kidnappers were sending him, sometimes following from a distance behind, while other vehicles sped ahead anticipating where the exchange would take place.

The message instructed him to head for 'The Dream'. He indicated left and pulled off the motorway. In the distance, he could see a huge black mound silhouetted against the yellow glow of streetlight pollution. The lights of the industrial town of St. Helens illuminated the night sky; the black mound, which blotted them out for miles, was the slagheap of a long defunct coalmine. When the mines closed, the council spent fortunes planting grasses and trees. They built footpaths and tried to make them more aesthetically pleasing to the eye. The site of Sutton Manor colliery had been transformed into acres of parkland, crisscrossed by wide footpaths, all leading to a huge sculpture, called 'The Dream'. The Dream is a white, twenty metres high sculpture of a woman's head. A huge bust situated on top of the old mine. It can be seen from miles around, and it's sited next to the M62 motorway, where it is seen by over a million drivers every year. It had become a landmark.

Ashwan had seen it a thousand times in the daylight, towering above the tree line. At night it looked eerie, the huge white face seemed to hang in mid air, like a giant ghost. He looked in his rear view mirror, trying to make out if his men were close behind. There were three sets of headlights, but he had no way of knowing if they were his backup or other motorists heading for the nearby town, and the sprawling housing estates that surround it. He forwarded the text message to Malik's phone, as he pulled into a car park which serviced the site. The car park was unlit, and deserted. The mobile beeped again.

GET OUT OF THE CAR NOW AND TAKE THE RIGHT HAND PATH TO THE TOP. IF YOU TOUCH THE KEYPAD ONCE MORE MAMOOD DIES

"Shit," he muttered. They were watching, and they knew that he had forwarded the message, or were they bluffing, and assuming that he would be sending the directions to his backup? Whatever, he couldn't take the risk. Ashwan put the phone on the dashboard, opened the door and climbed out. He flicked the driver's seat forward and grabbed the case of money. A car drove by slowly on the main road but Ashwan didn't wait to see who was driving. There was no way any of his men could enter the car park without being spotted. It was too dark and secluded. Ash thought it was ideal; good planning by the men that held his son. He grabbed the phone, slammed the door closed and ran toward the path. A metal sheep gate gave access from the car park and it clanged loudly in the darkness as he stumbled through it in the driving rain. He looked up at the giant head. It loomed out of the darkness, at least a half mile away up a steep path, which wound its way through bushes and trees to the top. The path disappeared in the inky blackness just yards from the entrance where the streetlights could not penetrate. Ash looked behind him briefly, before sprinting into the night; his only thought was to get Mamood back home safely.

David Bernstein watched Ashwan Pindar running up the path toward the statue. His progress was slow, hampered by the dark and the rain. He appeared as a green human shaped blob through his night-sights. David had used such surveillance equipment many times before in the Holy city, Jerusalem, watching for suicide bombers crossing the Jewish borders. He had chosen 'The Dream' as the ideal site to separate Ashwan from his men. There was no doubt that heavily armed men were following him. Taking them out of the equation was vital, if they were to take Malik Shah's money and drugs from him, and remain unscathed and anonymous. This was only the beginning. The statue was sited in an elevated position, with panoramic views of every direction. If Aswan had backup, he could see them coming a mile away. The only access from the road network was from the west, where Ashwan had parked. A six-lane motorway protects the south entrance to the park. The north and west approaches were open farmland, which stretched for miles, with no vehicle access. He waited until Ashwan was half way up the hill, and then he called Nick on a closed coms unit.

"He's on the way, no sign of any backup yet." The coms unit clicked twice, a sign that the message was understood.

He scanned the path again. Ash was five minutes from the statue when David heard tyres screeching He turned west to face the car park. A BMW stopped opposite the entrance, closely followed by a black Range Rover. Both vehicles were full of men. A third vehicle double-parked next to them, and the sound of raised voices drifted through the night to him. He couldn't hear what was being said, as the sound of motorway traffic drowned out the words. Articulated lorries roared by every few minutes. The lateness of the hour meant the traffic had thinned to a minimum. It was obvious that Malik Shah was debating whether to follow Ashwan Pindar into the park, risking ambush, or scaring the kidnappers away. The convoy was stationary for long minutes as the gangsters discussed their options.

One of the men leaped from the Range Rover and ran into the car park, stooping low to lower the risk of being hit by a hidden gunman. He checked that the Porsche was empty and then ran onto the sheep-gate. A quick reconnaissance of the park beyond it told him all he needed to know. Their choice was not an easy one. The old colliery was miles wide, wooded and pitch black. There were three different pathways, which split and forked dozens of times as they crossed the parkland. Ashwan had entered the park alone, while Malik Shah and his cronies waited for a text message that never arrived. They'd lost sight of him and the money, and there was nothing that they could do about it.

4 3

The Dream

Ashwan Pindar was out of breath and soaked to the skin as he reached the summit of the old slagheap. The rain was pelting down, running in rivulets over his head and into his eyes. His cosmetic hair gel was dissolving into the rainwater and making his eyes sting. He stopped as he turned a bend on the path, and the giant white head towered above him in a clearing ahead. His eyes had adjusted to the darkness, but he couldn't see anything unusual. The mobile phone beeped in his pocket. He took it out and covered it with his fingers to stop it getting wet. The message on the screen made his heart sink, and he screamed in frustration.

"You fucking bastards!" The words carried across the old pit before being soaked up in the motorway noise.

TAKE THE MIDDLE PATH DOWN THE HILL TOWARD THE EAST. OPPOSITE TO THE WAY YOU CAME. 1 MILE ON THERE IS A STILE LEADING INTO THE FARMLAND. CLIMB OVER IT. YOU HAVE 15 MINUTES. TOUCH THE PHONE PAD AND MAMOOD DIES.

The thought of dragging the suitcase another mile was gut wrenching. He was exhausted, wet through and freezing cold. His breaths were coming in short gasps as he looked at his wristwatch. Ash knew that Mamood was in mortal danger because of his business dealings, especially because of his connections to Malik Shah, or so he thought. He looked at the giant face once more and then ran across the clearing toward the opposite path. He noticed a dark rectangular shape at the bottom of the statue. It stood out against the white head. Ash thought nothing of it as he pulled his coat tightly around him and set off down the hill.

David Bernstein heard Ashwan cursing, and so did Malik Shah and his men. It carried down the hill on the wind. They stopped talking and looked up the hill toward the giant statue. David heard raised voices, and there was a flurry of activity. Someone was shouting orders and three men leapt from the BMW. Malik Shah was the driver, and he remained in the car, as did his passenger. The Range Rover and a Ford of some kind, wheel spinned into the car park. They screeched to a halt either side of Ashwan's Porsche, and men poured out of the vehicles as they came to a halt. Malik Shah and his passenger drove away from the scene as the men split into three groups and started up the hill toward the statue. David Bernstein smiled to himself as he slipped into the undergrowth and climbed down the slope toward the motorway.

Dipak Pindar sprinted ahead of the group. He was twenty-two years old, fit and ambitious. His family were originally from Pakistan, three generations before, and he wanted to be a permanent member of Malik Shah's organisation. He was keen to impress at every opportunity he could. Dipak put his head down and ran as fast as he could. He wanted to be the first to arrive at the statue. His imagination was working overtime, and images of rescuing his cousin Ashwan Pindar, killing the kidnappers and recovering the ransom money were playing through his mind. Malik Shah would offer him a fulltime position for sure. He covered the half mile in just over five minutes. The others were way behind him.

Dipak turned the last corner and the tree line parted to reveal a wide oval clearing. At the centre, the twenty-metre high head dominated the area. The smooth white surface seemed to glow in the darkness, reflecting the lights from the distant passing traffic. He crouched as he reached the clearing and looked deep into the shadows of the trees that surrounded it. Nothing moved.

"Ash," he whispered. Rain trickled down his back.

"Ashwan!" he called a bit louder. There was nothing moving.

Dipak could hear the rest of the men nearing the clearing. He scanned the area again and his eyes were drawn to a dark oblong shape at the base of the statue. Whatever it was, it shouldn't be there. It looked out of place. He darted from the cover of the trees and ran across the clearing to the base of the 'Dream'. The colossal head dwarfed him as he neared it. As he reached the base, the rectangle took another shape; it looked like the suitcase that Ashwan had used to carry the money. The money hadn't been picked up yet. Maybe the kidnappers got cold feet, or maybe Ash had struggled with them and frightened them away. The other option was that the kidnappers were still there, watching and waiting. He knelt next to the suitcase and tipped it onto its side, so that he could unzip it. If he could confirm with Malik Shah that he had recovered the money, then he'd be made a part of the team sooner than he had hoped for. As the suitcase tipped, a vial of mercury became horizontal, making a connection between an electronic charge, and a detonator. The case exploded. The blast ripped Dipak's limbs from his torso, and his body was blown thirty yards away into the trees.

44

Mamood

Ashwan stumbled down the hill in the pouring rain. The wind was blowing toward him driving the rain into his face, and his clothes were soaked to the skin. He shivered against the cold, only the thought that his son was out here somewhere kept him going. The suitcase felt like a dead weight, the further he dragged it, the heavier it felt. Malik had fitted a tracker in the lining, so that they could follow the kidnappers after the handover. It was an obvious move, but Malik was insistent. He was beginning to think that he had missed the stile, when the shape of a dry stonewall appeared from the darkness. Ashwan followed it to the left as the slope ran that way, and fifty yards on, he found the stile. There was a wooden signpost pointing across the farmland, declaring it a public footpath. He felt like crying as he climbed over the stile, dragging the battered suitcase behind him. The field was freshly ploughed, and grassed around the perimeter. He could just about make out a narrow path of flattened grass, running toward the motorway, to the right. The phone beeped in his pocket.

BENEATH THE STILE IS A HAVERSACK. TRANSFER THE MONEY AND DRUGS INTO IT. FOLLOW THE PATH TO THE RIGHT, THEN FOLLOW THE MOTORWAY UNTIL YOU REACH THE RAILWAY BRIDGE. TOUCH THE

KEYPAD AND HE DIES. YOU HAVE TWENTY MINUTES.

"Fuck! Fuck!," Ashwan kicked the suitcase and stubbed his toes painfully in the process. He looked up the hill toward the statue, wishing that Malik and his men would come and help him. He thought about Mamood, and it spurred him on. There was a reason he was here, and that was to save his son's life. He reached beneath the wooden stile and found a black plastic bin liner. Stuffed inside was the haversack. Ashwan unzipped the suitcase, grabbing bundles of used notes and stuffing them into the rucksack. Then he grabbed the cocaine from the holdall. Malik's tracker would be rendered useless by the switch. The rain hammered down on his back all the time he worked at repacking the ransom. Within minutes, the money was transferred. He placed his arms through the straps and pushed them over his shoulders. The rucksack sat snugly against his shoulder blades, and it was almost a relief not to be dragging the suitcase behind him. He was about to set off when a blinding flash of light dazzled him. The sound wave hit him milliseconds after. He looked up at the hill, and the sound of men wailing in agony drifted through the night.

"Fucking hell!" Ashwan whispered to himself. He stared at the giant head as he set off running toward the motorway. A half a mile ahead of him, a constant stream of traffic roared past in either direction. Ash could see a steep embankment leading up to the road, and he assumed that the footpath would run parallel to it. The noise became louder as he neared the motorway, but he was sure that he could hear sporadic bursts of automatic gunfire in the distance. Whatever had happened near the 'Dream', he was convinced that Malik and his men were not coming. He was alone. Whoever had Mamood was completely in charge of the situation, despite Malik's superior firepower. They'd picked the perfect spot to separate the money from his escort. Ashwan could only guess that the explosion he had witnessed was a booby-trap, designed to deter anyone from following him further. The rain became a downpour as he set off across the farmland.

Twenty minutes on Ash saw the field was angling down away from the motorway. To his right hand side the six lanes of traffic climbed away from the fields as they spanned a canal and a railway track. To his left were miles of agricultural land. He walked forward until he reached the perimeter fence, which marked the junction of the famer's land, and the railway embankment that carved through it. Ash climbed between two strands of barbed wire, catching the rucksack as he stumbled through. He tripped and fell into the long wet grass, cursing the rain and the darkness. His breath was coming in deep bursts as he climbed up on his feet. The motorway was deafening above him, and he could see the dull train tracks below him, disappearing miles away into the darkness. The embankment opposite separated the railway and the canal. He couldn't see the water, nor were there any narrow-boats moored nearby. The mobile vibrated in his pocket.

CLIMB BENEATH THE BRIDGE. WAIT ON THE LEDGE NEXT TO THE CENTRE STANCHION. TOUCH THE PHONE AND HE DIES.

"Fuck you!" Ash whispered. He peered into the night and looked at the embankment to his right. There was a steep concrete wall, supported by the stanchion that held up the arch. He headed along the embankment to the point where it met the bridge structure. From the distance, he could hear another noise, different to the engine noises on the motorway. Ash paid no heed to it as he looked for the ledge. He ducked low as he walked beneath the bridge, and escaping the rain was a relief. The darkness was different there, and his eyes struggled to adjust to it. Above him, a concrete beam spanned the railway, but it was smooth. There were no lips or ledges on it. Ash wondered if there was anyone lurking the blackness that engulfed him. Was his son nearby, tied up and gagged, cold and frightened? He moved deeper beneath the bridge as the traffic roared overhead. Progress was difficult as the huge concrete slab that he was edging along was set at such a steep angle. One wrong footstep and he would be tumbling toward the rails at high speed. He wasn't convinced that he could climb back up the slab if he were to fall.

Ashwan reached the centre of the bridge supports, and he could see a ledge about two feet wide. He stepped onto it where it met the embankment, and began to sidestep his way beneath the structure. His progress was steady, and he looked down. He was directly above the rail tracks. The distant engine noise was becoming louder by the minute. He looked to the east and he could see the lights of an approaching diesel tractor unit. The engine noise was booming, louder and louder as it neared. Ashwan couldn't understand why the train carriages that it pulled were in darkness. He could see the train behind the engine, yet it was black. The train seemed to be moving in slow motion, sluggish and certainly in no rush to keep to a timetable. The mobile phone beeped and vibrated. He reached for it and looked at the screen.

DROP THE BAG ONTO THE FIFTH CARRIAGE. TOUCH THE PHONE AND HE DIES

"What about Mamood?" Ashwan shouted in the darkness. His voice was lost as the diesel locomotive trundled toward the bridge. As he stared at the train, he could see that the carriages were open and piled high with a black substance. "Coal? The train is full of coal."

Ash laughed nervously in the dark. His mind raced through his options at a million miles an hour. The engine roared beneath him and his mouth and nostrils filled with fumes.

"Where is my son?" he screamed into the night. The second wagon went by. If he dropped the money then it was irretrievable, and the kidnappers hadn't told him where Mamood was. If he didn't drop the money then his son would be killed, he had no doubt about that. The third wagon full of coal roared beneath him. He slipped the rucksack off, and lowered it toward the train. "Where is my son?" Ash shouted as he dropped the bag of money onto the fifth wagon. It disappeared from his sight in a second, and he was left alone in the darkness as the train rattled on into the night.

45

L a n a   P i n d a r

Lana twisted her wedding band and turned off the flat screen television with its remote. The wind and rain hammered at the bedroom window. The howling wind intensified the feeling of emptiness and loneliness that she felt. Mamood was missing and Ashwan was out there trying to find him. The death of his business partners was still sinking in to her already befuddled mind. They had known each other since their school days, and stayed together through their adult lives, with Malik as the lynch pin. The police arrived at her front door looking for Ashwan yesterday morning. They had an arrest warrant, but they wouldn't tell her why they wanted to talk to him. She told them he had gone away for a few days. She didn't know why she lied, but she did. She knew that he was with Malik, that's where he always was. Ashwan was the only hope she had of getting her son back alive, and he was no use to her in a police cell.

If that wasn't bad enough, they returned with bomb squad officers and searched her car for explosives. They even checked her mobile phone for a bomb. They looked for a bomb in her car or her phone; what was going on? Whoever Ash really was, she wanted nothing to do with it. They were finished, of that she was absolutely certain. She planned to see a solicitor and file for divorce.

'Why do you want a divorce Mrs Pindar?'

'Oh, that's an easy one to answer. I've just found out my husband is a gangster. He sells drugs, pimps prostitutes, smuggles arms, and he can also have dead teenagers removed from our lawn.' She thought.

She checked her mobile for the tenth time in as many minutes. There were no missed calls or messages. Mamood was missing, her husband had been questioned by the police, and his business associates were being systematically blown up. A tear ran down her cheek as she put her head on the pillow. She lay fully clothed on the bed that she had shared with her husband for nearly twenty years. The man she loved and respected, once, but no longer. He was an imposter, a liar, a murderer even?

The doorbell rang and she sat up so fast that she felt dizzy. Her stomach tensed and filled with butterflies, and her throat felt dry suddenly. She looked at her watch. It was an Armani, a present from Ashwan for her wedding anniversary one year. The time was three in the morning. Ash still had his keys. She could tell that he had been home that afternoon sometime. His dirty washing was in the laundry basket. Would the police call this late at night? If they had bad news, they would.

Lana jumped off the bed and headed for the bedroom door. Ashwan's dressing gown was hanging from it. The smell of Aramis drifted to her as she walked by. She switched on the lights in the hallway and looked toward the front door. There were no silhouettes or shadows there. She ran down the stairs and looked through the glass. Her heart sank and she felt weak at the knees. She wanted to cry out but she couldn't. Her throat restricted and she felt nauseous. Lana pulled the bolt on the door and threw it open.

"Mamood," she screamed, eventually finding her voice.

"Mum," he said. He stood with a blanket wrapped around him. He was soaked to the skin and the wind threatened to rip it from his shoulders.

"Are you hurt?" She held his face in her hands, and pulled him inside out of the elements.

"No, Mum," he sobbed. He was still in shock. "They said bad things about my dad."

"Where is he?" Lana asked herself. "How did you get back here?"

"They put me in a van and then dropped me off down the road."

"I wonder where your father is?" Lana didn't think that she should care anymore, but she did. She looked across the lawns and down the road, but Ashwan wasn't there.

46

Ashwan

Ashwan Pindar climbed out of the tunnel and he looked at the mobile phone the kidnappers had given to him. There were no messages to tell him where his son was. The money and the crack were gone, but there was no sign of his son anywhere. They had stuck to their part of the deal, and delivered the money and drugs. Where was his son? He had to get out of there quickly. The rain drilled into him as he emerged, and he climbed up the steep embankment toward the motorway. He couldn't stumble back across the fields, it was too far and too dark. Exhaustion had caught up with him. The motorway above him was the easy answer. He reached the barrier and tumbled over it. Headlights glared at him from both directions. The traffic was relatively light but the noise of the engines was still deafening.

Ashwan knew that the next exit was about a mile away to the west. That was the nearest point that he could be picked up. He dialled Malik.

"Where are you?" Malik answered. He sounded annoyed.

"I am on the hard shoulder of the motorway, about a mile from junction nine."

"Why didn't you tell us where you were?"

"They said they would kill him if I touched the keypad."

"Where have you left the money and the drugs?"

"I had to drop it onto a coal train from under a bridge. It must be headed for Fiddlers Ferry power station."

"Did you get Mamood?"

"No."

The line went dead as Malik smashed his i-phone to pieces on the dashboard of his BMW. He wasn't angry about the money and the drugs; it was the fact that they had been tricked again, and they'd missed the opportunity to trap his tormentors.

Ashwan put the handset into his pocket and headed west toward the exit. His own mobile was inside his jacket, and it began to vibrate. He pulled it out and checked the screen. It was his wife, Lana.

"Lana thanks for ringing," he began to waffle. He took the fact that she'd called as a sign that she was coming to terms with the situation, but he was wrong.

"Mamood is home, Ash, and I want a divorce. This will never happen again," Lana had never been more determined in her life. The safety of her son was paramount.

"He's home?" Ashwan looked to the sky and said thank you. His relief was indescribable. "Lana I can make this right."

"Your son was kidnapped because of who you are and what you do. Your partners are dead. What will happen next, Ashwan?"

The line went dead and he stared at the screen for a while before trying to redial her. It clicked straight to answer phone. He tried again, same thing. Ash clicked Malik's number and dialled him, at least the news that Mamood was safe might calm him down a bit. The call didn't connect because Malik's handset was smashed to smithereens in the foot-well of his BMW. He would have to deal with Malik when he returned. Mamood was his priority. Mamood and Lana. He had to try to rebuild things back to the way they were. He jumped as a horn blared loudly behind him. Headlights approached him, but they weren't on the main carriageway. They were on the hard shoulder. The vehicle slowed down as it approached and he squeezed against the barrier to let it draw level with him. It was marked with green chevrons down the side panels, and Highway Patrol was printed above them. It was a transit van, with a crew cab at the front and a sliding door at the side, which accessed a van section. The passenger window went down and the driver touched his peaked hat as he spoke.

"Are you okay, Sir?"

"I'm stranded, it's a long story."

"Breakdown?"

"Something like that," Ashwan replied.

"Do you want a lift to the next exit?"

"Yes please," Ashwan was relieved. He opened the passenger door and climbed in to the van. The driver was fat. "Thanks for your help."

"Oh, it's my pleasure," Richard Bernstein put the vehicle into first gear and pulled away from the hard shoulder.

47

MIT

"Sorry to wake you at this time in the morning, Guv," Will Naylor sounded like he had just woken up too. His voice was thick with sleep. "We've got reports of another explosion."

"Where?" Alec reached for the glass of water that he kept on the bedside table and he checked the time on his watch.

"Up at Sutton Manor colliery. They think it was near the site of the Dream, Guv."

"What the bloody hell is going on?"

"That's not all, Guv. I've called the DI at the scene, Tom Chance from the St Helens nick," Will paused.

"I know him."

"They got reports of an explosion from residents nearby and several calls from drivers on the sixty two, reporting a fireball shooting into the air above the statue."

"Well, it sounds like an explosion."

"They are bringing in portable lights to help search the area."

"Have they found anything?"

"Not yet, it's too dark and the rain isn't helping, but there is a Porsche parked in the car park at the bottom of the hill, Guv. It belongs to Ashwan Pindar."

"That doesn't sound good." Alec tried to make sense of

the pieces of the puzzle, but it was a mess. They were missing something. His wife moaned and sat up. She was used to these late night phone calls. It was one of the downsides of being married to a police detective. She climbed out of bed and pulled on her towelling robe. Alec noted that her legs were still in good shape, and her behind was still firm. All that time and effort in the gym had paid off. She went down stairs and put the kettle on. Alec wouldn't go back to sleep now that he had been disturbed. His mind would be too active to sleep. She grabbed two mugs and made decaffeinated coffee for her and a strong regular brew for Alec.

"There's no sign of him yet, but listen to this. We put an officer on the Pindar residence today. In the early hours of this morning, he called in that a teenage boy walked into the front garden, and knocked on the front door. He was soaking wet and wrapped in a blanket."

"Pindar has a son, right?"

"Right, Guv. Mamood Pindar."

"Did he speak to the mother?"

"She wouldn't speak to him, Guv. She said everything was fine and slammed the door in his face."

"None of this makes any sense, Will."

"What time are you going in?" Will asked, already knowing what the answer was.

"I'm on my way to the Dream, It'll be light in an hour or so."

"I'll meet you there, Guv."

48

Nick

Nick waited patiently as the coal train approached. It was taking fuel to Fiddlers Ferry, a huge coal powered electricity-generating station, situated on the banks of the River Mersey. The rail track was dedicated to keeping the furnaces burning. The coal train slowed down as it neared, and the brakes squealed as they struggled to stop a thousand tons of moving steel. The wagons clanked as they rolled over the points. A signal showed red. The power station was fed by a single rail track. That meant that there was a siding where arriving trains, fully loaded with fuel parked, so that departing empty wagons could be shunted away. Nick waited for the train to stop completely before making his way to the fifth wagon. He reached into the long grass, which grew on the embankment, and retrieved an aluminium ladder. The ladder was hidden months earlier when they were prepping their plan. It took mere seconds to retrieve the haversack, and hide the ladder back in its place.

Nick climbed halfway up the embankment, and disappeared into the long grass. To anybody watching it was as if he'd been swallowed up by the grassy slope. He ducked low and walked through a concrete tunnel, which led to a storm drain under the embankment. The huge drain ran through concrete pipes four metres in circumference for a half mile where it joined the river beneath the colossal cooling towers at the power station. The water ran fast, but it was only a metre deep. Nick slipped a head torch on and switched on the light. He slipped the haversack on and dragged a plastic resin canoe toward the water. Twenty minutes later, he was in the Highway Patrol van with the Bernstein brothers. The unconscious body of Ashwan Pindar was layed out and handcuffed in the back of the van, and there was a faint whiff of chloroform lingering in the air.

4 9

The Dream

Alec Ramsey pulled into the car park that serviced the old colliery. A uniformed officer stood guard at a yellow tape, trying hard to keep back a growing throng of reporters. The Shah Corporation bombings had hit the news, and every satellite channel and red top newspaper in the country was carrying the story. It was fast becoming the hot story across the globe, as the press blamed right wing extremists for the anti-Muslim bombing campaign. Alec was under growing pressure from the Commander to come up with a line of enquiry that he could communicate to the press. Right now Alec didn't have one to give him. Malik Shah was the victim in the press, yet Alec knew that he was the cause of the problem, everything revolved around him. As he crawled through the reporters, camera flashes made strobe light in the dawn glow. The sun was coming up.

Alec ignored the questions shouted at him through the glass, and he waved at the constable as he lifted the tape. Across the car park he spotted Pindar's Porsche. Forensic officers were crawling all over it, and a white gazebo was in the process of being erected above it, to shield it from the prying cameras. At the top of the hill, 'The Dream' hung above the trees, almost floating in the dawn mist. Alec sighed as he brought his

Shogun to a halt. Whatever the missing pieces of this puzzle were, he needed to identify them quickly. The case was getting away from him. Will pulled up in his Audi TT convertible. It suited him down to the ground.

They exited their vehicles and DI Tom Chance spotted them and headed toward them. He grabbed a couple of paper suits from a crime-scene support vehicle and jogged over to them.

"Superintendent," he greeted Alec with a handshake.

"DI Chance," Alec returned the greeting. Will and Tom exchanged handshakes and nodded a silent hello. The detectives struggled into their protective clothing while DI Chance briefed them. "The Porsche belongs to Ashwan Pindar, as you know. We've spoken to his wife this morning, and she says that he isn't home."

Alec looked up the hill and wondered if Ashwan Pindar was up there somewhere. Was it his teenage son that arrived back at the family home in the early hours of the morning wrapped in a blanket? Why would Pindar visit the statue at night, unless he was meeting somebody subversively? What was he doing there in the first place, and why would anyone plant a bomb there? They walked toward the Porsche.

"There's nothing untoward about the Porsche so far, except the driver's seat was left forward. Either a passenger climbed out or the driver removed something from the backseat. It's a different story up the hill though."

"What have you got so far?" Alec was keen to start slotting the evidence into the relevant boxes in his mind.

"We've found one fatality, but we can't identify him yet because of his injuries."

"Is there any ID on the body?" Alec asked.

"We haven't found the body yet, Guv. Well not all of it."

"What have you found?" Will pressed the issue. He was as frustrated as the Superintendent was about their lack of progress. Every avenue they went down was a dead end.

"We have an arm, and a left foot. The skin is dark, probably Asian or Middle-Eastern ethnicity." Tom Chance pointed to the Porsche as they climbed the hill. "At first I thought the chances are that it's Pindar, but now I'm not so sure."

"Why?"

"See the markers there?" Tom pointed to numbered yellow markers that were dotted along the path. "There are nine millimetre shell casings all over the place."

Alec stopped and looked around. There were dozens of markers, clumped in six or seven different parts of the hill. It appeared that multiple gunmen stood still and fired up the hill at an unseen enemy. As they reached the clearing, the markers became more numerous. The giant bust towered above them as they neared it. The white face was scarred with a black scorch mark the shape of a candle flame. It stretched from the chin to just above the forehead.

"The base of the statue is where the bomb was planted, and we found the limbs twenty yards away, over there. If you look back down the hill, you can see how the shell casings are concentrated into seven areas."

"With our dead man, that makes at least eight people that were here, the victim and seven shooters."

"I agree, Guv." Tom Chance nodded his head.

"What were they shooting at?" Will asked.

"As far as we can see up to now, they hit nothing. They were firing blind, and probably panicked by the explosion," DI Chance surmised. "It would have been pitch black here last night, and the weather was terrible."

"Why would you come up here without artificial light of some kind, a torch or something?" Will said. "Unless, you didn't want to be seen, of course."

"DI Chance!" A voice called from the tree line to the east. A forensic officer waved a gloved hand to attract his attention.

"Looks like they have found something," Alec nodded.

They walked toward the officer. In the bushes that lined the clearing, the head and torso of a man lay face down. He was dressed in dark combat clothing, the remnants of which were reasonably intact. The forensic team lifted the body gently and photographed its position, and the injuries. The face was gone, only red mush remained. They searched the body with gloved hands.

"We've found a wallet in his trouser pocket," the forensic said. He flipped open the tan leather wallet. There was about a hundred pounds in twenty-pound notes, and a visa card. He pulled out the credit card.

"Dipak Pindar, Guv."

Alec and Will exchanged glances. Pindar had driven to this site, followed by at least seven heavily armed men. A bomb was detonated and a firefight ensued, but why?

"We need to speak to Pindar's wife, Will, and we need to do it now."

50

L a n a   P i n d a r

Alec pulled up his vehicle next to the driver's window of a Vauxhall. He didn't know what model it was as they all looked the same to him. They spoke to the Commander on the way to Lana Pindar's home, and the Commander was happy to authorise an arrest warrant if she failed to cooperate. The situation was becoming desperate, and desperate measures were required to deal with it. Lana Pindar wasn't a suspect in any investigation, but she was withholding information, of that Alec was certain.

"Has there been any more comings or goings?" Alec asked the detective that was assigned to watch the Pindar residence. The Vauxhall was his home for the foreseeable future. He was new to the team and looked surprised to see the Superintendent at his stakeout. He consulted his notebook before he replied.

"No, Guv."

"Take a break for a few hours; get some breakfast and a few hours' kip."

"Thanks, Guv."

Alec steered the Shogun across the road, and he parked on the driveway in front the Pindar residence. The curtains were closed in the windows.

"The answer lies with Malik Shah, and Ashwan Pindar, Will.

They know what is going on, and so does Lana Pindar," Alec switched off the engine and opened the door. Will Naylor did likewise. "I am not leaving here until we have answers."

"Are we going to tag team them?" Will referred to a technique of interrogation were two people were questioned at the same time. It caused confusion and led to mistakes being made. It wasn't something that they could employ in a formal interview with legal representation present. They had to make the most of this opportunity.

"Yes, whatever it takes," Alec replied. He reached the front door and rang the doorbell. He stared at his shiny brogues while he waited long seconds for a reply, but none came. His fist rapped four times loudly on the door. He waited only five seconds or so and then banged on the door again. They heard the bolts being drawn and the door opened an inch.

"What do you want?" Lana asked. "Why don't you leave me alone?"

"We need to speak to you, Lana, it's urgent," Alec pushed the door open with his right hand. "We can do it here, or we can do it at the station and get social services to look after Mamood while we talk, it's up to you."

She opened the door in silence, and looked at them suspiciously, as they entered. Alec spotted Mamood sat on a leather settee in the living room area. Lana walked toward the kitchen away from the living room, tying to steer them away from her son.

"We'll talk in here if that's ok. We need to speak to Mamood too."

Lana tried to protest but Will gently took her arm and guided her toward where her son was sitting. Mamood looked like a frightened rabbit. He had dark circles under his eyes and his face looked gaunt and drawn.

"Hello, Mamood," Alec said. "Sit down, Lana." He pointed to an empty armchair. "Did you have a late night, Mamood?"

257

Mamood looked at his mother for help. She twitched her head slightly, almost imperceptibly. She told him to be quiet without saying a word to him.

"Leave him alone."

"I can't do that, Lana," Alec sat on the arm of the settee. "You see someone is killing your husband's business partners, and I need to know why that is."

"I don't know anything about his business. I don't know anything about him anymore." A tear ran down her face, and Mamood got up and crossed over to her. He sat on the arm of the chair and put his arm around his frightened mother. She looked worn down and tired.

"Do you know where he is?" Will asked.

"No."

"Do you know where your father is, Mamood," Alec asked. Mamood kissed his mother's head and ignored the police detective. "Where were you last night, Mamood?" He looked up, but stayed silent.

"You came home wrapped in a blanket. Where were you, Mamood?" Will asked.

"Leave him alone," Lana demanded. He doesn't know anything, neither of us do. "Ask his father or Malik Shah."

"I would if we could find him, Lana," Alec teased. He could tell from her reaction that she was concerned. She pretended that she wasn't, but she was.

"What do you mean?" Lana wiped her eyes.

"We found his car abandoned in a car park," Will said.

"There was another bomb, Lana," Alec added. Her eyes widened in shock. There had been so much to take in over the last few days. It was a lot to absorb.

"Is he..?" She asked.

"We don't know, he's missing."

"I thought you said there was a bomb?" Mamood spoke for the first time.

"There was, near where we found your dad's car," Will explained. "We found the body of Dipak Pindar at the scene."

"Oh!" Lana put her hand over her mouth and looked stunned by the news. "He's Ash's cousin, Mamood called him Uncle."

"Tell them, Mum." Mamood stroked her hair and looked into her eyes. "All dad's friends from school are dead, and now Uncle Dipak too. You have to tell them."

"Tell us what, Mamood?" Alec looked into the boy's eyes. He looked terrified. "We can't protect your dad unless you tell us what's going on."

"I was kidnapped."

"Is this true, Lana?" Will asked incredulous.

"Is it?" Alec added pressure.

"Yes, yes!" She broke down in tears. "They said we couldn't tell the police or they would kill Mamood."

"Who was it?" Will asked. "Who kidnapped you, Mamood?"

"I don't know who he was," he said. "I only saw one, but I heard more of them."

"When did they let you go?" Alec played with the cleft on his chin while he pieced things together in his mind.

"Last night," Mamood said. "They chucked me into a van. The floor was metal. I was blindfolded. Then they untied me, gave me a blanket and dumped me on the pavement about half a mile away from home."

"Where did they take you from?"

"The reservoir near my school," Mamood blushed. "They sent me a letter from a girl at school. I went to meet her."

"What can you tell me about the man that took you?"

"He was big. He shot me with a stun gun thing." Mamood lifted up his sweatshirt and showed them the burn marks on his chest.

"Did he say anything to you?" Alec asked. The boy's voice was quivering as he remembered the ordeal.

"He asked how my dad was, and he said he was a wanker. Then he shot me."

"Wait a minute, did he ask you how your dad was, or did he use his name?"

"He said, 'how is Ash, is he still a wanker?', and then he shot me."

Alec looked at Will. The kidnapper knew his father's name, and used a shortened version of it. It indicated that they had a level of previous contact, and they were someone that knew him, even vaguely.

"What else did he say about your father," Will asked. "It doesn't matter how insignificant it is to you, it could be vital if we are to find out who did this to you."

"He said lots of bad things; he spent hours taunting me with newspaper cuttings and stories about him and uncle Malik."

"Tell me some of them, whatever you can remember."

"He said my father was a gangster, a drug dealer," Mamood stopped, his voice broken. He coughed and carried on. "He said my dad was a rapist, and that all his friends were rapists too."

"Did he say why or how he knew that?"

"No, not that I can remember, but he kept on saying that he had always been a bad man."

"What newspaper cuttings did he show you?"

"All kinds of stuff, mostly about drug addicts and dealers being killed."

"We need to get Mamood to the station, Lana. I want to have him checked over by our doctor, and he needs to be interviewed by our youth trauma team," Alec said. Lana nodded her agreement. She had no more fight left in her. "If Ashwan contacts you, then you must call me straight away. Do you understand?"

"Yes," she started to cry again. Alec made the call and within minutes, a marked police car was driving away with Lana and Mamood Pindar on board.

Alec and Will climbed into the Shogun. They hadn't said much while Lana and Mamood were still there, but they both had a different view of things now.

"I think we've been focusing on the wrong man," Alec began as he started the engine.

"You mean Pindar is the key?"

"Maybe not the key, but he's the weak link. We need to refocus the search onto Ashwan Pindar, dig back as far as the records go. We're still missing something, Will."

"I agree, Guv." Will frowned and shook his head. "What did he mean rapist?"

"I know that stuck in my mind too," Alec put his mobile onto hands free.

"I've been through Shah's record with a fine toothcomb, and there's no mention of any rape allegations, Guv. I wouldn't have missed that."

"He said that all his friends were rapists too."

"There was nothing in the records, Guv."

"You said the records went back to Shah's late teens, right?"

"Yes, Guv, eighteen I think."

"We need their juvenile records, Will. I think something happened before their adult records began," Alec's mind was racing. He speed dialled the MIT room.

"DC Wright, MIT," the voice answered the call.

"Jayne, it's Alec."

"Hello, Guv, what's up?" Jayne Wright was constantly perky. She was an officer that it was a pleasure to be around.

"I need the juvenile records pulling for Malik Shah, Ashwan Pindar and the rest of his corporate directors, and start with Pindar."

"Okay, Guv, I'm all over it, what am I looking for?"

"Look for allegations of rape, or anything that links them all."

"Okay, Guv, anything else?"

"Yes, pass a description of Ashwan Pindar to uniform. I want him brought back in for questioning." Alec wasn't sure where this new information would take them, but his senses told him that it was worthwhile following the lead. The kidnap could explain many things, the torture of Bruce Mann, and Kenny Richards for a start. Someone wanted answers to questions, and now he felt that he knew what they were asking. Who had kidnapped Mamood Pindar, and why?

51

David Bernstein

David Bernstein sat and waited. He was good at waiting. His time in the Israeli military taught him that waiting and watching was one of their best weapons against the insurgents. People are creatures of habit, and if you waited long enough you could learn their patterns of behaviour. Once you know how they behave, then it's easy to predict when and where they will be at their most vulnerable. Malik Shah was no different to the many targets he had tracked and killed in the Middle East. They were all much the same. He watched and learned their movements, identified their weaknesses and then neutralised them when they least expected it. Malik Shah had a weakness. Women. He had been abusing Malinda Singh since she was fourteen years old; David knew this after watching him closely. Malinda was his Achilles Heel. He had a thing for meeting women in hotels, and it was the only time he was separated from his goons.

Malinda Singh was sixteen now. For the last two years, she met Malik Shah at a Travel Inn every Thursday at two o'clock. Her father owed Malik money for a drug deal that went bad, and when he couldn't pay the money back Malik told him that his daughter could halt the interest on the debt. He refused at first but when two heavies beat him to a pulp in front of his wife and children, they realised that there wasn't really any other option. Malinda was beautiful. Her hair was jet and her eyes were brown. She was slim at the waist and curvy where she should be. At fourteen she looked like an Asian Barbie doll. Malik was an animal, and he ravaged her innocent body for all it was worth every week. Malinda cried every time he took her but it had little effect on Malik, if anything it turned him on. Malinda told him that she was going to kill herself if he didn't free her from her father's debt, but Malik told her that the debt would pass to her younger sister, and that thought was the only thing that kept her alive. Her life was a hell on earth and if she could have ended it all then she would rather than let that evil man touch her ever again. That was before she met David Bernstein.

David was tanned and handsome, and his body was wiry muscle, lean and defined. He watched her at the hotel, and followed Malinda home one day, waited a while and then knocked on her door. It was clear that this pretty, young girl wasn't meeting Malik Shah because of his magnetic personality. He had a hold over her family. She wept openly every time she left the Inn, and David could only guess what obscenities Shah enforced on her week in and week out. David introduced himself to her family, and bluntly offered them a way out of their nightmare. They were cautious at first but David was articulate and persuasive. He told them what Shah had done to his younger sister, and her suicide convinced Malinda that there was no way that she would be free of him. He was a monster. There was no other way out for them, and he pointed out that it was only a matter of time before Malik turned his attention to their younger daughter too. She was blossoming and he would take her as well. The debt would never be paid no matter what atrocities they endured as a family.

Malik Shah pulled into the Travel Inn car park in his BMW. He had a scowl on his face and he looked angry. The tyres screeched as he slammed the vehicle into a parking space. He got out of the car and reached inside for a bottle of red wine, and then he slammed the door closed and headed into the Travel Inn. Malinda shivered visibly in the passenger seat as she watched him go in.

"He looks so angry," she said quietly. He hurt her when he was in a good mood, but it always hurt much more when he was mad, and he was mad a lot. "I'm frightened."

"You don't have to be frightened. I'm right here and I'm not going anywhere, okay," David soothed her nerves. "You know what to do, right?"

Malinda nodded her head. She took the small vial that he had given her earlier, and she gripped it tightly in her hand. All she had do was put a few drops into his wine, and it would be lights out, and then her ordeal would be over forever. David Bernstein promised her, and she believed him.

"What if he pours his own wine?" she was desperately trying to be brave, but she was terrified.

"Does he ever do that?" David shook his head. He had the same pattern every time he met Malinda. They had been through it a dozen times. "He never does that, does he?"

"No, he makes me undress, and then I have to pour his wine. He drinks it while I," she looked embarrassed and ashamed. "Well, you know what I have to do."

"I know, and you don't have to do it ever again," David touched her hand to reassure her. She recoiled from his touch. It wasn't that she didn't like David, she did, but she couldn't bear to be touched by anyone anymore. Malik Shah had ruined her. She looked at him and gave him a nervous smile, and then opened the door and got out. David Bernstein watched her as she walked across the car park and into the reception.

5 2

MIT

"Shah is not at home, Guv, uniform have left an officer there in case he comes back," Will Naylor explained. A knock on the door interrupted them. "There's still no sign of Pindar."

"We're just about done going through this, Guv," Jayne Wright popped her head around the door. "I think we're ready to review."

"Okay we'll be there in a minute, Jayne," Alec stood up from the desk. Will unbuttoned his shirtsleeves and rolled them up as they walked. "I hope this isn't a waste of time."

The team were getting used to disappointment on this case, and the department was being flogged to death by the press. They were still following the line that Malik Shah and his business partners were being targeted by a right wing extremist group because they were Asian Muslims. For now, MI5 and the police department were happy to keep a lid on things by letting them speculate. Making a statement that they didn't have a clue what was going on would not instil the general public with confidence.

"Okay Jayne, what have we got?" Alec pulled a chair out and sat opposite her desk. Will leaned against the edge of the desk and folded his arms. He'd already seen the information that they'd gathered in snippets. Hearing how it all slotted together, if it did at all, would be interesting.

"You were right, there was an allegation of rape, Guv, made by a Sarah Bernstein, when they were still at school," she looked up from her computer screen. "That's why we didn't spot anything in their records."

"Who did she allege raped her?" Alec was thinking that it must be Ashwan Pindar, because of what the kidnapper had said to Mamood.

"All of them, Guv," Jayne raised her eyebrows. "She claimed that she was drugged and gang raped by them all at a party."

"Go on," Alec had a sick feeling in his stomach. He wasn't sure why, but he knew that they were on to something.

"She was dating Shah at the time of the incident. They were all brought in for questioning, and the files were sent to the CPS. They had a hearing and threw it out of the window. No charges were ever filed."

"Why not," Will asked. He grabbed a chair and sat next to the Superintendent.

"The girl admitted having consensual sex with Malik Shah, earlier that night, but she said that he had drugged her afterwards, and that's when the others abused her. The problem was that she had previously done sexual favours for them all at some time or another, at Shah's bequest. The Crown Prosecution didn't think that it would hold up in court."

"That could be what the kidnapper was referring to when he taunted Mamood," Will turned to Alec.

"Maybe," Alec said thoughtfully. "What happened was traumatic for the family, but it was decades ago. I'm not sure it has a bearing on our case, are you?"

"It could be enough for a motive back then, but I'm not sure about now, Guv."

"Have you traced the girl?"

"She's dead, Guv, suicide," Jayne flicked her computer screen. "She was pregnant when she jumped from Runcorn Bridge."

"Jesus," Alec shook his head and the lines around his eyes deepened. "Who's was the baby?"

"Have a guess."

"Malik Shah," Alec smiled.

"Give the man a cigar. According to the hearing notes she refused to have the baby aborted, claiming that it was Shah's, and that she loved him," Jayne shook her head incredulous at the thought. "That poor young girl, how desperate must she have been to have jumped off that bridge?"

"Was there any inquest into the suicide?"

"Yes, Guv. Malik Shah and his cousin Saj Shah were the last ones to see her alive. They claim that they took her out for a drive in Saj's Capri, got her stoned, had sex with her and then dropped her off at Runcorn train station. It's a short walk to the bridge, and no one recalls seeing her walking or jumping, although a lorry driver saw her on the pedestrian strip. At the inquest the turning point was her diary. The last entry in her diary said that she would rather die than be sent to Israel."

"Israel?"

"According to the social worker's notes, her father planned to send her to extended family over there while she had the child, to save the family any more embarrassment. The judge took that as a sign of intent to commit suicide."

"There were no witnesses to prove otherwise?"

"No, Guv, but this is where it gets really interesting," Jayne said.

"Come on, come on," Alec gestured with his arms. This was serious stuff, but he needed to lighten the mood a little. The information was shocking. Could it be reason enough to investigate further? Not so far, it was too long ago.

"Sarah had two brothers, Richard and David. They attended the same school as Shah and the others. Richard Bernstein was attacked and badly beaten, the year before Sarah's rape. He was on the way to school when the attack took place. He was stabbed numerous times, and nearly died."

Alec Ramsey didn't need to hear who was responsible, he already knew who had done it, but was it relevant to their case now?

"A witness made a statement that he saw a group of Asian teenagers attacking the Bernstein boy, and that they had the same school ties on as him," Jayne flicked the screen again.

"Malik Shah and the others?" Will asked.

"The police didn't know at the time, but they were the prime suspects, and they were questioned, but the witness withdrew his evidence. The police notes say that his house was vandalised and his dog was set on fire, by a group of Asian teenagers."

"They set his dog on fire?"

"According to the police files, it was the final straw and he withdrew his evidence, game over."

"I think our kidnapper was correct, they have always been bad," Alec frowned. There were plenty of motives for revenge here, but the time lapse was too great for it to be believable.

"Following the attack, Richard Bernstein couldn't remember, or he was too scared to tell the police who his attackers were, but when Sarah's case was thrown out, so was the assault. He eventually blamed Ashwan Pindar for the stabbing. The prosecution felt that Richard may have fingered Ashwan for the assault as a result of his sister's rape case collapsing."

"That is a family that must have a grudge against Shah and his amigos," Will said. "If it was my sister then I wouldn't be responsible for my actions"

"It doesn't end there," Jayne held up her hand to stop him jumping in at the deep end. "After Sarah's death, the older brother David was attacked in the park by Malik Shah's cousin Saj Shah and two of his friends. They alleged that David had smashed the windscreen of their Capri with a brick."

"The Capri that Sarah was in on the night she died?" Will was angry just listening to this. "I'm not surprised."

"Yes, they chased Bernstein and there was a fight. Witnesses reported that David Bernstein knocked Saj Shah unconscious to the ground, and was then knocked out himself by another boy. He was with a friend, Nick Cross. When David was knocked out, Cross swung a lead pipe, fracturing one boy's face, before he turned it on Shah. Shah was still out of it when he fractured his skull and ruptured his brain."

The team were silent as they listened to the story unfold. Jayne looked at their faces and she could see the impact that this story was having on them.

"Cross got a life sentence for murder, and Bernstein was charged with affray."

"Where are they now?" Alec asked.

"We are still checking that out, Guv."

"Find them. I want to know where every member of the Bernstein family is and I want to know today."

53

M a l i k   S h a h

Malik Shah was a troubled man. He was past angry, he was livid The men attacking his organisation were skilled and determined, there was no doubt about it. The problem was that he didn't know who the perpetrators were, or why he was being attacked. The ransom paid for Mamood was peanuts to him, and his enemies would know that. Why didn't they ask for more? He was the head of the crime family, so why hadn't they tried to assassinate him? His directors were dead. They had worked together since their school days. Now there was only Ashwan remaining. Could it be Ashwan plotting all this? Was he setting Malik up to take over the business? He didn't think so. The businesses that they owned would all revert back to the corporation, so he wouldn't lose financially. The pay and bonus payments that would have been paid to his dead associates would mean his personal income would significantly increase, as would Ashwan's share, but that wasn't the point. The point was that someone was picking him off from a distance, and they were doing it well. The ransom drop was the only opportunity they'd had to get near to the enemy, but they had planned it too well for them to get near the pickup. A knock at the door disturbed his thoughts. It would be Malinda. She would take his mind off the chaos for a while. She wasn't going to enjoy what he had in mind, but he didn't care. She would do as she was told.

"You're late," he snarled as he opened the door. Malinda stood in the doorway shaking. She always did when she was near Malik, but that was okay. He liked it when women were frightened of him it was so much more fun. "Come in, hurry up."

Malinda kept her eyes fixed to the floor. She could never look him in the eye. Her hands were shaking as she put down her handbag. The drug that David Bernstein gave her was hidden in her underwear.

"Get undressed," Malik ordered. She looked good. She always did. Her figure was perfect for now, but it would spoil as she aged, especially if the bitch had a few kids. He didn't care anyway, he'd have her while she looked good. Malinda peeled off her shirt and folded it onto the chair. Her breaths were coming in short gasps and her skin covered in Goosebumps. "What's the matter with you?"

"I'm not feeling well," her voice was shaking too. She wasn't sure if she could go through with this. What would she do if he caught her? He would kill her for sure. "I'm on my period." She lied. Sometimes it stopped him, other times it didn't.

"Shut up and get undressed, you're getting what I give you, bleeding or not," Malik grabbed a handful of her hair. He pulled it hard and yanked her head toward him. She gasped and closed her eyes as he forced his tongue into her mouth. He held her head in a vice like grip and pushed his mouth hard to hers. She gagged unable to breath. "Do you like that?" He pulled her hair harder and sneered in her face. "I said do you like that, you slut?"

Malinda knew from past experience that the answer was yes. He would get violent if she didn't. "Yes, I like it." She felt sick.

"Take this off," he slapped her backside hard and pulled at her skirt. Malinda closed her eyes as she unzipped the back.

The skirt fell over her hips onto the floor. She stepped out of it and tried to turn away from him, but he held her tight. He slipped his free hand down her back and squeezed her buttocks hard. His fingers made for the middle and he fumbled with her roughly. Malinda was cringing inside as he unclipped her bra. She bit her top lip as he squeezed her nipples painfully hard. "Do you like that?"

"Yes," she sighed desperate to get away from there. She wanted to cry, but that turned him on and she needed to slow things down. Her fear was exciting him. "I need the toilet first."

"Fucking hell! Hurry up you stupid bitch." Malik let her hair go. He walked to the dressing table and opened his red wine. Malinda ran into the bathroom wearing only her knickers. She was sick with worry. What if he poured his own wine, what then? She couldn't let him use her body again, she just could not. Her stomach was knotted with angst and she felt like she would vomit. She looked at herself in the mirror and breathed in deeply. She had to get a grip if she was to break this cycle. David Bernstein offered her a way out of this hellish situation, and she could see no other choice. Her mascara had run and she pulled toilet roll off and wiped it away from her eyes. A few more minutes, that's all she had to do and she would be free of him forever, David promised. Another deep breath and she was ready to face him for the final time. She reached for the door handle and opened it.

Malik was naked, sitting on a two-seater couch under the window. He grinned at her as she looked at him. Malik revelled in her discomfort. He grabbed her hand as she walked by, and forced her to touch his erection. She tried to pull away but he wasn't letting go. Reluctantly she pulled him for what seemed like an age. In reality, it was a minute at most.

"Get me my wine," Malik released her. He wanted her mouth around him and he liked to sip his wine while he watched her sucking. Malinda knew the routine well. She hoped that he wouldn't see her slipping the Flunitrazepam into his drink, and she hoped that it would take effect before she had to go near him with her mouth. Despite being forced to do it more times than she could remember, she didn't think that she could do it again, not even for a minute. She slipped the vial out of her knickers and snapped off the top. She tipped it into the glass before she poured the wine. A trickle of sweat ran from her hairline across her temple and down her cheek. David told her to let the drug saturate the wine by leaving it a few seconds before giving it to him. Her hands were shaking as she turned to face him.

Malik was right behind her when she turned. Her eyes widened in shock and she gasped in surprise. She put her hand to her mouth. He took the wine glass from her hand and held it under his nose. He sniffed the red liquid and stared into her eyes. A sneer crossed his lips.

"This is my favourite wine," he whispered as he grabbed her hair again. "Smell it." He pushed the glass to her face. Melinda closed her eyes and sniffed at it. It smelled like red wine to her, nothing else. She prayed that he thought the same. Had he seen her put the drug into his drink? Was he standing behind her watching as she did it? If he was then she was as good as dead. "Taste it." He put it to her lips.

"No." She tried to be assertive. "You know I don't drink at all."

"Oh, yes, I forgot," he answered sarcastically. "Melinda the little angel." Malik took a swallow of the wine and then forced his lips onto hers. He twisted her hair around his hand and pulled it painfully. Melinda knew what was coming next. He would push her head down. She felt her stomach turning at the thought. How could she stop this? In her mind she wanted David to kick the door in and rescue her, but that wasn't going to happen. She was on her own with the beast that had stolen her innocence time after time, after time, and relished every minute of it. He took another long swallow and grinned. Malinda put her hand down and gently stroked him. She smiled at him and squeezed it harder, trying to pleasure him while the drug took effect, and she pushed the glass to his mouth playfully. He tipped back his head and emptied it in one mouthful.

Malik felt strange. The anticipation of the sex that was to come always made him high. Melinda seemed to be compliant, which was unusual. She was stroking him without being told to, and that was giving him a rush, but something was wrong. His head felt numb for a moment, as if everything had stopped in time. When it restarted, it was in slow motion. The sex was his priority, and he wanted her to kneel down in front of him.

"Aaah," Malik tried to speak, but it came out as a sound. It was an incoherent gurgle. It came as a surprise to him that he couldn't speak. He could see Malinda look at his eyes, as if she was aware that something was wrong. She studied his face with interest. His muscles felt weak and they tingled. He wanted to move but he couldn't. His eyes were open, but the world seemed to elongate as he looked around. A wardrobe throbbed like a giant heart against the wall, growing bigger and then smaller with every beat. Melinda pushed him backward slowly toward the bed. Somewhere in his mind, he thought she was going to have sex with him, but another part of his brain screamed that something was very wrong. In his peripheral vision, he could see the bed behind him. It seemed to be creeping up on him. He tried to speak again, but his jaw wouldn't respond to his brain's commands. His tongue seemed floppy and useless. Melinda was smiling now, and a look of contempt came over her face. She looked at him with a hatred in her eyes that he couldn't understand right now. How dare she look at him like that, the bitch? He would make her suffer for that, if he could move his muscles, but he was immobile. What was going on?

"You bastard!" Melinda slapped him across the face. His lip split and a trickle of blood dribbled at the corner of his mouth. He felt the slap, and he felt the pain, but he couldn't respond. A part of his brain couldn't comprehend what was happening to him, but another section knew exactly what was going on. She had drugged him. Something was in the wine. The bitch had drugged him. She was dead, her family were dead, and he would crucify them all to a telegraph pole. Melinda pushed him hard, and he flew backwards onto the bed. His muscles had no density to them and he felt like he was made from jelly. Melinda kneeled over him and punched him in the nose. He saw the punch coming but he couldn't move out of the way. His eyes watered with the pain and he could feel his blood running down the back of his throat, but he couldn't move. She moved out of his field of vision, but he could hear her dressing, and he could hear her breathing. Her breathing sounded like wind blowing through an alleyway, almost a whistle. Sound became exaggerated as the drug took hold of his mind. When the drug wore off, he would slit her throat.

It was a strange feeling being aware of what was happening, but not being able to do anything about it. 'Rohypnol,' his mind screamed. She has tipped you Rohypnol. How many times have you used that drug yourself? How many woman have you raped and abused using that drug? Their faces flashed through his mind, teenagers mostly, frightened confused expressions and tears, lots of tears. How many young lives did you shatter using Rohypnol? He'd lost count. One of them killed herself, the stupid Jewish slut, Bernstein. They all had her while the same drug that immobilised you now, paralysed her. Melinda had given him the date rape drug that was for sure. His mind now asked the question why. Why would the bitch drug him? It was then that he felt real fear.

"It's done, he's on the bed," he heard Melinda's voice. She was calling someone on the telephone, but who? Was she talking to the people that paid her to drug him? Could it be her father? What about the men that had killed the others? Whatever the answer was, it wasn't good. He heard her talking and tried to make sense of it. "Shall I call them now?"

"Hello reception, I need an ambulance to room thirty-nine please, it's an emergency," she made another call to reception. Why drug him then call an ambulance? What was she doing? The room was spinning, but he could sense that she was still there. Time seemed to warp. He didn't know how long he'd been on his back when a knock on the door came.

"Tell me what happened?" A voice said.

"Thanks for getting here so quickly, I've only just placed the call," the manager looked nervous. The idea of losing a customer on site had him in a panic. It was his first posting as a hotel manager, and he didn't want any major incidents to mar his record.

"That's okay, sir, we were only around the corner when we responded."

"I'm the manager, is there anything we can do?" Another voice spoke, but he couldn't see any of them.

"No, thank you, we'll take it from here," the first voice spoke again. Malik was feeling worse. His hearing was echoing, and the voices distorted. The ambulance men were here now. He would be safe. That bitch was dead when he came around.

"You can leave it to us now, Melinda," a man's voice said. There was the hint of an accent, just a faint one, but he couldn't place it. "It's all over, go home, Melinda."

What was over? Who was telling the bitch to go home? Malik felt nauseous, and he was frightened that if he vomited he would choke. Rough hands pulled him into a sitting position. Two men held him upright. They wore lime green paramedic jumpsuits and hi-viz waistcoats. He watched Melinda reach the door. She turned and looked at him. It was the first time he'd ever seen her smile, and he was surprised how pretty she was.

There was a sparkle in her eyes that he'd never seen before. A voice called him.

"Malik," the voice echoed. He looked toward the voice and a fat medic was talking to him through the drug-induced haze. "Malik." He said again. The fat man held him while the second man pushed a trolley toward the edge of the bed. Between them, they lifted him onto it, half sitting half lying. "Malik."

Malik looked to the voice again as they strapped him to the gurney. The fat paramedic grinned at him, and the grin warped in his mind to a nightmare clown face. "Hello, Malik, remember me?"

Malik was confused. The words echoed through his mind, 'remember me?' 'remember me?' 'remember me?'. The drugs were slowing his thoughts, but his instincts screamed that he was in terrible danger. The fat face filled his vision. It was familiar, but it was in a part of his brain that handled distant memories.

"I'm Richard Bernstein, do you remember me?" the medic whispered in his ear as they pushed the trolley across the hotel room. "Sarah's brother, Richard, do you remember?"

Malik tried to get up but his muscles were useless. His head lolled to one side and his tongue poked out of the corner of his mouth. His memory cells sparked and the names rang through his brain like a peel of bells. Bernstein, Bernstein, Bernstein. The fat Jew that they battered in the park, and his sister, a little slut she was.

"You remember Sarah, Malik?" The fat medic tormented him as they trundled down the corridor. "You raped her, remember?"

'Remember?' Remember?' Remember?'

He remembered the bitch killed herself, and the inquest, and he remembered that the older brother and his friend had killed his cousin, Saj. The friend went down for life and Malik paid money for him to be hit while he served his sentence, but the hit man ended up dead himself, and Malik lost interest as his empire began to make demands on his time.

"Hello Malik," the other medic smiled at him as they reached the corridor. His face morphed into a long scream, the eyes were black holes and the mouth a gaping black hole. "I'm David," He said. "David Bernstein, you remember?"

Malik tried to shout for help, but he couldn't. He could hear other voices as he past reception and then he felt the breeze as they exited the hotel.

"Will he be okay?" the hotel manager asked as they left. Malik wanted to shout to him, and tell him that he wasn't okay at all. He was far from okay. His mouth flopped open and nothing came out.

"Oh, he'll be fine. We'll look after him well, wont we, Mr Shah," David Bernstein said as they lifted him into the back of an ambulance. They switched on the siren and drove out of the car park with their patient on board. Nick followed them off the car park in Malik Shah's BMW.

The hotel manager was relieved that the guest was in safe hands, but his relief only lasted for a short time. It was fifteen minutes later when the real ambulance crew arrived.

5 4

M I T

The Divisional Commander sat at his desk and listened intently to what his Detective Superintendent was telling him. The press were right, someone was targeting Shah's people, but not because of their religion, it was a purely personal motive. That was the way the evidence that MIT had uncovered was looking.

"So you think that the Bernstein family are responsible for the bombing campaign?" The Commander found it hard to take in.

"I wasn't sure until we traced their current whereabouts," Alec explained. "It adds up if you look at the evidence."

"Run it by me, what changed your mind?"

"We traced them and pulled their personal records," Alec began. "Richard Bernstein went to university and became a PHD in chemical engineering. He holds several patents for fertiliser based mass crop production. His second subject for his Honours degree was the history of Irish politics and terrorist mentality."

"You think he's our bomb maker?" the Commander asked.

"He's a chemical expert with a detailed knowledge of terrorist tactics. The van bomb was made by someone with an intricate knowledge of Irish republican explosive devices."

"Okay Richard Bernstein has motive, and the knowhow.

I'll accept that part of your theory for now."

"His older brother, David went to Israel when he left school," Alec changed the page he was reading notes from. "He joined the military on a commission, and became a Captain, in the Special Operations Unit known as the Sayeret Duuvedevan."

"That means nothing to me, Alec," the Commander shook his head. His double chins folded over his crisp white collar, and Alec noticed that the grey hairs, which grew from his ears, were out of control.

"They infiltrate enemy states, identify, track and then neutralise terrorist leaders."

"Bloody hell!" the Commander raised his bushy eyebrows. "Assassins?"

"Israel's finest, Commander."

"I'm assuming that he is still in the army?"

"They never really leave, they become reservists, but David Bernstein is listed as being on active duty, whereabouts unknown," Alec raised his hands as he spoke. "The Israeli military were not very forthcoming I'm afraid."

"I bet," the Commander, agreed. "So he could be here."

"We're checking flight lists into the country for the last six months. Nothing so far, but I think he's here."

"Is that it?" the Commander mulled over the information. It was compelling evidence and definitely put the Bernstein family on the suspect list. MI5 had nothing on extremists or rival gunrunners and the organised crime units had drawn a blank too. The only tangible evidence of a suspect was the events of decades ago.

"Not quite," Alec sat forward and showed the Commander a picture of Nick Cross. "This is Nick Cross. He went down for the murder of Saj Shah, the cousin of Malik Shah after a fight over Sarah's death."

"I read that bit in the report," the Commander wasn't sure what the relevance of Cross was.

"He was released on licence seven months ago from HMP Kennet," Alec said. The Commander looked up from the picture. "We checked his visitation records and the only visitor he had outside of his immediate family, was Richard Bernstein. He saw him every month without fail, all the way through his sentence."

"He was young when he went to prison."

"Yes, he was. The only blip on his record was the death of Asian prisoner three years into his term. The prisoner was found hanging in his cell, but there were concerns that it may not have been suicide. There were rumours that he'd been paid to kill Cross, but he got wind of it and took the guy out before he could try anything. There was an investigation, but nothing proven."

"Why wait so long to avenge what happened to their sister?" The Commander asked.

"I think they were waiting for Nick Cross to be released from jail," Alec replied.

The commander sat back in his chair, He placed his palms together in a praying position, and he leaned his chin on the top. The motives were plain to see now they had the information in front of them. Nick Cross's release from incarceration, coincided with David Bernstein's disappearance from the military radar, and both were a matter of a few months before the trouble started. That would account for a detailed planning phase.

"Do you know where Bernstein is?"

"We have an address for Richard. It's a farm on the outskirts of the city. I'm guessing we'll find all three of them there," Alec said confidently.

"If they are responsible for this, Alec you'll need armed backup and the bomb squad with you."

"They are on standby, Commander."

"Bring them in, Alec," the Commander slapped his fist

on the desk. The death and destruction over the last ten days was unprecedented. It brought an unprecedented number of headaches along with it. Alec stood up and headed for the door.

"Superintendent," the Commander called as he left.

"Yes, Sir?" Alec turned.

"You be careful."

Alec nodded but he didn't reply. They were going to walk into the lion's den, and he had a sneaking suspicion that the Bernsteins would be ready for them when they arrived. He had a hunch that they were working to a timetable, and time was running out.

55

Runcorn Bridge

It was dark when Ashwan woke. He could feel the wind buffeting the car, but he couldn't remember what car he was in. Rain bounced off the roof and it sounded like he was in a car wash. There were flashing lights all around him and he couldn't understand why. His head ached and his limbs were stiff, as if he had pins and needles everywhere. He was in the driving seat of a BMW. The brand emblem in the centre of the steering wheel told him that. He wasn't one hundred percent sure, but it smelled like Malik's car. His strong Armani cologne lingered in the vehicle. Above him, a colossal steel archway was illuminated against the night sky. He looked left beyond the handrail, and the abyss the other side of it. A dark sandstone railway bridge stretched off into the distance. Huge medieval shields adorned the giant towers, Britannia's crest emblazoned on them. He was parked on Runcorn Bridge, but he couldn't for the life of him think why. To his left was a highway patrol vehicle, an officer was placing plastic cones around the vehicle to guide the traffic into the outside lanes. His memory began to come back to him. He remembered the kidnap, and he remembered accepting a lift from a highway patrol. It was a blank after that. Had Malik come for him after the ransom drop?

"Hello, Ashwan," Richard Bernstein said. He sat in the back of the BMW. "You don't look so good."

"Who are you?" Ashwan tried to turn around in the seat, and then he realised that he was strapped to the seat with thick elastic bungee cords. "What the fuck is going on?" he struggled against the restraints.

"Oh, don't you remember me, Ash?" Richard put a silenced Mac-10 against the back of his head and smiled at him in the rear view mirror. "I remember you every time I take a shower. I still have the scars."

Ashwan stared at him in the mirror. His face was in the shadows but the flashing lights illuminated it momentarily. He was dark haired and fat. There was something familiar about him, but he couldn't place it.

"I don't know you," Ash began to think that this was part of the kidnap. His head was beginning to clear a little. "Did you take my son? Where is he? What do you want, more money?"

"Your son is home, safe and sound, only now he knows what a murdering rapist tosspot his father is."

"He's home?" Ash looked confused. They had lived up to their side of the bargain. "So why am I here, you going to ransom me now too?"

"No, we're past the money stage, Ash, we want to see you rot in hell with your rapist friends. I just want you to know who is behind this, before you die."

"Rapists?" Ash frowned. "What are you talking about?" Then it hit him like a steam train travelling at full speed. "Richard Bernstein?"

"Well done."

"Look, I had nothing to do with your sister dying."

"You did, Ashwan. You are as guilty as Shah is. You raped her at that party didn't you?"

"I didn't," Ashwan realised what it had all been about now. They were clueless why they were being wiped out and now he knew. "The others did, but I didn't touch her."

"Bye, Ashwan," Richard pressed the muzzle hard against his head. "Mamood and your wife will know the truth about you by now, and I bet they don't shed a tear over you."

"Wait," Ashwan, gasped. "Wait, please, look I'll give you whatever amount of money you want. I'm sorry for what I did to you and I'm sorry about your sister."

"Sorry doesn't cut it, excuse the pun." Richard leaned forward pressing the muzzle harder behind his ear. "Admit the truth. Did you rape Sarah?" Richard hit him with the gun. "Think very carefully what you're answer will be, you have got seconds to live you maggot."

"Okay, okay, please," Ashwan was panicking. His eyes filled with tears and his lips started quivering.

"Are you scared?"

"What?"

"Are you scared?"

"Of course I am, you've already murdered the others, but I can give you millions. You could call it compensation. I have a wife and child, Richard. I've changed."

"Sarah had a family and a child inside her when you maggots raped her. I don't think your wife is going to be around very long when she finds out the truth, do you?"

"Name your price, three million, four?"

"Did you rape Sarah, last chance?"

"Yes, and I'm sorry, Richard," Ashwan Pindar was about to apologise again when Richard pulled the trigger. A nine-millimetre bullet drilled its way through the seat and tore through the base of his spine. It ricocheted off his pelvis and travelled down his thigh, tearing muscle and ligament tissue, before ripping of a chunk of kneecap off as it exited. Ashwan tried to scream but Richard gagged him with a gloved hand.

"You're sorry, Ash?" Richard yanked his head sideways. "Do you see that safety rail?"

Ashwan nodded his head rapidly. Tears flowed freely down his face and mucus bubbles blew from his nostrils.

"Sarah jumped from there. Can you imagine how scared she was when you fucking pigs raped her one at a time?" Richard pulled his head backward hard. "Can you imagine how scared she was before she tossed herself over there, can you?"

Ashwan gritted his teeth and tried to fight through the pain barrier. His clothes and the seat beneath him were soaked with his blood. He was going to bleed to death in minutes, and he knew it. The highway patrol officer looked in the window and saw the gun and the blood. Ashwan thought he would intervene and call him an ambulance, but he ignored his pleading expression and laughed. An ambulance pulled alongside and the highway patrol officer moved the cones and let it pull in. Ashwan was confused when the officer looked at him and winked his eye. He lifted a hand and waved goodbye to him as darkness crept through his mind. Richard Bernstein unclipped the elastic cords and let him slump against the steering wheel.

5 6

The Farm

The decision was made to raid the farm under the cover of darkness. Ashwan Pindar and Malik Shah were both missing and concerns for their safety were not shared by everyone. Alec Ramsay was convinced that they were either hiding, kidnapped as Mamood had been, or they were the latest victims of the Mosque bombers. The farm owned by Richard Bernstein was situated in a wide valley with gentle grassy slopes leading down to the stream, which flowed through it. Thick woodland formed the perimeter of the farm. The armed response unit were ready to move, but Alec wasn't happy. There were no lights on in the farmhouse or any of the other outbuildings.

"It looks to me like there's no one home," Alec said, looking through night sights. Thermal imaging was picking up nothing either. "I'm concerned that the place will be booby trapped."

"They could be in the cellar system," Will commented, looking at the plans of the building. "We wouldn't see a heat trail down there would we?"

"No, not with this equipment," Inspector Green, replied. He was the unit leader on call with the armed response team. "We could check the outbuildings first, Alec, and then take it from there?"

"Okay start with the stable block here, and keep your eyes open. This bomb maker is in a different league," Alec frowned, deepening the creases in his face. He swept the blond fringe from his face and let out a deep breath. There would be plenty more grey strands on his head when this case was all over, that was for certain. "The bomb squad have finished with the yard, yes?"

"Yes, Guv, they've swept it and found nothing."

"Move in."

Alec and Will donned bulletproof jackets and followed the armed unit as they advanced toward the farm buildings. The farm was silent apart from the sound of the water running through it. Armed officers wearing full body armour, Kevlar helmets and combat boots moved silently in a four by four, cover formation. One unit approached the stables, while another unit readied by the barn.

"Black one, ready to penetrate," came over the coms unit.

"Black two, ready," the second troop called in.

"Roger that, you have a green light."

The doors were opened and the armed officers swooped through them with practised ease. Torch light flickered as they moved through the buildings.

"Black one, clear."

"Black two, clear."

"Roger that."

Alec and Will looked through the outbuildings they had searched, as the troops prepared to search the workshops and enter the farmhouse. They were empty. There wasn't a cobweb or a layer of dust to be seen.

"This isn't right," Alec said. "The place is spotless."

"It's the cleanest farm I've ever seen," Will said. "Not that I've seen many, but this place has been scrubbed from top to bottom, recently."

"I think whatever they were doing here is already done,"

Alec said. They walked across the farmyard and waited for the armed officers to breach the farmhouse. Alec remembered the van at the Mosque. It was clean as were the other devices that the bombers had used. They left no evidence behind them wherever they operated. He didn't think that the farm would be any different, unless they had left any nasty surprises.

"Superintendent, we're ready to move into the workshop and the farmhouse," the Inspector called on the coms.

"Move in, but leave the cellar areas for now," Alec had a bad feeling about it. The lengths that the Bernsteins had gone to not to leave any evidence was just one indicator of how much planning they had put into the attacks.

"Roger that."

"Black one, ready."

"Black two, ready."

"Roger that, green light."

The armed officers moved like shadows and the support teams held their breath and waited for the 'clear', call to come. Long minutes went by as the teams searched the workshop.

"Black two, workshop clear."

"Roger that."

Alec glanced at his watch as torchlight flickered from inside the farmhouse. Eventually the call came through the coms.

"Black one, the farmhouse is clear."

"Roger that."

Alec skipped the workshops and headed into the house. It had been stripped of furniture and ornaments, and cleaned from top to bottom. There wasn't a light bulb or lampshade left anywhere.

"Is it the same upstairs?" Alec asked.

"Roger that, Guv, It's empty. It doesn't look like it's been used for years up there."

"Mamood said he thought he might have been underground, because there were no windows, and no noise," Will thought aloud. "Ashwan Pindar and Malik Shah could be down there now, and so could the bombers."

"I don't like this, something isn't right," Alec turned to Will. "Get everyone out of here. I want the bomb squad in to sweep the cellars first."

"We should check that it's safe down there first, Superintendent," Inspector Green was disappointed that his teams wouldn't be the first in. "I must insist armed response sweep first, Sir."

"Get your men out of the building and pull everyone back a hundred yards, and do it now," Alec growled across the coms network. "Captain Bishpam, I want one officer in the blast suit to check out the basement. There's something not right here and the bombers haven't put a foot wrong so far."

Captain Bishpam was an officer in the Army. The Royal Logistics Core were the world's foremost Explosive Ordinance Disposal experts. He was seconded to the police bomb squad, as an advisor, and a trainer. Bishpam had three tours of Iraq, and two tours of Afghanistan behind him, and he missed being in the front line. He felt as if he was letting his Army unit down being on secondment with the police. Members of the logistics core were dying every week trying to make safe improvised devices in Afghanistan, and he felt that he should there alongside them. His police team were good, loyal and brave, but they had little real experience of locating and defusing terrorist devices. He was the most experienced member by far, and as such, he would wear the suit. The blast suit was a full body armour kit designed to protect technicians who were looking for or defusing bombs. They were nicknamed Demon Suits, because of the high number of men that died wearing them. The reality of the situation was that if you were in the blast radius of a bomb, with or without the Demon Suit, then you were dead. Bishpam wouldn't allow anyone to don that suit in live theatre, except himself.

"Roger, Superintendent, I'll check it out myself, give me ten minutes to climb into it," the Captain said. He was aware of the skill of the bomber, he'd been called to every scene to inspect the devices, or what was left of them. "You got a hunch, Alec?"

"It's not right, Captain. Why clean down the outbuildings and the stables?"

"You've got me there," the Captain sounded muffled as he struggled into the heavy suit. The clumsy suit offered bomb technicians a small amount of protection during reconnaissance procedures. It protected from fragmentation, blast pressure and the thermal and tertiary effects of an explosion, but their effectiveness was limited if a device detonated in close proximity. "What are you thinking?"

"Let's say they were done here. If they were going to level the place and they had left anything in the buildings above ground, then there would be evidence left in the rubble, right?" Alec explained his hunch on the coms. The officers of every unit there could hear them, and he made sense. "Anything below the buildings could be destroyed with say, incendiary devices maybe?"

"You think the bomb factory was below ground?"

"Where would you build them if you were the bomb maker?"

"In the cellar, no doubt about it," the bomb squad Captain agreed. Five minutes later, he was suited up and ready. The rest of the teams were pulled back away from the house. The Captain checked the plans one more time before he neared the house and he noticed a shaded area beneath the workshops.

"Superintendent," the coms clicked into life and the voice of the Captain came over.

"Go ahead, Captain."

"I think the cellars run beneath the workshops too, Alec. There's a shaded area on the plans, best to move your men away from that building."

"Roger that, move everyone back from the workshop area," Alec ordered. "You're green light to go in, Captain."

"Roger that." The Captain and his bulky suit squeezed through the doorway sideways, and he disappeared into the darkness.

57

The Bridge

Ashwan was bleeding heavily, but he would live for a while. He couldn't move, that was the point in shooting him in the back. Nick and David carried Malik from the ambulance and they plonked him in the back of the BMW. He was doped and compliant, and unable to move for now. His surroundings were confusing to him, but he knew that he was in trouble. The wind and rain blew into the car as he was manhandled into the back seat. The world was spinning, and he closed his eyes to steady his mind. The door slammed closed and everything became quiet. The wind stopped blowing and he could hear traffic passing by but the sound was soothing. He opened his eyes and saw the flashing lights of an ambulance. The vehicle was pulling away. A highway patrol truck was parked alongside his BMW in between it and the traffic. It blocked the view of passing motorists. The engine started, and it too pulled away. The passenger window opened and a hand waved goodbye to him as it drove away.

Malik tried to get his bearings. He was in the backseat of his own car. He recognised the dashboard and the leather seats. Why was he in the backseat, he couldn't remember. Next to his right hand was a reactivated Mac-10 machinegun. He bought them and sold them in their thousands, but he rarely saw them.

The police had been chasing him for decades, but he'd been too clever for them to be caught. Everything had been perfect until the bastards that planted bombs turned up. He remembered the hotel room. He was about to fuck Melinda, wasn't he? Yes, he was right. She'd drugged him, and then the ambulance turned up. Bernstein, remember me? The ambulance men kept repeating it. Bernstein, remember me? He did remember them, they'd taken him from the hotel, it echoed, remember me? They were at the hotel. Why?

He remembered that Sarah Bernstein was their sister. Her face flashed into his mind. She was pretty, but then it warped into a frightened face. She was crying, but she couldn't speak, and Ashwan was on top of her paralysed body, pumping her while she sobbed. The faces of is school friends were there, holding her down, probing her and squeezing her body. They were laughing. The sound of laughter echoed around his brain, and then it turned to screaming.

The image disappeared, and he looked at the machinegun again. Sweat ran down his face. His hand twitched and he touched it with his fingers. If he could reach it, he would shoot the fat ambulance man, Richard fucking Bernstein in the face, and then he would kill his brother. Fucking Bernsteins, they'd been a pain in his arse from day one. They should have killed the fat Jew when they had the chance. What were they doing now? Where had they gone? He remembered the ambulance pulling away. Were they in it? His mind was processing information a little quicker than it had. The effects of the Flunitrazepam seemed to be wearing off. Where was he? He looked up and around, taking in detail for the first time since he'd arrived. How long was it since the ambulance men closed the door and left him? Time had no meaning for now.

Malik suddenly realised that there was someone in the driver's seat. They were slumped over the wheel. The sound of passing engines became louder, and he recognised the fact headlights were flashing by, illuminating the interior of the BMW every few minutes. He was at the side of a road. Intricate steel framework surrounded the road and it disappeared into the sky above him. Runcorn Bridge echoed from the far edges of his mind. He was in his car on the bridge. The car was surrounded by traffic cones, each one fitted with a flashing yellow light on top of it. He needed to know who the driver was.

Malik moved his right hand and then tried his left. His motor neurone functions were returning to him. He made a fist with his hands as the movement returned. The man in the front looked like Ashwan Pindar. Malik leaned forward, his head between the front seats.

"Ash," Malik said. It came out as a gasp. "Ashwan." This time it sounded like he had marbles in his mouth. He reached forward and grabbed the back of his jacket. He tugged as hard as his muscles allowed him to. Ash groaned and slumped back in the seat. "Ashwan, what's wrong with you?" Malik looked at his hand. It was covered in Ash's blood. He looked down and noticed the bullet hole in the seat, and the corresponding wound at the base of his spine. "Shit!"

Malik looked around for something to stop the bleeding. Next to him on the backseat was a sports bag. He reached for the zip, his limbs responding better now. His head was woozy but he felt in control of his body. He unzipped the bag and opened it. His eyes struggled in the dark; the passing headlights offered him some help as they lit up the interior of the vehicle. He reached inside and fumbled with the contents. His hands touched a tightly wrapped package. The plastic wrapping crackled as he handled it. He pulled it out. Cocaine. Malik reached in again and pulled out a second package with the same result. Cocaine. It was the cocaine from the ransom drop. Three kilos of it, which would equate to about fifteen years in jail.

"Ashwan, wake up!" Malik felt alone for the first time in his adult life. There had always been someone there to help him out of trouble, help him fight his battles, or to take the blame. He looked around the car. On top of the dashboard was another Mac-10. It was wedged above the steering wheel resting on the heater vents. Malik assessed the situation in his befuddled mind. He was sat in his car with a machinegun in his hand. The driver had been shot through the back, and there was three kilos of cocaine on the seat next to him. It was then that he heard the first police siren approaching.

58

The Farm

Captain Bishpam reached the top of the cellar stairs. There was a light switch on the left, fixed to the wall, but it was an obvious place to fix a booby trap, so he ignored it. He switched on a head torch, which was fitted to the blast suit. The stairs were crafted from pine and stained with a clear varnish. The torch light swept the floor space that he could see from the top of the stairs. There was a gel substance spread evenly across the floor. The floor seemed to be a concrete base, covered in self-levelling cement. It had been painted red with floor-paint and the gel made it look wet in the torch light.

"Black three," Bishpam made his call sign. He took the first two steps slowly, looking for tripwires or fine metal filament, which could be a trigger for a bomb.

"Go, ahead, Captain."

"The floor is coated in a gel, I'm guessing it's an accelerant of some type, or a Hypergolic liquid. The place stinks of chemicals."

"Roger that, Captain, get out of there," Alec knew the cellar was rigged, and the Captain had confirmed it.

"I'll get half way down the staircase then I can get a proper view of the cellar," Bishpam held the handrail and moved awkwardly down the steps. He ducked and scanned the cellar with the head torch. A camera fixed next to it relayed pictures back to the bomb squad command vehicle. There were workbenches lined up symmetrically along the length of the cellar, and the walls were lined with shelving. The shelves were packed with electrical gadgets. Stereo systems, video recorders, and televisions were piled high. "Are you getting this?"

"Roger, Captain, we're seeing it. It's an Aladdin's cave of electronic spare parts, right?"

"Right," Bishpam replied. There were three blue lights glowing in the darkness across the room. He knew it was a bomb, even from where he was stood.

"Superintendent Ramsay," a call came over the coms unit. It was Inspector Green from armed response.

"What is it, Inspector?" Alec sounded irritated by the interruption at such a critical moment, but he knew the Inspector wouldn't be using an open channel unless it was important.

"We've got an Armed Response Unit en route to an incident."

"Go ahead," Alec was irritated now.

"A shooting was called in anonymously an hour ago. The first teams at the scene reported two men in a BMW, armed with MAC-10 machineguns. One of them is shot and wounded. The other man is holed up in the backseat. The vehicle registration plate has its owner listed as Malik Shah."

"Where are they?" Alec scratched his chin.

"Runcorn Bridge, Guv."

"Roger that, Inspector." Alec didn't know what was happening, but something was. He had to get the Captain out of there.

"Can you see the lights across the room?" Bishpam said when the other conversation was done.

"Roger that, I want you out of there now, Captain," Alec repeated. The accelerant gel had been put down for one reason only. To spread fire evenly throughout the cellar and to destroy everything that was down there. There were a million and one ways to set up a trigger device that would detonate a bomb, or start a fire.

"Roger that, I'm on my way out of here," Captain Bishpam said as he turned on the stairway. He moved his left foot off the fourth step down, and released the pressure in a pressure pad. The pressure release closed a live electric circuit, which was causing a magnetic field around a steel ball bearing. When the magnet was turned off, the steel ball rolled down a metal track and then slotted between two connectors, and completed a circuit. The trigger detonated a series of explosive devices, which were designed to destroy everything in the cellar, and start a firestorm, which would cremate any remaining evidence. Captain Bishpam didn't stand a chance.

59

End Game

"Drop the weapon and get out of the vehicle," an amplified voice travelled across the bridge to him. Malik was surrounded by armed police units at the front and rear of his car. They had closed the bridge to traffic and set up roadblocks seventy-five yards back from his position. Ashwan smelled of excrement, which told him that he was dead, and his bowels had relaxed and emptied. His options were limited. He was in possession of two machineguns and three kilos of cocaine. Ashwan was dead, probably shot with the gun that he had in his possession. The police would lock him up and throw away the key. He wouldn't see the light of day ever again. The Bernsteins had stitched him up good and proper, and he knew it. The police would know it as well. Would they admit it was a set up and miss the opportunity to lock him up? Malik doubted it very much. MI5 tracked him for years because of his arms dealing. To catch him in possession of two reactivated weapons would be six numbers and the bonus ball.

"Throw the weapon out of the vehicle, and come out with your hands up," the voice sounded more urgent this time. "You have nowhere to go, throw your weapon down."

A helicopter roared over the railway bridge to his left. It soared above the suspension bridge and then hovered a hundred yards above him to the right. Malik looked up, and saw a sniper taking aim at the vehicle. He closed his eyes tightly when he saw the muzzle flash.

There were two loud bangs as the driver's side tyres exploded, and the BMW rocked violently and lurched to one side. The sniper fired three more rounds, and ragged holes appeared in the bonnet as the high velocity bullets fractured the engine block, sending sparks high into the air. Malik had nowhere to go. He was trapped and surrounded by his very own produce, cocaine and reactivated weapons. Another helicopter appeared a distance away and floated above the river, level with the bridge. Malik guessed it was the television cameras, trying to get a good shot of the action.

"Throw the weapon out of the vehicle." The voice repeated. If they wanted him dead then they would have shot him by now. They wanted to take him alive. It would look good on the TV if they could capture an armed drug dealer alive. Britain's top gangster is snared in a shoot out, caught red handed with the dope in his possession. He would get life. There was no doubt about it. Malik thought it through. If he surrendered, he'd be put behind bars in a maximum-security prison for life without parole. His companies assets would be seized, and he would be penniless. If he had no money, then he had no power. There was no one left to conjure up a daring escape plan to spring him from jail, and there would be no money to fund legal challenges. The prisons were full of his enemies, rival gangsters, bitter drug dealers, and dozens of heavies that had been on the wrong end of Malik's justice over the years. He was untouchable a month ago, now he was nothing. Life in a prison cell taking one beating after another, ending up as someone's bitch in the showers was about all he could expect.

The Bernsteins had brought him here because of Sarah, the silly bitch. She jumped off the bridge years ago, and they wanted him to do the same thing now, or rot in a six by four cell stinking of his own piss. There was another option though. He could go out in a blaze of glory. Malik checked the magazine. It was full bar one round. He put his hand on the door and took a deep breath. As he yanked it, the wind took it and blew it wide open. He ducked low and ran toward the pedestrian walkway.

"Drop the weapon or we will open fire, do it now!" the officer on the megaphone bellowed the order. Malik ignored him and turned toward the helicopter. He raised his weapon, so did the sniper. Malik pulled the trigger to unleash a maelstrom of nine-millimetre bullets at the aircraft. This was his last stand.

'Click.' The reactivated weapon jammed. He tried again. 'Click.'

The sniper fired. Two high velocity slugs slammed into the pavement a yard in front of him.

"This is your last chance, drop the weapon!"

Malik turned and ran full pelt at the railings. He threw the Mac-10 behind him and vaulted the barrier. The wind whistled by his ears as he plummeted into the abyss, and his desperate last scream resounded off a million tons of steel.

60

The Bernsteins

"Shah jumped off the bridge, Superintendent," the armed response officer in charge of the standoff said as they arrived at the scene.

"I heard it on the coms. Did anyone get hurt?"

"No, Sir, his weapon jammed."

"There's an ironic justice in there somewhere," Alec shook his head and the deep wrinkles on his face creased.

"Sir?"

"I'm thinking out loud, Inspector, don't worry."

Alec Ramsay felt like he'd been punched in the guts by Mike Tyson. The explosion at the farm killed a good soldier, a real war hero. Losing an officer under those circumstances was hard to take, especially when it became obvious that the farm was rigged to blow. He knew it would be, and so did Captain Bishpam, but he still went in there to try and make it safe for others to do their job. Alec had no sympathy for Malik Shah or Ashwan Pindar. The world would be a better place without them in it. The fact that the Bernstein brothers had a personal axe to grind with them did not excuse what they had done. They were murderers too, and in Alec's book, that made them just as evil as Shah and his mob. He had to find them and bring them in, or Bishpam had died for nothing,

304

and the case would eat away at him forever.

He walked through a melee of police officers and ambulance men toward the BMW. There was a chattering of voices on the wind, and everyone had an opinion about Shah jumping.

"What do you think, Guv," Will Naylor caught up, and was a step behind him.

"I think this scenario was planned from day one, Will." Alec looked up at the steel girders above him. An icy wind blew through him as he tried to make sense of it all. "The vehicle was parked here and surrounded by traffic cones, now how could they pull that off without alerting the other road users that something was amiss?"

Will looked at the set up. Ashwan Pindar was still slumped back in the driver's seat. Shah was in the back before he jumped. They picked the bridge because of their sister, and Will could understand their choice.

"How did they get them into the car in the first place, and why did they stay in it?" Will mused.

"There are traffic cameras at both ends of the bridge, right?"

"Yes, Guv."

"Get them looked at pronto, I want to know how they set this up like that, without anybody noticing what was going on," Alec ordered. Will took his mobile out and punched numbers in. Less than a minute later, the stored footage was being sent electronically to the MIT offices. Alec had his own theories. He guessed that they were using a vehicle that wouldn't look out of place, something that is almost wallpaper to a passing car. He was also of the impression that Shah and his sidekick were drugged when they were placed into the BMW. They couldn't have transported them there in the vehicle, someone would have found it suspicious, two men unconscious.

Alec approached the BMW.

"Step away please, Sir, we haven't checked it over yet," one of Captain Bishpam's bomb squad officers shouted. Alec looked and waved in acknowledgement.

"Okay, let me know when it's clear."

He skirted the vehicle knowing that there was no bomb in it. The Bernsteins set this up like a game of chess. They nipped and prodded Shah relentlessly, picking off his people like pieces on a board, upsetting the balance. The kidnap was genius. They ruffled his feathers so much that he began to run in circles, attacking shadows and demons that didn't exist. They pushed him to the edge, and then brought him back to where it all began. To the place where their beloved sister committed suicide carrying his child. They used the farm as their base until the game was over, and then they destroyed the evidence. Alec reached the railings and looked over. The River Mersey looked steel grey from up there. Below the bridge, the waters merged with the salt water of the Irish Sea as the tides ebbed and flowed. A river police launch trawled the waters looking for Shah's body. He was dead no one could survive a fall like that. The tidal undercurrents would drag him down and take his body miles before it would surface, if it ever did at all.

"It's clear, Superintendent." The bomb squad officer finished checking beneath the floor plan and wheel arches. "You can approach the vehicle, but please don't press anything, or switch anything on."

Alec nodded and walked around the car. It was an odd request to make to an experienced senior officer, but he had just seen his commanding officer blown to bits and charcoaled in a firestorm, he was doing his job the way he'd been taught to. Alec looked in the windows. Ashwan Pindar bled to death slowly. The foot well was pooled with congealing blood. His trousers were blown away at the knee, and most of the joint was splattered over the dashboard. There was a reactivated machinegun on the driver's side heater vents. Alec didn't think that Pindar ever used it. Why would he put it in the window in plain view? It was put there for a reason, probably for the benefit of the police officers that arrived first at the scene. There was an anonymous tip off about a shooting, and a Mac-10 in the windscreen of a parked vehicle. It was bound to provoke an armed response from the police. That's exactly what they got. The rear door was still open, and the sports bag was clearly visible. Alec clocked the three packages of white powder. Cocaine he guessed. Malik Shah was far too shrewd to transport dope around in his own car. It was another piece in the game created by the Bernsteins.

"They've watched the footage, Guv." Will called him. He was twenty yards away with his phone to his ear. Alec had seen enough in the car to know what happened, but he wanted to know how.

"Go on, don't keep me in suspense."

"The cameras show the BMW being stopped by a highways vehicle. They flanked it and then an ambulance turned up and reversed up to the front of the vehicle. The ambulance men go back and forth while a third man in uniform places the cones around the scene. Everything is obscured from the road by the way they parked them up."

"They brought Pindar and Shah here in the ambulance, drugged I bet."

"They can't take those vehicles back to the farm, Guv. We need to find them."

"Get the plates to traffic and airborne. They won't be far away, I'm sure of that." Alec looked west toward Liverpool. Planes were taking off and landing less than three miles up the river. "How far is it to the airport from here by road, four miles, five at the most?"

"Yes, no more than that."

"They worked to a timetable, Will, and now we know why. Tell uniform to check the airport parking facilities, all of them, off site and on site."

"I'm on it, Guv," Will took his mobile and dialled.

"What time did the cameras show them leaving the bridge?" Alec asked when he'd finished his call.

"Forty minutes before the first officers arrived."

"Forty minutes, plus an hour stand-off. They could be in the air already. I want every bit of camera data at the airport checked, and find out which flight they got on. I want everyone we have at our disposal at the airport."

61

John Lennon Airport

Alec had every detective available at John Lennon Airport, along with over sixty uniformed police officers, an armed response unit and the bomb squad. The ambulance was found parked on a housing estate a mile from the airport, and the highways truck was left on an unmanned long stay car park. The police helicopter spotted them as it scoured the area for the vehicles. Alec was convinced that they were gone already. Their planning was meticulous, and it would be naive to assume that they would foul up their escape. The airport was the nearest transport hub, and their obvious means of escape, but is that what they wanted him to think? Park the vehicles near to the airport, and then get a ferry or a train instead.

"Have we got the passenger information we need yet?" Alec called Smithy at the office. The data was supposed to be sent direct to him from the airport security systems analysts, but there was an irritating delay for a reason yet unknown.

"Nothing has come through, and they won't tell me why, Guv."

"What do you mean, Smithy, who won't tell you?"

"I called airport security, and they've referred me to the Divisional Commander."

"What?" Alec screwed up his face in a scowl. "The Divisional Commander, what exactly did they say?"

"I told them the information was vital, and it was on Detective Superintendent Ramsey's authority. They said it would be with me in ten minutes, but when it didn't come, I called back, and they said there was an issue with the request, and that it was with the Commander, Guv."

"Get the Commander on the blower, Smithy and patch me through to him." Alec was furious. Had the Commander taken over the case, or assigned another Superintendent? He ran the possible scenarios through his mind while he waited. All the time they messed about the Bernsteins were putting distance between them. The line clicked and Smithy's voice came back over the phone. "Guv."

"What is it Smithy?"

"He said he can't talk to you now, Guv, and get this, we're to stand down!"

"What the hell is he playing at?"

"What do you want me to do, Guv?"

Alec thought for a long time before answering the question, and when he did his stomach turned. "If the Commander says that we are to stand down, then that's what we'll have to do."

6 2

M I 5

There was a feeling of outrage running through the law enforcement teams working on the case. Confusion, frustration and resentment were running high. There was no communication coming down the ranks as to why there was a stand down ordered at the airport. It was as if someone pulled the plug on the entire investigation at the last minute. If they'd identified which flight the bombers had boarded, then they could have had them arrested at the other end. Alec Ramsey couldn't fathom the reason why.

Alec was shell shocked by the decision to stand down, and not being able to explain it to his troops made things worse. He'd demanded an immediate briefing with the Commander when he finally returned his calls, which was granted, but he was told it would be the following day, and he was to go alone. He hadn't slept a wink that night, and his long suffering wife Gail kept him supplied with coffee and organic sandwiches as he made call after call to his high ranking colleagues digging for information. Either no one knew anything, or they weren't saying anything. He dressed in his best navy blue suit, and chose a tie to match the colour. If he was to be kicked off the case then he would step down as the head of the Major Investigation Team. Gail said she would stand by him, whatever decision he made. The drive to work took forever, and the charcoal clouds reflected his mood. He went direct to the top floor without calling into his office, it was better not to see his own officers before he'd had the briefing with the Commander. The elevator ride seemed to take forever, and when he stepped out of it, he needed to pee. He pushed open the door of the gents, thick black marble tiles covered the floor and walls, white porcelain sinks, and stainless-steel fixtures complimented them. Agent Spence of the MI5 was using a urinal. Alec stopped in his tracks and shook his head in disbelief. Who else could have blocked his request for information from the airport, apart from MI5 that was?

"Superintendent," Spence said without turning his head. His face blushed red and Alec didn't think it was because he'd seen him pissing.

"Agent Spence, are you here to shed some light on my investigation, or are you loitering with intent in the executive toilets again?" Alec thought about smashing the agent's face into the tiles.

"Oh, I didn't realise that investigations were owned by individual officers, no matter how high up the food chain they are."

Agent Spence shook it dry and tucked himself back into his grey trousers, before leaving without saying another word. He wasn't wearing a suit jacket, which told Alec that he'd been there for sometime already, and it was only nine o'clock in the morning. Alec finished and stood in front of a basin. He looked into the mirror and frowned at what he saw. His blond hair was greying fast, his worry lines were firmly entrenched around his forehead and eyes, and they were spreading rapidly. The fact MI5 had an agent on the top floor didn't bode well for the meeting he was about to have with the Divisional Commander. Chief Carlton wasn't invited either, which worried him further. He washed his hands and splashed his face with cold water, and then headed for the Commander's office.

"Commander," Alec knocked and opened the door at the same time. His superior was sat behind his desk, and he didn't look happy. His face was dark with worry.

"Alec, come in," the Commander said. He left the formalities aside for now. "You and Agent Spence are familiar with each other by now, so let's get down to the nitty-gritty, shall we?"

"That suits me," Alec closed the door and sat opposite the Commander. He positioned himself so that he could look both men in the face without moving.

The Commander coughed nervously, and cleared his throat. "I'm sure that you have lots of questions, Superintendent, and I intend to answer them as honestly as I can, with the help of Agent Spence, however I must remind you that whatever is discussed in this meeting is top secret information."

Alec didn't like the sound of that. He could smell bullshit and cover-up coming over the horizon; they usually travelled together. He decided not to comment and to remain silent for now.

"I must reiterate, Commander, this is an ongoing operation, and as such I'm limited as to what I can divulge." Agent Spence smoothed his grey hair backward. He was already nervous, before they'd started. Alec was pleased that he was uncomfortable.

"Yes, quite," the Commander waved his hand face down as if he were waving him away. "Alec, what do you need from me?"

"Why did you block the security information that I requested from the airport?" Alec asked casually. He was keeping his powder dry. There would be plenty of time for getting annoyed, he was sure of that. The Commander looked at Agent Spence.

"I didn't block it, Alec, MI5 did."

Alec looked at Spence for a reply to his question, but none was forthcoming. Spence didn't look at him.

"Why did you block my request Agent Spence?"

"I'm afraid that's classified, Superintendent."

"Why?"

"Why what?"

"Why would footage from check-in desks and boarding gates be classified information?" Alec wasn't going to be fobbed off. "We were in pursuit of dangerous criminals, that's what we do, and you stopped me doing my job."

"You have no solid evidence that the Bernstein brothers were in the airport, let alone that they boarded a plane. We will release the passenger manifest and the camera evidence to you tomorrow."

"Thank you, now it's virtually useless." Alec raised a finger to his lips and looked confused. He was playing Spence. "Why did you mention the Bernstein brothers?"

"I beg your pardon?"

"You said we had no evidence that the Bernsteins were in the airport, why mention their names?"

"We were following your investigation." Spence looked down at the floor, another lie.

"I thought you were following Malik Shah and his gun running business?"

"We were."

"How do the two things collide?"

"I don't understand your problem," Agent Spence was on the back foot. He had slipped up mentioning their names, and he knew it.

"The Bernstein investigation uncovered a tragic family history connected to Shah and his cronies when they were teenagers, but nothing to do with gunrunning or arms deals."

"We are aware of your findings, Superintendent." Spence straightened his tie, and sat rigid. He wanted to look composed, but he wasn't at all.

"Then how would Shah's gunrunning be connected to the Bernsteins?" Alec frowned again.

Agent Spence smoothed his hair back again. He had blushed again. The Commander remained quiet while Alec made the agent squirm. "I'm sorry, Superintendent but that is classified."

"I'll ask you again, Agent Spence, why would the Bernstein family have anything to do with your arms dealing investigations?"

"It's classified."

"So it is connected?"

"You're repeating yourself, Superintendent."

"You're damn right I am." Alec turned the volume up a few notches. "The Bernstein investigation revealed a family grudge, a bitter campaign of revenge against a group of men that raped their sister, now tell me what the fuck that has to do with international arms deals?"

"It's classified."

Alec turned to the Commander, and tried to read his face. He couldn't look him in the eye. Alec's brain was working overtime, and he wasn't enjoying the answers that it was coming up with.

"You didn't want us to capture the Bernsteins did you?"

"Don't be ridiculous." Spence tried to be aloof and bat the question away, but he failed miserably. Alec was all over his reaction immediately.

"You blocked our request for information at the airport, because you didn't want us to capture them, why else would you block it and then release it to us when it's useless?"

"The reason is classified."

"The reason speaks for itself, Agent Spence."

"I'm not sure there is any point in continuing this line of questioning, Commander," Agent Spence looked for a way out.

"You couldn't nail Malik Shah could you?"

"What are talking about now?"

"You couldn't nail Malik Shah, but the Bernsteins could use methods that you couldn't."

Agent Spence shifted in his chair and crossed his arms. Alec was driving him into a corner and he wasn't articulate or intelligent enough to fend off his questions. "I think we've accomplished all we can from this meeting."

"You let them go, why would you do that?"

"What, that's ridiculous!" Spence looked shocked by the remark, but Alec was onto the truth.

"Are you that stupid, or do you think that I am?"

"I've had enough of this, I'm calling it a day. If you need anything else do it through the proper channels. We're done." Agent Spence tried to stand up, but Alec was too quick. He closed the gap between them and grabbed Spence by the tie, and twisted it tightly. Spence tried to relieve the pressure on his throat, but Alec squeezed harder. The Commander raised a hand to intervene, but he was gobsmacked by the accusations Alec was making, and the credibility that they had.

"I think the least you can do, Agent Spence, is listen to me for a few minutes. You see I'm just a bog standard detective. I follow the evidence and try to put the bad guys in jail, no bullshit, no cover-ups. I have to play by the rules, and I want to know what happened."

Agent Spence held up his hands in surrender and Alec relieved the pressure on his necktie. He brushed down the agent's suit with the back of his hands, and straightened his tie sarcastically. Stepping back, he sat back down in his chair.

"I'm pissed off, Agent Spence, because I watched a good man get blown to bits by the lunatics that you let walk. Now I want to know why you would let them leave the country, why?" Alec was beginning to put the pieces together himself, but that didn't mean he was about to let the MI5 man off the hook.

"That's classified." Agent Spence looked jumpy. Alec had him rattled, but he wasn't going to spill the beans.

"So you did let them walk?" Alec pressed, looking for a chink in the armour. "Did you know David Bernstein was here all along?"

There was a flicker of recognition in his eyes as Alec mentioned it. It was enough to cement Alec's theory in his head. David Bernstein was an operative in one of the world's most secret military units. The Israelis denied that the unit actually existed at all, and so would MI5 if they were asked. Alec could tell by his reaction that he knew David Bernstein was in the country.

"That's classified." Agent Spence wanted to make a bolt for the door, but he could tell Alec wasn't going to let him walk out. He had to stand his ground though. "I really can't say anymore on the subject of the Bernsteins, Superintendent."

"Fucking hell!" Alec looked at the Commander and slapped his knees with his hands, as if he'd had a Eureka moment. "They knew he was here, and they knew he was Israeli Special Forces, and that's why the Israeli military wouldn't cooperate when we asked them where he was."

"I can see where you are coming from, Alec, I'm not so sure there's anything that we can do about it now," The Commander wobbled his jowls as he spoke. "If this is true then it will have been approved by the top brass."

"Was David Bernstein sent here by the Israeli government?" Alec turned back to Spence and jabbed a finger toward his face. The agent looked away.

"I'm not saying anymore, Superintendent."

Alec sat forward in his chair. He was calm because he was amazed at what he'd discovered.

"Was Malik Shah selling weapons and munitions to Israel's enemies?"

"Yes, that I can confirm." Agent Spence looked relieved that he could answer a question at last. "He was supplying Hamas with reactivated weapons"

"I thought Shah was a non-religious Muslim?" the Commander looked to Alec for confirmation.

"He was," Alec agreed. "This was all about money, not religion, wasn't it?"

"In the Middle East there are a lot of incentives on offer to those who support the Arab struggle against the Jews."

"Yes, I bet there are," Alec laughed sarcastically. "Shah has business interests in Dubai, Saudi and Qatar, not bad for a drug dealer from Liverpool, eh?"

"That's the way business works there, Superintendent. Support is rewarded with money."

"So Shah was targeted by the Israelis as a legitimate target, and David Bernstein is one of their operatives?"

"My God," the Commander whispered. "He was sent here."

"He wasn't sent here," Spence said curtly.

"He wasn't sent here officially, you mean?" Alec taunted him. "The Israelis knew where he was, but they didn't try to stop him, it would kill two birds with one stone."

"All I can tell you is that he wasn't sent here."

"Bullshit!" Alec sat forward and shook his head in disbelief. "Mossad highlighted Shah as a legitimate target on their list, and David Bernstein was made aware of the fact, and allowed to disappear for six months. In the meantime no one knows where he is, conveniently?"

"We were not aware of the Bernstein connection, until you uncovered it, Superintendent."

"No, maybe not, but you knew there was an Israeli agent in the country stalking Shah, didn't you?"

"Anyone supplying Hamas is an enemy of the Israeli state, and so they should be."

"If only we could all just assassinate our enemies, Agent Spence," the Commander chipped in. He was shocked but not surprised.

"I'll bet David Bernstein jumped at the chance to take Shah out of the game, and you lot at MI5 jumped at the chance of letting them do it as well. You couldn't do it yourself so you let a foreign government do it for you, David Bernstein happened to have a history with Shah, and his brother was only too willing to go along with it. He'd planned revenge for decades. How neat for you. All you had to do was cover their escape from the country when it was done, or am I wrong?"

"We didn't know about his brother, I can assure you of that. We didn't expect bombs, and we weren't sure it was them when they started." The Agent coughed nervously. "I can't comment anymore."

"You really don't need to, Agent Spence. Tell me were any of your agents killed investigating Shah or the Bernsteins?"

"Yes."

"Then you and your superiors are disrespecting every one of them and their families. You let killers off the leash to kill one of your most elusive targets, and then you let them escape."

"I think we're going around in circles, Superintendent."

"Where did you let them go to, Agent Spence, are they all in Israel now?"

"I'm leaving, Commander, and if there's any repeat of your behaviour earlier, then I will press charges, is that clear?"

"Perfectly, leave, because I won't be responsible for what happens if you stay," the Commander snarled. "I will be speaking to the director later today, and you can tell him from me that we will be raising this case with the Home Secretary."

"Fine, do that, he's very familiar with the case, if you know what I mean," Spence stood up and winked at Alec, smoothed his suit and left in silence.

Alec felt enlightened, but numb. Either the Intelligence Services, worked with the Israelis or they knew David Bernstein was here and chose to ignore it, despite his history with Shah. There were times when the politics involved in his job made him puke. The door closed loudly as the agent slammed it behind him.

"What are we supposed to do with that, Commander?"

"Absolutely nothing, Alec, there's nothing that we can do."

"What do I tell my team?" Alec shrugged. "We were shafted by our own people, and the whole fucking investigation was a smoke and mirrors operation by the Israeli Secret Service?"

"Whatever you decide to tell them Alec, they'll believe you, and the next bad guy that you investigate will get their undivided attention. Put this one to bed, you couldn't have done anymore than you did."

"I'm not so sure, Commander," Alec felt drained. Was it time to pack it all in? "This time around, I am just not so sure."

63

Checkmate

Richard Bernstein was sweating profusely in the front seat of a battered Mercedes as it hurtled through the Moroccan desert toward the thirteenth century city of Touradant. The compacted sand road was more than a match for the aged suspension of the rusty old taxi, and he was bouncing about like a space-hopper in a giant salt pot. His shirt was sticking to his back, and there were dark patches spreading beneath his arms. All four windows were down but it had no effect on the soaring temperature in the ancient vehicle.

"How much further is it?" Richard asked, wiping sweat from his brow. He was hungry. The breakfast at the hotel in Agadir was paltry; bread rolls and bland cheese were not his idea of a good start to the day. There was no bacon to be had in this godforsaken country.

"See there," the driver, pointed to the east with enthusiasm. His toothless smile and sundried skin made him look a hundred years old. Richard was immediately sorry that he'd asked the question as the driver's body odour wafted over to him when he raised his arms. He smelled and looked like he hadn't bathed for decades. "Ten minutes!"

David Bernstein was asleep in the back seat, as was Nick. They had been up until the early hours of the morning drinking local brand whisky, and it had caught up with them now. The flight from Liverpool to Agadir was under three hours, but it felt much longer. The anticipation of armed police greeting them at the gate was gut wrenching. It had been a huge relief when they breezed past customs and walked out of the airport unhindered. David said they wouldn't be stopped, but it was still a worry. Their documentation was forged, but they were top of the range quality, and impossible to spot. They stayed two nights at the beach resort, before heading off to Marrakesh, via Touradant. David had contacts in Morocco, and they'd arranged sea passage for them across the Mediterranean to Israel. They had to meet their contact the following day in Marrakesh, and decided to see some of the country on the way there. Richard couldn't be bothered. It was a shithole of a place, sand and more sand, and no bacon.

David woke up when the taxi hit a pothole at thirty miles an hour. He was jolted violently and his head hit the window frame. The desert wind blew in his face, which would have been pleasant if it didn't carry the scent of the driver with it. He opened his eyes and wiped the crusty sleep from the corners. They were approaching the walled city, and red-ochre fortified ramparts stretched into the distance as far as he could see. The size of the fortifications were testament to the skill of the thirteenth century Muslim engineers. They drove by groups of local woman, all dressed in blue robes and matching headscarves and veils. The men they saw held wooden staffs, which they used to guide their goats, or whip their donkeys. Their leathery faces were full of loathing and suspicion for foreign visitors that earned more money in a day than they did in five years. As they approached the huge gates the smells and sounds of the city drifted into the car.

It was Friday, and the city was packed with locals heading to Friday prayers. The narrow streets were awash with colours, as traders showed their produce to the faithful as they passed by to their Mosques. Fruit and vegetables of every shape and colour were on sale, and the smell of rotting meat hung heavily in the air as the butchers plied their trade too. The Imams could be heard wailing from the minarets, calling the faithful to prayer. The smell of spices was powerful as they drove near to the Souk, and shoppers flooded out of the exits as prayer time neared. David watched the crowds with his head resting on the backseat. His head was tilted so that the breeze would blow into his face and cool him. He couldn't care less about the sightseeing, he needed to contact his colleague here, pick up documents and find somewhere that they could drink. The previous months had been hard work, mentally and physically, but they'd been worth every second. Shah and his nest of rats were annihilated and they were nearly a million pound richer. He would call it compensation for his loss. His superiors would be pleased that Malik Shah was no longer in business, but another arms dealer would take his place immediately. The Israelis would also have a place for Richard. He was a very talented man in many ways. Israel is nothing but an arid, salt encrusted desert. The only water supply was the River Jordan, and all the farming and agriculture were created by extensive manmade projects. Richard's fertiliser expertise would be worth millions there, as would his talent for making explosive devices. Unfortunately, David's superiors were not happy about the way he had taken Shah out of circulation. The bombing campaign attracted far too much attention, and the world's media were still focusing on it. It was only a matter of time before the blame was laid at Israel's door, and an international scandal was on the cards, but David didn't care. He would face the music when the time came.

The taxi slowed to walking pace as the crowd thickened, and the driver honked the horn constantly to no avail. Locals called abuse and spat at the car as it crawled alongside them. David recognised a barbershop where he'd been shaven once before, it was a block away from the hotel they were heading to. A trader proffered his selection of fruits through the window and David waved him away. The wrinkled old man fired a string of abuse at him for his troubles.

"Turn down here," David tapped the driver on the shoulder. He wanted to get out of the crowds. The road would take them the back way to the hotel. "Down there!"

The driver nodded and gave him a gummy smile in the mirror.

"This way, only five minute! Five minute!" He grinned as he repeated himself.

"Turn here, it's quicker, you bloody idiot," David leaned forward and pointed to the barbershop. "Here by the barbershop."

"Barbershop?" the driver grinned again. "You want shave?"

"No, I don't want a shave turn this way!"

"I know best barbershop, good price for you, Asda price for you!" The driver carried on pushing his way through the crowd and David gave up giving directions. They would be there soon enough. The crowd began to thin out as they turned off the main street to their respective places of worship, and the hotel was in sight.

"I turn, I turn." The driver drove by the hotel entrance and he eyed David in the mirror. David was immediately suspicious.

"Stop the car!" He leaned forward and grabbed the driver's seat.

"I turn around, okay boss man!" he grinned like an idiot again, but he looked nervous and his eyes darted all over. He slowed and turned the wheel full lock. The turning circle was too tight for the taxi to make it in one movement, and the gears crunched painfully as he engaged reverse. "I turn around."

David relaxed a little as he attempted a three-point turn in the narrow street. A haggard face appeared at his window, and a wooden board filled with melon slices was thrust toward him. He jumped. "Fuck off!" he shouted at the old woman.

"I'm starving," Richard turned around. "How much are they?" He shouted to the woman but she was gone, only to be replaced by another blue clad figure.

David Bernstein was about to tell her to go forth and multiply when the taxi driver pulled on the handbrake, opened his door and bolted. The blue robes parted for a second and he caught sight briefly of an Israeli manufactured suppressed Uzi nine-millimetre machinegun. The first rounds ripped David's jugular and larynx out of his throat, and arterial blood spatter soaked the interior of the taxi. Nick didn't get time to wake up as four rounds smashed his thickened brow bone and sprayed his brains all over the back window. Richard Bernstein opened the passenger door and tried to get out but he was too fat and awkward to do it quickly. Not for the first time in his life, he wet his pants in fear as the assassin reloaded. His troubled life flashed before him as they emptied the second clip into his bloated body, and he lay twitching half in and half out of the taxi. His blood soaked into the Moroccan dust. A Nissan truck pulled up and the assassin jumped into the back of it, while two men emptied the boot of the taxi. A gallon of four-star petrol was splashed around the Bernstein brothers and the taxi became a raging inferno as the Mossad team sped away. The last remaining evidence of the embarrassing events in the United Kingdom was erased from memory, and the Israeli government were off the hook. The Bernstein family were officially extinct.

64

Major investigation team

Alec Ramsey folded his newspaper in half so that he could read it without it falling into his breakfast. He was enjoying a Sunday morning off work for a change, as they were rare. His organic sausages tasted like cardboard, and apparently, there was no such thing as organic black pudding.

"Are you sure black-pudding is bad for me?" he moaned as he slotted another piece of tasteless banger into his mouth. He slurped his tea to wash it down.

"Positive, Alec, it's disgusting, don't you dare ask for that," Gail raised her eyebrows and gave him that look, the look that could turn the milk to cheese in an instant.

"What about free range black pudding, now that can't be bad for me can it?"

"Shut up and eat your sausage."

"I'm not sure this can be called a sausage, it doesn't taste of meat and it's a little bland."

"There is no meat in it."

"What?"

"It's vegetable and soya, organic vegetables of course."

"Of course," Alec stared at the sausage on his fork and decided not to bother. He dunked a piece of wholemeal toast into his free-range fried egg instead.

He was about to moan again when a piece in the paper caught his eye. It was a paragraph long and very brief. It described the murder of three western tourists in the Moroccan city of Touradant. They were robbed and burned to death in a taxi, and local bandits were being blamed. According to the reporter, their belongings were stolen, and they had no identification on them. Alec felt the hair on the back of his neck tingle. He didn't know why, but he knew it was the Bernstein brothers and their friend. Flights to Morocco from Liverpool were scheduled every day. He took another mouthful of toast and reached for the phone.

"I thought you were having a day off?"

"It's these sausages, I'm going to have to call it in." Alec joked as he dialled. "I am charging them with attempting to impersonate a sausage, and for assaulting my taste buds."

"Silly man."

"Silly sausage," he stuck his fork into one and held it up.

"DI Naylor," Will answered the phone.

"I thought you were having a day off?" Alec scolded him.

"Morning, Guv, I thought you were."

"I am," Alec looked at the article again. "Get Interpol on the blower and see what you can find out about a triple murder in Touradant last week."

"Where?"

"Touradant," Alec spelled it out for him.

"Any particular reason, Guv, or are you being nosey?"

"Just my spider senses tingling again."

"Leave it with me, I'll make a few calls."

Alec hung up and went back to his newspaper for ten minutes. He played with his breakfast, but his appetite had gone. He kissed Gail on top of the head and put his plate on the side.

"Thanks for that, it was very interesting," he joked. "I'm going for a shower, Darling."

"You'll thank me for looking after your cholesterol one day."

The telephone rang.

"That'll be for you," she frowned and picked up the breakfast plates. Alec grabbed the phone and connected the call.

"Hello."

"You were right, Guv." Will smiled at the other end of the phone. Alec could tell he was smiling.

"What am I right about?"

"Three western tourists robbed and murdered in the street. Their belongings were stolen and they had no identification on them. The police don't know what country they were from. They identified their ethnicity by DNA."

"Is that it?" Alec was disappointed.

"The only thing not damaged beyond use was a wrist watch. The strap was destroyed but the body protected the back of it."

"Go on, go on, don't wind me up, and excuse the pun."

"There was an engraving on the back of it. Happy birthday Einstein."